I0823073

RECKLESS

Also by Lauren Roberts

Powerless
Powerful: A Powerless Story

RECKLESS

LAUREN ROBERTS

THE POWERLESS TRILOGY

SIMON & SCHUSTER BFYR

NEW YORK AMSTERDAM/ANTWERP LONDON
TORONTO SYDNEY/MELBOURNE NEW DELHI

An imprint of Simon & Schuster Children's Publishing Division
1230 Avenue of the Americas, New York, New York 10020
This book is a work of fiction. Any references to historical events, real people, or real places are used fictitiously. Other names, characters, places, and events are products of the author's imagination, and any resemblance to actual events or places or persons, living or dead, is entirely coincidental.

Simon & Schuster: Celebrating 100 Years of Publishing in 2024
For information about special discounts for bulk purchases, please contact Simon & Schuster Special Sales at 1-866-506-1949 or business@simonandschuster.com.
The Simon & Schuster Speakers Bureau can bring authors to your live event. For more information or to book an event, contact the Simon & Schuster Speakers Bureau at 1-866-248-3049 or visit our website at www.simonspeakers.com.
The text for this book was set in Bembo.
Manufactured in the United States of America
8 10 9 7
Library of Congress Cataloging-in-Publication Data
Names: Roberts, Lauren, 2002– author.
Title: Reckless / Lauren Roberts.
Description: New York : Simon & Schuster Books for Young Readers, 2024. | Series: Powerless ; book 2 | Audience: Ages 14 up. | Audience: Grades 10–12. |
Summary: After she conspires with the Resistance and kills the king, Paedyn Gray faces a perilous game of cat-and-mouse with Prince Kai, whom she once loved, as she uncovers revelations about her past that make her question everything she thought was true.
Identifiers: LCCN 2024011331 (print) | LCCN 2024011332 (ebook) | ISBN 9781665955430 (hardcover) | ISBN 9781665955454 (ebook)
Subjects: CYAC: Fantasy. | Survival—Fiction. | Government, Resistance to—Fiction. | BISAC: YOUNG ADULT FICTION / Fantasy / Romance | YOUNG ADULT FICTION / Social Themes / Class Differences | LCGFT: Fantasy fiction. | Novels.
Classification: LCC PZ7.1.R5936 Re 2024 (print) | LCC PZ7.1.R5936 (ebook) | DDC [Fic]—dc23
LC record available at https://lccn.loc.gov/2024011331
LC ebook record available at https://lccn.loc.gov/2024011332

For the reckless souls who dare to love and be loved

Izram
The Shallows
North
E
N
S

met
Sanctuary of Souls
Dor
The Scorches
Tando
The Whispers
lya

The Brave, Benevolent & Brutal
Pallias Azer
Ari Caelix
Seraphina Azer
Galen Raye
2s 2d
Harlan Azer
Mareena Ophir
Tristan Azer
Elowyn Moyra
Cedric Azer
Adeline Caelix
Arabelle Azer
Terrance Ophir
2s 1d
Azer Family Tree

AZER
Roland Azer
Tyra Caelix
3s
Elara Azer
Aiden Hayes
1s 3d
Ava Azer
Favian Azer
Samora Ophir
Edric Azer
Myla Rowe
Kai Azer
Landan Azer
Aspen Moyra
Kitt Azer
Iris Moyra
{Plague begins}
{First wife of Edric Azer}
{Edric Azer banishes all Ordinaries}
Valery Azer
Koen Moyra
1s 3d
Legend
Tandan Royalty
Izrami Royalty
Dorian Royalty
s ~ son
d ~ daughter
Deceased

PROLOGUE

Kai

The halls are eerily empty at this hour.

Just as they are every year.

I take my time walking down them, stealing this sliver of peace for myself. Though stolen bliss is little more than smothered chaos.

I choose to ignore that thought as I turn down a dark hall, my footsteps soft atop the emerald carpet. A sleeping castle is comforting, solitude a rarity among royals.

Royal.

I almost allow myself to laugh at the title. I frequently forget what I was before what I became. A prince before the Enforcer. A boy before the monster.

But, today, I am no one. Today, I simply get to be with who should have been.

A soft light leaks from beneath the doors of the kitchen. I manage a slight smile at the sight.

Every year. She's always here every year.

I gently push open the doors and step into the puddle of light cast by several flickering candles. The sweet smell of dough and cinnamon hangs in the air, swaddling me in warmth and memories.

"You're up earlier every year."

I meet Gail's smile with a small one of my own. Her apron is dusted with cinnamon, her face streaked with flour. I lift myself onto the same counter I've sat atop since I was big enough to reach it—my palms flattened behind me, scars sticky from the countertop.

There's comfort in the normalcy of it all.

I smile at the woman who all but raised me, a single shoulder lifted in a lazy shrug. "Every year I sleep less."

When her hands find her hips, I know she's fighting the urge to scold me. "You worry me, Kai."

"When have I not?" I say lightly.

"I'm serious." She wags a finger, gesturing to the whole of me. "You're too young to be dealin' with all this. It seems like only yesterday you were running around my kitchen, you and Kitt. . . ."

She trails off at the mention of him, forcing me to resuscitate the dying conversation. "I actually came from Father's"—I pause long enough to sigh through my nose—"*Kitt*'s study."

Gail nods slowly. "He hasn't left it since his coronation, has he?"

"No, he hasn't. And I wasn't in there long, either." I run a hand through my disheveled hair. "He was just informing me of my first mission."

She's quiet for a long moment. "It's her, isn't it?"

I nod. "It's her."

"And are you—"

"Going to complete the mission? Do as I'm told?" I finish for her. "Of course. It's my duty."

Another long pause. "And did he remember what today is?"

I look up slowly, smiling sadly as I meet her gaze. "It's not his job to remember."

"Right," she sighs. "Well, I only made one this year anyway. Figured he wouldn't be able to join ya."

She steps aside, revealing a glistening sticky bun beside the oven. I slide off the counter, smiling as I walk over to her. Only after I've kissed her on the cheek does she hand the plate to me.

"Now, go on," she shoos. "Go spend some time with her."

"Thank you, Gail," I say softly. "For every year."

"And the rest to follow." She winks before shoving me toward the door.

I glance back at her, at this woman who was a mother to me when the queen could not be. She was warm hugs and affection, well-deserved scoldings and much-desired approval.

I fear where the Azer brothers would be without her.

"Kai?"

I'm halfway through the door when I stop to look back at her.

"We all loved her," she says quietly.

"I know." I nod. "She knew."

And then my feet are carrying me out into the shadowed hallway beyond.

The sticky bun sitting atop the plate in my hand is tempting, smelling of cinnamon and sugar and simpler times. But instead I force myself to focus on walking the familiar path to the gardens, the same one I take this time each year from the kitchens.

It's not long before I'm heading for the broad doors that separate me from the gardens beyond. I barely glance at the Imperials standing guard or the ones sleeping uselessly beside them. The few who are awake pretend not to notice the sticky bun I'm carrying into the darkness with me.

I follow the stone path between the rows of colorful flowers I can't make out in the shadows. Statues covered in ivy litter the garden, several missing chunks of stone after taking one too many topples that certainly had nothing to do with me. The fountain ripples at the center of it all, reminding me of stifling days and understandable stupidity that had Kitt and me jumping into it.

But it's what sits beyond the gardens that I'm here for.

I step out into the soft stretch of grass that was once layered with colorful rugs for the second Trial's ball. Not allowing myself to reminisce any further on that night, I follow the moonlight that strokes its pale fingers over the outline of her.

The willow tree looks hauntingly alluring, her leaves rustling in the soft breeze. I run my eyes over each drooping branch. Over each root breaking through the dirt. Every inch is beautiful and strong.

I push through the curtain of leaves to step beneath the tree I visit as often as life will allow it—but always on this day with a sticky bun in hand. I run my fingers along the rough bark of the trunk, following its familiar grooves.

It's not long before I take my familiar seat beneath the towering tree, draping an arm over my propped knee. Balancing the plate atop a particularly large root, I pull a small matchbox from my pocket.

"I couldn't find a candle this year, sorry." I strike the match, staring at the small flame now sputtering on the stick. "So this will have to do."

I push the match into the center of the sticky bun, smiling slightly at the pathetic sight. I take a moment to watch it burn, watch it paint the massive tree in a flickering glow.

Then I look down beside me, running a hand over the soft grass there.

"Happy birthday, A."

I blow out the makeshift candle, letting darkness swallow us whole.

CHAPTER 1
Paedyn

My blood is only useful if it can manage to stay inside my body.

My mind is only useful if it can manage to not get lost.

My heart is only useful if it can manage to not get broken.

Well, it seems I've become utterly useless, then.

My eyes flick over the floorboards beneath my feet, wandering over the worn wood. The mere sight of the familiar floor floods me with memories, and I fight to blink away the fleeting images of small feet atop big booted ones as they stepped in time to a familiar melody. I shake my head, trying to shake the memory from it despite desperately wishing I could dwell in the past, seeing that my present isn't the most pleasant at the moment.

. . . sixteen, seventeen, eighteen—

I smile, ignoring the pain that pinches my skin.

Found you.

My stride is unsteady and stiff, sore muscles straining with each step toward the seemingly normal floorboard. I drop to my knees, biting my tongue against the pain, and claw at the wood with crimson-stained fingers I struggle to ignore.

The floor seems to be just as stubborn as I am, refusing to budge. I would have admired its resilience if it weren't a damn piece of *wood.*

I don't have time for this. I need to get out of here.

A frustrated sound tears from my throat before I blink at the board, blurting, "I could have sworn you were the secret compartment. Are you not the nineteenth floorboard from the door?"

I'm staring daggers at the wood before a hysterical laugh slips past my lips, and I tip my head back to shake it at the ceiling. "Plagues, now I'm talking to the *floor,*" I mutter, further proof that I'm losing my mind.

Although, it's not as if I have anyone else to talk to.

It's been three days since I stumbled back to my childhood home, haunted and half-dead. And yet, both my mind and body are far from healed.

I may have dodged death with each swipe of the king's sword, but he still managed to kill a part of me that day after the final Trial. His words cut deeper than his blade ever could, slicing me with slivers of truths as he toyed with me, taunted me, told me of my father's death with a smile tugging at his lips.

"Don't you want to know who it was that killed your father?"

A shiver snakes down my spine while the king's cold voice echoes through my skull.

"Let's just say that your first encounter with a prince wasn't when you saved Kai in the alley.'"

If betrayal was a weapon, he bestowed it upon me that day, driving the blunt blade through my broken heart. I blow out a shaky breath, pushing away thoughts of the boy with gray eyes as piercing as the sword I watched him drive through my father's chest so many years ago.

Staggering to my feet, I shift my weight over the surrounding floorboards, listening for an indicating creak while mindlessly spinning the silver ring on my thumb. My body aches all over, my very bones feeling far too fragile. The wounds I earned from my fight with the king were hastily tended to, the result of shaky fingers and silent sobs that left my vision blurry and stitches sloppy.

After limping from the Bowl Arena toward Loot Alley, I stumbled into the white shack I called home and the Resistance called headquarters. But I was greeted with emptiness. There were no familiar faces filling the secret room beneath my feet, leaving me with nothing but my pain and confusion.

I was alone—have been alone—left to clean up the mess that is my body, my brain, my bleeding heart.

The wood beneath me groans. I grin.

Once again I'm on the floor, prying up a beam to reveal a shadowy compartment beneath. I shake my head at myself, mumbling, "It's the nineteenth floorboard from the *window*, not the door, Pae. . . ."

I reach into the darkness, fingers curling around the unfamiliar hilt of a dagger. My heart aches more than my body, wishing to feel the swirling steel handle of my father's weapon against my palm.

But I chose the shedding of blood over sentiment when I threw my beloved blade into the king's throat. And my only regret is that *he* found it, promising to return it only when he's stabbed it into my back.

Empty blue eyes blink at me in the reflection of the shiny blade I lift into the light, startling me enough to halt my hateful thoughts. My skin is splattered with slices, covered in cuts. I swallow at the sight of the gash traveling down the side of my neck, skim fingers over the jagged skin. Shaking my head, I slip the dagger into my boot, stowing away my scared reflection with it.

I spot a bow and its quiver of sharp arrows concealed in the compartment, and the shadow of a sad smile crosses my face at the memory of Father teaching me how to shoot, the gnarled tree behind our house my only target.

Slinging the bow and quiver across my back, I sift through the other weapons hidden beneath the floor. After tossing a few sharp throwing knives into my pack, where they joined the rations, blanket, water canteens, and the few crumpled garments I'd hastily tucked inside, I struggle to my feet.

I've never felt so delicate, so damaged. The thought has me swelling with anger, has me snatching a knife from my waist and itching to plunge it into the worn, wooden wall before me. Searing pain shoots down my raised arm when the brand above my heart pulls taut with the movement.

A reminder. A representation of what I am. Or rather, what I'm not.

O for Ordinary.

I send the knife flying, plunging it into the wood with gritted teeth. The scar stings, gloating of its endless existence on my body.

". . . I will leave my mark upon your heart, lest you forget who's broken it."

I stalk over to the blade, ready to yank it from the wall, when the board beneath my foot creaks, drawing my attention. Despite knowing that flimsy floorboards are anything but foreign to houses in the slums, my curiosity has me bending to investigate.

If every creaky board were a compartment, our floor would be littered with them—

The wood lifts and my eyebrows do the same, shooting up my forehead in shock. I huff out a humorless laugh as I reach into the shadows of the compartment I didn't know existed.

Silly of me to think that the Resistance was the only secret Father kept from me.

My fingers brush worn leather before I pull out a large book, stuffed with papers that threaten to spill out. I flip through it, recognizing the messy handwriting of a Healer.

Father's journal.

I shove it into my pack, knowing I don't have the time or safety needed to study his work now. I've been here too long, spent too many days wounded and weak and worrying that I'll be found.

The Sight who witnessed me murder the king has likely displayed that image all over the kingdom. I need to get out of Ilya, and I've already wasted the head start *he* so graciously gave me.

I make my way to the door, ready to slip out and onto the streets where I can disappear into the chaos that is Loot. From there, I'll attempt to head across the Scorches to the city of Dor, where Elites don't exist and Ordinary is all they know.

Reaching for the door and the quiet street beyond—

I halt, hand outstretched.

Quiet.

It's nearly midday, meaning Loot and its surrounding streets should be a swarm of swearing merchants and squealing children as the slums buzz with color and commotion.

Something's not right—

The door shudders, something—*someone*—ramming into it from the outside. I jump back, eyes darting around the room. I contemplate ducking down the secret stairwell to the room beneath that held the Resistance meetings, but the thought of being cornered down there makes me queasy. That's when my gaze snaps to the fireplace, and I sigh in annoyance despite my current situation.

How do I always find myself in a chimney?

The door breaks open with a bang before I've barely shimmied halfway up the grimy wall, my feet planted on either side of me while bricks dig into my back.

Brawny.

Only an Elite with extraordinary strength would be able to smash through my barricaded and bolted door so quickly. The sound of heavy boots has me figuring that five Imperials have just filed into my home.

"Don't just stand there. Search the place and convince me that you're useful."

A shiver runs down my spine at the sound of that cool voice, the one I've heard sound like both a caress and a command. I stiffen, slipping slightly down the sooty wall.

He's here.

The voice that follows is gravelly, belonging to an Imperial. "You heard the Enforcer. Get a move on."

The Enforcer.

I bite my tongue, whether to keep myself from letting out a bitter laugh or a scream, I'm not sure. My blood boils at the title, reminding me of everything he's done, every bit of evil he's committed in the shadow of the king. First for his father, and now for his brother—thanks to me ridding him of the former.

Except he's not thanking me. No, he's come to kill me instead.

"Maybe when I rid myself of you, I'll find my courage. So I'm giving you a head start."

A lot of good his head start has done me.

I can't risk being heard scrambling up the chimney, so I wait, listening to heavy footsteps stomping through the house in search of me. My legs are beginning to shake, straining to hold me up while my every wound has me wincing in pain.

"Check the bookcases in the study. There should be a secret passage behind one," the Enforcer commands dryly, sounding *bored.*

Once again, I find myself stiffening. A Resistance member must have confessed that little secret after he tortured it out of them. My pulse quickens at the thought of the fight after the final Trial in the Bowl when Ordinaries, Fatals, and Imperials clashed in a bloody battle.

A bloody battle that I still don't know the outcome of.

The steps of the Imperials grow distant, the sounds of their search softening as they head down the stairs and into the room beneath.

Quiet.

And yet, I know he's still in this room. Only a feeble amount of feet separate us. I can practically feel his presence, just as I've felt the heat of his body against mine, the heat of his gray gaze as it swept over me.

A floorboard creaks. He's close. I'm shaking with anger, revenge coursing through my blood and desperately wishing to spill his. It's a good thing I can't see his face because if I were to catch sight of one of his stupid dimples right now, I wouldn't be able to stop myself from trying to claw it from his face.

But I steady my breathing instead, knowing that if I fight him now, my fury won't be enough to beat him. And I intend to win when I finally face the Enforcer.

"I imagine you pictured my face when you threw that knife." His voice is quiet, considering, sounding far more like the boy I knew. Memories of him flood my mind, managing to make my heart race. "Isn't that right, Paedyn?" And there it is. The edge is back in the Enforcer's voice, erasing Kai and leaving a commander.

My heart hammers against my rib cage.

He can't know I'm here. How could he possibly—

The sound of a blade ripping from splintered wood tells me he yanked my knife out of the wall. I hear a familiar flicking noise and can practically picture him mindlessly flipping the weapon in his hand.

"Tell me, darling, do you think of me often?" His voice is a murmur, as if his lips were pressed against my ear. I shiver, knowing exactly what that feels like.

If he knows I'm here then why hasn't he—

"Do I haunt your dreams, plague your thoughts, like you do mine?"

My breath hitches.

So he doesn't know I'm here, not for certain.

His admission told me as much.

As an Ordinary who was trained and tailored into a *Psychic,* I was taught by my father to read people, to gather information and observations in a matter of seconds.

And I've had far more than a matter of seconds to read Kai Azer.

I've seen through his many masks and facades, glimpsing the boy beneath and growing to know him, care for him. And with all the betrayal now between us, I know he wouldn't declare dreaming of me if he knew I was drinking in every word.

I hear the humor in his voice as he sighs. "Where are you, Little Psychic?"

His nickname is laughable, seeing that he and the rest of the kingdom now know I'm anything but. Anything but Elite.

Nothing but Ordinary.

Soot stings my nose and I have to clamp my hand over it to hold in a sneeze, reminding me of my many nights thieving from the stores lining Loot before escaping through cramped chimneys.

Cramped. Trapped. Suffocating.

My eyes dart across the bricks surrounding me in the darkness. The space is so small, so stuffy, so very easily making me panic.

Calm down.

Claustrophobia chooses the worst times to claw to the surface and remind me of my helplessness.

Breathe.

I do. Deeply. The hand still clamped over my nose smells faintly of metal—sharp and strong and stinging my nose.

Blood.

I pull the shaky hand away from my face, and though I can't see the crimson staining my fingers, I can practically feel it clinging to me. There's still blood crusted under my cracked nails, and I don't know whether it's mine, the king's, or—

I suck in a breath, trying to pull myself together. The Enforcer looms far too close to me, pacing the floor, wood groaning beneath him with each step.

Getting caught because I started sobbing would be equally as embarrassing as getting caught for sneezing.

And I refuse to do either.

At some point, the Imperials stomp back into the room beneath me. "No sign of her, Your Highness."

There's a long pause before *his highness* sighs. "Just as I thought. You're all useless." His next words are sharper than the blade he flips casually in his hand. "Get out."

The Imperials don't waste a single second before scrambling toward the door and away from him. I don't blame them.

But he's still here, leaving nothing but silence to stretch between us. I have a hand clamped over my nose again, and the smell of blood combined with the cramped chimney has my head spinning.

Memories flood my mind—my body caked in blood, my screams as I tried to scrub it away, only managing to stain my skin a sickening red. The sight and smell of so much blood made me sick, made me think of my father bleeding out in my arms, of Adena doing the same.

Adena.

Tears prick my eyes, forcing me to blink away the image of her lifeless body in the sandy Pit. The metallic stench of blood fills my nose again, and I can't stand to smell it, to look at it, to feel it—

Breathe.

A heavy sigh cuts through my thoughts. He sounds as tired as I feel. "It's a good thing you're not here," he says softly, a tone I never thought I'd hear from him again. "Because I still haven't found my courage."

And then my home bursts into flames.

CHAPTER 2
Kai

Flames lick at my heels as I leisurely make my way to the door. Waves of heat crash into my back; wisps of smoke cling to my clothing. I step outside into the cloudy afternoon, now further polluted by the billowing clouds of smoke wafting into the sky.

My lips twitch at the look of shock on my Imperials' faces, accompanied by the unhinged jaws they fight to clamp shut as flames consume the house behind me. Their gazes slowly flick to me, managing to reach as high as my collar before they're shifting uncomfortably on their feet.

They still when I stride toward them with ease.

They think I've gone mad.

Glass shatters when a window bursts behind me, sending shards of sharp edges scattering onto the street. The Imperials flinch, covering their faces. The sight makes me smile.

Maybe they're right. Maybe I have gone mad.

Mad with worry, with rage, with betrayal.

The tension continuously coiling through my body seems to be the only constant in my life, resulting in stiffened shoulders and a clamped jaw. My fingers drum against the dagger at my side, tempting me to take out my frustration on one of the many useless Imperials.

I trace the swirling steel on the hilt, the pattern familiar beneath my fingertips. How could I forget the dagger that's been held against my throat so many times?

How could I forget the dagger that I pulled from my father's severed neck?

It's been three days since I saw the hilt of this very weapon protruding from the king's throat. Three days to grieve, and yet, I haven't shed a single tear. Three days to prepare, and yet, no plan will truly free me from her. Three days to simply be Kitt and Kai—brothers—before we became king and Enforcer.

And now her head start is up.

Though it seems that she used it wisely—took advantage of my weakness, my cowardice, my *feelings* for her—and ran. I spin to face the flames, watching the colorful chaos as fire consumes her home in red, orange, thick black smoke, and—

Silver.

I blink, squinting through suffocating smoke at the collapsing roof. But there's nothing there, no hint of the shimmer I saw a moment ago. I run a hand through my hair before pressing the heels of my palms against tired eyes.

Yes, I've truly gone mad.

"Sir!"

I drop my hands, slowly fixing my gaze on the Imperial brave enough to shout at me. He clears his throat, likely regretting that decision. "I, uh, I think I saw something, Your Highness."

He points to the flaming roof, smoke shifting as a figure stumbles through the flames. A figure with silver hair.

So she is here.

I can't seem to decide whether I'm relieved or not.

"Bring her to me."

My command rings out, and the Imperials don't miss a beat. And, apparently, neither does she. I barely catch a glimpse of her before she jumps off the edge of the crumbling roof and onto the neighboring one, legs bounding as soon as she finds her footing.

Imperials run down the street below, Brawnies and Shields rendered utterly useless as she jumps from roof to roof. I comb a hand through my hair again before dragging it down my face, unsurprised by their incompetence.

I flip the knife I'd yanked from the wall in my hand before taking off down the street, quickly catching up with my Imperials. I feel each of their powers buzzing under my skin, begging to be released. But their abilities are useless to me unless I can get her on the ground, making me regret not bringing a Tele who could set her on the street before me with nothing but a thought.

She can only stay on the rooftops if she's able to jump between them. And that's why, with the flick of my wrist, I send the knife flying toward her.

I watch as it meets its mark, slicing through her thigh as she leaps. Her cry of pain makes me flinch, an action that is as frustrating as it is foreign to me.

She hits the flat roof hard, rolling in a feeble attempt to lessen the fall. I watch as she staggers to her feet, blood streaming down her leg. Her features are fuzzy from this distance, and I can almost pretend that she is simply a forgetful figure limping to the edge of a roof.

She's no fool. She knows she can't make the jump.

My gaze snaps to the Imperials gawking up at her. "Must I do everything for you?" My voice is cold. "Go get her."

But then my eyes wander back up to the roof. Empty.

Foolish of me to think she'd make this easy.

"Find her," I bark, gritting my teeth against a slew of curses. The Imperials split up, sprinting in opposite directions down the streets I ensured would be practically empty for this exact reason. A thief's ability to blend in is alarming, allowing them to get swallowed in chaos, lost in a crowd. And she would do just that if I hadn't cleared Loot for the day.

I stride down the street, glancing into the adjacent alleys jutting off it. Muffled shouts ring out, echoing off the run-down homes and shops. I silently continue my search, feet faltering when I spot a figure slumped at the end of a shadowed alley.

I crouch beside the Imperial, eyes wandering over his once-white uniform, now soaked with blood. Scarlet seeps from a throwing knife buried deep in his chest, oozing over the crisp folds of his uniform.

She is a vicious little thing.

My fingers are at his throat, checking for a pulse despite knowing I won't feel its familiar beat. I sigh, dropping my head into my hands. My whole body feels heavy with exhaustion, weighed down by my worries.

I buried someone who tried to kill her once.

Simply because I knew it was something she would have wanted. I carried Sadie's dead body through the dark Whispers Forest during that first Trial because I knew Paedyn was falling apart when I left her to spin that ring on her thumb. If it were up to me, I would have never buried the body of someone who tried to kill her. But I wasn't thinking of myself when I'd done it.

Death is familiar to me, both friend and foe, and far too frequent in my life. But for her, Death is devastation, no matter its victim.

I imagine she's spinning that ring on her thumb at this very moment, biting the inside of her cheek as she forces herself to run from the man she just killed rather than dig him a grave like I know she desperately wishes to.

"She would have buried you if she weren't so busy running from me, you know," I murmur to the body beside me, confirming that I have, in fact, gone mad. I lift the Imperial's white mask from his face, giving me a better view of his glassy brown eyes before I brush his lids closed. "So the least I can do is bury you for her."

I'd never given a second thought to what became of my soldiers' bodies. And yet, here I am, hauling a man over my shoulder because of a girl who despises doling out death. I grunt under the Imperial's weight, wondering why the hell I'm even bothering with this.

What has she done to me?

His limp body swings over my shoulder with every step I take.

Will her grave be the next I dig?

CHAPTER 3
Paedyn

I'm shocked he can't hear my pounding heart, feel my burning gaze as it trails over him.

I shift, my stomach sliding across the rough roof as I peek over the edge. Pain sears down my leg, drawing my attention to the crudely bandaged slice on my thigh. I bite my tongue, holding in a cry along with a string of colorful curse words. The hastily torn hem of my spare shirt is already a revolting shade of crimson atop the wound, forcing me to turn my attention on the figure below, unable to stand the sight of it.

But I can't stand the sight of him, either.

I already know what his remark would be if I'd told him that to his smirking face—*You're a terrible liar, Gray.*

My eyes roll at the thought before they travel over him, taking in his messy black waves falling wherever they please across his brow. He's crouching beside the Imperial I'd gifted with a knife to the chest, his profile grim, gray eyes skimming over the man's face. Then he drops his head into his hands, looking equally frustrated and fatigued.

The sight of the Enforcer fills me with rage, but I force myself to focus on him rather than the blood blooming across the Imperial's white uniform.

I swallow, suddenly feeling sick at the thought. Tears stung my eyes when I let that knife fly into the man's chest, blurring my vision as his body crumpled to the ground.

I'm sorry. I'm so, so sorry.

I don't know if he heard my pleading apology, don't know if he saw the sorrow in my eyes before I dragged myself onto the roof of a shop when the sound of footsteps echoed off the walls.

I blink away the memory, the tears, and instead choose to focus on the Enforcer mere feet away from me.

I could kill him. Right here, right now.

There's suddenly another throwing knife clutched between my stained fingers, my trembling hand.

"Promise me you'll stay alive long enough to stab me in the back?"

His words to me after that first ball echo in my mind.

I could make good on that promise.

With the way he's positioned, his back is exactly where I would bury this blade. The hilt of the dagger grows sweaty in my palm, but I tighten my grip.

Do it.

There's suddenly a lump in my throat that I furiously try to swallow. The boy beneath me killed my father, has killed dozens of Ordinaries in the name of the king. And I am his next target.

I hate how I'm hesitating.

Do. It.

I raise my arm, fingers trembling around the knife. The movement makes my brand burn, stretching the skin and the reminder engraved there.

O for Ordinary.

He suddenly shifts, lifting the Imperial's mask and closing his unseeing eyes with a gentleness that doesn't belong to the Enforcer—a gentleness I wish I hadn't witnessed.

"She would have buried you if she weren't so busy running from me, you know."

My breath hitches; my heart hammers.

He's right. I would have dragged this man to the nearest patch of dirt and dug him into the ground if I could have. As if that would right the wrong I'd done. As if that would make up for the fact that I never buried my best friend or father.

The symmetry in their deaths was sickening—both of them bleeding out in my arms before I *ran*.

"So the least I can do is bury you for her."

That one soft sentence cuts through me like a knife, making me nearly drop the one clutched in my hand. I stare, stunned, as he heaves the man over his shoulder and staggers to his feet.

Kai.

That is who I see before me. Not the Enforcer. Not one of the many masks he slips on. Just *him*.

I hate it.

I hate that I got to see a glimpse of that boy again. Because it is so much easier to hate him when it's not *him* I'm hating at all, but the Enforcer he was molded into.

I watch as he makes his way out of the alley with the man I killed slung over his shoulder. Kai does nothing without reason, leaving me to baffle over his kindness.

And when he disappears around the corner, I'm suddenly wondering why I showed *him* kindness.

The stars are flirtatious things, always winking down in the darkness.

But they make for good company, surrounding me with their countless constellations. I've been lying on the roof of this run-down shop for hours, watching day melt into dusk and dusk fade into darkness.

The sun had sunk deep into the horizon before the Imperials' echoing shouts slowly sputtered out. Eventually, the sounds of their shuffling boots on uneven cobblestone died as I stared at the sky, willing it to darken.

When the last streaks of purple bleed from the canopy of clouds, leaving a black blanket smothering all of Ilya, I finally stand to my feet and stretch. My body aches—a feeling I've grown familiar with—but the fresh wound I earned today is especially painful. At the sudden movement, blood begins to trickle down my thigh, carving a crimson path down my leg. I can't stand the sticky feel of it, reminding me of the blood I will never be able to wash off my hands.

Climbing down from the roof is an embarrassingly slow process, but as soon as my feet hit the street, I'm slipping into the shadows. I limp through quiet alleys, avoiding the homeless who have begun to hunch back into their familiar corners for the evening.

There are Imperials crawling everywhere. They quietly pace down the streets, heads swiveling, eyes searching the darkness for me. That makes things both complicated and completely annoying. I dodge them in the dying light, doing my best not to drip a trail of blood across the cobblestones while weaving through alleys.

I turn down a dark street littered with uneven stones—

A rough hand clamps down around my shoulder, the grip anything but gentle. I duck my head, catching oiled black boots out of the corner of my eye as the scent of starch slams into me. I don't hesitate before hooking my foot around the man's ankle and tugging, sending him sprawling to the ground, startled. I'm on him in a matter of seconds, slipping the dagger from my boot and sending the hilt of it down against his temple, silencing his strangled cry of surprise.

The thin Imperial is barely more than a boy, now lying in an unconscious heap on the shadowed cobblestones. My heart beats wildly, forcing me to take a breath before I struggle to drag him farther into the alley, hiding him deeper in the darkness.

Reaching the outskirts of the Scorches Desert is a slow and severely frustrating journey. I never imagined that I would be relieved to see the wide stretch of sand before me, but after hours of slinking in the shadows and narrowly avoiding getting caught, the sight is enough to make me smile despite the pinch of pain it causes.

There are very few Imperials stationed on the border of the Scorches, seeing that the citizens of Dor and Tando know better than to visit Ilya and be mistaken as an Ordinary. Isolation is what Ilya does best, ensuring the Elite society continues to thrive without being tainted by those without abilities.

The thought makes me angry. The truth of it makes me sick.

And with fury fueling each one of my steps, I begin stomping my way through the sand. It shifts under my boots before eventually slipping into them, making this journey impossibly more uncomfortable.

The hours tick by as I trudge forward. I occupy myself by racking my tired brain, trying to recall the maps my father would spread before me as a child. I'm not entirely sure how far the desert spans, which makes me feel entirely foolish for thinking I could survive this with my injuries.

As if I have any other options.

I sigh, submitting to the fact that Death has cornered me on all sides, forcing me to face him head-on. My memory of the maps is vague, but I suspect that if I continue at my current pace, I'll make it to Dor in roughly five days. That is, if I can manage to walk for nearly the entire time—which could potentially end in me collapsing, allowing Death to finally claim me.

Well, there's only one way to find out.

The night grows cold, the temperature plunging as I head deeper into the desert. My dirty, pocketed vest is far more useful for thieving than it is for warmth—and that's exactly why she made it. I run my thumb over the rough, olive fabric, remembering the soft, brown hands that stitched it together.

"Promise you'll wear it for me?"

The image of Adena dying in my lap, whispering her final request, flashes in my mind, only forcing my feet faster. Even if I had the time, I know I wouldn't be sleeping much on this journey—or ever.

Because, in the quiet moments before sleep steals me, I watch Adena die all over again. As if my eyes shutting is an invitation to relive that horror. The blunt branch through her chest, her bound and broken fingers, her body covered in *blood* . . .

My own blood begins to boil at the thought of Blair's smirk as she guided the branch through Adena's back with nothing but her mind.

I'm going to kill her.

I'm unsure of how, or where, or when, but Adena wasn't the only one who wouldn't make promises unless she could keep them.

I rummage through my pack before pulling on the worn jacket that belonged to my father. It's far too large, and yet, nothing has ever fit me more perfectly. I shove my hands into the pockets, shivering slightly as I continue pushing through the sand.

The hours creep by, stealing the darkness and replacing the sky with streaks of orange and the promise of a sweltering sun. My breaks are brief, only long enough to rest my sore legs as I eat my rations and drink my warm water. I frequently inspect my wounds, taking extra care with the fresh one along my thigh.

A gift from *him.*

The bloody gash is his handiwork—I'm sure of it. The sheer accuracy of the throw alone could only belong to him, along with the idea to slice me open in order to get me off the rooftops. I would expect nothing less from the calculating Enforcer who's so desperate to catch me.

All the more reason to pick up the pace.

I push my sore legs faster as I try to push him from my thoughts.

He's coming for me.

My lips twitch at the thought, tugging at the scar trailing from my jaw.

And I won't hesitate again.

CHAPTER 4
Kai

"You look like hell."

Kitt's eyes skip over the scarlet splotches staining my shirt, courtesy of the Imperial he doesn't need to know I buried.

For her.

Borderline treasonous at best.

Pathetic at worst.

The king's scrutiny finally meets mine, our eyes locking, laced with amusement. Familiarity forms a smile on my lips involuntarily, simply at the feeling of being brothers. Brothers who don't have titles wedged before their names. Brothers who, for this blissful moment, ignore their allegiances tethered by blood.

It's the first time he's let me look at him in days. Really look at him.

He's traded tears for tiredness, smiling eyes for haunted ones, accompanied by slightly sunken cheeks and a stubbled jaw. My inspection snags on the same wrinkled shirt I've seen the past three days—half-unbuttoned, sleeves splattered with ink.

"Yeah, well, you don't look much better," I say, something akin to a smile still surprising my lips.

Kitt blinks, taking in his stained hands and the smudged papers sprawled out before him as if seeing the scene for the first time. Then he sighs, slowly shuffling the papers he's been so engrossed with into a sloppy pile. "I'll be fine. Just a little tired, that's all."

"You are aware that there is a simple solution to that—correct?" I sound annoyingly timid as I try to walk the fine line between lightening the mood and attempting to talk some sense into him.

Kitt is different. We are different. I no longer know where my brother ends and my king begins.

When he doesn't respond, I finish with a quietly concerned, "You should try to rest. Get some sleep." I nod toward the worn leather seat he's inherited. "I haven't seen you leave that chair in days."

"Sleep is for the dead." The noise Kitt follows his blunt statement with can only be described as a choking scoff. "Sorry," he half laughs, shaking his head with what seems to be amusement. "Too soon?"

I force a smile while facing what feels like a stranger. In another life, I can hear those same words falling from Kitt's mouth, only they are lacking the bitter edge, the crazed crack of his smile. Grief has morphed him into a man I'm wary of.

"Fine," I sigh, "sleep is for the dead. Though it doesn't seem you're living much either." My eyes search his, pleading in a way I never would with words. "You haven't left the study since your coronation. We could take a walk through the gardens, go see the queen." I swallow at the thought of what grief has done to her. "The physicians say she's getting worse. She hasn't left her bed, and they fear . . . They fear there may not be much time left."

He stills, silent long after my suggestion. I shouldn't be surprised by his reluctancy. Kitt has no bond with my mother. Because she is exactly that—*my* mother. Not his.

Clearing my throat, I quickly change the subject to more appealing endeavors. "We could visit Gail in the kitchen. She won't stop asking to see you until you eat one of her sticky buns—"

"I'm quite happy here, thank you."

I blink at him. A kingly dismissal if I ever heard one.

I nod slowly, taking a step back toward the door. "Well, if there is nothing else . . ."

Your Majesty.

I swallow the words before I can spit them out at the end of the sentence. My hand reaches for the door, ready to make my escape—

"Is that her blood?"

I falter, turning to face him.

His green gaze is fixed on the splotches soaking my shirt. I'm still, silent for a long moment, simply allowing him to study me while I try to decipher what it is looming behind his eyes.

When I finally speak, it's the question I'm avoiding answering myself that falls from my lips. "Would you be more disappointed if it was, or if it wasn't?"

He swallows. Takes a deep breath. Smiles in a way that is anything but happy. "I don't know." Another long, lingering silence. "You?"

"I don't know."

Pathetic.

"Is it?" Kitt doesn't look at me as he says it. "Hers, I mean."

I sigh, suddenly tired at the reminder of this morning. "No."

Relieved? Disappointed? It seems I suddenly cannot tell the difference between the two as I say that seemingly simple word.

"I see," Kitt mutters. "But she was there, I take it?"

"She was. I forced her out of the house." Kitt quirks a brow before I finish, "Burnt it to the ground."

"I see."

We watch each other warily. She is a topic better left untouched, and yet, she's never further than a thought away. Torture for the two of us.

"The blood?" Kitt nods toward me expectantly.

"Belongs to the Imperial she stabbed. Killed him near Loot."

There's that lifeless laugh again. "She does have a nasty habit of stabbing people, doesn't she?"

I clear my throat, careful not to cross the line I no longer know where to find when it comes to Kitt. "Yes, well, so do I. And she didn't escape unharmed—I made sure of that."

"So," Kitt drawls in a tone all too familiar. I see Father reflected in his gaze, reincarnated in his words. "What are you telling me, Enforcer?"

I stiffen slightly. "I believe she is headed to the Scorches, attempting to make it across to either Dor or Tando. Though I'm not sure she will. Then again, she does also have a nasty habit of staying alive." My tone is flat, embodying the Enforcer he wishes me to be. "I will ready some men and desert horses to head into the Scorches after her. We will leave as soon as we are able." I pause. "Your Majesty."

Dammit. I just couldn't help myself, could I?

Kitt studies me, seemly less than unsettled by the title. Rather, curious. "And then you'll bring her to me."

I nod.

"Will you?"

I stare at him, breathing slowly. "Do you have reason to believe I won't?"

Kitt shrugs a shoulder before leaning back to cross ink-stained arms over his wrinkled shirt. "It's just that, well, I know your . . . history."

I stiffen. We eye each other, silently communicating the one thing we never used to utter aloud. Kitt's comment was subtle, but his lack of faith in my fulfilling his command was anything but.

My reply is distant. "That is different. And you know it."

"Is it?" Kitt's tone is unsettlingly innocent. "You had no attachment to those children, and yet, you still spared them their punishments despite their crimes."

"Kitt—" I start before he abruptly cuts me off.

"Look, I'm not saying that saving children was the wrong thing to do." He laughs, devoid of humor. "I'm not a monster. Banishing the Ordinaries with their families instead of outrightly executing them was a kindness, however small. But"—his eyes darken—"you repeatedly disobeyed Father's orders. Again and again."

I sigh through my nose, exasperated. At the mention of Father, I've lost the argument before it's even begun. In Kitt's eyes, nothing I say can justify an action against the previous king.

"I always obeyed orders," I sigh. "And I always will. That was an exception."

"Was?" Kitt repeats, his expression equally scrutinizing and skeptical. "What, do you not plan to continue that exception because I am king? Because I know?"

It's a struggle to not openly gape at him. "Do you want me to execute the children, then?" My chest heaves, heart hammering against sore ribs. "By all means, just say the word and it will be done, my king."

Shit.

I bite my tongue hard enough to focus on the burst of pain and not the surge of anger sweeping through me. The last thing I want is to view Kitt as nothing more than my king, to treat him how I treated the one before.

Kitt is easy to love until he begins resembling the father who had little love for me.

"Kai." The king's harsh gaze softens with his voice. "I know this isn't exactly a simple order to follow. I suppose I'm just . . . paranoid. I've witnessed you go against orders in the past." At the look I give him, he hastily adds, "For good reason. Which is why I worry when asking you to bring *her* back to me." His eyes find mine, full of an emotion I can't determine. "And what better 'good reason' to disobey orders than your feelings for her."

We stare at each other, eyes locked and throats lodged with unspoken words. I want to protest, beg my mouth to open and spew a convincing string of words that contradict his accusation. But he's right, and we both know it. My feelings are what freed her in the first place.

The thought jolts me, has me jumping to the conclusion that Kitt knows this, knows that I already let her go once—and he resents me for it. But nothing on his placid face proves this, and I bury the thought before it can do the same to me.

"This can't be easy for you, either," I say quietly, testing the rocky water that is Kitt's flood of feelings for the same girl.

He almost laughs. "Oh, so now we're going to talk about this?"

We'd skirted around the touchy topic even before she decided to tear the tendons of our father's neck with the very dagger I have strapped to my side. She was a risk, something we avoided voicing as though that could stop her from driving a wedge between us.

Falling for her was fatal.

"Whatever I felt for her died the day she killed him," Kitt says simply.

Lies.

I've been telling myself the very same thing, convincingly calling it the truth.

"I know the feeling," I nod.

Lies.

We eye each other, both content to drown in our shared delusions. But we say nothing else, not bothering to confront the fact that we're lying to both ourselves and each other.

"I will bring her back to you, Kitt." My voice is quiet, earnest. "Before I was your Enforcer, I was your brother. My loyalty is to you and no one else." I'm silent for a long moment, allowing my words to sink in. "She killed my father too, you know."

More silence stretches between us.

"Alive," Kitt says finally. "Bring her to me alive."

His tone doesn't suggest that this is exactly a mercy.

Pulling off the thick ring I was given the day I became Ilya's Enforcer, I place it on his desk. "Give it back to me when I've earned your trust again."

CHAPTER 5

Paedyn

Sand scrapes the inside of my mouth, grinding against my gums. I run my tongue over dry teeth, feeling the same coating of grit I've had for the past three days. Spitting is no longer an option, seeing that every drop of saliva is needed in my struggle to survive.

My throat aches. My feet. My legs. My head. My *everything.*

Sand shifts under my feet as I continue shuffling onward. With a sore neck shouting in protest, I lift my swimming head toward the setting sun above. It sinks toward the horizon, daring to dip behind sand dunes and rip its rays from the sky.

My palm strays to my forehead, sticky and burnt from days spent trudging through the desert. A shiver runs down my spine, racking my aching body. With a sigh, I convince myself it's the rapidly cooling desert that's chilling me to the bone and not a fever settling beneath my sticky skin.

I've been walking for days—and most nights that follow.

The desert is an unforgiving beast. Each night I plead with the sand, begging it to allow me a few hours of rest. Despite my desperation,

the desert has yet to grant me little more than an hour or two of sleep at a time. Whether it's sand in my ears or scorpions at my feet, I can't manage more than a paranoid nap.

"I'm the only one keeping you company, so the least you could do is let me sleep through a single night," I say through cracked lips, my voice little more than a croak. I scan the vast desert, seeing nothing but sand and hearing no response but the whispering wind. I huff, breaking off pieces of crumbling bread before popping them into my equally dry mouth.

"I'm going crazy." I throw my hands up, letting them fall down again to slap my sides. "I've been talking to sand for three days," I grumble, feet dragging deep lines beneath me. "It's not fair to blame the entirety of my insanity on you, I suppose. I've been going crazy for a while now." I laugh, practically coughing. "I mean, just stepping foot out here is crazy to begin with. Right?"

I look around, despite knowing that the dunes won't deign a response. Though what's worse than me talking to the sand is suddenly hearing the sand talk back. That is when I'll truly be worried.

My water supply is running dangerously low, and simply knowing that fact makes my throat even drier. The canteens clanging in my pack will be empty in no more than two days. Self-control is far less appealing when surviving on a limited number of sips.

I find myself scanning the horizon for the dozenth time this hour, hoping to catch sight of a city. Catch sight of anything.

Nothing.

No outline of buildings or smoke puffing from a chimney. I struggle to swallow, feeling so small in the vastness surrounding me. Feeling like a single grain of sand in a sea of dipping dunes.

Insignificant.

Lost.

Lonely.

I swipe at a bead of sweat threatening to sting the eyes that are already being blinded by a setting sun. The waves of sand are cast in golden hues, mirroring the shifting sky above them. Admiring the beauty of the treacherous terrain I'm tramping through is a bittersweet way to end my nights. Dusk in the desert is devastatingly breathtaking, and yet, the very last place I wish to be.

My gaze snags on something glittering in the distance, glinting enticingly in the sun. I blink in the blinding light, my eyes dry. The pool of water shimmers, winking invitingly at me. I shake my head, only managing to make it pound harder.

Mirage.

Teasing, tempting things. They tend to taunt in the form of crisp water and pools I ache to plunge into. I sigh, bending slightly to rub my sore legs. Blisters hide inside sweaty boots, my feet sticky with sand.

The things I would do for some water . . .

I spend the rest of my evening buried beneath the folds of my father's worn jacket, the dropping temperatures numbing my toes. After surviving a surprisingly friendly encounter with the largest snake I've ever seen, I walked long into the night, talking to the sand and feeding my insanity.

My eyelids droop, feeling as heavy as the rest of me. I manage to keep my eyes open long enough to find a flat stretch of sand to stumble toward. Slinging my pack from my back, I struggle to free the scratchy blanket from within.

I've barely spread it across the sand before my body ungracefully follows. I collapse atop the blanket, pulling my jacket tight around my aching body. Clutching a piece of stale bread, I take my time nibbling at it before swishing sips of hot water around my dry mouth.

"You know," I whisper into the darkness, "it's not all your fault I can't sleep at night. The nightmares certainly don't help."

As if summoned by the mention of them, flashes of Adena plague my thoughts. The feel of her blood oozing between my fingers. My tears as they splattered across her smooth cheek. The bloody branch skewering her through the back . . .

A shudder snakes through me. I swallow hard, feeling sick but unable to afford spilling the little content that's occupying my stomach. "I might blame you for my lack of sleep"—my voice is little more than a choked whisper—"but I don't think I want to sleep at all if it means I'll see her like that. Again. I just can't . . . I can't—"

I haven't realized I'm crying until the tear rolls down my nose. I swipe it away with a huff before curling my fingers around the green vest swallowed beneath my jacket. My nail traces the even stitching of the pockets, feeling the folds of her painstaking work.

If I want to keep my promise to Adena, I have to survive. I have to live in order to wear this vest for her.

And I'm determined to do just that.

I mumble once more into the night, my eyes sealing out the world before I slip into sleep.

"And I'll get my revenge. For her."

CHAPTER 6

Kai

Silver glints in the dying sunlight.

I drink in a flash of blue eyes, quenching my thirst.

Her freckles like the sand surrounding us.

A silver dagger, sharp as her tongue, flipping between swift fingers.

It's her.

There she is. Just standing there. Watching me like I'm no more than a stranger she's sizing up. Like I'm worth nothing more than the coins she's preparing to steal from my pocket.

Like I'm not the man who ruined her life. Like she's not guilty of doing the same to me.

She strides toward me, the sight so familiar that I find myself fighting a habitual smile, the muscle memory yet another memento of her. Something aches when she finally stands before me, her hands tucked behind her back. I absentmindedly rub a hand above my heart as I look her over, feeling a trickle of urgency for reasons I can't place.

I shake my head in a futile attempt to clear it.

I was supposed to do something. What was I supposed to do with—

Her lips split into a smile, her eyes roaming over my face.

There goes the ache in my chest, feeling like a blunt knife.

"Hello, Prince."

Her voice is silky, soothing in a way that sends shivers down my spine. "I have a gift for you," she says smoothly, smiling sweetly. "Something to remember me by."

She pulls her hands from behind her back, presenting them to me. Her fingers are fisted around a drooping bundle of dull, blue flowers.

Forget-me-nots.

I start to smile, but the emotion snags on my lips. My gaze drops to the fist of flowers—the same ones given to her on our final night together in the rain. And then I'm suddenly staggering back at what I see, clutching my chest and the pounding pain there.

"What is it?" she asks, far too innocently. "What's wrong, Malakai?"

I gasp, gaping at the sticky blood now drenching her hands, dripping down her arms. Each flower stem is stained a sickening red, dulling its vibrance, wilting in her palm.

"You . . . ," I stutter, shaking my head at her. "His blood. That's his blood, isn't it?"

The look on her face mirrors mine, shocked and sketched with hurt. "I did what I had to. I *do* what I have to." Her gaze hardens, as does her resolve. She steps toward me, dropping whatever flowers aren't sticking to her bloody hands as she reaches for my face. I jerk away, practically tripping over my feet in my attempt to escape her touch.

"What have you done?" My voice cracks. "Look what you did. What you are making me do."

I suddenly identify the ache emanating from my chest.

It's my heart.

That's when I remember what it is I must do with her.

"What have you done, Enforcer?" Her voice trembles, bitter and biting. "So it's okay when you kill? Hmm?" She takes a step toward me, but I hold my ground. "You have just as much blood on your hands, Kai. The difference between us is that you refuse to see it."

I'm shaking my head, beginning to back away again.

"Oh, you don't believe me?" She's practically laughing, finding this amusing. "You're covered in it."

I look down, raising red hands from my sides. My breath comes in fast pants as my eyes sweep over my body.

I'm dripping in death.

Blood clings to my hair, pools in my boots, coats my teeth. I'm spitting, sputtering, spiraling as I stagger backward. "No, no, no . . ."

"Go ahead," she challenges, her voice quiet. "Spill my blood and wear it with the rest."

I scream.

My eyes fly open.

I'm blinking blindly at the inky sky above, sand shifting beneath my back. My heart pounds as I scan the makeshift camp, eyes adjusting to the darkness. A dozen dozing Imperials litter the desert ground, all scattered around the dying fire.

My throat is raw.

Had I been screaming?

If I woke any of my men, they're smart enough to act as though I hadn't. I sit up slowly, my back aching from nights spent on uneven sand and days sitting atop stiff saddles. Dirt-streaked hair tickles my forehead, and I run my fingers through it before warming them beside the fire.

I've been in this damn desert for four days now.

And not a single trace of her anywhere.

Well, no physical trace of her anywhere.

And yet, I see her everywhere. She haunts me. Half the time I'm wondering whether she's already dead, whether the desert has claimed another, swallowed her whole and spit her out as a phantom to ensure my suffering.

No one else glimpses the gleam of silver hair in the sunlight, or the outline of her figure atop a dune.

Because no one else is going insane.

I'm losing my mind, feeling lost in this desert despite knowing we'll reach Dor before tomorrow's sunrise. We'll scout out the city first, and if we find nothing, we'll head toward Tando to continue our search.

She can't have made it to a city yet.

Right?

Despite my denial, I've seen what she is capable of. Seen how she can survive; heard how she *has* survived her whole life. I doubt even the desert is a strong enough force to take her from this world before she's ready. The Scorches will soon learn of her stubbornness.

I raise my head from the remaining glowing embers of the fire, fixing my gaze on the shifting sky above. Dawn dances along the horizon, creeping up on the clouds to cast them in faint, golden light. My eyes shift to the slumbering men surrounding me, their snores the only sound filling this corner of the desert.

Sighing, I stand to my feet, stretching my sore limbs. "Up. Now." My command echoes, stirring even the desert horses tied several feet from our makeshift camp. I'm greeted with groggy grumblings as I begin pacing the messy circle of Imperials. "Good morning," I say lightly, though the toe of my boot nudging them in the ribs is anything but.

At that, they don't hesitate to obey my demands. The disheveled bunch is up and milling about in a matter of minutes, some tending to the horses while others round up our scattered supplies. We're gnawing on stringy, dried rabbit and sipping warm water before mounting our horses and setting off at a steady pace.

The rabbit rations have me swooshing sandy water around my mouth. It's not just the taste I'm attempting to erase, but also the memory that accompanies it. I distantly wonder if I twisted my mouth as I ate it, just as I had in the Trials when she watched me close enough to notice.

It's dangerous, how much I think of her. How much everything reminds me of her. How much I wonder if everything was a game to her, a ploy to help the Resistance. To help the Ordinaries overthrow the kingdom. To kill the king. To kill my *father.*

Do I really care that she killed him?

I shake away the thought, shifting in the saddle and rolling my tense shoulders.

I'll find out soon enough. Find *her* soon enough.

And when I do, I'll get my answers.

CHAPTER 7
Paedyn

I swear the scorpion scuttling dangerously close to my worn boots blinks in response to my question.

That's it. I'm actually insane.

With that thought in mind, I sigh and repeat my question. "I said, if you could eat anything—and I mean *anything*—what would it be?"

To say my voice is raspy would be an understatement. My throat feels as scratchy as the sand crunching beneath my feet, so dry I can hardly think straight. I shake my aching head at the creature while carelessly stepping around it, practically stumbling. "Fine. If you won't answer, I will." I trip in the sand, tripping over my words. "I—I could go for an orange. Yeah. A fat, juicy orange. Or . . . or some butterscotch."

I look back at the scorpion, finding it scurrying close behind. The sight should be far more alarming to me, but I can't find the energy to care at the moment. "You know, my father loved butterscotch." I make a sound that only slightly resembles a laugh. "Sometimes I wonder if I even like the candy, ya know? Like, maybe . . . maybe I just convinced myself I liked them because he did."

The scorpion stares up at me.

Or maybe it doesn't. I've had some trouble deciphering what's reality recently.

Is this my fifth or sixth day in the desert?

I almost laugh.

Maybe I'm dead already. How am I to know the difference?

I stumble, sand suddenly flying up to meet me. My knees sink into the gritty ground as I pant, the sinking sun still burning my raw skin. With a shaky breath, I slowly stumble to my feet, forcing my sore legs to continue their unsteady march.

I'm tired. So very tired.

My eyelids droop, mimicking the sun as it begins dipping behind dunes for the night.

Stay awake.

Suddenly, I feel as though I'm back in the Whispers, stumbling in the dark while trying not to bleed out from the deep slice beneath my ribs. That is when *he* found me. Saved me.

I shake the thought away and scan the horizon for the hundredth time, my eyes tracing the outline of each shadowy building that litters the city beyond.

I'm almost there.

Where "there" is, I haven't the slightest idea. I'm not sure which city I've happened upon, whether it's Dor or Tando, but I'm not exactly in any position to be picky.

I just need to make it *there*.

Licking my chapped lips does nothing but add more sand to my mouth. Now would be the time to gulp down some grainy water, except that I greedily drank the last of it this morning.

I'm dying of thirst.

Maybe just dying. Maybe just dead already.

My ragged laugh at the thought rapidly morphs into a racking sob, seeming to rattle my brittle bones.

Keep walking. Just keep walking.

But I don't want to. What I want is to lie down, shut my eyes, and *rest.*

My feet slow, my whole body feeling sluggish.

Keep. Walking.

I know if I stop now, I'll never start again. Dehydration, fatigue, and the many injuries still scattering my body have finally caught up to me. If I lie down, it will be on my deathbed.

Would that be so bad?

That little voice in my head, the only one I've heard for days besides my own, has grown rather convincing.

What am I living for? Why am I putting myself through this agony?

Every inch of me aches. Every inch of me begs for the mercy that is giving up.

"N-no," I stutter. "No, I can't." Talking to myself has never been a good sign, but it's the only thing that will keep my eyelids from shutting out the world and my body from shutting down. "I've . . ." Another ragged breath. "I've survived too much to die by desert."

I press a calloused palm to the stubborn beat of my heart, proof that broken things can still serve a purpose. My fingers trail up to the familiar letter carved there, teasing me with the reminder of just how fragile I am.

O for Ordinary.

"O for 'on the brink of death.'" My attempt at a joking tone sounds scarily similar to a dying whisper. "This is not the way I imagined my end. I'm . . ." A fit of dry coughs has me slumping. "I'm embarrassed to not die in a more dramatic manner."

I really thought it would be him who did the honor. Him who

shoved my beloved dagger through my chest. Or maybe my neck, simply for the sickening symmetry.

He'll be so disappointed to learn he was robbed of his revenge, that it was the desert where death finally caught up to me.

My vision is blurry as it sweeps over the city so close, catching something shifting in the distance. Squinting, I struggle to make out what seems to be a figure. I blink. Is this my mind playing tricks on me? Teasing me one last time?

My knees are suddenly sinking into the sand once again, my palms sliding out before me.

I guess I'll never know.

My temple meets warm sand, and I hum at the feel of it.

Why was the desert never this comfy before?

My fingers clutch the crumpled seam of my vest, pulling the promise around me.

I wore it every day, A. To my very last.

"I'm just . . . I'm just closing . . . my . . ."

My eyes flutter closed; the world shut out by a single blink.

And for the first time in days, I don't dread the sleep that awaits me.

A heartbeat thuds beneath my ear.

I stir in the strong arms surrounding me, my senses sluggish.

Strong arms. I'm being carried.

My eyes fly open.

I'm smothered by darkness, swaddled in a blanket of blackness that the sky has thrown atop us. With eyes made utterly useless at the moment, I focus on the feel of a rough hand beneath my knee, its twin encircling my shoulders.

It's him. He found me.

I jostle with each uneven step, trying desperately to calm my hammering heart and force my foggy head to formulate a plan. But he's too close, too *solid*, as though he's walked straight out of my nightmares and into the very real night before me.

I suddenly can't remember how to breathe.

He found me. He found me. He found me.

My mind screams the three words I've been so terrified of, drowning out any hope of a rational thought. I'm paralyzed in his arms, powerless in his hold that once felt so safe. His chest rises and falls against me, a feeling that was once so familiar. Now it is foreign. Frightening.

How did he find me?

I'm still trying to puzzle out why I'm still alive, despite being carried to my doom by Death itself. He's holding me. He's taking me back to Ilya. Back to Kitt and the wrath I'm sure is waiting for me—

He killed my father.

That one thought saves me from insanity.

I will not hesitate. Not again.

Forcing myself to breathe, I hone in on the hand around my shoulders, easily assessing the best angle in which to snap his wrist bone. It's his legs I focus on next, the fatigue in his stride, the unsteadiness that will aid in sweeping him off his feet. How long has he been carrying me? Where are his men? I scan the inkiness surrounding us, seeing nothing but the city we are walking into.

I can feel a thin blade strapped to his belt, and my heart skips over itself. But the hilt is plain, smooth against my hip. I take a moment to swallow my disappointment at the loss of my father's dagger before forcing myself to focus.

Take him down. Then finish the job you haven't been able to.

After that, I'll simply blend into the city, camouflaging myself with the chaos I'm so used to. No one will ever find me again. He is the only one who could, and after tonight, he will no longer be a threat to my existence.

Envisioning every move before I attempt to make it, I suck in one final steadying breath.

And then I'm moving.

A scream tears from his throat when his wrist snaps under my palm. He stumbles, all but throwing me out of his arms. I anticipate his ungraceful toss and drop to the ground, sand sticking to my sweaty palms as I sweep my leg back to catch his ankles.

He topples to the ground with a grunt. I'm straddling his chest within the next breath, my knees pinning down his arms, pressing my weight onto his broken bone.

My words cut into his strangled cry. "I'll admit I'm a little disappointed." I tug at the dagger on his hip, freeing it from its sheath before settling the infuriatingly dull tip against the throat I can hardly see. "I was hoping you'd put up more of a fight."

"W-what? Look, I saw you in the desert from my post, and I thought you were dead, but when I got there you were breathing." His words come out in a rush with a voice that is very much not *his*. I blink as my eyes begin adjusting to the darkness, revealing the very frightened face of a young guard. "I was just carrying you to the city, all right?" He's panting now, pleading with me to understand.

"I . . ." I blink again, taking in his messy brown hair and crumpled red uniform beneath me. "I thought you were someone else."

"Yeah, well, clearly you don't need my help." His eyes dart to his hand. "And if you'd get off my broken wrist, I'll gladly leave you be."

"Oh." I smile sheepishly. "Yeah, sorry about that." I slide off him after returning his dagger to its sheath, watching as the guard stands to his feet, cradling his hand. I'm suddenly fighting the urge to sprawl back onto the sand as the adrenaline slowly begins to seep from my body. "Thank you for coming out here for me. Truly. I'm sorry that is how I repaid you for the kindness."

He grunts a response, stepping back toward the city we are now bordering. "I need to get back to my post."

"Right." Feeling incredibly awkward, I begin walking beside him at a safe distance. "Um, sorry, which city are we walking into right now?"

He throws me a bemused look. "Dor." Another questioning glance. "What were you doing in the desert anyway?"

I swallow. Imperials may not be a problem in Dor, but there will still be guards with pressing questions for me to avoid. And I haven't the slightest idea if Ilya's surrounding cities know of my reputation. As I open my mouth to spew a relatively convincing lie, his gaze sweeps over my ragged body in a way that has me bristling. He scans my face, seeming to scrutinize, to search.

"Hey, you look . . . familiar." He pauses, pondering what he sees. I turn away, aware of the suspicion in the subtle movement. The whisper of fingers through my hair has my gaze snapping back to his. "Silver," he says softly, as if it were a thought that slithered its way out of his mouth. "Interesting."

"Is it?" I ask lightly, attempting to discern what it is he knows.

"Well, such a color wouldn't be unusual in Ilya." His skeptical gaze has shifted into something far more confident. "But here . . ." The hand that slowly grazes the hilt of his dagger doesn't go unnoticed. "You wouldn't happen to be that king murderer, huh? You know, the 'Silver Savior'-turned-killer?" The dagger is gripped in his hand now, angled toward me. "You are worth a pretty penny, you know. Ilya has a hefty price on your head." I take a step away, my gaze glued to the blade inching closer to my chest. His next sentence is strung together with a smirk. "Dead or alive."

Moonlight glints off the steel he swipes at my chest.

I twist, saving my heart from the blade but not the shoulder it drags across. I bite back a scream at the searing pain, feeling hot blood begin to gush from the gash. The guard doesn't waste a single second before sending his knife stabbing upward toward my stomach. I dodge again, feeling sluggish as I'm forced on defense. Every bit of exhaustion and accumulated ache comes flooding back, reminding me that I slipped between Death's fingers yet again. Perhaps he's come to finally finish the job, claim his vengeance.

"Look," he pants between gritted teeth, "just come quietly, and I won't have to hurt you."

I duck under another attack from his blade. "I'd believe you, but you seem pretty eager to repay me for that broken wrist."

The guard all but growls at me, throwing his weight behind a stab intended to slash my ribs. The two quick breaths he always takes warn me of his swing before I see the flashing steel. I twist, grabbing his wrist before stepping behind him to roughly bend the arm against his opposite shoulder blade.

The dagger slips from between his sweaty fingers, stabbing the sand beneath us. He doesn't scream until I grab his broken wrist with my free hand and squeeze, his severed bone jutting into my palm. The guard sinks to his knees, shaking violently as I slowly lower myself behind him, his hands still clasped between mine.

My lips nearly brush the shell of his ear as I murmur, "Who else knows about me?"

He thrashes against my hold, only earning him another twist of his broken wrist. He cries out before spitting his next words. "You're a crazy bitch, you know that?"

"Yes," I sigh, "I know that, and you know that. See, what I'm asking is if anyone else knows that."

He huffs out a pained laugh. "Everyone knows you're a crazy bitch. You have quite the reputation."

I stiffen at his words. "What about Tando? Does Ilya have a price on my head in both cities?"

"As far as I know," he breathes, a smirk hidden in his soft words, "even Izram has a poster of your face plastered on every surface."

I scowl at the back of his head. Stowing away on a ship heading for Izram sounded far more appealing than trekking through the Scorches. And I would have done just that if it weren't for the fact that it's been years since anyone has journeyed across the Shallows' treacherous waters. This is partly due to Ilya's immense isolation from the other kingdoms, though the dozens of shipwrecks have further discouraged anyone from the perilous journey.

But none of that matters now, because it seems my reputation traveled to Izram before I could.

"Well," I sigh, "let's hear it. How much am I worth?"

The greed in his voice slips between his grinding teeth. "Twenty thousand silvers."

I nearly choke on my laugh, my whispered words more to myself than the guard at my mercy. "Kitt wants me that badly, huh?"

"He does." The guard's voice is suddenly cold, calloused. "Dead or alive."

And then the back of his skull collides with my nose.

I cry out, already feeling blood beginning to gush, the steady stream spilling into my mouth.

There are suddenly rough hands at my throat.

The guard throws me onto my back, his weight pressing down on me nearly as hard as his hand crushing my windpipe. Spots begin swimming in my vision, and I'm oddly grateful that I can barely see what it is I do next.

The blade slides easily into his heart.

He blinks above me, a look of disbelief painting the blank canvas that is his face, now completely drained of color.

The hand around my neck loosens and falls away, his body following. He slumps to the ground, clutching the fatal wound delivered by his very own weapon. He grunts, his final words a growl. "Crazy . . . bitch."

I'm shaking.

The dagger slips from my hand despite being held between sticky fingers.

Sticky fingers.

I look down, taking in the blood coating my hands.

No, no, no . . .

The feel of it has me gagging, even with the lack of contents in my stomach. I crawl toward the guard, mumbling my apologies as I wipe blood from my palms with his already scarlet-stained shirt. Lifeless eyes look up at me while I can barely see through the tears in my own.

I stare at the young man as I stagger back, the heels of my palms sinking into the sand.

I killed him.

I killed *again.*

In a short amount of time, I've managed to take the life of three people. The thought has my stomach churning once again, and I twist to retch into the sand.

I never wanted to kill anyone. I never wanted—

But I had. I did. I *do.*

What have I become?

The tang of blood stings my nose, so potent I would puke again if my body had anything left to give. Taking a deep breath through my mouth, I slowly stand on shaky legs to turn away from the scene.

I need to get out of here.

Blood is leaking into my mouth, forcing me to spit with every step I take into the city. I gingerly lift a hand to feel my nose, recoiling at the pain but relieved to find it isn't broken.

One foot in front of the other.

I left him there.

One foot in front of the other.

He'll rot in the sun.

One foot in front of the other.

I'm a monster.

One foot in front of the other.

CHAPTER 8

Kai

Stabbed through the chest—her signature move.

I crouch beside the crumpled guard, blood-stained sand crunching beneath my boots. A face that can't be much older than my own looks up at me, dark eyes leached of the life he barely got to live. Running a hand through my disheveled hair, my gaze travels over the bloody splotches staining his red uniform. Each one tells a story.

After drawing blood your whole life, every stain begins to speak, if only you listen.

Or maybe I'm just insane.

The wound to his heart seeps crimson across his chest, spilling over to puddle beneath him. The sand surrounding him shows signs of a struggle, a fight portrayed in footprints.

Well, she had a reason to kill him at least.

My eyes trail back to the man beneath me, skimming over the smeared blood on the hem of his shirt, opposite his wound. I inch my face closer, nearly choking on the metallic and morbid scent.

"This was her," I say, without bothering to look up at the men

circling me. "She was here. She *is* here. He's only been dead for a day at most." I eye the blood on his shirt where she hastily wiped her hands.

She must have been in bad shape to leave evidence like this in plain sight.

At that thought, I sigh, running dirty hands through dirtier hair for what is likely the dozenth time. If she's hurt, then she can't have gotten far. If she's hurt, then I have an advantage.

If she's hurt, I need to be okay with that.

I shake my head, pitying the man who got too close to her. "Grab him. We'll hand him off to his fellow guards to deal with."

A few Imperials exchange glances, silently inquiring who among them will have the unfortunate task of dragging the decaying body. I stand, shaking out my sore neck before turning my back on them to stroll toward the looming city. "If you need some encouragement, I'm happy to . . ."

Uncomfortable coughs and shuffling feet drown out my words, the Imperials wasting no time before following with the dead body in tow. But we don't have to trudge much farther before we're swallowed by the swarming city.

I push aside a sun-bleached banner hanging low between crumbling buildings, offering me a better view of the city that is nearly as harsh as the people who inhabit it. Glowering glances greet us, eyes speaking of suspicions that the people of Dor are smart enough not to voice to the Elites strolling through their city. It's like they can smell the abilities in our blood all while looking down their noses at us.

I offer a curt—and borderline cocky—nod to a few, not shocked in the slightest by their reaction to me and my men. It's not as though Dor is subtle about their loathing for the Elite kingdom, seeing that they have taken in the most Ordinaries over the decades.

Ilya hasn't had allies since before the Plague. Since before the kingdom isolated itself to hoard its Elite powers. Since before Ilya suddenly became a threat to anyone outside it.

Spotting a guard that looks entirely too bored to be doing his job even remotely right, I push through the crowded market street we've stumbled upon and make my way toward him. Inch by inch, the guard straightens with every moment his eyes rove over us.

"I believe this belongs to you," I say, gesturing to the dead guard now laid at the feet of the wide-eyed one before us. "We found him on our way into the city. He was stabbed in the chest." The guard blinks. "And I know who's responsible. My question is whether or not you've seen her stumbling around."

"H-her?" the guard stammers. "A *woman* did this?" His eyes widen slightly with recognition. "It was *her*? The Silver Savior?"

It's a struggle not to visibly cringe at the title. "Yes. *Her.* The girl you have plastered all over your city." I gesture to a tattered poster beside the guard's head, barely sparing a glance at the face I'd once memorized. No, what catches my eye is the script scrawled across the bottom: TWENTY THOUSAND SILVERS FOR PAEDYN GRAY'S ARREST. DEAD OR ALIVE.

Dead or alive.

And Plague knows she wouldn't go easily. It's unlikely she'd allow anyone to return her to Ilya alive. Though, that is what Kitt wants, despite what he tells the surrounding cities.

I turn my attention back to the baffled guard before me. "You didn't answer my question. Have you seen her?"

"If I had, I'd have already dragged her back to Ilya for them silvers." He laughs, half snorting. "So, your king's really got all the cities lookin' for her, huh?"

Yes, he does.

"If you see her, or anything of suspicion, you are to report to me," I say, dismissing his question.

Another snort. "Like hell I'll report to you. Who are you to steal my twenty thousand silvers from me?"

I inch closer, studying him long enough to make his throat bob. "I'm the man with the twenty thousand silvers."

Watching the realization make his jaw drop is comical. "You're . . . you're . . ."

I turn on my heel before he's even finished stuttering my title.

Enforcer.

The word hovers in the air, turning heads as I pass. My appearance is well-known throughout the neighboring cities, seeing that they view Ilya and its royalty like a bedtime fairy tale. We're idolized in the way that mutual dislike brings people together, providing petty gossip when there's a lull in conversation.

I scan the street for anything edible, searching for a merchant's cart. I'm drained and beginning to feel dizzy, as though all the frustration filling my body has finally settled in my head. I set off toward a cluster of carts, content to shove anyone standing between me and my appetite.

But the crowd parts as though the Plague walks among them.

Whispers wash over me, my name falling from lips pulled into firm frowns. I ignore them and their accompanying scrutiny. Judgment is a familiar feeling, almost comfortable with its predictability.

Though I am regretting my lack of composure that has so quickly identified me.

"Do you have any meat?" The merchant's back is to me when I place a few coins atop his cart and begin grabbing stale loaves of bread, each of them nearly as solid as the wood they're stacked upon.

The merchant twists, roaming his dark eyes over me and the coins sprawled before him. "Just wild boar." His voice is exactly what I'd imagine it to sound like, as gruff as he looks.

I nod once. "I'll take enough for my men and me."

My request is met with a long stretch of silence. "For you"—the man's eyes narrow at the coins—"double."

I duck my head, a humorless laugh slipping past my lips. The merchant shifts, his body tense when I rest my palm atop the rough wood. I nod down at the coins. "You and I both know that meat isn't worth half of what I've already given you."

"Double," he grunts again.

"And why"—my voice is lethal—"is that?"

"Because I don't like you or your kind."

I almost laugh at that.

Your *kind*.

To think that anywhere other than Ilya, I'm the enigma. The unnatural thing to dispose of. I stare at him, this man who is essentially an Ordinary himself, though he lacks the Elite-weakening disease running through his veins. It's no wonder the surrounding cities despise us for banishing the Ordinaries who are just like them.

"So you know what I am," I say quietly, "and yet, you still choose to charge me double?"

"You don't scare me. Not here." His bearded face does little to hide the smirk tugging at his lips. "I know yer used to Elite privilege, but you won't get none of that here. This'll prolly be the most respect you'll get from anyone around here."

"Noted," I say, far too stiffly for my liking. I don't exactly relish the idea of people being aware of their ability to ruffle me. With a slight roll of my neck, I exhale the frustration from my lungs—a familiar, well-practiced action. "Well, if this is the most respect I'll receive in Dor, then I suppose you're cutting me a good deal."

The man blinks, slightly taken aback by my swift shift in tone. I almost smile at that, enjoying the reactions of those who are not yet accustomed to the many masks I slip on and off at will. My smile is sharp as I dump more coins onto the wood, joining the several I'd already placed there.

It's not long before my Imperials are passing around dried strips of what I was told is wild boar, though I'm hardly convinced. "Make yourself scarce," I order. "We'll meet back here at sundown."

The men exchange confused looks, an expression that never seems to leave the planes of their dirty faces. "But, sir—" Matthew starts, stepping forward from the cluster of crumpled uniforms. He's one of the few Imperials I bother to remember by name—one of the few I don't have a constant itch to leave behind in the desert.

The glance I cut in his direction has the words dying in his throat. "We're drawing far too much attention to ourselves. We'll never get the information we need, or food and board for that matter, if people know who I am and where we are from." Matthew nods alongside the other men, understanding dawning on them. "Split up. Learn what you can."

I nod curtly to the group before turning on my heel and slipping into the crowd, suddenly no one of importance.

Ordinary, if you will.

CHAPTER 9
Paedyn

"Oh, come on. You and I both know this is not worth two shillings, let alone three."

I knock the stale loaf of bread against the merchant's cart for emphasis. *Thunk, thunk, thunk.*

"In fact," I add with more than a little amusement coating my tongue, "you should be paying *me* to eat this, Francis."

The older gentleman hides his grimace behind the folds of fabric encircling his nose and mouth. The west winds are harsh today, blowing bits of grainy sand and debris from the desert to thoroughly coat the city and its inhabitants. It only took two days in Dor to learn how very essential scarves are to my wardrobe if there is any hope of keeping the constant film of sand from my mouth.

"Three," he grunts for the fourth time, his thick accent muffled by the filthy fabric. "Wheat shortage."

I groan. I've spent days trying to get this man to warm up to me, so I don't have to keep robbing him blind. Curse that damn conscience I still have.

"Francis," I begin slowly, watching how the scowl I can't see narrows his eyes. After seeing his name carved crookedly onto the top of the wooden cart, I've been using it in an attempt to build some sort of rapport with the merchant. So far, I've failed miserably. "Let's be reasonable. You know I don't have that kind of money to throw around on bread that will likely break a tooth."

He doesn't bother responding with more than a gravelly growl.

I shut my eyes, taking a deep breath that has sand slipping between my lips.

I'd come to pride myself on the fact that I understand these people. People like me. People who struggle to survive, rely on scrappiness to feed their growling stomachs. In another life, I could have considered the slums of Ilya my home, if it weren't for the lack of power flowing through my veins.

Maybe that's why I'm so desperate to start over here. Here, in Dor, where I'm Ordinary in a whole new sense of the word. One cannot be considered powerless if everyone else is as well. No, here, I'm considered equal. And nothing has ever sounded so unique.

"Fine," I sigh, feigning defeat. "But only because I like you, Francis."

Only because I want you to like me.

His golden eyes seem to be fighting the urge to roll at me. I smile sweetly, hoping my own gaze portrays how badly I crave companionship while simultaneously hating how willingly the wanting shows.

I clumsily toss another coin atop his cart, willing it to roll off the worn wood. Silver glints in the lazily setting sun before the coin hits the ground with a satisfying clink. "Oh, I'm sorry, Francis! I'm not yet used to the heat and my hands are disgustingly sweaty at all times."

He blinks, his tanned face blank beneath his scarf, aside from the obvious disdain for me. When he bends to pick up the silver that is my current partner in crime, I snatch two more loaves from his stand with deft hands, one from each tower of dough so as not to draw suspicion. "I mean, I am never *not* drenched in sweat," I continue casually while Francis straightens, brushing off the dirty coin with his thumb. "Seriously, how do you stay cool under all those layers? I feel so sticky that I—"

"This is our winter season," he grunts, cutting me off.

I blink at him. "Oh. Well, that's . . . terrifying."

Despite Dor being fairly close in proximity to Ilya, I grew up with revolving seasons, though our winters were thankfully mild. I hadn't realized how drastically the weather could differ beyond the expanse of a desert. While the west winds blow cool air from the Shallows toward Ilya, Dor is blessed with the grainy heat of the Scorches constantly wafting into its city. Heat is a familiar inhabitant of its home.

"You will never survive famine season, pale thing." He stares at me for a long moment in which I silently struggle to get my voice to work.

A dry laugh breaks the unbearable silence, and my eyes shoot up to his. Francis places a sun-soaked hand atop his belly, shaking with rough laughter. I hesitantly join him with an uncomfortable laugh of my own. "You are funny, pale thing," he adds between chuckles.

I sigh in relief, sagging with the hope that my ignorance will earn Francis's favor. "Glad to hear my sweaty suffering is humorous to you," I say lightly, taking the loaf he extends to me.

His chuckling continues as he tears another loaf in half with more than a little effort. "Here." He waves it at me before I tentatively take it. "Go find some shade to eat this under."

I offer him my thanks, swallowing guilt at the feel of two stolen loaves weighing down the inside pockets of my vest. Francis is still laughing as I turn away, causing a small smile to tug at my lips behind the fabric swallowing most of my face.

Perhaps he is warming up to me, after all.

I look down at my arms, now far tanner than they were a week ago, prior to trudging through the Scorches. Even despite that, I'm still fairer than most of those who have spent their lives in Dor. Scanning the busy streets, I admire their dark skin, smooth and shining in the sunlight—like the rays themselves are old friends, stroking their skin with familiar fingers.

Tugging the thin fabric lower down my forehead, I push through the mass of bodies swarming the streets. My eyes snag on a crinkled poster, hung precariously against a crumbling shop wall. I scowl, sliding through the crowd to stand before the face that mirrors mine. I stare at the girl reflecting my own features, her eyes full of terror and rage.

I swallow, blinking back tears I refuse to let fall.

This must be a replica of what the Sight recorded after spotting me moments after killing the king—the crime I'd committed written all over my weary face. I can almost feel the blood that drenched my hands, covered my broken body. My hand drifts to the scar trailing below my jaw, my fingers fumbling to the letter carved above my heart.

I can't bear to look at it any longer, can't bear to relive that moment more than I already do.

I can't bear to look into the face of a murderer.

With shaking fingers, I rip the poster from the wall, crumpling it in my fist before shoving it into the pack slung over my shoulders. When I stumbled into the city that first night after my tussle with the guard—

The man you killed and left to rot.

—I'd nearly run into a wall plastered with my face. My silver hair gleamed in the moonlight, and even while being dulled with sand, there was no mistaking that I was the perfect replica of the wanted Silver Savior staring back at me. Any sort of oddly colored hair is a dead giveaway as to having Plagued blood running through your veins, whether you are Ordinary or Elite.

And after spending a life of insignificance and hiding in plain sight, I stuck out like a sore thumb. I've never felt so exposed, so *out* of the ordinary.

I spent the night atop the crumbling roof of a shop, nursing my wounds and hiding until an early sunrise painted the streets golden. Only then did I brave slipping a scrappy scarf from a merchant's cart to wrap around my face and traitorous silver hair. Lucky for me, it's not at all unusual to protect your face from both the sun and whipping sand throughout the day. And, just like that, I was blissfully invisible again.

A shoulder collides with my own, startling enough to shake me from my stupor. The young boy tosses what I think is an attempted apologetic nod before he's back to shoving through the crowded street. Taking a deep breath, I tug at my scarf while pretending to look like I belong here. The people of Dor are more than a little rough around the edges—dare I say akin to the jagged scraps of metal Father used to have me pelt at the gnarled tree in our backyard.

My eyes skim over the street, finding countless confrontations and their accompanying shouts. Sparring, both physically and verbally, is clearly a common occurrence. And if the guards aren't yawning with boredom or barely batting an eye, they've likely joined the fight themselves.

These people are as gruff as the sand they crawled out of.

I spot a tattered awning hanging precariously from a shop wall, promising a tempting sliver of shade.

Might as well take Francis's advice.

After nearly tripping over a cluster of children weaving through the streets, I ungracefully fold myself into the splinter of shade, rubbing my sore muscles. Chewing is a generous term for the effort it takes to swallow the stale bread, seeing that I can now add my jaw to the ever-growing list of aches and pains. But I spend what little remains of the day hiding from the scorching sun and incriminating posters leering at me.

I need money.

That one thought has plagued my mind, pounding through my head with every hour spent in this new city I'm desperate to make a home. The coins clinking in my pack feel far too light for my liking, and unfortunately for me, Dor's inhabitants are anything but careless with the livelihood that lives within their pockets. My attempts at thievery outside what decorates the merchants' carts has been minimal, to say the least. I'm almost embarrassed.

With the sun setting and the heat retreating with it, I zigzag through the city in search of the roof I've grown fond of sleeping atop.

I need money. Money means shelter. It means food. It means . . .

A will to live.

". . . three silvers Slick will win. The bastard's undefeated."

The rumbling voice distracts me from my spiraling thoughts. Boredom and curiosity mingle to create a dangerous concoction of intrigue that has me leaning against an alley wall, intent on eavesdropping.

Another man scoffs, his accent thick. "Undefeated, eh? Maybe 'cause the mate's only fought 'n three matches. Lucky bastard is what he is."

"You bettin' on a rookie then, aye?" The first man leers.

"I'll decide when I see 'em." He laughs then, a gruff sound I doubt he makes often. "Maybe I'll get in the ring. Show 'em how it's done, eh?"

Rough laughter drifts down the alley as I casually step away from the wall to stroll at a safe distance behind them. Every bit of me itches for excitement, for something to occupy me other than my troubling thoughts.

And where there are bets, there is money to be won.

And where there is money to be won, there is money to be stolen.

An elbow sinks into my stomach, sucking the air from my lungs.

I push through the crowd, trying my best not to drown in the sea of sweaty bodies. Shouts and sneers ripple through the cellar, all directed at the caged violence on display, though I can hardly see it.

I'm being suffocated by sticky bodies, forced to peek through slivers of space in the wall of shoulders. Annoyed, I whip my head around, nearly smacking it into the one directly behind me. I've already lost the two men I followed down here after copying the sequence of knocks they rapped on the hidden door. I drum the pattern on my leg, engraining it in my memory even as I attempt to weave through the crowd.

I recognize the sound of fists finding flesh, though I'm far more interested in the pockets of those I'm wedged between. I attempt a subtle swipe of my hand toward the body beside me, only to be shoved from the back by a bellowing man.

I blow out a breath, feeling people pressed against me.

How am I supposed to steal if I can barely move my arms?

My fingers curl into a fist at my side while I fight the urge to throw it at someone.

I blink, eyes flying toward the cage and bloody brawl within.

I can get paid to throw a punch if it's in there.

An entirely new, foolish plan begins to form as I attempt to push through the crowd once again. I'm greeted with more elbows to the stomach and shoulders to the face that I ignore in my search of whoever runs this illegal fighting ring.

The fight finishes in a final bloody blow by the time I stumble to the front. Curses and cheers echo through the cellar, everyone's mood suddenly dependent on who they did or didn't bet on.

"Betting tickets! You lot know the drill. Bring up your betting tickets and we'll get your cut sorted out!"

I follow the crudely formed line leading to a rickety table beside the cage. A strand of silver hair threatens to slip from beneath my scarf, and I quickly tuck it back with the rest as I strain to see the man exchanging tickets for coins.

His slicked ponytail shines in the dim light he stands beneath, his back bent over a mound of tickets. He wastes no time plonking the appropriate number of coins into each hand, barely bothering to glance at the person before him.

"Your ticket?"

I blink at his outstretched hand, stunned by how quickly I'm suddenly standing before him. "No, sorry, I actually wanted to talk to you about fighting in the ring."

"No ticket," he sighs without looking up at me, "no talking."

I shake my head, stepping closer until my hips meet the edge of the table. "But—"

"Next!"

His shout has a woman stepping beside me without a second thought. After being shoved aside when she hands over her ticket, I plant my feet at the end of the table.

"Let me fight."

"Listen, kid." He rubs a hand over his tired eyes before inspecting the next ticket. "I don't just let anyone fight in my ring. Besides"—he throws me a glance—"you'd get eaten alive in there. So, scram."

Flattening my palms on the table, I lean in close enough to catch the flash of a gold watch on his wrist and the smell of cologne on his skin.

He's better off than half this city.

"I want a fair cut. Whatever the rest of your fighters are earning," I say smoothly. "Though I expect to be making more than them in no time."

At that, he reluctantly lifts his head, meeting my gaze as he holds a hand up to halt the line. "I said scram, kid. While I'll still let you."

I tilt my head innocently, eyes narrowing slightly. "It would be a shame if the guards were to find out about the illegal cage-fighting you're running down here." I nod toward the shiny watch decorating his thick wrist. "It seems you've become quite accustomed to wealth. I doubt it would be easy for you to readjust to the poverty you crawled out of."

Though fighting is clearly not outlawed here in Dor, considering how common of an occurrence it is, gambling on said fighters is where they decided to draw the line—explaining the cramped cellar with a fancy knock to allow you access.

A smile begins to form at the corner of his mouth, as though he possesses a sort of corrupted charisma. "Are you threatening me?" He laughs, harsh and biting. "You can't threaten me, kid. I'll have my men tear you to pieces. I practically own this city."

"You've never seen me fight." I shrug nonchalantly. "So, if I need to return them to *you* in pieces just to prove myself, I suppose I'll have to do just that."

The thought of ripping anyone to pieces makes me queasy, but the look I pin him with says anything but. Several slow seconds tick by before a smile spreads across his lips. "I like your spirit, kid."

I swallow my relief. "Is that a yes?"

"You fight in an hour." He pulls out a sheet of parchment inked with the names of previous fighters and how much they earned him. "I'm givin' you a shot, so don't disappoint me, kid. You don't wanna know what happens when I'm disappointed."

I nod, hiding my smile. "I doubt I'll ever find out."

He shakes his head in disbelief, looking as though he already regrets his decision. "Yeah, we'll see about that. I'm Rafael." His eyes flick up to my concealed face. "And what should we call you, kid?"

My eyes skim over the cage and the flickering lights above it. A small smile manages to curve my lips, tugging gently at my scar.

"Shadow."

CHAPTER 10

Even the moonlight feels warm here.

Pale silver rays slip between the cracks of buildings and banners, like frail fingers desperate to claw through anything in their way. I tug at the bandanna tied around my mouth and nose; the blood-red fabric intended to keep the blowing sand from my mouth, though it grinds between my teeth nonetheless.

I've abandoned my Imperials for the night, just as I've done the previous four since we'd arrived in Dor. I spent most of the day alone, scouting the streets along with any possible crevice she could have climbed into. Every time I pull back a banner, push open a decaying door, ask if someone has seen the Silver Savior, she evades me at every turn.

She's a phantom in human form. Like trying to clutch the wind in your fist, unable to see it even while feeling it slip between your fingers.

And the knowledge of that has me feeling something pathetically too close to relief.

Tonight is warmer than most, leaving me sticky with both sweat and sand. I turn down a quiet street, feeling slightly unsettled by the silence that swallows this city each evening. If I were to take a wild guess, I'd say it's because everyone is worn out after a long day of fighting in the streets and pushing through the current of bodies.

I glance at a passing guard who looks anything but alert. I take a deep breath, swallowing the urge to pick a fight out of sheer curiosity as to what the lazy bastard would do. They're worse than most of the Imperials back home, and that's saying something.

My lack of power here weighs on me, a dull buzz in my blood. I feel oddly heavy despite missing a piece of myself. Unlike the other Elites, my ability relies on those around me, and the Imperials I brought to Dor are the only bit of power I have to feed off. After spending the entirety of my life surrounded by Elites, the absence of them and their accompanying powers is so foreign, it's frightening.

I've never felt so exposed.

A sudden, slight pressure at my hip has me tensing, tentatively reaching for my concealed dagger. Well, *her* concealed dagger.

The coin pouch.

That's what they're after.

That's what she was after too, that first day I met her.

Could this be her? Could she be repeating history without even realizing it?

There's no way in hell that even she'd be ballsy enough to steal from me knowing that it's *me.* My heart pounds, both my head and pulse racing.

Turn around.

I swallow, savoring the seconds in which I still stand within the unknown.

Turn around and look at her. Look at the face that took your father's life. The face that didn't just steal your money, but also your h—

I hook a foot behind me, catching an ankle of the thief silently stealing my silvers. With a tug, I send them tumbling to the ground.

Sloppy. Not her style.

Sure enough, the body sprawled before me doesn't belong to a woman, but a girl. My eyes widen, both in surprise and in an attempt to see through the thickening darkness. In a matter of moments, the girl's palms are pushing her backward as she tries to put some space between us, her worn boots kicking up dust as they scrape against the ground.

I take a light step toward her, crouching slightly to get a better look at—

The tip of a blade is suddenly pointed at my face.

I blink. That was . . . unexpected, to say the least.

Raising my hands slightly in surrender, I start to take a step away, my eyes pinned on the weapon clutched within a delicate hand. My gaze narrows on the engravings peeking between the small fingers wrapped around the hilt.

I know this knife.

My eyes shoot up to the tousled hair crowding around a pale face.

Red.

"Abigail," I breathe.

She's alive.

It's a miracle she made it across the Scorches after I banished her and the family who harbored her.

The knife is shaking in her hand now, but her voice has a steady sort of softness. "How—how do you know my name?"

I pull the bandanna from my face before slowly inching closer to her, my hands held where she can see them. As way of answering, I say, "It seems you've been putting my knife to use."

Her eyes widen with something akin to childlike wonder, though her awe is anything but pleasant. "You," she says, her tone bordering accusation. "What are you doing here?" I open my mouth to respond, but her small voice fills the silence before I have a chance. "Are you here to kill me? For real this time?"

The twinge of hurt I feel at her words sends a shock through me. I shouldn't be surprised by her assumption. My reputation leaves no room for speculation. I am the very thing I was created to be—a killer.

"No," I say quietly. "It's not you I've come for."

She considers me for a moment, only slightly lowering her weapon.

Smart girl.

"You remembered my name," she states.

"Of course I did."

I tried to forget, trust me.

I clear my throat, crouching to look her in the eyes while ignoring the blade still pointed at me. "Maybe you can help me find who I'm looking for?" She pins me with a skeptical stare. "The . . . Silver Savior. The woman on the posters all over the city. Have you seen her? Heard anything about her?"

Abigail slowly lowers the knife, having decided it's best not to use my own weapon against me. "I dunno." She shrugs. "Haven't heard a peep."

I heave a sigh.

Well, that was totally unhelpful.

The girl's fiery red hair ripples when she swivels her head to the right, looking down an especially dark street with anticipation. "If I'm keeping you from something, by all means . . ." I gesture to the stretch of darkness she seems so intent on running into.

"I've got to get there before the match ends. I haven't made much today, and the bets should be pretty high tonight." Words tumble out of her mouth while I struggle to keep up. "There's a new favorite, so that means lots of people."

She starts to step away, my question only halting her for a heartbeat. "A new favorite? What's the new favorite?"

"Not what." A childish grin lights her face. *"Who."*

"Abigail," I say, my voice deceptively calm, "I'm going to need a little more information than that."

"Ugh." I can practically feel her eyes roll in the darkness. "Come on. I'll just show you." She spins to point a tiny, accusing finger at me. "But keep your hands to yourself. These coins are mine. I need shillings to bring back to Momma."

I bite back my smile. "Ah, yes. You're quite the thief now. Though you still need some practice. Your hands are too heavy." A frown tugs at her lips as we walk, so I simply add, "The best thieves know how to distract who they're stealing from. Get their mind off the money in their pocket, and it's yours."

She looks up at me, head tilted. "How do *you* know so much about stealing?"

I'm silent long enough to let my thoughts wander back to the person who distracted me more than any other. "Because," I sigh, "even I've been the victim of a great thief."

She stops before a crumbling building and the cellar door that opens beneath it. With a tiny fist, she wraps her knuckles in a series of knocks. I look around, seeing no one in the dark alleyway while wondering what the hell this child is leading me into.

"So," Abigail says confidently, "once I can steal from you without noticing, then I'll be one of the best?"

The corner of my mouth kicks up. "That's wishful thinking, kid."

She scowls. "Hey. I still have a knife, remember?"

The doors to the cellar suddenly swing open with a clang. Tying the bandanna back around my nose and mouth, I watch Abigail spin on her heel before descending the stairs beneath.

I shake my head at her retreating form.

The fire in her eyes. The thieving instincts. The blade with a hilt engraved with swirls.

What have I created?

The similarities between them are startling.

Was this what *she* was like so many years ago? Teaching herself how to survive on the coins from another's pocket? Refusing to focus on the fear she felt?

I can't seem to escape the thought of her, the sight of her in those surrounding me.

It's infuriating.

And what's worse is that I may have just helped craft what will soon be another version of the thief who got the best of me.

CHAPTER 11
Paedyn

I now know why they call him Slick.

My knuckles drip with sweat that was once coating the man's jaw before I forcefully wiped his face with my fist. Slick's blood coats my hands, stinging the raw knuckles I shake out as we circle one another.

The crowd jeers, their shouts echoing in the cramped underground cellar. Faces I don't have time to focus on press against the wired ring separating us from the rowdy audience beyond. The bets are especially high tonight, emboldening the onlookers to rattle the cage or stomp in time to the rolling thunder outside. Considering how anticipated my match against Slick has been since spending the past several nights defeating each of his opponents, I would expect nothing less.

He's suddenly charging at me, and I fumble to comprehend a suitable adjective to describe his sheer size. Slick may be the largest and most slippery man I've ever encountered—but also the slowest. I duck under the giant fist he swings at my head, narrowly avoiding the second one aimed at my stomach. My foot connects with his bare

side, his body so solid that I may have done more damage to myself.

A sweaty hand clamps around my ankle before he yanks me forward with a grunt. Slick is about as predictable as he is gigantic. With the leg that's still planted on the ground, I drive my knee up into his groin. At that, he does more than grunt while the surrounding crowd sympathizes with a synchronized oof.

The tussle has my tightly wrapped scarf shifting atop my head, threatening to expose a strand of damning silver hair. I back away, panting as I adjust the cloth around my face. After three nights, it's a miracle I've managed to stay anonymous.

Maybe it's the thrill that keeps me coming back for more. That, and the money.

A fist connects with my ribs, forcing the breath from my lungs. I stumble from the impact, sputtering through the fabric around my face as I try to catch my breath. Slick stalks toward me, grinning in response to the shouting crowd.

I scowl at the sound. He's a fan favorite after all, no reason to take it personally. It's a shame the crowd can't see the girl of nearly eighteen who's been kicking the asses of men twice her size and age. Then again, attention is the last thing I need, which makes these fights all the more dangerous. I need to remain the faceless rookie, a passing piece of intrigue to fuel the whispered gossip on the streets.

But I don't intend to leave. Or lose.

No, I've made more from winning these matches than I ever did in a month of thieving back in Ilya. Even with Adena selling her clothes, we never could have managed enough to afford real room and board. A twinge of pain shoots through me at the thought, though it has nothing to do with the injuries I've earned. It pierces me right through the heart that aches without her—the one that broke the day she did.

For you, Adena. All for you.

Slick is persistent, raining down blows I barely avoid. He clips the side of my head with his fist, and stars burst in my vision. I'm sluggish. Tired and . . .

Starving. The things I would do for an orange right now.

I shake my head, trying to clear the murky mind inside.

Focus now. Food later.

Slick has thoroughly worn me out. I'm trying to get a read on him, trying to tap into that *Psychic* ability of mine and find the best way to quickly take him down.

Father would be disappointed at how long it's taking me to read him.

He blocks my jab before barreling into me, pushing me hard against the cage. The loose wire rattles, and I barely register the chants of the crowd beyond.

"Finish him! Finish him! Finish him!"

Right. I almost forgot I'm a him.

My baggy clothing and covered face have helped to keep my identity to that of the male species. I would be slightly offended if that wasn't exactly what I wanted.

Focus.

He's pressing me against the rusty cage, winding back a giant arm to strike me. When the fist comes flying toward my face, I twist to the side, watching it deliver a blow to the metal where my head once was.

He only fights with his upper body.

Sure enough, he cocks his arm again, intent on only hitting his mark with a fist. With that knowledge in mind, my foot finds the inside of his knee, kicking hard enough to send a jolt up my leg. Slick bites down a scream as he drops to one knee before me, clutching what is likely a dislocated kneecap.

A collective gasp echoes through the crowd at the sight of their champion so vulnerable. Those gasps grow into something much louder when I drive my knee into his gut.

Once. Twice—

Suddenly I'm being thrown to the ground.

He's grabbed my leg and ungracefully thrown me off my feet before swinging my body onto the barely padded floor of the ring. I stagger to my feet, bones aching as I charge the still-kneeling man. Then I'm using his propped, uninjured leg as a step stool before he has a moment to react. Swinging my legs over his shoulders, I hook a knee around his neck and use my momentum to send us crashing to the ground.

Not my most graceful takedown.

I brace for the impact, keeping my leg locked against his neck, squeezing his throat. He grapples blindly behind him, his hands flailing in the hopes of hitting something of importance. I take the opportunity to catch one of his wrists, pulling it hard behind his head and pressing it down to my chest.

This time he does scream. Though it's strangled, thanks to my leg still choking the sound from his throat.

His elbow strains as I pull his arm down unnaturally, hyper-extending the joint. His excessive sweat has me at the disadvantage as I struggle to keep my grip from slipping. I hold him there, panting as he writhes, my own back sweaty against the rough mat beneath us. The crowd closes in around the cage, rattling the metal and shouting things I don't have the energy to process at the moment.

It took Slick nine seconds to smack the mat aggressively with his free hand, succumbing to his defeat.

I've won.

I untangle Slick from my many limbs, rolling away from the puddle of sweat outlining his panting form. My sore fingers fiddle with the snug fabric around my face before I slowly stand to my feet, feeling unsteady. I scan the cheering crowd, more than a little satisfied by the mix of surprised cheers and scowling faces belonging to those betting on my defeat. I raise a triumphant hand into the air, smiling with cracked lips they can't see.

"And there you have it. Shadow's won!"

I turn my attention to the man who won't admit just how fond of me he's grown. Rafael raises a hand, shouting a variation of his usual lines above the buzzing crowd. "If you bet on the rookie, it's your lucky day. Bring me your tickets and . . ."

I don't bother listening to the rest of his repetitive speech. As soon as I get my cut, I'll be on my way and sleeping as soundlessly as one is able atop a roof.

Just a few more nights, and I'll have enough for a real bed.

The hope of that has me clinging to the last shreds of my sanity. Rubbing my sore knuckles, I push my way out of the ring and into the cluster of bodies beyond. Hands are clapping me on the back, congratulations following in the form of various grunts. That is the peak of politeness among this crowd.

"Ah, Shadow." Rafael nods his congratulations, watching me shove my way over to his rickety table covered with tickets and coins.

"How'd we do tonight, Rafael?" And by *we*, I mean me. I keep my voice low, my parched throat helping to make the sound far gruffer than I intended.

He shakes his head at the messy table, whistling low. "Pretty damn good, kid."

I smile despite the angry split in my lip, ignoring the blood beginning to pool in my mouth. "What are we talking? Twenty? Thirty?"

"At least." Rafael glances up at me with a sly grin while the gray streaking his slicked hair shines in the flickering light.

"How's that for proving myself, hmm?" I say slyly, just as I do after each one of my wins.

"Yeah, yeah. Listen, you have a future here, kid. The people will wanna see more of ya after tonight's show." He straightens, beginning to count out coins before placing them into my greedy palms. "I could set you up consistently," he continues as I slip the silvers into my pocket. "Say, a fight every night?"

My smile is smug enough for him to see it in my eyes. "Perhaps I'll consider it after hearing an apology for doubting me."

"You're a pain in my ass, ya know that?" The words are harsh, but his tone is anything but. "Fine. I'm sorry. There, you happy now?"

I open my mouth to reply, to tell him that I accept his pitiful apology and expect a higher pay cut.

But it's not my voice that echoes through the cellar.

No, it's a voice that chills me to the bone, though it used to set my blood ablaze. Used to have me hanging on every word and aching for the next time I'd hear it.

But now? Now I'd hoped to never hear that cool voice again. Hear the command lacing each word, the calculation accompanying every sentence spoken.

Yet there it is, strong and sure and so damn cocky as it snakes its way down my spine.

"So, is *Shadow* up for another round?"

He's found me.

CHAPTER 12

Kitt

It's been nearly two weeks.

No, definitely longer than that. Maybe.

I scrub a hand over my face, now rough with the remnants of forgetfulness. I can't remember the last time I shaved, let alone the last time I stepped outside this office. Well, two weeks ago would be a safe bet. Because, presumably, that's all the time that separates me from what was once my normalcy to my now-reality, though I can't quite remember what's happened between this life and the one I lived prior.

Parchment litters the desk I'd used as a pillow last night, covering the dark wood with paper cuts waiting to happen. Drooping eyelids make for scribbled handwriting, and I glare down at the slanted letters staring up at me.

Such angry words. Such bitterness squeezed between the lines of crumpled paper. Who would have thought I'd be capable of such cruelty, such crippling sadness?

Maybe Father would like this version of me.

The thought is a bitter sort of betrayal, a whisper of truth tickling

my ear. Because this—this shell of a man and silhouette of a monster—is exactly what he wanted. Not the meekness he mocked, the Achilles' heel that is my kindness.

I run an ink-stained hand down my face, scribbling between the deep lines of my skin. My eyes catch a cursive that doesn't belong to my hand, scrolled across the parchment resting beneath my elbows. Kai's harshness can be found even in the slant of his letters, the heaviness of the ink.

I don't envy him. Not truly. Not intentionally.

Kai was the king Father wanted. It was as clear as the obvious distaste they shared for one another. Kai is every bit the brutal, the bold, the foreboding—every bit the king's son. And I think that was exactly the problem between the two of them. Father hated that he wasn't the heir. Hated that the king he wanted was thwarted by the son he had first. I wasn't Kai, and it killed him.

And I know that part of him despised my brother because he was everything I wasn't.

I stand, feeling nearly as shaky as the sigh I let out. Pacing to and from the window has been my routinely exciting excursion for the past two weeks. But today, today I'm feeling rather bold. Today I open the curtains before immediately regretting that rash decision.

I'm blinded by the dull light streaming through the cloudy window. Between blinks, I scan the grounds beyond, the home I've felt like a hostage in as of late. My eyes trail to where I know the Scorches stretch far beyond, to where I sent Kai to find her.

Her.

I think about her more than I should. Write about her when my thoughts can no longer contain her. Pore over every detail of our short, shared existence. Every deliberately deceptive word. The persistence of her playing with me. Father and his subtle encouragement to spend time with her. The feelings Kai is fighting while hunting her down.

The flood of thoughts has me pulling a relatively clean sheet of parchment from beneath its marred brothers and sisters.

And then she's spilling onto the page again. A variation of words I've strung together before. A ballad of betrayal, a sonnet of sorrow.

I'm tired of writing from the villain's perspective.

CHAPTER 13

Rai

I've found her.

In the middle of a damn fight, of all things. I shouldn't be surprised.

"Finish him! Finish him! Finish him!"

The cellar is damp, echoing with the shouts of a cramped crowd. After pushing past sweaty bodies, I let my eyes drift over the various heads of dull colors, still unaccustomed to the lack of vibrant hair among them. That's when I turned my attention to the man stalking circles in the cage, shockingly large in comparison to his opponent.

His opponent.

The one who moves like a dancer, not always in fluidity, but in calculation. As though anticipating each step, mapping out each movement.

The one who fights with a familiar kind of fire, a fierceness that's been fueled and honed for years.

The one with the covered face, hidden hair, concealed identity.

I know the face behind that fabric. Know the freckles that fleck

that nose, the silver hair that glints in the sun. Know the lean body hidden beneath layers of clothing, concealing the waist where my hand fits perfectly, ribs scarred by a spear in the Whispers Forest.

It's her.

"And there you have it. Shadow's won!"

Shadow. How fitting.

Though I can't see her face, I can practically feel the pride radiating off her as she stands in the ring, fist lifted in triumph. I'd barely focused on the match, too consumed with the realization that it's *her.* But I spot the blood soaking through the scarf she keeps tightly wrapped around her head and face, concealing the criminal who lies beneath.

All too quickly, the match is over. The crowd is clapping. The Shadow is leaving.

No. I need her.

The thought almost has me laughing bitterly. Two weeks ago, those words would have held a very different meaning, one I'm not allowing myself to ponder any further.

She's standing beside the announcer now, collecting her pay and what looks to be his praise.

Think.

I should follow her. I should follow her and take her by surprise. I should be smart about this. Every bit of training screams at me to handle this delicately, deliberately.

But where's the fun in that?

I'll handle her as delicately as she did my father.

I want to see her squirm, fumble to keep up her facade. And with an audience at my disposal, her identity is at stake, forcing her to focus on both me and the role she's playing.

And that's when I open my mouth.

"So, is *Shadow* up for another round?"

It's as though I had screamed.

Her head whips in my direction with such fervency that I struggle to ignore the memory of how she used to relax at the sound of my voice. Her eyes drift from face to face. Searching. Frantic. Afraid.

And then those ocean eyes crash into mine.

It's electric, this look, though not like it used to be. The invisible tether between us is now charged with our past, our present, our future—with everything we once were and everything we now are. It's a hostile sort of harmony, both of us finally fully aware of what we are to each other—nothing. Just the shell of what was; what could have been.

I used to welcome the idea of drowning in those blue eyes of hers. But now, seeing the disdain she stares me down with, I realize that drowning alone wasn't what I craved, but sinking together.

"And"—the announcer's voice doesn't manage to tear my gaze from hers—"who might you be?"

Her gaze narrows atop the folds of fabric concealing the face I know too well. A challenge. I can practically hear her taunting voice echoing in my skull.

Go on. Tell them who you are, Prince.

"Flame," I say, my eyes never straying from hers.

Her eyes leave mine long enough to roll. My smile is sharp, though she can't see it behind the bandanna concealing the bottom of my face.

If she is Shadow, then I am Flame.

This girl is the very thing I can't seem to escape—can't seem to go anywhere without the remnants of her following. Where I am, she is. Whether it's in the flesh or in the fragments of my mind.

And where there is a flame, there is always a shadow.

She is my inevitable.

The announcer rubs the back of his neck, contemplating. "Well, *Flame*, we weren't planning on another match tonight. . . ."

"Ah, of course." I raise my hands slightly, appearing apologetic. "I understand. Shadow can't handle another fight tonight. Wouldn't want him to lose his winning streak, now would we?"

When my eyes slide back to her burning gaze, they narrow slightly. A challenge of my own.

Your move, Shadow.

The eavesdropping crowd finally breaks its silence with scattered whispers. The announcer glances sidelong at her, speaking volumes with the single movement. I've backed her into a corner, threatening the image she's built. Her reputation is now at risk if she refuses my obvious challenge.

Her eyes bore into mine, threatening to set me ablaze. And then she nods, slow and sure and single-handedly sending the room buzzing in anticipation.

"Looks like we have another match, folks!" I barely hear the announcer's booming voice through the blood pounding in my ears. My feet begin carrying me toward the ring and every moment after. Every moment after I touch her again.

"Let's give Shadow a quick breather, aye? That's only fair."

My head whips in the announcer's direction, feet stalling. My gaze flicks to the figure beside him, relief smoothing her crinkled brow, eyes sifting through the crowd.

Because she's going to disappear.

And I can't let that happen.

The man smiles, likely thinking of every coin he'll make off us. "We'll begin shortly." The crowd resumes their idle chatter, already beginning to bet on their champion.

But my eyes never stray from her covered face, though I've memorized every inch of what lies beneath the folds of her scarf. If I knew her any less, I might not have seen the signs. Might have missed the way she takes a casual step around the table, right into the path of some bickering onlookers.

It's as though she truly is made of shadow.

I take a step toward her, shoving people aside before she can melt into the madness. Catching the ripple of her scarf, I slide between bodies, attempting to keep up with her. Heads turn as I curse colorfully. The crowd has swallowed her whole, but I fight my way to the cellar door I know she's slinking toward.

Steel screeches, informing me that she's about to slip away into the night. Murmurs follow as I continue pushing my way to the door, only cracked wide enough for her familiar frame to slip through. Prying it open, I bound up the steps and into the darkness beyond.

My ears ring in the sudden silence while my eyes attempt to adjust. The muted echo of heavy strides has my head whipping to the right before my feet begin racing.

I can just make out the outline of her form before it turns down another alley. I'm sprinting—legs pumping, heart pounding.

But she can't outrun me. And what worries me the most is that she knows it.

I'm gaining on her, tailing each of her turns meant to throw me off. Only seconds separate us from the fate we've both found ourselves in. Only seconds before she's haunting me outside my nightmares.

She turns another corner, and I follow.

. . . darkness.

I skid to a stop, head swiveling in search of her shadowy figure.

Nothing.

"What the hell . . . ?" I murmur under my breath, taking slow steps across the stones. I scan the walls around me before my gaze climbs up to the flat roof above. A window resides in the center of the bricks, acting as the perfect step stool.

Found you.

Wedging my foot atop the windowsill, I pull the rest of my limbs up until I'm balancing on the ledge. I stand there for a moment, palms sweaty and throat dry. The seconds slow. Even time seems to hold its breath in anticipation of our reunion.

And then it exhales. Time resumes. And I curl my fingers over the edge of the roof to lift myself up.

I swing my legs up in one swift movement, standing in the next.

First, there is nothing.

Second, there is everything.

There is her.

"Move, and I'll sink this dagger into your heart."

No. There is hatred.

Moonlight glints off the blade between her fingers. She's poised to strike, her arm cocked and voice steady.

That voice.

It's exactly as it was. Neither of us changed, and yet, here we stand—strangers.

I swallow, opening my mouth—

"That includes your lips," she says sharply. I blink, struggling to bite back the scoff she begins talking over. "The only reason I haven't thrown this knife yet is because I have a proposition for you."

Humoring her, I nod slightly, lips twitching beneath my bandanna.

She takes a step toward me, never lowering her weapon. "We go back to the cellar. We fight. I win."

Before I've even finished scoffing, she's suddenly closed the distance between us. As if to remind me of her threat, I feel the cool tip of a blade pressed roughly against my throat.

"I *win*," she continues, deceptively calm, "and you let me go."

I stare down at her, at the face swallowed in shadow.

"And if you win"—she swallows, adjusting her grip on the dagger still digging into my skin—"I'll . . . I'll go quietly back to Ilya."

Silence hums. The moon bears down on us, leaning in to hear my answer. I clear my throat. "Am I allowed to speak now, or will you be stabbing me?" I bow my head closer to her, ignoring the sting of a blade at my throat. "I know how good you are at that."

She sighs through her nose. "You are welcome to speak so long as it's to accept my offer."

"I hadn't realized you were in any position to negotiate," I say coolly.

"You should be thankful I'm even *bothering*."

"And why is that?" I murmur, ripping the bandanna from my face. "Why not slit my throat?"

I can hardly see her face, but I hear the suppressed rage in her voice. "Careful what you wish for."

I inch dangerously close. "You can't do it, can you?"

"You of all people should know better than to underestimate me," she breathes.

"So do it, Gray."

A flash of steel flies toward my stomach, leaving my neck bare besides the thin line of blood beginning to bloom there. She sends the blade arcing upward, intending to slip it between my ribs and pierce the heart that once beat for her.

Only, she's already done that. Already mutilated whatever part of me wasn't yet a monster. Now here I stand, a mosaic of a man—all sharp edges and shattered pieces.

I catch her wrist, anticipating this exact move. She sucks in a breath when I twist her arm outward, giving me room to step in against her body. "Oh, come on," I breathe against her ear, "your heart wasn't in that."

Steel sings against its sheath, hissing in the silence.

And once again I'm staring down the length of a blade, its point angled up beneath my jaw.

She hasn't held that dagger since she buried it in the king's neck. I should have known she would pull it from the sheath at my side, its familiar swirling handle now back in her palm. All it took was a distraction and the flick of thieving fingers.

Her chest heaves, brushing mine with each heavy breath. "Don't think for a second," she whispers, "that I won't be the death of you."

She's dangerous with this dagger in hand. I've seen what she can do with it, had it held against my throat enough times to memorize the thickness of the blade slicing into my skin. At my throat is the very weapon that sliced through my father's, held there by his murderer. Held there by *her.*

I smile slightly. "I doubt there is any more damage you can do to me."

I can feel the heat of her gaze boring into mine, though I can only make out shadowy features in the moonlight. And I'm thankful for it. Thankful for the blessing that is being unable to behold her.

Because when darkness hides those blazing blue eyes, I can pretend that she is nothing to me. Just a shadowy figure that feels like her, smells like her, talks like her. Just a stranger in this strange place that I will never see again.

But the moment the sun comes up, shedding light on my dark reality, I can no longer pretend. Can no longer steal what I want when duty has me bound by a leash, dragging me back to my destiny.

But here, she is no one.

Here, I am nothing.

Here, we are forgotten.

The dagger shakes in her hand, prodding at my skin with each quiver.

"I hate you," she whispers.

The reminder of her lack of feelings only spurs on my sudden stupidity. My sudden need to finish what we started, no matter how doomed it was from the beginning. Because here, nothing between us matters.

With one of her wrists still grasped in my palm, ensuring the other knife won't slice my skin as well, I lift my free hand toward her face. It's slow, soft even, so as not to startle her. I hold my breath, heartbeat pounding in my ears.

She seems to still, to melt under the feel of my fingers pulling the scarf from around her face. Her breath catches, her body tensing against mine. I scan the face that is now uncovered, seeing nothing of the girl I cared for. The girl who killed my father. The girl I've been ordered to bring home.

I see none of that, because I see nothing at all.

She is no one.

I am nothing.

We are forgotten.

And this is meaningless.

I gently tuck a strand of hair behind her ear. A strand that is shadowed, not silver. A strand that belongs to this stranger I will never see again. "You promised to be my undoing," I murmur, lowering my head close enough to hear her sharp intake of breath. "So, prove it."

Her face angles up toward mine, our noses brushing. She never lowers her dagger, and the point of her blade still draws blood from my throat. "Prove it," I repeat, voice quiet. "Hate me enough to make me want you." I cup her jaw, feeling her eyes burning into mine. "Ruin me."

Our mouths crash together.

I can taste the loathing on her lips, the anger in each swipe of her tongue. She spells out a promise, leaving it to linger on my lips. A vow to undo me. And she's already begun.

She kisses me hard, biting my lip to draw blood like the dagger she still presses against me. I tighten my grip on her other wrist still clutching the small knife, hard enough to have her palm opening and the blade clattering onto the uneven roof. With her hand now free, I lift it over my shoulder, guiding it around my neck.

Her fingers are buried in my hair while mine dig into her hips. I ignore how familiar she feels, ignore every one of my screaming senses. Because this is a stranger. We are nothing to each other. And that means anything is allowed.

This kiss is deep and anything but tender. It is betrayal. It is bitterness. And nothing has ever tasted so sweet.

It is ruin.

She suddenly jerks away, dropping the dagger that was pressed against my throat. Pushing hard at my chest, she staggers back, breathing heavy. I blink in the darkness, trying to ignore the heavy weight of reality crashing down on us.

"Don't . . . ," she pants. "Never again."

I lick my lips, tasting a trickle of blood from her bite. She sways on shaky legs, and I watch as she fixes her attention on the roof between us. The blades lie forgotten at our feet, winking up at us in the pale moonlight.

She stiffens at the sight. And then she lunges.

I manage to grab her swirled dagger before she can snatch it, forcing her to settle for the knife she greeted me with. Her shoulders heave as she takes another step away from me, shoving the blade into her boot.

My lips tingle from the taste of her; hands trembling from the feel of her. I take a breath, shocked by my own actions. Shocked that I found a way to justify them. Shocked that she wanted to as much as I did.

It was hatred, but it happened.

I look up to find her seemingly composed, tucking her hair and face back into its cocoon of fabric.

"Do we have a deal?" she says evenly, as though nothing has changed between us. And nothing has. She is still my mission, and I am still her monster. What happened between us, past and present, was nothing more than a mistake. A lapse in judgment. A spark between two strangers in the night.

But when she turns her face toward the rays of moonlight dripping from a starry sky, I see the girl who ruined me. The planes of a face I've held in my hands, freckles I've counted a dozen times. The hands that drove a sword through the king's chest, a dagger through his throat.

And now I can no longer pretend.

I pull my bandanna up and walk toward the edge of the roof. "Deal."

The crowd splits, creating a path to the cage.

She beat me back to the cellar after practically jumping off the roof to get away from me. I take my time strolling inside, staring at her through the wired cage, though she looks in any other direction than mine.

When the door swings shut behind me, shouts erupt. The crowd is already gambling on the outcome of the match, shouting what they must believe to be words of encouragement at their chosen fighter.

She wastes no time before beginning to circle me. This is not the same girl I kissed on the roof, and it feels as though we are meeting again for the first time. Though a public reunion in which we are both hiding our identity is not exactly ideal.

I watch her as we slowly circle one another, each of us attempting to anticipate the other's move. Words stick in my throat, unable to say something worth the weeks of silence between us. Because what happened on the roof hardly counts as a reunion. Hardly counts at all.

"Took you long enough, *Flame*."

Her words are laced with bitter amusement, void of whatever emotions we left on the rooftop.

Good. We are carrying on as normal. As enemies.

"What," I ask, "finding you or coming to my senses?"

"Well, clearly you haven't really come to your senses, considering you stepped foot in this ring. With me inside it." Her hands twitch at her sides, itching to connect with my face.

I almost laugh. "I could say the same to you, *Shadow*." My voice drops to a whisper I'm not even sure she can hear over the crowd, though I know my eyes shout the title at her. "Or should I say, *Silver Savior*?"

"I'd watch your tongue, *Prince*." I can see the sharp smile in her eyes. "Unless you'd like to swallow it."

"Have you been practicing that little line?" I drawl. "You know, for when I inevitably found you? Or did—"

Her fist finds my jaw. Hard.

I don't even have time to react, to dodge, to do anything other than take the blow as it whips my head to the side. "No," she answers sweetly, "but I have been practicing *that*."

I spit blood onto the mat, drawing a roar from the crowd. "It seems I won't need to remind you how to punch correctly. Again."

This time, I duck before she can break my nose. Her arm swings over my head, and I take advantage of her unguarded stomach to send a quick jab below her ribs. She staggers slightly before filling the space between us with a foot flying toward my temple. I twist, blocking her kick and pushing her leg away from me.

"Are you prepared to let me go when I win this fight?" she pants, pelting me with a combination of punches I scarcely block. She's persistent, as per usual, and far less fatigued than I figured she'd be. I suspect our time on the roof likely added to her bloodlust.

After exchanging blows, most of them blocked, she drops into a crouch to swing her leg out. I jump, narrowly missing her attempt to send me sprawling onto the mat. But she's up in an instant, twisting with a back kick that has her heel careening toward my skull.

This time, I block before catching her leg. Using the momentum of her kick, I have her flipping onto the mat before her next blink. She rolls, her back colliding with the cage wall, making it rattle while the crowd roars on the other side.

I wipe an already bloody hand across the line of crimson trailing from my split lip. "Look," I pant, moving to stand over her. "Here's what's going to happen. You're going to—"

Both of her booted feet fly into my stomach, thoroughly knocking the air from my lungs. I stagger with the sudden force of it, my back slamming into the cage wall. She's on me in a moment, her hands on my shoulders and . . .

We're dancing in the Whispers.

Pale moonlight streams through the trees, illuminating the eyes staring up into mine, sparkling like an indigo pool I'm all too willing to dive headfirst into.

Her hands anchor me, tethering us together with a tentative touch. Soft but sure. Steady but seemingly timid. Unsure what this means, but sure that she wants it.

Her hands are on my shoulders and . . .

And her knee is driving into my stomach.

Once. Twice. Three times before I come to my senses and block with one arm before swinging the other at her jaw. Her head snaps to the side, and I take advantage of the second of shock she allows. I have her gripped by the collar and pressed against the cage within the next heartbeat.

That's when she knees me in the groin.

The crowd grunts right alongside me. "Classy as always," I choke out, still clutching her tightly.

"Oh, that was nothing, Prince," she hisses through gritted teeth. "Now, get the *hell* out of my ring."

I laugh dryly, my face close to hers. "Oh, I'll get the hell out of this Plague-forsaken city so long as you come with me. I'll drag you back to Ilya if I must."

"Over my dead body, Prince."

"That would make things a hell of a lot easier, so trust me when I say I'm considering it."

Her body tenses, and I feel the punch she's about to throw before she even moves. My hands pin her wrists to the cage, pressing her hard against the wire. "Here's what is going to happen," I breathe close to her ear, eying the crowd enjoying this immensely. "We're going to wrap this little show up, and you're going to come *quietly*."

Her eyes are ablaze. "You haven't won yet."

"Oh, I haven't?" I trail a hand up to her face, tugging at the fabric there. "All I have to do is slip out a single strand of silver hair, and everyone in this room will be trying to kill you for that hefty price on your head. And I'm tempted to let them do just that. It would make my job far easier."

Lies.

I have strict orders to return her to Ilya *alive*, despite what the posters say. But she sure as hell doesn't need to know that.

I smile enough for her to see it in my eyes. "So, yes, I won the second I stepped into this ring."

She swallows, the only sign of worry she'll allow me to see. "You're awfully confident for someone who's also hiding their identity."

"Yes, well, there's not a price on my head."

"You're the prince of Ilya. There will always be a price on your head."

And with that, she rips the bandanna from my face.

CHAPTER 14
Paedyn

His face is jarring in the way that déjà vu can be, like seeing a figment of your imagination materialize outside your mind.

I could barely see him atop the roof, draped in darkness. And that was dangerous. Dangerous to pretend that he was anything but the man who murdered my father. It was pathetic. It was a distraction. And I will never be so weak again.

But I see him now for what he is to me—dead.

Stubble shadows his sharp jaw, accompanied by the blood leaking from his lip, reminding me of how I'd bitten him. I shake the thought away, vowing to never think of it again.

His dark brows rise in shock, his gray eyes piercing mine. He has a sort of rugged look to him, like the face I grew annoyingly fond of in the forest.

He's horrifyingly exactly how I remember him.

Every dark lash lining those silver eyes. Every twitch of his too-familiar lips. Every lock of ebony hair falling in waves atop a tanned brow. Every piece of him perfectly in place, exactly how I'd left him.

The sight of him so preserved, so seemingly the boy I came to care for, feels like a taunt. Like a mockery of every moment that amounted to nothing.

I can barely make out the muffled voices in the crowd, barely focus on the many fingers pointing at the prince. I'd heard the rumors in the streets. Heard whispers of the Enforcer slinking through the city in search of the Silver Savior, though I wasn't sure they were true until I laid my own eyes on him.

Flame.

The cocky bastard called himself Flame. The fire to my shadow.

Insufferable son of a bitch—

The knuckles he sinks into my cheek catch me by surprise. My head whips to the side as pain laces through my face and down my neck.

He's definitely not holding back anymore.

Before I can repay the favor, his hand grips my chin, roughly turning my face back toward him. "That was a mistake, darling."

Darling.

The title is now void of endearment, empty of all empathy.

When his hand pulls down the fabric covering my nose and mouth, I do the classiest thing I can think of.

I bite him.

"Shit," Kai hisses through his teeth, snatching his hand away from my wicked smile. "What the hell was *that*?"

I shove him hard, pushing him toward the center of the ring. "What? Not classy enough for you?" I throw a punch I know he'll duck beneath. When he jabs for my stomach, I catch his wrist as I spin behind him to press it to his shoulder blade. He sucks in a breath, biting his tongue against the pain I know is shooting up his arm.

"It's shocking that anything you do still surprises me," he grits out before hooking a foot behind my own and tugging. The bastard has me tumbling to the mat. He's straddling me before I have a moment to catch my breath, pinning my arms beneath his knees. I writhe under him as he grips the scarf still covering my traitorous hair. "Move again—*bite* again—and everyone will see what a fascinating hair color you have."

I pant, livid, frantically searching for a way out of this. "Fine. I'll come quietly. But we need to end this fight." I relax my body, willing myself to look defeated. "Let me tap out."

I wriggle a hand that's trapped beneath his knee. He gives me a skeptical look before slowly lifting the pressure off my arm. Then I move my hand to the side, giving the crowd full view of the palm I'm about to smack against the mat.

Except that instead of hitting the mat, it's his face my hand connects with.

He curses loudly, not wasting a second before pinning my wrist above my head. I smile. His legs have loosened their hold just enough for me to thrust my knee up into his groin once again. He grunts, but I'm already using the distraction and my free leg to flip us over.

I press my full weight atop his chest as I slip the short, wicked blade from my boot. The same one I should have sunk into his chest the minute he climbed onto the roof. Leaning close to his face to conceal the illegal weapon, I press the knife onto his cheek. The shock that slips through his mask of cold indifference, settling in his wide eyes, has me smiling down at him.

"You're going to cut me open? Here, with a room full of witnesses?" His voice is steady, but I can feel his betraying heartbeat pounding against the ribs where my legs are pressed. "You should have killed me on the roof."

I break skin at the mention of what should have never happened between us. "It would have certainly saved me the trouble of having to do it later."

"Go on, then." He lifts his head slightly off the ground, pressing the blade harder against his skin. Taunting. Testing. "Do it. Wouldn't be the first time you spilled royal blood."

His eyes flick between mine, seemingly haunted by the very sight of me. By the sight of his father's murderer on the brink of becoming his own. I vaguely wonder if he can even stand to touch me, to brush the hands that are covered in his father's blood. I wonder if he can barely look at me in the light without seeing the brutal way his father died.

Because that's what he feels like to me. Like a constant reminder of my father's fate.

"Go on, my *Silver Savior,*" he muses bitterly. "Be my undoing."

And this time, I will. I'll do what I should have done on that roof.

The hilt grows slick in my sweaty palm.

Do it. Damn the consequences, the crowd, and do it.

I told myself I wouldn't hesitate again. And yet, here I am. His life cupped in my bloody hands while my head and heart haggle for control.

Do. It.

My throat has gone dry. Blood pounds in my ears, drowning out the rumbling crowd along with any rational thought. I grip the handle tighter, pulling back slightly as I prepare to swipe the blade—

A calloused hand catches my wrist, the one I'd been too preoccupied to notice slipping out from beneath my legs. He pushes my arm away from his already bleeding throat while his other hand lifts up, up, up. . . .

No, no, no—

I'm powerless to stop him from ripping the scarf from my head.

CHAPTER 15
Paedyn

Silver tumbles from the fabric, dull in the dim light but undeniably identifiable.

"Careful, Gray," he murmurs. "I was beginning to think you cared about me."

Gasps travel through the crowd as whispers evolve into pointing fingers and shouted accusations.

No, no, no.

Even if I'm able to escape the Enforcer, I can't outrun every person in Dor. And now that they've seen my hair, seen that I'm here, I can't fight in the ring anymore. Can't earn enough money to start over.

Something akin to amusement lights his eyes, making me regret not slitting his throat when I had the chance. And I've certainly had that chance, more than once.

"You bastard." My voice is little more than a whisper, even as I struggle to shove myself out of his grip.

He suddenly has both my wrists clutched in calloused hands, yanking me closer to him as the dagger slips from my sweaty palm. I prac-

tically topple over his chest before his mouth is at my ear. "What are you going to do, hmm? You won't make it one step outside this cage before being torn apart—"

"Oi, come on out, little Silver Savior!"

Before the words have even left his mouth, taunting shouts ripple through the crowd.

"*That's* who's worth so much?"

"Pretty little thing worth a pretty penny, eh?"

People are rattling the cage now, shouting at the stunned Silver Savior. "Great observation, Prince. You could pass for a Psychic." I'm all but baring my teeth at him. "We had a deal."

"And I won."

"Oh, is that what you're calling it?" I scoff. "How exactly are you planning to get me out of here, then? Why the *hell* did you do that?"

He smiles. It's a simple, soft lift of his lips that feels like a punch to the gut. Like a piece of the past slipping its way into my present. A piece of him I didn't think I'd witness again. "Because," he answers calmly, "I needed you to need me."

I choke on a humorless laugh. "And you think today is the day I suddenly decide I need you?"

"I think today is the day you don't have any other choice." He starts to sit up, my wrists still gripped between his fingers despite my incessant yanking. "The only way you're walking out of here in one piece is with the Enforcer at your side. Unless you think the Silver Savior can take down every person in this cellar? Then, by all means, be my guest."

I glare at him—a last resort when I refuse to say what he wants to hear. Because he's insufferable and intolerable and annoyingly right. The Enforcer is my only way out of here. But one person is far easier to evade than the entirety of this packed room.

I'll use him to get out, and then I'll deal with him alone.

I swallow, my throat dry as I try to gulp down my growing pride. "Fine," I grit out. "Get me out of here."

"There are those glowing manners of yours," he says dryly. "You may need to get out of my lap, though, if we plan on leaving anytime soon."

I startle, my cheeks burning with the sudden realization that I'm perched atop his lap, my wrists pinned down. He's far too close, the feel of him far too familiar. I can't stand it, stand him. Which is why I ungracefully slide from his lap to stand with him.

He releases one of my wrists but makes up for it by gripping the other all the more tightly. Turning to face the crowd, his voice is even as he announces, "I'll be taking the Silver Savior with me, and no one here is going to give us any problems." The crowd erupts in an outrage that the Enforcer refuses to acknowledge as he continues, his tone every bit the commander. "As Ilya's Enforcer and second to the king, she's my property. *Mine.* Which means if anyone so much as lays a hand on her, you'll learn firsthand just how brutal the Elites can be."

Silence.

The cellar is thick with it, drawing attention to the ringing in my ears. I shift uncomfortably, spinning the band on my thumb while his words sink in.

"She's my property."

I swallow my scoff and instead scan the room, fear hiding among the crowd in the form of flickering eyes and furrowed brows. No matter their feelings about Ilya, fright runs deeper than detest. Just the mere possibility of an Elite's wrath raining down on them has their imaginations running wild. I doubt most of them have yet to even encounter someone from Ilya, let alone hear anything but horrors about the powerful population isolated across the desert.

They don't even know what they're afraid of, what it is the Elites can do. What *he* can do. The Enforcer only has abilities when there are others to wield them from, though he's a weapon himself. And yet they cower from the potential of his power, from the threat of an infamous Elite.

Maybe the unknown is half the horror.

He used their ignorance against them.

"Stay close," he murmurs, reaching for the cage door. "Or don't. It's your life at stake."

I fight the urge to roll my eyes while simultaneously trying to ignore the fact that I look and feel like a toddler. He has me pressed close to him, not out of protection but something far more predatory. It's the possession radiating off him that has the people parting to make a path, has them gawking as he guides the girl worth their livelihoods from the room.

Eyes follow us up the stairs and into the world above the cellar. The streets are dark with the dead of night, and a warm breeze whips at my unbound hair. I fight the sigh that threatens to slip past my lips at the feel of wind kissing my scalp.

This is the freest I've felt in days.

A rough tug on my arm has my unfortunate reality resuming.

I'm not free at all.

"This way, Little Psychic. No time for a moonlit stroll tonight."

I bristle at the mocking title. "So, what's the plan?"

He throws a bemused look over his shoulder while tugging me down a narrow street. "You know, I try not to make a habit of informing criminals of my plans."

I snort at that. "You know damn well I was a criminal long before that final Trial. And yet"—I smile slyly at his tense shoulders—"I seem to remember you informing me of much more than just your *plans*."

I knew you. Knew your past, your present—and your future that we were foolish enough to think I'd be a part of.

He turns, forcing me to skid to a stop before my face meets his chest. "I know." His voice is soft, sorrowful in a way that makes me squirm. "And I'm trying not to make a habit of repeating the same mistakes."

Mistakes.

The seemingly simple word is like a slap to the face, no matter how fitting it is. Because that's exactly what it all was—a mistake. Every shred of ourselves shared in silent looks and whispered stories under willow trees only contributed to the slow death that was us. And now we can add the rooftop to that ever-growing list of mistakes.

We were inevitably imperfect for each other.

"Come on," he urges, all but dragging me down the street. "You can pick up the pace, even with that sloppy footwork of yours."

"Maybe it wouldn't be so sloppy if you'd let me keep my feet on the ground," I shoot back at him, stumbling when he pulls me around a crumbling corner.

"Would you rather I throw you over my shoulder? It's not as though I haven't done it before."

"No, I wouldn't—"

I skid to a stop midsentence, midplotting, before planting my feet as best I can against his persistent pulling.

Maybe I would rather he throw me over his shoulder.

"I'm not budging until you tell me what's going on," I say simply.

He turns slowly, amusement hidden among the annoyance tugging at the corners of his mouth. "Is that so?"

I yank at my wrist still grasped in his unyielding grip. "It is. So I suggest you save us both some time and fill me in on my fate."

He chuckles darkly. "Aren't you entitled for a criminal."

"And aren't you righteous for being no better?"

We stare at each other, still connected by his rough hand encircling my own. Our unspoken sins seem to stretch between us, swallowing the insignificant words burning in my throat. We are one and the same, this Enforcer and me. Both numb, both burdened, both covered in the blood of each other's fathers.

An Elite and Ordinary have never seemed so similar.

His next words are delicately dangerous in that devastating way of his. "Everything I've done has been for the king, and you're the one who killed him, not me."

"I killed a father," I say, stepping closer to him. "And so did you."

His brows crinkle, confusion creased between them. "What are you—"

His grip has loosened, his guard has fallen, and I don't think twice before taking advantage of his distraction. In one swift movement, I twist so my back is against his chest and hook my free arm under his shoulder. With a combination of momentum and his sheer shock, I have him suddenly flipping over my shoulder.

It's not exactly a smooth takedown, and Plague knows Father would raise his brows in that way he always did during training. After all, it was he who taught me to take down a man three times my size, so the sloppiness in which the Enforcer rolled over my shoulder just now would have him shaking his head with that exasperated smile of his.

The prince hits the ground with a trail of curses. I'm on him before my next thundering heartbeat, slipping my last thin blade from my boot. "Did you really think I wouldn't have another knife on me?" I pant, pressing it to his ribs.

Something sharp bites into my back, and I shudder at the familiar feeling of a blade pricking my spine. I'm getting careless. I haven't the slightest idea where the weapon came from, or when he pulled it out, and my lack of focus is frightening.

Sorry, Father.

"Did you really think I'd underestimate you after everything you've done?" His eyes bore into mine, burning like the unspoken words trying to claw their way up his throat.

"Go on!" The shout surprises me, the words far harsher than I intended them to be. "Say it. Say what I've done."

His chest heaves beneath me. "You killed the king."

I shake my head at him, my eyes never breaking from the betrayal in his gaze. "Yes. I killed the king. But more importantly, I killed a wicked tyrant. I killed a man who has killed countless. I killed a man who tried to kill me just because power doesn't run through my veins." I heave a breath, my teeth bared above him. "But I'm forgetting one other thing. What else did I kill, Prince?"

His throat bobs. "You killed . . . my father."

"Yet another thing we have in common," I breathe. His brows crinkle as I hover the knife above his stomach. "Should I drive this through your chest like you did my father? That seems only fitting, don't you think?"

He shakes his head at me, disbelief drenching his features. "Your father . . . ? I didn't—" His eyes widen slightly with something that resembles realization. "How many years? How many years ago was he killed?"

I refuse to believe he didn't know whose life he'd taken that night. Refuse to believe he wasn't deceiving me all these months, tricking me into trusting him after all he's taken from me. Refuse to believe he didn't know it was my heart he shattered the night he slid a sword through my father's.

"Five," I croak. "In my house." My words are little more than a whisper. "I watched you kill him."

He shakes his head at me, horror slipping through the cracks of his mask, the crevices of his crumbling walls. "Paedyn, I—"

It's the first time he's said my name, and some pathetic part of me would have liked to hear him say it again. But I don't even get the chance to hear anything he says after.

"He's over here!"

A shout that can only belong to an Imperial echoes off the walls, followed by the thundering of a dozen pairs of booted feet. My eyes shoot up toward the sound, finding shadows shifting closer. Then I'm looking at him again. He opens his mouth to say something, but it's a strangled grunt that slips out instead.

The clean slice to his shoulder buys me a few seconds, and I don't dare waste a single one.

I'm running again, like I always seem to find myself doing.

And I don't look back.

CHAPTER 16

Kai

A pain in the ass does not even begin to describe this girl.

She has me running through unfamiliar streets, stumbling over uneven cobblestones in the cramped darkness. My hand is coated in blood, pressed to the surprisingly shallow wound she offered as a parting gift.

She had the chance to kill me. More than once.

And yet, for all her talk of slitting my throat, she's failed to do it multiple times now. Then again, I've failed to uphold my promise of burying her own dagger in her back, though I blame that on the strict orders I have to keep her alive.

I'm panting in the Plague-forsaken heat that constantly envelops this city. I turn down an empty street, nearly running into one of my men before I signal for him to turn left while I take right. Even with the thirteen of us split up, she's managed to evade every one of my men for nearly half an hour.

A pain in the ass is an understatement.

The moon stretches its pale fingers across the city, casting every-

thing in a dull glow that has done nothing to help find her. If shadows are her friend, then the moon may be her accomplice, with its silver rays streaming through her blood to stain the hair that masks her in moonlight.

I turn another corner, wincing at the wound on my arm. My feet pound against the uneven path like the thoughts racing through my mind. Her words echo in my head, stealing my focus from the streets I should be searching.

"I watched you kill him."

Five years.

Five years ago, I killed for the first time. Five years ago, I plunged a sword through a man's chest for the first time. Five years ago, I watched a man crumple to the floor before running from the first of my many crimes.

Five years ago, it was her father who was my first kill.

How did she know this, and I didn't? Why was I sent to kill him in the first place? Maybe she's mistaken. Maybe she's looking for yet another reason to loathe me. I think back to that haunting night, the one that forced my fate upon me. I can almost see the room, the blood, the shakiness of my hands. . . .

The room.

I nearly stumble when the realization crashes into me.

Her house. The one I burnt to the ground. That room I was standing in . . .

That wasn't the first time I had been there. The pieces begin to fall into place, connecting that shadowy house where I had my first mission with the one illuminated by flames.

It was me. I killed her father—

Movement has my head jerking toward the shifting shadows.

I know it's her even before I glimpse the figure darting across an alley. I have a throwing knife in hand, aimed at her before she can melt back into the darkness.

Her scream is strained, as though she barely has the energy to express her pain. I take my time walking over to her, watching her slump against a grimy wall before sliding to the ground beneath. She's panting in pain with a bloody hand pressed against the healing wound I've reopened on her thigh.

"What?" she huffs. "Slicing my leg open once wasn't enough for you?"

"Well," I sigh, "apparently it wasn't enough for *you*, considering you're still trying to run away from me."

"Get used to it."

"Oh, I'm beginning to."

Her head is propped against the wall, eyes fluttering with fatigue. She looks tired. Too tired. As though teetering on the edge of something more devastating than sleep deprivation. I tilt my head, examining her in the veiled darkness. "You feeling all right, Little Psychic?"

Her laugh is breathless. "You just cut me open with a knife. What do you think?"

"Oh, come on, I barely grazed you."

She pins those blistering blue eyes on me. "Yeah, you *grazed* a wound that's still healing. One you gave me in the first place, might I add."

I almost smile. "You knew that was me, huh?"

"Of course it was you," she huffs. "You're the only one with aim almost as good as mine."

"Almost?" I say dryly. "Really?"

"You heard me, Prinçe."

I see her fingers flinch toward the knife in her boot before I have her wrist clutched in my hand. “Enough,” I sigh. “I’m tired. You’re tired. Let’s call it a night. Not to mention that you’ll bleed out if you don’t get that wound wrapped.”

“If you think I’m going to go without a fight—”

“I think,” I cut in while pulling the dagger from her boot, “that you won’t have any fight left if you don’t get some rest and bandages.”

“Isn’t that what you want?” Her voice cracks with the weight of accusation in it. “To stop fighting you? Come quietly to my doom?”

I study her for a moment, study the stubbornness sketched into the scowl she wears. The truth has my chest tightening, my heart heaving a sigh when my lungs cannot. Because I can’t seem to decide what’s more frightening—watching her stop fighting or watching her die.

What is she without her fire fueling her? A shell of the Silver Savior she once was? The ghost of a girl I was willing to ruin myself for? If she fights for nothing, she lives for death. But if she burns for something, she lives for *hope*.

I want her to fight me.

I want her to burn for me, even if it means with hatred.

I sigh, exhaling the emotions accompanying each dizzying thought, and instead say, “Where’s the fun in that?”

“This is ridiculous.”

Her mumble is muffled, and when I tug on the cloth covering her face, her gruff grumble is equally so.

“No, it’s necessary. You look great.” Try as I might, I can’t keep the laughter from lacing each word. I can practically feel her glare through the scarf I tossed over her entire head, partly to cover her highly recognizable hair and face, though mostly because I was far too lazy to wrap the fabric around her.

"I hate you," she hisses.

"Yeah, you and everyone else in this kingdom, darling."

The innkeeper waves a hand, beckoning me to his counter. I give her a little push forward, resulting in a reluctant limp. "Just one room. We'll take whatever you've got," I say, offering a tight smile hidden behind the bandanna covering the bottom half of my face.

"Yer in luck," the man huffs. "A room just opened up on the third floor. Little thing."

As way of answering, I roll a few coins onto the chipped counter, watching as he counts them before giving me a gruff nod. Then his eyes land on the girl being swallowed by a scarf. "What's wrong with her?"

I feel her shift in anticipation of some smart-ass comment about to spew from the mouth I can't currently see. "Terrible accident," I cut in with a sad shake of my head. "You don't wanna see what's under there." I lean in, giving him a knowing look. "She's a little self-conscious. Rightfully so."

The innkeeper nods, looking like we've just shared a hilarious joke. "Then by all means, keep 'er covered up!"

He laughs. I laugh. I bite my tongue when the heel of her boot meets the toes inside mine.

I know better than to laugh again as she blindly stumbles up the creaky stairs, blood dripping down her leg and threatening to splatter on the wood beneath. The door on the third floor groans when I push it open, revealing a room the size of my closet back at the palace. With the bed taking up nearly the entirety of the space, the washbasin in the corner seems to be the only other accessory in the crude excuse for a room. A musty window sheds just enough dull light to display the grime decorating the space.

"I'm going to *kill* you." She's ripped the scarf from her face, huffing at the hair falling around it in a heap.

"Are you, now?" I muse. "You had trouble with that even before you were injured."

She turns away from me, shaking her head. Her voice is distant, as though the words were intended to remain a thought. "I'm always injured. Always a little broken." I watch her take in the room, if only because every response that comes to mind seems to be stuck in my throat. "This is it?" she asks, gesturing around. "What, are all your men going to pile into bed with you?"

"Funny," I say without a hint of humor. "No, my men will stay out in the city tonight. Such a large group draws unwanted attention. Don't worry though—they'll meet up with us in the morning when we head out."

She gives me a look that slightly resembles one of those sly smiles she used to show me. "You really think you can handle me on your own?"

I shrug. "I think I'm the only one who could handle you on their own."

"Still a cocky bastard, I see."

"I have a reputation to uphold."

She snorts, struggling as she limps past me to slump onto the edge of the bed. I eye her bleeding wound and the quilt folded beneath it. "By all means, please bloody the bed I'll be sleeping in."

She barely spares me a glance. "And what makes you so sure that you'll be sleeping in this bed?"

"What makes you think I won't be?"

Ignoring me, she begins gingerly examining the wound on her thigh, completely content to disregard my existence. The sight of her rolling up the loose pant leg, revealing a tremendous amount of tanned skin, seems suddenly more significant in the shadowy room.

She hisses through her teeth when the fabric tugs at the sticky wound, and I watch her struggle to keep the pain from pinching her features. I run a hand through my hair, sighing out a quiet "Come here."

"I'm good, thanks," she says blandly.

"You're such a pain in my ass, you know that?"

"If that's the case," she says sweetly, "you could simply let me go. Problem solved."

"You and I both know that's not an option."

"Right." Her voice is harsh. "Because your new king has you chasing me down."

A handful of heartbeats pass before I say, "Well, you did kill his father, the king. And played a key role in the Resistance's uprising. Not to mention that you used Kitt to help do it."

"And I don't regret a thing." She looks me right in the eyes as she says it, not a trace of remorse reflected in her gaze. "Everything I did, everything I fought for, was for Ilya."

My jaw tightens. "And that includes killing Ilya's king?"

She shakes her head, looking away from me. "I didn't go into that Trial planning to kill him when I came out of it. He came after *me*." There's something scarily similar to a plea in her eyes, not because she's begging forgiveness for what she did, but because she needs me to understand why she did it. "But that doesn't mean I hadn't thought about driving a blade through his black heart a dozen times before."

Even with the hatred coating each word, this is the most honesty I've received from her. I can hear it in the hoarseness of her voice, see it in the hands now trembling. Everything prior to this moment may have been fake, a facade, a fairy tale spun to lure me in. But starting right now, I've never seen anything realer.

I sigh, content to let the silence stretch between us before grabbing the small washbasin from the floor. I'm not worried about leaving her alone while I trek downstairs to fill the bin with freezing water, not with the injuries that have her trying her hardest not to tremble in front of me.

Water sloshes over the rim with each step back up the steep stairs, and after I push open the door with a damp boot, the girl slumped on the bed before me looks different from the one I left there. Her hair seems to bleed into the body beneath, blending with her very being now leeched of all color, save for the crimson staining her trembling hands. She stares unseeingly at the blood coating her fingers, swallowing hard at the sight, shaking with each shallow breath.

Something is very wrong with the Silver Savior.

And I'm not supposed to care.

I've seen trauma take on worse forms. Seen it cripple courage, devour dreams, and spit out the shell of a person. Trauma and I are well acquainted.

"Come here."

The command is softer this time, sympathy seeming to smother the sternness in my voice. Her eyes flick up to mine, unfocused and filled with panic. She blinks, her voice cracking as she begins, "I . . . I can't . . ."

"I don't need to know," I cut in quietly. Because I don't. I don't need to know what keeps her up at night, what haunts her dreams, what has her trembling like this. Because knowing that involves knowing *her.* And that's something I swore I wouldn't do again.

She is the history I'm desperately trying not to repeat.

And I've failed enough at that for one night.

I watch her swallow, watch her slide off the bed to sit beside me on the worn floorboards. She doesn't waste a moment before dunking her bloody fingers into the freezing water, scrubbing vigorously with numb hands.

My eyes skim over her, using her distraction as a chance to let my gaze linger on the jagged scar down her neck. I don't bother asking because I already know it was my father's doing. I can practically feel the exact amount of pressure he used to carve into her skin.

But I say nothing of it, knowing that the wound likely runs far deeper than its physical form. The thought reminds me of just how careful I still am of her feelings. It's maddening.

She's so entranced with the task of ridding herself of her own blood that I have to grab her wrists and reel her back to reality. "Unless you're hoping to scrub your skin off, I think that's enough."

With a slow nod, she's pulling her dripping hands from mine to wipe them on a crumpled shirt I tug from a borrowed Imperial's pack. Rolls of dingy bandages tumble to the floor when I shake them from the bag, frowning while fiddling to unravel one.

"Why are you doing this?" she asks, voice hoarse.

I don't look up at her. "Well, I can't have you bleeding out on me, now, can I? It's selfish really. I don't want to have to carry you all the way home."

She huffs halfheartedly at that. "He has big plans for me, then? Plans I need to be alive for?"

I'm quiet for a long while, taking my time cleaning the wound with a sopping bandage. The only sounds shared between us are the hushed hisses of pain and the steady drip of water.

When I finally deign to respond, it's with the answer to a question she hadn't asked. "I didn't know."

Her gaze struggles to meet mine. "Didn't know what?"

"Your father. I didn't know. Not then, and certainly not until now."

She stills beneath my touch. I take my time prepping her thigh for the bandage, swallowing as I gently push the thin pant leg higher. I quietly thank the Plague when she finally speaks, giving me something to focus on other than my current task.

Her voice is surprisingly soft, and I'm not sure whether to be alarmed or at ease. "You didn't know who you killed that night?"

I bite back my bitter laugh. "I didn't even know I would be killing anyone that night. Didn't know my fate was starting so soon."

"Don't be cryptic," she murmurs. "Not when it comes to this."

I sigh and slowly begin wrapping the bandage around her thigh. "I was fourteen. Right in the midst of my . . . training with the king. I'd grown up knowing exactly what my future would look like, but that didn't mean there would ever come a time when I was ready to face it." She flinches when I tighten the bandage. "When I woke up that day, I didn't know I'd be killing a defenseless man in cold blood. Didn't know my father would threaten to do the same to me if I didn't go through with it."

"He didn't . . ." She swallows, taking a deep breath. I doubt the agony on her face has much to do with the wound I've now finished wrapping. "He didn't tell you why you were killing him?"

I offer her a slight shake of my head. "For the first three years of my *missions*, I was given no information on who I was killing. He'd call it blind obedience. Told me that the Enforcer didn't need to know anything more. That the king's commands are never to be questioned."

Her eyes flick between mine, burning like a blue flame. "You could have been killing innocent people. You *did* kill innocent people." Chest heaving, she turns away from me, scoffing as she stares at the wall. "And to what? Test your allegiance, your willingness to blindly follow orders?"

My eyes never stray from her. "I think you know that's exactly why."

She shakes her head like I knew she would. "It's a shock no one's thanking me for what I did."

I stare at her, something constricting in my chest that might just be my heart. The thought of thanking her for driving a sword through my father's chest may be the cruelest thing I've ever considered. And yet, each scar scattering my body sings with the memory of cold hands and hot anger. Each one of my many masks a reminder of the man who molded them.

Maybe I should be thanking her.

I don't remember loving him when he was alive. But now? Does death divulge deep-rooted devotion? I can't seem to differentiate grief out of love and guilt out of the lack thereof.

She bites the inside of her cheek against a wince as she begins unrolling her pant leg. "I suppose I should thank you."

I study her, silence stretching between us. When she says nothing more, I raise my brows at her. "I'm waiting."

"Don't get too excited. I said I *should* thank you."

I harrumph in a way that suggests I might have found that humorous, while she lifts her lips in a way that suggests she might be smiling. When she struggles to her feet, I follow, holding her stare from where she stands before me.

"Turn around," she orders.

"Excuse me?"

"Turn around. I want to change." She waves her hands at me, signaling for me to obey.

"I don't know," I sigh, crossing my arms as I lean against the wall, "how do I know you won't jump out the window when my back is turned?"

She grabs the borrowed, damp shirt with a scowl. "The only thing I'm considering doing when your back is turned, is shoving a dagger into it."

"You're not helping your case—"

The pack hits me square in the stomach before I catch it. "Just turn around," she huffs, eyes flashing with challenge.

I take my time turning to stare blankly at the wall ahead. She doesn't bother making conversation, leaving me to listen to the rustling of clothes before they hit the floor. And now that I've had a taste of her lips, it's difficult not to crave them, especially when I know I shouldn't. So this certainly isn't helping.

"Can I turn around now?" I ask with a sigh when the bed creaks behind me.

"Shh, I'm trying to sleep."

I spin to see her sprawled atop the quilt, the stolen gray shirt swallowing her whole. With arms and legs stretched wide, she attempts to take up as much of the bed as possible. The sight is so unexpected that I nearly choke on a laugh. "What is—"

"Sorry," she says, her eyes closed and lips crooked. "There's no more room on the bed."

"I can see that," I respond dryly.

Her eyes fly open when I tug at the quilt she's toppled on. "What are you—"

"I'm compromising," I cut in. "If you get the bed, then I at least get a blanket."

"Fine." She nods curtly from the flat pillow her hair is fanned messily atop.

I snatch the other from beside her head, trying and failing to fluff the miserable excuse for a pillow. "And I get this, too."

She shoots me a glance before curling onto her side and burrowing into the sheets. "Deal."

With that, I'm banished to the hard floor beside *her* bed. The quilt is scratchy, the floor is rough, and the pillow is practically pointless—but I've slept in worse conditions.

Yet, I can't help but think that in another life, another time, another chance to choose each other—I would be in that bed beside her.

CHAPTER 17

Paedyn

"I'm going to smother you with a pillow in about five seconds."

I groan, blissfully ignoring the prince's threat and burrowing farther into the rough sheets. This is the third and supposedly final warning he's willing to give me. With that in mind, I happily disregard the demanding Enforcer beside the bed.

When a lumpy pillow hits my face, muffling the string of curses spewing from my mouth, I raise a hand to show off my middle finger. He responds to my unspoken words with two of his own. "Get. Up."

"If you're escorting me to my doom," I grumble beneath the crumpled cotton, "the least you could do is let me enjoy my last time in a bed."

"You've had plenty of hours to enjoy, don't worry."

I pry the pillow off my face, peering into the shadowy room. The cloudy window reveals an equally cloudy sky beyond, still splotched with darkness. "The sun's not even up yet, so I don't see why I should be either."

"Compelling argument," he says dryly. "Up. Now. We can't spend too

much time in one place. I'm shocked we haven't been recognized yet."

I sigh through my nose, staring blankly up at the ceiling. I had planned to spend the night plotting my escape from the Enforcer, but there was no fighting the wave of drowsiness that crashed over me the moment my head hit the pillow. Sleeping so soundly is scary when it's beside someone so willing to stab you in the back.

Peeling myself from the worn sheets, I ungracefully slide from the bed before wincing at the forgotten wound on my thigh. Kai's eyes track the movement, trace the crease between my brow, the catch of my breath. "How are you feeling?"

I scoff, pushing the stray strands of silver hair from my face. "Don't pretend to care about my well-being, Prince. I'm just another mission for you to complete."

He seems to stiffen slightly at that, but his words don't match the wariness he wears. "Yes, and my mission needs to be well enough to endure the trek home."

Home.

The word stings my eyes, burns in my throat, just as the smoke had when I escaped the fiery fragments of my childhood. Each one of my homes is gone—my father, my Adena, my house on the corner of Merchant and Elm.

I am homeless. Hopeless. Hollow.

"That's not my home." I hadn't meant for the words to be whispered, though he looks at me like I've screamed them.

"Ilya?" he asks slowly. "Ilya isn't your home?"

"Nowhere is my home. No *one* is my home. Not anymore." I hold his gaze, raising my head high as I add, "You and your king made sure of that."

We stare at each other, his scrutiny sliding over my face. "You're not the only one who knows loss."

"I have you to thank for that."

"As do I," he fires back. "Have you forgotten that I'm now fatherless as well? Or did you not consider that when you drove a sword through the king's chest?"

"You killed a father," I practically growl, stepping close enough to see the storm brewing in his gray eyes. "I killed a *monster.*"

His eyes flick between mine, simmering with something I can't quite place. "Have you forgotten everything he did to you?" I whisper, pleading with him to remember the crimes of his childhood. "Everything he made you do? Not to mention what he did to this kingdom—"

"Enough." His voice cuts through my own, commanding and quiet. "That's enough."

"What? You can't handle hearing the truth?"

He grabs my arm, his grip callous like his next words. "I said *enough*. We're leaving."

With that, I'm fumbling for my pack before being pulled behind him down the narrow staircase. As we reach the bottom, I'm being roughly swaddled in my scarf, batting away the prince's swift hands as he wraps the fabric around my face and hair. As soon as his feet hit the creaky floor, he tosses a coin at the grumbling man behind the counter, not sparing him another glance before tugging me beyond the run-down inn.

I blink in the blinding light of the rising sun, stumbling slightly as he steers me through the sea of people. The streets are flooded with merchants, drowning in mayhem. The Enforcer weaves us through the crowd, his eyes flicking from face to face above the bandanna covering the lower half of his own. I envy his ability to disguise himself so easily, what with his lack of identifiable hair.

I wiggle my wrist in his grip, testing my many options to break his hold.

"Don't even think about it," he murmurs, not slowing his stride.

I roll my eyes at his back. He's increasingly insufferable.

He turns us down a tight alleyway, pausing long enough to throw a glance at me over his shoulder. "You holding up back there?"

"You ask as though you'd stop if I weren't."

"You truly know me so well," he croons, pulling me down another bustling street. After several sharp turns, I'm slowing behind him, struggling to keep pace with his long strides. My leg burns, the dull pain growing into something far more demanding.

He must hear my panting, feel my dragging feet, because he slips into a shaded side street and slows to a stop. "Out of shape, Gray?"

I glare at him before directing my gaze to the gash across my leg. "Yes, my pace has nothing to do with the fact that I'm actively bleeding out."

"Oh, don't be dramatic." His words are light, but his gaze is anything but as it travels down my body, finally landing on my thigh. And then he's suddenly crouching before me, hands braced on my leg. I can do nothing but blink at the bent head of messy black hair beneath me. He fiddles with the bandage peeking through the ripped pants atop it, fingers skimming my skin. "Are you really bleeding out on me, or just too stubborn to admit you need a break?"

"Maybe," I grit out through a false smile, "I need a break *because* I'm bleeding out. Which is because of you."

He's distracted by my now-exposed wound, offering me an amused "Hmm." I wince when he dabs at the hot blood trailing down my leg in red rivulets. His touch is so gentle, so disguised with something akin to care. I swallow when his hands roam the sides of my thigh, silently reminding myself why I'm injured in the first place. Why I'm running in the first place. Why I'm so broken in the first place.

Then his hands slide from my skin to tug at the bottom of his shirt, leaving me frustratingly cold in the shade. He rips a piece of cloth with ease before tugging my leg toward him to rest atop his own from where he kneels. I find myself committing the sight to memory with a smug smile.

I feel anything but Ordinary with the prince on his knees before me.

"Hold still," he murmurs. "You're swaying like a drunk."

I frown at the ebony hair tumbling over his brow. "You stole one of my legs."

"Yes, a leg. Not your balance."

I shake my head at the wall I've planted a hand against. "You're insufferable."

I catch the corner of his smirk as he ties off the new makeshift bandage and gently lifts my leg onto the ground. He stands, towering over me so suddenly that I find myself taking an unsure step back against the grimy wall.

"Better?" he asks, noting my skittishness with the softening of his gaze.

"Fine," I manage. "I'll make the trek to my doom, don't worry."

His eyes roam over me, scrutinizing with a sense of uncertainty. "Then we best be on our way."

CHAPTER 18

Kitt

Fresh air feels foreign to me.

Standing beside the cracked window, I breathe in the cool unfamiliarity beginning to blow into the stuffy study. The grounds sprawled beneath me are blanketed in a vibrant bed of grass, glowing in the cascading sunlight.

I don't stand here often. Don't open the curtains long enough to be perceived by the gossiping staff. But it's warranted after my meals.

Tipping my half-eaten plate out the window, I watch the contents spill onto the grass far below. Each vegetable hits the ground with a soft plunk—potatoes, carrots, a stringy sort of bean I've come to dislike—all adding to the growing pile of scraps I've discarded.

It's the part of my routine that needs refining. At first, it began as a way to clear my plate and appease the servants. Well, appease Gail with the proof that I digested her food. But, as of late, the whispers outside my door have only grown louder before each delivered meal. Perhaps my pile of uneaten food has finally been found, and it's only a matter of time until Gail storms in here to spoon-feed me herself.

A knock on the door has me assuming that day is upon me.

"Come in." Running frantic fingers over my tousled hair, I attempt to smooth down the standing strands. My crumpled shirt is the next concern that captures my attention, but I'm barely able to run my hand down the fabric before the door swings open.

Looking up, it's not Gail who meets my gaze.

"There's my secluded cousin."

The smile I muster surprises even myself. "Hello, Andy."

She steps farther into the study, her honey eyes sweeping over every inch of it. I clear my throat before stiffly sitting back into my seat. "Is there a reason for your . . . visit?"

Tearing her gaze from the open window, she allows it to settle on me. "Right. Well, I'm obviously here to fix your, um . . ." She trails off, visibly attempting to concoct some sort of scheme. "Your window?" She nods, trying to convince the both of us. "Yes, your window."

"You're here to fix my window?" I repeat slowly.

"That's what I do!" She gestures to the belt of tools around her waist, nose ring flashing in the light. "I know it's easy to forget that I'm still a Handy around the castle, what with my many other talents."

My eyes skim over the worn leather encircling her waist, every inch of it occupied by the heap of tools thrown haphazardly inside. I remember the days when the top of Andy's wine-red hair barely reached her father's hip, though she was practically attached to it, following him everywhere.

So, naturally, he taught her everything she knows. The art of fixing, mending, creating—all part of a Handy's role. Even despite the unique shifting ability running through her veins, she chose to pursue what most believe is a lowly passion.

Plopping hands onto her hips, she sighs. "But someone needs to clean up after you and Kai, and I have plenty of experience with that."

I nod along with each word, reminiscing on the many things we've broken during our impromptu brawls. Back when we were just brothers, unburdened by these shiny new titles we now bear.

Unable to stand the feel of her heavy scrutiny, I preoccupy myself with pretending to be busy. Shuffling papers in my hands, I attempt to straighten the scattered contents of my cluttered desk. "There is nothing wrong with my window, Andy. If you wanted to see me, you could have just asked."

A sorrowful shadow shades her face. "And you would have let me? See you, that is."

Here we go.

It was foolish of me to think I could avoid this conversation for much longer. Sighing, I offer, "I've been busy."

"Right." She nods, her gaze distant. "You're a king now. You're *my* king now. I can't imagine how difficult it has been to adjust." A pause. "Especially after how it happened."

You mean, how my father was brutally murdered? How I knelt beside his bloody body, staring at her dagger severing his neck? Is that what you meant to say, cousin?

I bite my tongue against the slew of spitting thoughts. "Yes, it has been . . . difficult."

"Jax misses you. And he's driving me insane, so feel free to take him off my hands." She says this with that bright smile of hers, despite the sadness clouding her gaze. "All right, fine. We both miss you. And I know you've been dealing with a lot lately, but it might be really good for you to get out of this study—"

"Andy." I hold up an ink-splattered hand, silencing her with a single movement. "I'm fine here. Really."

My words are so steady that I almost believe them myself.

Andy stills. Smiles. Sets a quick pace toward the window.

"You know," she says with that familiar edge in her voice, "I do think your window is broken, actually."

I don't look up from the stack of papers piled before me. "And why is that?"

I can hear the challenge in her voice. "Well, food always seems to be falling from it."

Silence falls, filled only by the drum of my fingers against the desk.

Her arms are folded above her work belt when I turn to face her. She raises a scrutinous brow. "You want to explain this to me?"

I think about this for a moment. "No."

She scoffs. "Come on."

"You're right. The window must be broken."

"Kitt."

"King."

She blinks at my correction, straightens at my suddenly stony complexion. "It is *king* now. Things are different—I am different." Shaking my head, I whisper, "He is gone, and I don't even know how to breathe if he does not command me to do so. Command me to eat. To *live*."

My hands are shaking. Papers slide from their sloppy piles while unshed tears burn my tired eyes.

Andy's face crumbles, pity pinching her burgundy brows. "Oh, Kitt . . ."

I stand stiffly before she has a chance to kneel at my side. Clearing my constricting throat, I murmur, "That will be all, Andy."

"Kitt, wait—"

"That will be all."

She stands, sucking in a breath. "Let me help you fix the window. Please. It doesn't have to stay broken."

I look at her then. Let her look at me.

It's only when she's examined every crack in my calm facade that I say, "I'm afraid it's beyond repair."

CHAPTER 19
Paedyn

"Is this really necessary?"

I raise a brow at the coarse ropes currently constricting my wrists, rubbing them raw. By way of response, the Enforcer smiles slightly in the shadows before tugging the ties impossibly tighter. I scoff, gesturing with bound hands to the barrenness surrounding us. "Now you decide to tie me up? In the desert with all your Imperials breathing down my neck?"

But the prince has already lost interest in me, turning to take the reins of one of the many restless horses. "All of this for an Ordinary?" I raise my voice so the blanket of sand can't smother it. "Who would have thought I'd have you so scared?" I open my mouth again, ready to spit something else that will most definitely get his attention when a shove at my back has me stumbling, biting the tongue that was about to get me into trouble.

"Bitch."

It's a hiss in my ear, a shiver down my spine. The Imperial has my hair twisted in his fist before I've even found my footing, yanking me

into his chest with a growl. I gasp at the pain, wince at the feel of his lips against my ear. "Filthy Ordinary. I should slit your throat right here. . . ."

"You know, I haven't even bothered to learn your name, Soldier. That is how little I value your life."

The Enforcer's drawl has the Imperial stiffening behind me, straightening slightly when the prince takes his time strolling toward us. I stare at the broad chest looming before me, watching it rise rapidly despite the deceptively calm words falling from his lips. "So imagine," he says casually, "what I would be more than happy to do to you if you ever lay another finger on her."

It's a struggle to keep from stumbling into the Enforcer with how forcefully the Imperial shoves me away from him. Then he's muttering a poor excuse for an apology, nodding to orders veiled as a threat. As soon as I find my footing, I'm staggering back from the prince and the callous scrutiny coating his face.

That wasn't care or concern or anything close to kindness. No, it was possession. The threat was territorial. I am his prey, his prize, his prisoner. His and his alone.

I hate it. Hate that I *belong* to him.

"Come here."

I blink at the blunt order, the blatant disregard for the fact that I was ever anything more than his captive to control. His command has the opposite effect, forcing my feet farther from him. He responds with a tilt of his head, eyes roaming over what must be the remaining disgust written across my face. "We're leaving," he says slowly, taking an equally slow step toward me. "If you'd prefer to walk across the desert, be my guest. Otherwise, I'm going to need you to get on a damn horse."

My eyes flick to the snorting creatures scattering the sand. I swallow. "I'm good, thanks."

Another step. "Is that so?"

I'm shifting on my feet now. "I'd rather walk."

"The *Silver Savior*?" He's smiling. "Scared of horses?"

Light laughter meets my ears, mocking me. I ignore the surrounding snickers and instead settle my gaze on the silently amused bastard before me. "Well, I was never privileged enough to ride one growing up, was I? So I think I'm allowed to find them . . . unsettling."

"We all have our fears, Gray," he murmurs, stepping closer for only me to hear. "Though I was beginning to believe you didn't have any. Least of all horses."

"I'm not afraid," I say between the teeth I'm flashing at him. "Just in need of some exercise."

I can barely make out the twitch of his lips in the darkness before he tethers my bound wrist to his horse with a long lead. "Try to keep up, Gray. I don't want to have to drag you across the desert."

I roll my eyes at his back but quickly avert them from the muscles straining against his shirt as he pulls himself up onto the saddle. At the sight, my mind wanders to the rooftop before I'm shaking my head and shoving the thought back down.

It's not long until I'm stumbling beside him, trying to put as much distance between myself and the beast looming beside me. The Imperials scattered around us are cast in shadow, draped in the darkness we waited to fall before setting foot in the desert. Spending my afternoon with the prince and his entourage was equally as miserable as the blanket of heat smothering us. That is, until the sun finally grew tired of its torture and sank into its bed of clouds, allowing the moon to guide us as we began our trek across the desert.

Time ticks by, indicated only by the ever-growing pain pulsing from my wound. Every step burns, scorching like the sun we managed to evade for a few hours. It's not long before a limp manages to slip into my stride, despite my best efforts to smother it.

But when he clears his throat beside me, I force myself to straighten, biting my tongue against the pain. "You're slowing down, Gray." His voice is quiet, gruff from hours of disuse.

"Would you like me to run, Your Highness?" I manage, keeping my eyes on the shifting sand beneath my feet.

"I'd like to see you try. It would be entertaining, to say the least."

I throw him a glance. "I live to amuse, Your Highness."

A cough catches in his throat, the closest to a laugh he'll allow himself. "Stop," he commands, pulling his horse to a halt. I stagger beside him, almost tempted to lean against the beast. The parade of Imperials pull on their reins, stopping to circle us.

I watch the prince swing gracefully from his saddle before closing the distance between us. Swallowing, I trace the muscle that ticks in his jaw, the path his gaze trails down my body. And then he's crouching before me once again, looking up with hands braced on either side of my injured thigh.

I ignore the prickle of a dozen prying eyes roaming over the scene we've created, unable to find a single reason to care. His eyes are on mine, and for a single, bittersweet second, it's Kai I'm looking at—not the monster meant to hunt me down.

Then his brow is furrowed, his mind captured by the task at hand. With swift fingers, he's tracing the jagged cut, threading skin and tissue together. I sigh, relief flooding me with every pass of his fingertips. He looks up at me then, eyes wandering over my face in a way that makes me feel stripped bare before him.

"Better?" His voice is barely more than a murmur.

"Better," I breathe. Tearing my eyes from his, I look up to scan the Imperials, silently wondering which one of them is the Healer he's drawing power from. "You couldn't have done that twelve hours ago?"

The corner of his lips twitch. "Twelve hours ago we were in a bustling city I knew you'd be able to easily disappear into. That is, if you managed to get away from me." He almost shrugs. "Call it a precaution."

I mimic his shrug with one of my own. "You seem to be taking a lot of precautions for a mere Ordinary."

"I think we both know that nothing about you is *mere*."

We watch each other for a long moment, wary in the way that we know we are supposed to be. Everything about him is sharp and cold and piercing me with that glasslike gaze. Even crouched beneath me, he's every bit the prince and creation of the king. A puppet of the crown disguised with a fancy title.

I wonder how often the Enforcer kneels before anything. *Anyone.*

"You're afraid of me."

He meets my statement with a stare, steady but drawn out like a sigh. "I'd be a fool not to fear something so fierce."

I swallow. "And are you not? A fool, that is?"

He stands then, holding my gaze until he's the one looking down on me. "Not anymore."

I open my mouth, fumbling for words he doesn't care to hear. With a turn and a nod to his men, the parade lurches to life once again, dragging me along with it. I watch as he mounts his horse, glimpsing the glimmer of hope on his hip.

My heart skips a beat, tripping over itself at the sight of a dagger decorating his side, though the lack of swirling steel on its hilt tells me it is not mine. I force my thoughts to be rational, force myself to think like the thief I had to become. Having maimed any chance for a morsel of trust, every move I make is annoyingly under suspicion. It's a struggle not to mourn how easy getting close to him used to be, and how desperately I crave something not completely complicated.

I lurch forward with the huffing horse beside me, mind reeling and feet faltering.

Plagues, I need a plan.

The parade continues its melancholy march in the pale moonlight—little more than silver shadows painting the sand. "Plan" is a generous word for the idea that formulates, but desperation has me throwing caution to the wind. With a deep breath, I swallow my pride before forcing my feet to drag dramatically.

The rope tethering me to the beast grows taut, my heels grinding into the sand. At first, the Enforcer doesn't deign to acknowledge my obvious resistance, and the horse he's atop certainly doesn't either. But after several drawn-out sighs and stubborn steps—

"What now, Gray?" He sounds utterly underwhelmed by my display.

"I'm tired."

"Is that so?"

I scowl up at his shadowy shoulders. "It is."

"Hmm."

"Hmm?" I pant. "That's all you have to say? *Hmm?*"

"Fine." I can practically feel him smiling atop his high horse. "*Hmm*, it's a shame you're scared of horses."

"I am not—" I sigh, taking a deep breath to hide my smile. This is exactly what I wanted. "I'll get over it. I'm too tired to care at the moment."

Now he offers a glance over his shoulder. "Let's see it, then. Get on."

I swallow, a reaction that I wish was dramatized. He extends a hand to help me up, his mouth kicking up at the corner. "Absolutely not." I try to take a step back, straining against the rope. "I'm going to need . . . assistance."

Now he really does smile. "You mean, you need *help*?"

"I am asking nothing of the sort."

He shakes his head at me. "Still too stubborn to admit you're asking for help, let alone that you need it." I roll my eyes, looking anywhere but into his. "Go on, Gray. I want to hear you say it."

I shake my head, tilting it toward the stars staring down on us. "You're insufferable."

"That's not quite what I'm waiting to hear."

A noise of disgust slips between my lips, a groan sounding of regret. "Fine. I need . . . your help." I bite out the words, swallowing the bitter taste they leave behind.

He smiles at me then, startling in a way it shouldn't be—not anymore. In response, he easily slips from his saddle to stand before me. My heart hammers in my chest, eyes flicking to the weapon at his side. I hold out my bound hands expectantly, smiling sweetly at him.

He watches me, his piercing eyes gliding over my face. "One wrong move, Gray," he murmurs, "and I'll bind you to the back of this horse. Understood?"

"Understood, Prince."

He meets my mocking with the hint of a grin. And then he's cutting me free with the knife I so desperately want in my palm. I don't dare track his movements as he slides the small dagger back onto his hip, instead keeping my eyes locked on his. My wrists are red and raw, sore from hours of strain. I take my time massaging them, running fingers over the growing welts there until I'm sure his thoughts are far from the knife at his side.

Time for a distraction.

Lifting my eyes to his, I take one last deep breath in preparation for the lack of plan I've conjured. "All right," I sigh. "Get me up there."

His smile is far too teasing for my liking. "All right, then." He steps behind me. His hands are hard on my hips before I can suck in another breath, sure and strong and sickeningly familiar. And then he's lifting me up, up, up—

"Plagues!" I squeal, thrashing in his hold like I intended to. Every limb is flailing, desperate to flee from his grip out of what I hope looks like fear. My back is pressed against his chest while feet fly in front of me and hands reach behind to grasp at anything—his face, his arms, his hip as I slip the dagger from its sheath.

"What the *hell* is wrong with you?" He lowers me back onto solid ground, dodging an elbow I throw back in his direction. As soon as my boots hit the sand, I turn and stumble against him, reaching the hand holding his knife behind my back. Unable to risk tucking the weapon into the band of my pants where he will likely feel it, I flip the blade so its handle faces downward and silently say a prayer to Plague-knows-who. Only then do I let the knife drop toward the mouth of my boot.

I bite my tongue against the sting of pain, feeling blood begin to prickle my skin where the blade nicked my ankle. But then I'm biting my tongue against a smile.

I did it. It worked. Maybe I should pray more.

"I—I wasn't ready!" I pant, taking a step away before smoothing out my rumpled shirt.

"Oh, I'm sorry," he mocks, exasperated, "I just assumed that 'get me up there' implied you were ready to *get up there*."

I glance up at the men around us, hidden in shadows. The blanket of darkness is the only reason I was able to get away with the sloppy stunt I just pulled without anyone seeing. "I'm just . . . nervous, okay? Give me a second."

"Take your time," he grinds out between clenched teeth, not meaning a single word.

I look away from the agitation so blatantly displayed across his face. Taking a deep breath, I play the part of the anxious captive, complete with fidgeting fingers and shifting feet.

"All right," I finally say.

"All right, what?" he asks slowly. "I want to hear you say it, so I don't get ambushed again."

I offer him a dull look. "All right, I'm ready."

"You sure about that? Should I expect a black eye or—"

"Just get me on the damn horse, Azer."

He takes a slow step behind me then, holding my gaze while sliding rough palms onto my hips. I swallow at the sheer intimacy of a moment that is intended to be nothing of the sort.

He's lifting me onto the horse that's carrying me to my doom, for Plague's sake.

And yet, my cheeks are heating in the middle of a sunless desert. And I hate it—hate him. *Right?*

He pulls me close, holds me like a breath, knowing it's only a matter of time before he needs to let me go.

And then he's lifting me, guiding my foot into a stirrup. I swing my other leg over the beast, shaky and slow. I'm clutching the saddle, every muscle taut and ready to throw myself off if need be. But right as I'm considering doing just that, he's suddenly behind me, solid and pressed against my spine.

"I think," I say quietly, "I'd be more comfortable in the back."

"Oh, I'm sure," he murmurs, so close to my ear, I suppress a shiver. "But I want you where I can see you."

He reaches around me then, forearms framing my waist as he grips the reins. I roll my eyes at where his hands rest on my thighs. "Is this really necessary?"

"What, you know how to steer a horse?"

I lean slightly against his chest. "I'm a fast learner."

He huffs, stirring my hair. "Yes, a fast learner that would head straight back to Dor."

"You think so little of me, Highness."

A laugh. "No, I think so often of you. Which is why I know exactly what you would do."

I swallow, slouching as I let the silence settle over us. Minutes tick by, tempting me to talk, if only out of boredom.

"What will he do to me?"

He's tucked so closely behind that I can feel his body tense when the question slips from my mouth. I suddenly have the prince shifting uncomfortably, sighing onto the back of my neck. I've tried not to think of Kitt, of how I may have helped mold him into a replica of the king I drove a sword through.

"I . . . ," Kai starts, ducking his head, "I'm not sure."

"What is he like?" I say softly. "My *king*?"

"He's like you left him." His voice is dull. "A shell of a man, stepping into the shoes of a king."

I sigh, looking up at the stars above. "Then I'm as good as dead."

CHAPTER 20

Kai

Her breathing is melodic.

Hypnotizing in a way I hate admitting.

She's pressed so close, so slumped against my chest that I can feel her rib cage expanding with each breath.

I doubt she's slept so soundly in days.

Another deep breath. Another jab of her ribs into my stomach.

. . . or eaten much, for that matter.

By the look and feel of her, she's likely survived off stale bread the entirety of her stay in Dor, all while fighting daily in the ring.

I should really make her eat more.

I shake my head at the thought, at the reflex that is caring about her. Because she is not my responsibility. She is my prisoner. My mission. My father's murderer.

A soft, sleepy noise slips past her lips, and I still at the sound. She's held between my hands, solid against my chest, head on the pounding heart of her captor. I've never seen such peace held so gently in the arms of Death.

I glance up at the sky, a blanket of blackness covered in constellations. The men riding beside me are nothing more than shifting shadows, silently treading through the sand. Heads bob around me, fighting against the sleep weighing heavy on their eyelids.

"Stop," I call hoarsely. "We'll camp here for the rest of the night."

I'm met with grunts of gratitude, followed by frantic fumbling and clumsy dismounts. I pull my horse to a halt, hesitating before resting heavy hands atop her thighs. I allow myself one moment. One selfish moment of my miserable existence committed to her. To a girl in the arms of a boy. To a facade.

And then the moment is over, shattering as I shake her awake.

Well, try to.

She grunts, unamused by my attempt to wake her. I try again, grabbing her waist this time to thoroughly jostle her. She protests, as per usual, throwing an elbow into my stomach with surprising strength for someone still half-asleep. I hiss between my teeth before pinning her arms to her sides. "Easy," I breathe. "Would you rather I have you spend the rest of the night on this horse?"

She sighs, her voice softened with sleep. "If it means I can ride it far away from you, then yes, I would love to."

"You wound me," I say dryly, easily swinging from the horse. She's eying me expectantly, looking down her nose to where I stand beneath. I smile pleasantly in return. "Is there something you need?"

Her nose scrunches, visible representation of the frustration finding its way onto her face. "No. I'm perfectly fine." And with that, she's gripping the horn of the saddle and attempting to swing a leg over.

"Is that so?" I'm smiling now. "Nothing you want to ask me?"

"I am *not* asking for your help," she huffs, teetering in the saddle. "Better yet, what is stopping me from turning this horse around and bolting?"

"Ability. Knowledge. Fear," I state flatly. "Would you like me to keep going?"

"I'd like to knock your teeth in."

"Oh, but then I wouldn't be able to smile in that way I know you like."

Scowling, she states, "Smile all you want. I don't like anything about you."

My rebuttal is quiet, ragged, as though it's been ripped from the depths of my mind. "I recall you liking the one that was meant only for you."

She stiffens at my words but doesn't deem them worth a response. Ignoring me, she instead turns her attention back to the task at hand. For someone so typically coordinated, watching her attempt to dismount a horse is comical. She all but throws herself from the animal, eager to finally be on solid ground.

"Where am I sleeping?" she asks, eying the many bedrolls now littering the sand.

"Beside me."

Her eyes fly to mine. "Absolutely not."

"Why?" I ask innocently. "It's not anything we haven't done before."

"And it's not anything I plan on ever doing again," she challenges.

"And why is that, Gray?" I sigh. "Worried you'll like it too much?"

The sound she makes is a cross between a scoff and disgust. "You're the one who should be worried. I just might strangle you in your sleep." With that, she plops down on the closest bedroll, watching an Imperial use his Blazer ability to light a fire.

I let my eyes wander over her, wander over the tan skin, the fingers fidgeting with the ring on her thumb, the silver hair mirroring the moon above. Everything about her is so very familiar, so very deceiving. No power runs through the veins beneath that tan skin.

No abilities guided by those fidgeting fingers. No Elite likeness in the silver strands of her hair.

And yet, she feels anything but Ordinary. I've been taught my whole life that the likes of her would be the ruin of Elites, but I've never felt anything stronger.

I move to sit beside her, combing a hand through my sandy hair.

"Careful," she mocks, "any closer and I'll start weakening your powers."

I throw her a glance. "That's not how it works, and you know it."

She laughs, harsh and hateful. "Please, enlighten me, then. I would love to hear how you think the Ordinaries will be the doom of all Elites."

"If you'd continued to live in Ilya," I sigh, "you would be. For more than one reason." I turn to take her in, eyes skimming over the obvious disbelief in the crease between her brows. "Do you not know our history? Where we came from and why it is so important we remain Elite?"

I catch the quick roll of her eyes in the flickering firelight. "Of course I know Ilya's history. I may not have gone to school, but my father made sure I wasn't completely incompetent."

"All right, then," I say casually. "Tell me."

She gives me a halfhearted scoff. "What, you want me to teach *you* of Ilya's history?"

"I want to make sure you know what you're talking about. So"—I gesture for her to proceed—"go on."

"This is ridiculous," she huffs, fidgeting with the bedroll beneath her.

"It's beginning to sound as though you don't know—"

"Ilya was a weak kingdom," she cuts in, annoyed to be entertaining me. "We always have been, even before the Plague swept through.

Being conquered was a constant fear for past kings, and when the Plague killed nearly half the population, the kingdom was quarantined, isolated, and more vulnerable than ever." She recites the information with her eyes trained on the sky above. "So, when the Elites were born from the Plague, the kingdom rejoiced at the power they suddenly had over everyone else." She glances back at me. "Satisfied?"

"Hardly." I smile. "Continue."

A huff. Then a heavy sigh. "Ilya has remained isolated ever since, in order to ensure we are the only kingdom with Elites. And then, after seventy years, your father decided to banish all the Ordinaries so he could have his Elite society."

"You are missing some very key points, Gray," I interject.

"Right," she sighs. "The *disease* that Healers discovered we Ordinaries possess. The one that will eventually weaken the Elites' powers."

"And?" I prod.

"*And* the fact that Ordinaries and Elites procreating will eventually cause the Elite race to go extinct. That," she adds with a pointed look, "I do believe." With a sigh, she wistfully continues. "Only Elites can make Elites. Though, one's abilities are not depicted by their parents. Some believe the level of power pertains to the very strength of the person."

"So you do understand why Ilya must remain the way it is."

"Yes," she says softly. "Greed."

I study her for a long moment, letting her words sink in. Hearing her perspective of Ilya is both jarring and intriguing. Having grown up as an Ordinary in the slums, she sees the kingdom vastly different than any upper-class Elite. And, unfortunately, I'm intrigued.

"Are you done quizzing me, or can I go to sleep now?" she asks, leaning back on her elbows.

I ignore her question to risk asking one of my own. "So what do you suggest, then?"

"Suggest for what?"

"Ilya," I say simply. "What other option is there but to carry on as we have for the past thirty years?"

She sits up slightly, seemingly surprised by my question. "I suggest we carry on with what we were doing for seventy years prior to the Purging. Back when Ordinaries and Elites lived side by side—"

"And the weakening of our powers? The disease?"

She sighs. "Has it ever occurred to you that maybe Elites weren't meant to be? That what the Plague *gifted* Ilya with is unnatural?" I stiffen at her words, but she pushes on. "Humans aren't meant to play God. And the Elites have played that part long enough. If their powers being weakened means no more isolation and killing of Ordinaries, then so be it."

I look away, shaking my head at the stars. "Ilya will be weak without its Elites. We could be easily conquered and—"

Her laugh cuts me off. "You think we aren't weak now? We are so isolated that there isn't enough food to feed those of us in the slums, let alone hold everyone, when there is no more land to expand into." Her voice is stern, but her eyes are pleading. "Without a single ally or kingdom that doesn't hate us, are we not weaker than ever? And we will only continue to crumble unless something, or someone, changes."

Someone.

She's thinking of Kitt. She's probably always thought of Kitt as that someone who could change Ilya for her. Someone with potential to be persuaded into seeing things differently.

I almost laugh at the thought.

The Kitt I left is devoid of any potential that wasn't a part of Father's plan. He'll do nothing but what the king wanted and wished for. Even dead he's controlling Kitt, ruling Ilya from the grave.

"Good to finally hear how you really feel," I say with a scoff.

"Well, there's no point in hiding it now. Treason is the least of my worries at the moment." Stretching, she scans the stars before curling onto her side. "Do you believe I'm diseased?"

I'm startled at how earnestly she asks the question. "I believe the Healers. And thirty years ago, they found something undetectable. Something that will deteriorate the Elites' powers over time." She's quiet, so I take advantage of it. "Do you believe you're diseased?"

"I'm biased, but no, I don't think so. My father was a Healer, and he didn't think so either. Maybe there is no way to know for sure," she says softly. "But I do know I deserve to live either way."

She quiets, favoring sleep over finishing this conversation. After a long moment, I feel her shiver before hearing the complaint slip past her lips. "Please tell me I wasn't kidnapped only to freeze in the desert?"

"You are a pain in the ass." I wave a hand at an Imperial as I lie down beside her. "Get me an extra blanket."

She doesn't bother rolling over to mock me to my face. "And I thought chivalry was dead."

When the Imperial throws me a blanket, I don't hesitate before tossing it over her head. "Oh, it is, darling."

With a huff, her head peeks over the folds of fabric, sending silver hair sliding across her face. The look she gives me promises a death I know she can deliver. Then she's turning her back to me once again, content to ignore my existence until sleep claims her.

No, she's likely plotting something. I suspect she rarely isn't. She makes for a difficult captive, needing to be watched even when there is nowhere to go. Because if anyone can find a way to—

"Shit, Gray!" I jump away from her, cursing colorfully.

"What the hell is wrong with you?"

"Wrong with *me*?" I'm exasperated. "Your feet are *freezing*."

She glances over her shoulder, clearly failing to conceal her smirk. "Well, I can't sleep with shoes on. Never been able to."

"Seems like you can't sleep with socks on either," I grit out.

She shrugs. "It's a curse, really."

"Well, keep the curse on your side."

Her face falls. "But you're warm." Before I can respond, she's nodding across the fire. "Me and my cold feet could always just sleep over there. Alone."

"Like hell I'm letting you sleep alone," I mutter.

And then I'm shaking my head, wrapping an arm around her legs, and pulling them against me.

She looks at me, shocked. And then she smiles, bright and big like the night sky hanging above us.

I fear she could rival the stars.

An arrow sinks into the sand beside my head.

I hear it land before I've even opened my eyes.

I roll, staying low to the ground as I scan the darkness for the source of this ambush. Arrows are pelting our camp, burying themselves into the flesh of my groggy men. Their screams fill my ears as I feel their powers flicker out from under my skin.

Blinking away sleep and the blackness blocking my view, I can just barely make out the figures stalking toward us in the sand. I shift onto my side, preparing to stand and use one of the few powers left at my disposal to—

Something cool and sharp meets the skin of my neck.

The feeling is all too familiar.

And so is her voice.

"One more move, and I won't hesitate again."

CHAPTER 21
Paedyn

The blade glints in the moonlight, hiding the pale line of blood it's drawn beneath.

"I don't even want to know how you managed to get that," Kai breathes, the muscle in his jaw ticking with frustration. I keep the knife firm against his neck as I hear the last of the Imperials fall to the sand with a muted thud.

"We are being ambushed, Gray. What do you think you're doing?" he mutters, eyes searching my face as I scan the sand and figures approaching.

I look down at him from where I'm casually sitting. "I think I'm getting rescued."

Confusion crumples his face while a smile spreads across mine. "How . . . ?" He pauses, disbelief painting his features. "How could you possibly—"

"Aye, Princess!"

My heart leaps at the sound of his voice. I've never been so happy to hear that ridiculous nickname.

His hair blends in with the ring of firelight he's just stepped into. It's a curly mess falling over his forehead, while the face below is splattered equally with dirt and freckles. The smile he gives me has tears springing to my eyes. I never thought I would see another friend, alive and well.

"What, you just gonna sit there all day or get over here and give me a hug?" Lenny asks, raising a skeptical pair of eyebrows.

I glance at the Enforcer glaring up at me when a sharp voice answers the question I hadn't voiced. "I've got him, Paedyn, don't worry."

Smiling, I look up to find Leena doing the same. She has a crossbow trained on the prince while a sly grin plays at her lips. Her long black hair is tied at the nape of her neck and flung over a shoulder. She is tiny and terrifying and I'm tearing up just looking at her.

I don't hesitate before scrambling to my feet. With my eyes locked on Lenny, I'm stumbling toward him, bare feet shifting in the sand. Then I'm staggering to a stop, staring up at the face I thought I'd never see again.

"All right." He spreads his arms open with a slight shrug. "Come here."

I nod, letting the knife slip from my hand before stepping into his embrace. My forehead meets his chest with a comical thump. I feel his laugh vibrate through me as he wraps his arms around my back to give me an awkward pat.

"I missed you, too, Princess," he says into my hair before pulling away to look at me. "I didn't know if I'd ever see you again. At least"—he looks away, suddenly serious—"at least not before the rest of Ilya saw you."

"Yeah, me too," I whisper, blinking back stubborn tears. Then I'm hugging Leena while she holds a loaded crossbow in hand, which somehow feels fitting.

"It's good to see you," she breathes. I nod, smiling as another figure steps from the shadows.

"No heartfelt greetings for me? I'll try my best not to take offense."

"Hello, Finn." I laugh, wrapping my arms around him and the bow now resting across his back. "I knew you were here before I even saw you." I turn to look at them all. "I knew I was safe."

"Oh, really?" Finn raises an eyebrow at me, his brown hair glinting auburn in the dying firelight.

"The arrows." I gesture to the dozen littering the camp and its former occupants. "Those are the Resistance's arrows. The ones you make with the red arrowheads." Finn smirks at my knowledge of his handiwork. "And I knew that you were the one firing them, because you always carve an *F* at the bottom of the shaft."

He shrugs. "Maybe I make the best arrows for myself. And maybe I want to make sure no one else takes them."

"Typical," Leena huffs from where she still aims at the Enforcer.

"What are you guys doing here?" I ask, turning toward Lenny.

He runs a hand over the back of his neck. "Why don't we take this conversation on the road. We've spent enough time in this desert." He glances at the prince who is looking anything but pleased. "Finn, do you have the rope in your pack?"

After fishing the rope free, Finn throws a smug smile over his shoulder at an already irritated Leena. "See, I told you we'd need to tie someone up on this trip."

"Yeah, I just hoped it would be you," she mumbles.

Despite Kai making no move to fight him, Lenny hesitates before binding Kai's hands behind his back. It's obvious he never dreamed he'd be taking his prince as a captive, seeing that he swore an oath to protect him. "I can't believe I'm actually saying this to you," Lenny sighs, "but if you run, we shoot."

Kai is silent as he stands and scans the scattered bodies. His expression is suddenly blank, apparently emotionless, as he looks at the men. I've watched him slip on dozens of his masks, so I recognize the moment he fixes another one into place.

I tug my shoes back on before helping stuff a few bedrolls into their packs while the three make quick work of untying horses for themselves. "What's the matter, Princess?" Lenny asks after noticing me shifting on my feet. "These horses not up to your standards?"

"No horse is up to my standards," I mutter before adding much louder, "Could I just ride with you?"

I can see the exact moment he realizes the Silver Savior is afraid of horses, and I'm not going to let him say a damn thing about it. "I'll hurt you, Lenny. You know I will."

He raises his hands in surrender, shrugging as he says, "I wasn't going to say a thing."

"Like hell you weren't," I mutter, watching as he frees the rest of the horses we can't take with us. After I find my knife in the sand and return it to my boot, Lenny struggles to smother his laughter while doing little to help me get onto the beast.

The prince walks in front of us as we leave the carnage behind to begin heading back toward Dor. "What is happening back in Ilya?" I ask into Lenny's back as I wrap my arms tightly around him. "And what happened in the Bowl after the final Trial? Oh, and the rest of the Resistance—"

"Easy, Princess," Lenny cuts in. "We have plenty of desert before Dor to answer all of your questions." His eyes flick between Leena and Finn riding to the right of us. "Uh, either of you want to tell her?"

"Not particularly, no," Finn says evenly.

Lenny reaches over and claps him on the back, smiling sweetly.

"We all know you're the best at telling stories. Go ahead, man."

"I am, aren't I?" Finn smiles before shaking his head. "Which is why you need the practice . . ."

"Can someone please tell me what the hell I need to be told?" I blurt, blinking at the both of them.

"Move," Leena orders before pushing her horse around Finn's to ride beside me. "Ugh, you have no idea what I've had to deal with." She combs small fingers through the length of her hair, composing herself. "Paedyn, the Resistance . . . the Resistance is done. It's over."

I run my fingers over the ring on my thumb, shaking my head at her. "What . . . what are you talking about? What do you mean it's *done*?"

Leena glances at the boys before continuing with a sigh. "The fight in the Bowl was brutal. We weren't prepared for the number of Imperials that rushed in. Every number we had calculated, every detail we had learned from our spies on the inside, was wrong. Nothing went right that day."

"Yeah, Calum was cut off before he could even deny that us Ordinaries are diseased and weakening the kingdom," Finn adds.

I nod, remembering how outraged the crowd was at learning how many Ordinaries had been living among them. "Is he alive? Calum? What about Mira?"

"We've heard that the king has them." Lenny shakes his head, rubbing a hand behind his neck. "They're probably being interrogated as we speak."

I shudder at the thought of what Kitt is doing to them, to the Resistance leader and his daughter. "And everyone else in the Bowl?" I ask softly, fearing the answer. "Were they all . . . ?"

Leena shakes her head at the sand. "Any Resistance members that weren't lost in the battle at the Bowl are on the run. Just like us."

A heavy silence settles over us at the thought of so much death. So many people that *I* led into the arena. So many innocent lives lost fighting for what they believed was right. What *is* right.

"So, that's how we ended up here," Finn says finally. "And how we found you."

I smile, shaking my head at the three of them. "How did you know it was me?"

"Well," Lenny chimes in, "it helped that the group of you was laying around a fire. Helped us see you while you couldn't see us—even if you were awake. As for knowing it was you . . ." He laughs, turning to tug at my unraveling braid. "Most of this was covering your face and reflecting the light."

"You were like a little beacon in the night," Finn says cheerily.

I laugh lightly, watching Leena roll her eyes before adding, "The Imperials weren't hard to take care of, considering they were asleep. Not to mention that you took care of the Enforcer for us."

"Yeah, well, none of them would have even woken up if Leena"—Finn throws a glance in her direction—"hadn't hit a guy in the arm and sent him screaming."

Even in the pale moonlight, I can easily see the fire burning in Leena's brown eyes. "That," she says through clenched teeth, "is because you bumped me."

"Whatever you say, Leeny," Finn singsongs, earning him a jab to the ribs.

I listen to the two of them bicker until Lenny leans back toward me. "How have you been, Pae? I mean, after everything?" He glances behind him, seeming to take in all of me with a single look. "I wasn't sure if you were even alive. We eventually went back to the Resistance house—your house—and it was—"

"Burned to the ground?" I finish for him. "Yeah, I was inside it when that happened." I glare at the Enforcer walking several yards ahead of us, hoping he can feel my gaze burning into his back.

Lenny shakes his head. "You are a little cockroach, you know that?"

"Plagues," I snort. "You really know what a girl wants to hear, don't you?"

"No, I mean, I'm convinced you can survive anything."

"Yeah, well, I'm convinced that's becoming a curse," I say quietly.

"Come on, don't say that," Lenny says softly. "Don't live to die. Die because you lived." A pause. "Or something like that. Listen, you've earned every breath. So enjoy it."

I sigh. "Well, there's not much to enjoy in the desert."

"My company."

"Like I said," I say with a smile. "Not much to enjoy."

"Watch it, Princess," Lenny warns. "I'm the one controlling this beast you're so scared of."

I roll my eyes at his back even while squeezing him tighter. We're silent for a stretch of sand before Lenny says, "At least I've been able to see your face every day. You're plastered all over Ilya."

"In Dor, too," I add. "Tando. Probably Izram."

"The price on your head is . . ." He lets out a low whistle.

"Yeah," I sigh. "That's what happens when you murder a king, I guess."

I can feel him preparing to ask before he finally opens his mouth. "Paedyn, how did that even—"

"I was running back from the castle," I say quietly. "I made a promise and couldn't leave without something." I fidget with the unraveling hem of my vest, feeling the phantom of Adena's skilled fingers. "And he was just standing outside the Bowl, bloody and holding a sword. Then . . . then he just attacked me, like he'd been waiting for the moment." I shake my head. "He said things about my dad and the Resistance, but it's mostly a blur now."

Lies.

I relive the moment every time I close my eyes.

Lenny turns, tracing the jagged scar down my neck with worried eyes. "He did that to you?"

I swallow. "You didn't see what I did to him."

The carving below my collarbone stings with the reminder, but I pull my vest tighter around myself. No one will see how he's ruined me.

"I'm sorry you were alone," Lenny says gently.

"Cockroach, remember? I always find a way to make it out alive."

He laughs quietly while I study the sky, spotting the first pink clouds crowding the horizon. Taking a breath, I ask, "How's our new king doing?"

Lenny shakes his head before running a hand over his face. "There . . . there are rumors."

"Rumors?" I repeat.

"The whole kingdom is talking about it," Finn chimes in, riding up beside us. "He's gone mad. Simple as that."

"That," Lenny throws him a look, "is the *rumor.* All we know is that he hasn't left his office since the death of the king, and servants talk. They say they can hear him mumbling through the walls and always find his food tossed from the window." He shrugs. "Maybe he's just grieving, and it will all be over soon. Or maybe . . ."

"Maybe this is the future of Ilya," Leena says softly.

It's suddenly difficult to swallow. I know firsthand how affected Kitt was by his father when he was alive. And now that I've killed him . . .

"How is Ilya? The people?" I manage after clearing my throat.

Lenny shrugs. "Well, not great. The Elites are also mourning the ruler that single-handedly made Ilya the strongest kingdom by banishing the Ordinaries."

"There are a lot of people who hate you—let's just say that." Finn's tone is joking, though the topic is anything but.

I look away, shaking my head. "I'm not surprised. Not only do they hate what I did, but they also hate what I am."

"The people are restless," Leena says softly. "Our new king has yet to show his face to the kingdom, and it's made many feel neglected in a way."

"The queen isn't doing well either," Finn adds. "They think it's only a matter of time now."

My eyes trail to the prince ahead of us. His eyes are on the sky, watching the darkness hint at the promise of pink skies. I let out a shaky breath. His mother is dying, and he was sent on a mission to retrieve me. A mission that is now taking far longer than anyone expected.

Did he say goodbye to her before he left? Did he make a promise he now cannot keep? Did he—

I push the thoughts from my head, bury the worry beneath my layers of loathing for him.

The prince's well-being is not my problem.

And with that, I turn my attention back to the boy before me and the beast beneath us. "Lenny, you need to teach me how to ride one of these things."

CHAPTER 22

Paedyn

"Where are you taking us?"

I duck before a fallen beam can connect with my skull. Fumbling in the darkness, I try my best to keep up with Lenny's lanky legs still several steps in front of me. My body aches after a full day of riding, and blindly navigating the backstreets of Dor is not exactly helping.

"You'll see. Just a little farther," Lenny calls over his shoulder at the group grumbling behind him.

Leena shoots me a skeptical look while Finn trails behind Kai with a crossbow in hand. We've been making our way through the outskirts of the city for nearly an hour now, though we still haven't been told exactly why.

"Watch your head here," Lenny warns before ducking through a partially boarded doorway. I spin, taking in the abandoned building we've just stepped into. What is left of the walls is draped in shadows, dappled in the moonlight streaming through a slatted roof.

Lenny doesn't bother slowing the long strides that carry him toward the dark corner. I squint after him, sucking in a breath. Blinking, I can barely make out the figures melting from the shadows Lenny approaches.

I open my mouth to shout a warning, call his name—

"Lenny!"

But it's another woman's shout I hear despite it being on the tip of my tongue. A flicker of flame paints the wall, shedding light on the scene. Dozens of bedrolls litter the uneven floorboards, most of which are occupied by groggy men, women, and children. A tall woman stands among them, her short red hair glowing like an ember in the flickering light. Lenny grins, pulling her into a crushing embrace.

"What the hell is going on here?" Finn murmurs beside me. I shake my head, unable to do anything but stare.

"Everyone," Lenny says after finally being released, "meet my mother."

We blink at him and the strangers beginning to stir awake. Leena is the first to move, extending a hand to the woman. "Hi. I'm Leena."

"Meredith," she says warmly, shaking her hand.

"Mom," Lenny says, "this is Paedyn and Finn and—"

"And the Enforcer," she finishes, her lips thin.

"Yes, the Enforcer." Lenny rubs the back of his neck. "We still aren't sure what to do with him."

"Well"—she flicks her brown eyes to me—"you are the Silver Savior, yes?"

"Unfortunately." I smile slightly.

She doesn't seem to be scared of me or what I've done. Instead, she returns my smile. "Then you use him to earn your freedom. The king needs his right-hand man more than a girl on the run."

Lenny nods slowly. "That could work. We'd need to figure out the exact plan but—"

"I'm sorry to interrupt," Finn cuts in, "but where are we? And who are these people?"

There are dozens of them now sleepily stirring in their beds or standing to join the greetings. "This," Meredith says with a smile, "is a refuge of sorts."

"Len Len!"

A squealing blur comes charging at Lenny before he scoops it into his arms. The little girl giggles uncontrollably as he spins her around, kissing her on the cheek. "There you are, little dragon!"

"Did you miss me?" she squeals.

"Depends on how much you missed me." Lenny smiles, pinching her nose.

She grins, eyes bright. "More than a little."

"Good," Lenny says. "I missed you more than a little too."

I watch her swat at his hair before hesitantly asking, "Is this your sister?"

Lenny shrugs. "In a way. Ma found her on the streets of Ilya and knew she couldn't stay there, so she brought her to live here. We've grown more than a little attached to one another."

"And where is *here*, exactly?" Leena asks, looking around at the crumbling building.

Meredith smiles. "It's a place for . . ." Her eyes land on the bound prince who's studying the little girl intently. "Well, he's certainly figured it out."

Kai takes a step toward the girl before Finn nudges him with the tip of his crossbow. "Easy, Prince."

The Enforcer ignores him to scrutinize the strangers surrounding us. "They're . . . partial. Percentages." He shakes his head, struggling to sort out what it is he's sensing.

Meredith nods, smiling slightly. "That's right. They're the outcome of Elites and Ordinaries. Some have more power than others, but all of them are here because they belong nowhere else." She speaks pointedly toward Kai, studying him as he swallows every word. "They cannot risk living in the slums of Ilya because their powers are too weak to be considered Elite, but they cannot live freely in the surrounding cities because the people loathe the power they cannot control." She steps aside, allowing us full view of the many figures now staring at us. "So, they sleep here and blend in as best they can."

"Show us what you can do, little dragon," Lenny whispers into the girl's ear.

She grins, showing us her palms and wiggling her fingers—the same fingers that suddenly flicker with flame. She smiles up at Lenny, who nods encouragingly. "Go on. Show 'em why you're my little dragon, Luna."

She nods, her dark hair streaked with firelight. Then she lifts her flickering fingers toward her mouth, taking a deep breath before blowing it out at the flames. They ripple from her fingers, stretching into the room as though she's breathing fire.

"Luna comes from a long line of Mixes, for lack of a better term, which is why her fingers are the only place her Blazer ability manifests," Meredith says softly. "I found her in the slums, no older than a toddler. I knew immediately that she didn't possess the full power of a Blazer, considering that Elite children can barely contain their abilities for several years. She should have been covered in flames."

She smiles sadly at the giggling girl in Lenny's arms. "I knew it wouldn't be long before it became clear to everyone that she wasn't fully Elite. And Ilya has no use for those weakened by Ordinaries." Her eyes skip over the Enforcer. "So I hid her for a while. Most Mixes are still strong enough to blend in with Elites, but Luna is far from the first Mix in her bloodline. Eventually"—she waves a hand to the group behind her—"I found more throughout Loot and took them in. That is, until I couldn't hold any more and eventually made the trek to Dor, where it is safer for them. Here, they are met with hatred if they are found out. There"—her sharp stare finds the prince—"they are met with death."

"There aren't many left in Ilya," Lenny adds. "Most of them fled to Dor or Tando a generation ago and live among everyone else. But if I happened to find any in the slums when I was stationed there, I'd send them to Ma."

A man clears his throat, stepping forward from the back of the group. "Lenny found me a few years ago." His hands are cupped together, holding the small flame that has been illuminating the dark room. "I'm also a partial Blazer. I have to cup my hands together like this, just to make a flame."

A woman clears her throat, stepping into the dim light. "I'm a partial Veil. So . . ." Her arms suddenly flicker out, disappearing before our eyes. "The rest of me stays visible."

Several others walk forward, sharing how they got here and the little they can do. Leena is nearly brought to tears as she profusely thanks Meredith for all that she's done, hugging her and anyone else who will allow it.

But it's the Enforcer who holds my attention. He studies them like a puzzle, deciphering the percentage of power each of them possesses. I vaguely wonder how many of these half Elites have passed him in the streets with him none the wiser.

"You're welcome to stay here as long as you like," Meredith says sweetly, turning her attention to me. "I can imagine it's hard to keep you out of trouble with that hair of yours."

"You have no idea," I say, smiling slightly.

"Make yourselves comfortable," Lenny says before turning toward his mother to inform her on where we left the horses while Luna plays with his hair.

I make quick work of unrolling a bedroll while gnawing on some bread Meredith begins passing out to us. "What are we doing with him?" I turn to see Finn nodding the crossbow at the prince.

"Put him by me," I say sweetly, though my smile is anything but. "We'll take shifts watching him."

When he sits down beside me, he's wearing my least favorite mask at his disposal—indifference. So I lean over, whispering softly in his ear. "Lucky for you, my feet are *freezing*."

CHAPTER 23

Kai

My hands are numb.

And they've been numb for nearly two days now.

I shift against the wall and attempt to rotate my sore wrists. I've been tied up since the ambush in the Scorches and, frankly, I'm not accustomed to feeling like my fingers are going to fall off. I huff, frustrated at my current situation.

"Something the matter, Prince?"

She's perched at the end of my bedroll, crossbow in hand and a smirk on her lips. It's alarming how much she enjoys this. "I don't know, maybe the fact that I'm still tied up?" I say dryly.

She gives me a falsely sympathetic look. "You'd better start getting used to it."

Oh, I've had plenty of time to get used to it.

I walked the entire way back from the Scorches with my hands bound behind my back. At least I had entertainment at the time. Eavesdropping certainly kept me occupied on the long trek, since no one seemed to remember that Lenny's Hyper ability was free game to me.

And that's when I heard how she killed him. I'd never asked, I realized, what it was like for her. Maybe I didn't want to know if she had a good reason for doing it.

My eyes linger on the scar trailing down her neck to slip beneath the folds of her vest. She tracks the movement, shifting uncomfortably under my scrutiny. Pulling the collar of her vest higher, she holds my stare. "What?"

I shrug, shaking my head at the ground. "Nothing. I just know how painful that was."

I've been cut up enough times by the king to know exactly how much pressure he uses with a blade.

She rolls her eyes. "Sympathy doesn't look good on you, Azer."

"Everything looks good on me, Gray." I flash her a smile. "Don't lie."

Her mouth falls open, and I'm greatly looking forward to what is about to come out of it when Lenny strides over instead. "You ready for tomorrow, P?"

She takes a deep breath, looking composed as she continues staring at me. "Oh, I can't wait."

"Great." Lenny nods. "We'll set off in the evening and ride through the night. Then, a few days later, once we get close to Ilya, I'll go ahead and inform the king that we have his Enforcer." With a sigh, he adds, "I'll tell him to meet us in the field near the Sanctuary of Souls with, what, no more than three Imperials? That should avoid the ambush that would certainly happen if we all tried to walk into the throne room. We will keep our crossbows aimed on the *leverage*"—a nod at Kai—"the whole time to ensure that there is no funny business. And that is when we'll exchange our prince here for your freedom." He claps his hands together, looking cheery. "After that, we return to Dor and live happily ever after."

I struggle not to shake my head at them. It's a terrible plan. They will lose all control over me as soon as I step close enough to an Elite. A real Elite. Not the strands of power I've been trying to grasp from this group for the past two days. The little bit of ability they possess is unpredictable, slippery under my skin, and I don't yet know how to use it.

I've never felt anything like it. But now that I have, I don't doubt it's been hiding right under my nose. I wonder how many Elites I've read who only contain a percentage of power, having come from a mixed line. It's frustratingly fascinating.

"Bread, anyone?" Meredith's making rounds with her usual basket of stale bread and warm cheese. Her power pulses in my veins, hers and Lenny's more potent than the rest. She's a Crawler, which would be more than helpful if my hands weren't tied behind my back.

"Yes, ma'am," Finn calls, jumping over a few sleeping bodies to grab a loaf. Taking a bite, he turns to Paedyn. "Hey, I'll take the first shift tonight." Even at this distance, I can see the crumbs flying from his mouth. "You get some sleep."

She smiles at him, looking relieved. "Thanks, Finn. Wake me in a couple of hours, okay?"

He's still chomping on his bread when he salutes her, takes the crossbow, and slumps against the wall a few yards away. Ignoring the corner he occupies, I scan the candle-scattered floor casting flickering shadows across the run-down walls and ceiling. I wriggle into the large bedroll, forced to lie on my side with my hands bound behind my back.

Paedyn hesitates before sliding in beside me. She always does. She's only ever timid when I'm close enough to touch her.

I shift in the bedroll, rustling enough to force a sigh out of her. "What is the matter with you?"

"My nose is itchy," I say, voice muffled with blankets.

She's silent in the way that makes me think she's struggling not to laugh. "Fine," she huffs. "Turn around."

With aching arms, I flip onto my other side so we're facing each other. I haven't gotten the chance to study her recently. She's close to me, her body warm despite the freezing feet inching their way closer to mine. Her blue eyes ripple in the candlelight, looking like the deepest corner of a lagoon. I can just make out the faint freckles that dot her nose, though I pretend to forget the exact number of them there.

She slips a hand from beneath the blanket, reaching for my face. "Um." She's timid again. "Where?"

"Bridge of my nose," I say, my eyes never leaving hers.

The tip of her finger meets my nose, and I can't help but be reminded of when she flicked it. Maybe she's thinking the same, because after a quick swipe of her finger, she snatches her hand back.

I clear my throat. "I didn't take you for the gambling type."

"I'm a thief," she says dismissively. "Every pocket I reach into is a gamble."

"Fine. I didn't take you for the ignorant type."

She gives me a dull look. "What is this about, Prince?"

"Your deal with the king." I hold her gaze. "Trading me for your freedom. It won't work."

Her eyes drift across the room, gaze haunted by memory. "Kitt loves you more than he hates me. It'll work."

I smile sadly. "You'd be surprised."

We fall silent, and I watch her eyelids flutter with sleep. She's unbearable, really. But not in the way that makes it any easier to look away. No, everything about her is a bold sort of beauty, like a rose proudly displaying its thorns. She's alluring in the way that most deadly things are. It's captivating.

No. No, it's terrifying. It's *supposed* to be terrifying, still thinking of her as something I'm trying to deserve. Still deeming her worthy of my desire.

But she's not. No matter what has already happened between us. She's my prisoner and my mission.

She is nothing to me.

And that's what I tell myself as I watch her fall asleep.

I follow her—into sleep, into oblivion, into wherever it is she's going.

I only wake up when something is thrown over my head, the air thick and choking.

I struggle against the strong arms strangling me before my body goes limp.

Then I'm dreaming again. And it might just be of her.

My hands are still tied behind my back.

Only now, they are also tied to hers.

Her head is slumped against the back of mine, hands twitching beside my own. She shifts slightly, the only warning that she's stirring awake. And then the back of her skull connects with my own, sending stars swimming in my vision.

"Ow," I groan, leaning forward as much as the ropes will allow.

"Oh, it's you," she says groggily. "I didn't know who I was tied to. I should have hit you harder."

"Funny," I say through gritted teeth. "Move closer to me. You're pulling my hands."

I can practically feel her eyes roll. "Yes, Your Highness. Is there anything else I can do to make you more comfortable?"

"You are just such a pleasure to be held captive with."

I feel her head turning to take in the cell we've been dumped into. There's nothing but cracked stone and grimy floors. The bars are made of simple metal, not Mute like I'm used to. Though, without an Elite to draw from, I'm just as powerless as the Ordinaries.

"Where the hell are we?" she finally asks, voicing the question I've been waiting for her to ask.

"Some sort of prison," I say. "Definitely underground." The stone floors covered in filth are freezing, and the only light in sight is halfway down the hallway outside our cell.

"How . . . how did we get here?" she asks, panic lacing each word. "I don't remember anything from last night."

"They must have drugged us." I lean my head back against hers. "So much for your friend standing guard."

She tugs at her hands, yanking on mine in turn. "No, no, no. This can't be happening—"

"Easy, Gray," I say lightly. "You're going to rip my arm out of its socket."

"Why did they . . . ?" She gulps down a breath. "Why did they put us in such a small cell?"

"Well," I say calmly, "it's not as though we can move around. . . ."

"Thanks for the reminder, Azer," she all but yells. "I can't do this. Do you smell blood? I smell blood. I can't. I . . . I need to get out of here."

I feel her hands grow sweaty around mine, feel her back expand with each shaky breath. The smell of blood is faint, but I'm so used to the scent that I'd hardly noticed. Why would that bother her so much?

When her breath hitches on what sounds to be the beginning of a sob, I know something is very wrong.

"Paedyn," I say softly. The taste of her name is intoxicating on my tongue. "Paedyn, are you listening to me?"

"When am I ever," she pants, "listening to you?"

I smile to myself. "Are your knees against your chest?"

"What?" she huffs. "Yes. Yes, my knees are against my chest."

"All right," I say slowly. "I want you to listen to me for once in your life and put your legs on the floor. Spread them out as much as you can."

"Why would I—"

"Listening, remember?"

Her breath is shaky, hands sweaty as she slides her legs across the stone. "Now," I say slowly, "I want you to see how much room you have. This cell is much larger than you think. My legs are on the ground too."

Lie. My knees are against my chest, and I'm staring into a stone wall.

"Feel how much room you have? This cell is plenty big enough, and it's not going to get any smaller." I swallow before lacing her fingers with mine, feeling her breath hitch at the sudden contact. But then her breathing is slowing against my back, her hand clutching mine like an anchor from her racing thoughts.

"Better?" I ask, breathless.

I feel her nod. "Better."

Silence stretches between us. She rests her head on my shoulder. Every bit of my being is focused on the way her fingers feel between mine. It's absurd.

The distant sound of clicking boots has her snatching her hand out of my grasp.

Good. Fine. I'm glad that's over with.

The man who appears outside our bars looks vaguely familiar with his streaked gray hair slicked into a tail, and bushy brows hanging over black eyes. But when I feel Paedyn stiffen behind me, I realize why it is I recognize him.

"Rafael," she sighs. "So it's your greed that's behind this?"

He opens his arms as though greeting an old friend. "Oh, come on, kid. Can you blame me? No one would be able to pass up the price on your head." His eyes flick to me. "And what I could get for the both of you is irresistible. Even I'd stomach stepping foot in Ilya for the gold I'll get for you two."

"How did you even find us?" Paedyn chokes out. The air has grown gradually thicker with a foul odor that is suddenly wafting toward us.

Rafael continues on, unfazed. "I've had my men stationed all over the outskirts of the city, keeping an eye out for you in case you ever escaped your prince." His smile is giddy. "But instead, you brought him with you."

The look on Paedyn's face has him frowning. "Oh, don't take it personal, Shadow. You may have made me a lot of silvers in the ring, but you'll make me a hell of a lot more for taking you back to Ilya."

He steps away for a moment to grab a dish from a nearby table. "I thought I'd bring this to you personally." He unlocks the cell door with a rusty key before bending to place a metal tray before us, filled with chunks of stale bread. "To thank you for finding your way back to me."

"Thanks, but I doubt I could stomach anything with this stench," Paedyn practically coughs.

"Ah"—Rafael nods—"that's the sewer under us." He nods to a grate several feet down the hall. "They fill up the sewer and flush it out every few weeks. Lucky for you two, it seems they will be doing just that very soon." He smiles as the door swings shut behind him. "I hope you enjoy your short stay in Dor's finest." Then he nods toward the plate of stale bread. "Have fun figuring out how to eat that."

His steps grow softer as he makes his way down the hall. I cough, trying to clear my throat of the thick air threatening to choke me.

Paedyn rests her head on my shoulder, forcing my attention back to her as she says, "We need to get out of here."

I nod before slumping my head on top of hers. "There is no way in hell I'm returning to Ilya as a prisoner." That alone would shatter the reputation I've been meticulously building since I was a boy. Every order obeyed, every mission completed, every death by my hand—utterly useless. Returning with a ransom on my head would make me look worse than weak, more pathetic than dying during a mission. It's simply not an option.

"Okay, then." Her voice is detached, determined. "Got any ideas, Prince?"

CHAPTER 24

Kitt

There's a knock at my door.

There's always a knock at my door. Always a servant, or Imperial, or someone else banging on the wood and begging for my attention.

Life of a king, I suppose.

I run a hand down my tired face, then down my crumpled shirt before remembering my inky fingers.

I don't look like a king.

I look like a boy who's trying to fill the shoes of a man, sitting in a chair that's swallowing me whole. Living in a kingdom full of people I'm too afraid to confront.

And yet, through it all, I pretend. Pretend to know how to live my life as a king.

"Come in."

The command is met with creaky hinges followed by soft steps on a worn rug. My eyes flick up from the papers littering every inch of the desk. The man slowly shuts the door, every movement calm and deliberate.

Not a servant. Not an Imperial. Not someone begging for my attention. In fact, I can't picture him doing anything of the sort.

"Shit, is it noon already?" I shake my head, attempting to clear the desk of its inky carnage.

"Well, it is hard to keep track of time with those curtains always closed," he says smoothly, nodding to the draped window.

"You know why I keep them closed," I sigh, gesturing for him to take a seat. "I don't need any more servants gawking up at my window from the courtyard. There are enough rumors going around as it is."

"For good reason," he says gently, in that way that makes it difficult to tell whether he's scolding me or not.

He has such a way with words. Confident enough to speak softly because he knows that everyone will lean in to listen. Each word is deliberate, delicate in the most demanding way.

"You have yet to address your people, Kitt." His pale blue eyes cut through mine, searching far beyond my gaze. "If you don't give them something to talk about, they will concoct their own version of the story."

"Yes, thank you for the wise counsel," I mutter, having heard it at every one of our meetings.

His gaze softens as he sits back, examining me from across the desk. "I'm only here to help, Kitt. Offer you my guidance."

"Right. Of course," I say with a nod. "And Plague knows I need it."

He smiles, and it's comforting. "Plague knows this isn't easy for you, either."

"Yes, well." I sigh. "You have advised me through much of this, and for that, I am thankful."

"And I will continue to do so." He shifts in his seat to lean over the desk. "Which is why I hope you will go through with my latest suggestion."

I stiffen. His latest suggestion was absurd at best. An absurdity that I'm foolish enough to consider. But before I can voice this or something else equally unwise, he's pulled a small box from his pocket and set it on the worn wood between us.

I blink at what I know is trapped inside the velvet case. My heart stutters beneath my ribs, my mouth following as it attempts to form his name in protest. "C-Calum—"

"It's the best way," he cuts in, combing fingers through the blond hair atop his head. "I know that it's not exactly the most appealing idea—"

"Not exactly?" I scoff, laughing at the insanity of it all. "Do you even understand what you're asking me to do?"

His sigh is heavy, as though he, too, wears the weight of the kingdom on his shoulders. And, in a way, he does. "You're the king. The life you live is no longer yours alone. This is a sacrifice that must be made for the good of the kingdom." He pauses, letting his words hang in the air between us. "This is how you help the people you still haven't confronted."

I look away, shaking my head at the ink staining every surface. "I will. I just . . ." Emotion traps the words in my throat, choking them until I'm finally able to spit the syllables out. "I just hurt. I'm not the prince they knew."

"No, you're not," Calum says softly. "Because now you are their king." With a hesitant hand, he slides the box farther across the desk, until I can no longer ignore it. "Which means you sacrifice who you were for who you need to be." His eyes bore into mine, reading more than just the emotion on my face. "And who you need to be it with."

I stare at the box, only looking up at him when he murmurs, "What was it your father would always say to the people? Something about what it is that makes a great king?"

Managing a sad smile, I supply, "Ah, yes. The three *B*'s."

Calum nods, humming at the memory. "That's what it was. I remember how he used to recite them when informing the kingdom of a new law or decision he had made."

"It was one of his many mottos," I reminisce. "He made me write it dozens of times during our tutoring sessions. I wouldn't be surprised if I mumble it in my sleep." Calum chuckles as I recite the phrase dully. "'To be a great king, you must first be brave, benevolent, and brutal. Only then can you rule a great kingdom.'"

Nodding, Calum leans back in his chair. "He's not wrong. It's a good motto to measure yourself by." He reaches for the box then, tapping a long finger against the velvet. "And doing *this* would take all three of those qualities he hoped to find in you. Bravery." A tap on the box. "Benevolence." Another. "And even brutality, depending on how you look at it."

He's right. Plagues, he's always right.

Swallowing, I pick up the box, fitting it into the palm of my hand. "The three *B*'s, huh?"

He smiles at me. "The three *B*'s."

CHAPTER 25
Paedyn

"Your clumsy footwork will be the death of us, you know."

A frustrated sound tears from my throat. "Well, you're not exactly the most encouraging person to be tied up with."

"Under different circumstances," he pants, "I promise you I'm much more fun tied up."

My cheeks flush as I roll my eyes, fully knowing he can't see them. "Not. Helping." I feel his back shake with laughter. Ignoring him, I plant my feet, preparing myself. "Okay, let's try this again," I breathe before pushing against his back to try to get my feet under me.

"There you go, Gray," he murmurs. "Come on, just a little more."

My legs are shaking as they strain to stand with him. This is far from our first try, making me both tired and frustrated all at once. Standing to my feet has never been such a challenge. I push against his back, inching my feet beneath me to ungracefully stand on the cold prison floor.

"It's about damn time," the bastard sighs. "Now for the fun part."

I glance at the jagged stone jutting out from the wall, nearly four

feet off the ground. He takes a step toward it, yanking me behind him in turn. "Ow," I hiss. "A warning next time would be nice."

"Fine," he says stiffly. "I'm walking to the stone now."

And with that, he all but drags me as I trip backward toward the wall. I huff when my feet are finally planted on the floor again, wishing he could see the glare I'm wearing. Then he's lifting our hands, guiding the rope to rest on the sharp stone.

My arms are pulled behind my back, bent at an uncomfortable angle. And it only gets worse when he begins sawing the rope against the stone. Back and forth. Back and forth. I hang my head toward the floor, watching my hair fall into a messy halo around my face.

"You all right back there, Gray?"

"Oh, I'm just great," I say, my voice muffled with hair. "My neck has never felt better."

I can hear the sound of rope rubbing against stone, feel Kai doing most of the work. "How about we play a game? To take your mind off things."

My head shoots up at his offer. It's startling—him caring. Didn't he vow to never do that again?

The Enforcer orders me a step closer to the stone.

But this isn't caring, is it? No, he's using me to escape and save his reputation. I'm a means to an end.

"All right," he sighs, still sawing at the rope. "I'm seeing something gray. Guess what it is."

I snort. "Everything in this Plague-forsaken place is gray."

"Well, then, you'd better be specific."

I sigh through my nose. "Okay. The wall."

"Guess again."

"The bars?"

He tugs at the rope, testing its strength. "Wrong again."

"The ceiling?"

"You're not very good at this—"

Echoing footsteps cut off his words. This time I'm silently tugging him back to our spot on the floor where I all but fall, pulling him down with me. The guard rounds the corner into the eerily empty hallway, stopping only to fish a key from his pocket. He doesn't look at us as he steps inside and places a metal bowl of water beside the barely touched stale bread.

It's a struggle to stifle my scoff. We're expected to lap up the water like dogs. Further proof of their hatred for us Ilyans.

The door locks behind him with a heavy click, and I watch his shadow slither down the length of the hallway. We are quiet for a long moment before I feel Kai's hand pat my lower back in silent command. I take a deep breath, preparing myself before struggling to my feet.

Then it's back to the stone and tedious sawing. I hang my head again, resting my sore neck as I mumble, "The tray."

"That's more silver."

I frown. "What about my hair, then?"

"I don't know, *Silver Savior*," he says slowly, "you tell me."

"I think it could pass for gray," I argue.

He laughs. It's deep and dark in a way I've come to recognize. "Your hair could pass for moonbeams before it passes for gray."

"Careful," I say slowly, "that almost sounded like a compliment."

I hear him huff out a laugh. "Maybe I'll give you a proper compliment if you can actually manage to guess correctly."

I glare at the floor. "I've named every gray thing in here."

"Obviously not."

He pauses his sawing long enough to tug on the rope. I feel it loosen slightly around my wrists and sigh in relief. Not much longer until I'm free. "What could I have possibly missed?" I huff, lifting my head to scan the cell again.

"That stone over there," he says casually, as though he doesn't sound insane.

I try to bite my tongue for as long as possible. I really do. But before I can stop myself, I'm blurting, "I'm sorry, do you mean the stone on the other side of the cell that I *can't see*?"

He's quiet for a moment. "That's the one."

"That's completely unfair."

"I told you to be specific," he says slowly.

A frustrated sound climbs up my throat, to which he has the audacity to laugh at. Shockingly, I manage to keep my mouth shut, slouching silently with my arms being pulled back and forth. When my eyelids begin to grow heavy, he stops to test the strength of the rope.

"I'll be able to break it now." His voice is gruff, body begging for sleep. "We can rest until the guard gets back."

Nodding, I sluggishly pull him back to the center of the cell and slide to the ground. "And then we'll get out of here."

"And then we'll get out of here," he repeats softly.

My head finds the back of his shoulder, slumping against him despite my best efforts. My body aches, every inch of my betraying being begging to curl up against him, to be held by him.

At my weakest, I wish for him. And at my strongest, I wish I could say it wasn't the same.

He rests his head on mine, gentle and grounding. I hate that he feels like that. Feels like comfort incarnate.

"Can we pretend that it's okay not to hate each other in these moments?" I ask quietly, if only to ease my conscience.

He sounds as though he might have laughed if he wasn't so exhausted. "Yes. Pretend."

I'm quiet until I'm not. "Do you regret any of it?"

His voice is soft, soothing. "Regret what?"

"Us?" A pause. "Regret what happened between us? Even the more recent things?" I whisper, recalling our moment of weakness on the rooftop.

He's quiet for so long that I doze off, only waking when he murmurs, "Sleep, Little Psychic. Regret in the morning."

I wake to the sound of groaning metal.

My eyes flutter open at the feel of Kai patting my lower back in warning. Through hazy vision, I watch the guard step into the cell, clutching a stale loaf. I blink awake, preparing for the plan that is about to unfold.

It all happens so quickly that I almost forget the part I'm meant to play. As soon as the guard bends to place the bread between us, Kai shifts his body and slips a foot beneath the tray. The metal meets the man's face when the prince kicks it up, hard enough to hear the guard's nose crack.

"Pull against me, Gray," Kai grinds out, straining as he tugs at the severed rope still binding us together. I throw my body weight forward, nearly smashing my face into the stone wall when the rope snaps, setting my wrists free.

I scramble toward the moaning guard now clutching his broken nose. I've slammed his head against the wall before his eyes have even widened at the sight of me. He's out cold as I fumble for his pocket, finding the rusty key within, and stagger to the cell door.

Kai is right behind me, watching as I reach a hand through the bars to unlock the door from the outside. We step through the open bars, rubbing our raw wrists. My eyes sweep over the wall of empty cells, relieved to find not a single familiar face within.

Lenny and the others aren't here. It seems that only the prince and Silver Savior were worth Rafael's trouble. And I'm momentarily comforted by that realization.

But it's the sewer grate at the end of the hall that now captures my attention.

"So far, so good," Kai murmurs, taking off at a soft sprint toward the sewer. I'm on his heels in an instant, head swiveling as I search for any sign of oncoming guards. My heart races, head pounding, as I focus on keeping my tired legs pumping toward freedom.

"Grab the other side," the Enforcer orders when I skid to a stop over the grate. My fingers slip on the grimy metal, but I lift as hard as my strained arms will allow. "Come on, Gray," Kai grunts. "You can do better than that."

The grate is impossibly heavy, and the growing sound of pounding boots isn't helping my focus. I take a deep breath before yanking upward, hoping Kai will do the rest. I'm tempted to thank the Plague when he manages to slide the lid halfway off the dark drop into the sewer.

We're greeted with the sound of rushing water, and the stench of bodily fluids. I gag despite my best efforts but manage to keep the few bites of stale bread down. Distant shouting has my head snapping up, eyes straining in the dim light to see just how many guards are racing toward us. I count seven before my eyes find Kai's across the yawning mouth of the sewer below.

And with a single nod, I step off the ledge and into darkness.

I land with a splash, thankful to find that it is mostly water sloshing around my calves. Kai quickly drops down beside me despite something clanking around his shoulders. He doesn't give me the chance to ask before he's grabbing my hand and sprinting through the tunnel.

"They're coming!" he shouts over the sound of rushing water. "We need to move fast!"

I give him a nod he can't see, all while trying to ignore the fact that this is the extent of our plan. This is as far as we plotted. Sever the rope. Knock out the guard. Get the key. Escape through the sewer.

Except, we don't have the slightest idea what awaits us at the end of this tunnel.

My legs feel heavy, like trying to run through honey. "The water is rising!" I yell, panic quivering my voice. It's rushing around my knees now, fast and forceful.

"Just keep moving!" His order echoes off the tunnel walls, forcing my legs faster in the current.

It's so dark down here that I can't see Kai wading through the water in front of me, but his hand is firm in mine as he leads me straight through the tunnel. Stretching out my stray hand, I drag my fingers across the grimy wall beside me, feeling every passage we could have turned down.

The thick water laps around my waist now. I can only see shadows and outlines, feel freezing water and paralyzing terror. I'm slipping with every step, trying to keep up with Kai as he pulls me behind him.

The liquid rises rapidly as we run, daring to drown us with every inch.

Drowning has never been ideal, especially not in a sewer. I know I'm moving, but I can hardly feel my legs beneath me. Chills rack my body, chattering teeth now joining the symphony of rushing water—rushing water that keeps rising.

"Just a little farther!"

I hear his shouted encouragement, but I don't bother to believe it. We're blindly running through sewers, being pursued by both water and guards driven by greed. Our odds are hardly favorable.

My hands are numb, fingers frozen by the water now circling my elbows.

Maybe this is a better fate than the one awaiting me back in Ilya.

Maybe this is where Death finally catches me, finally gets to cackle at the sight of me drifting into a watery grave.

Or maybe he'll embrace me like an old friend.

I slam into something solid, splashing freezing water over whatever part of me was still dry. Kai's back is blocking my path, but I'm close enough now to hear the string of curses he's spewing. "Dammit," he breathes, dropping my hand.

"What? What's going on?" I feel my way around him, pushing forward until . . .

My palms meet a grimy wall.

I slide frantic fingers in every direction, feeling for some sort of opening in the darkness.

Nothing.

Water is lapping at my rib cage, and I'm struggling to breathe from both the frigid water and fear tightening my chest. "No," I say simply. "No, there has to be a way out."

I can hear Kai running his hands across every wall, splashing as he searches the tunnel beneath our feet. Ignoring the echo of shouts growing closer, I continue to feel every inch of stone trapping us down here. My fingertips can barely brush the ceiling looming over us, forcing me to jump as I search for any sort of escape.

I'm panting, panicking, pounding on the walls. My fists find the stone in front of me, again and again. "There has to be a way!" I'm not sure who I'm shouting at. The wall. The prince. The shadow of Death I can feel looming over me.

I'm tearing at the wall with cracked nails, slamming raw fists into rock. I can't see anything, and I doubt I'll see anything again. The water reaches my breasts, beating against me as I struggle to breathe. I think I might be shouting with every slam of my hand into the wall. I think I might be scared of death.

"That's enough."

His voice is calm, so damn calm that I want to slap him across the face I can't even see. I ignore him, as per usual, and continue to pound against the wall. A tear slips down my cheek, mingling with the water splashing across my face.

"I said, that's enough." He grabs me around my waist, yanking me away from the wall. I fight against him, feeling like a feral animal as I thrash in the water. "Paedyn!" My name echoes off the walls, stilling me for a moment. Then his face is beside mine, his cheek wet and cold against my own. "That's enough."

I hear it then. Hear the defeat in his voice. He's giving up.

"No, it's not enough!" I shout, struggling against the arms wrapped around me. "No, there has to be a way out. There has to be a way. . . ."

His hands slide from my waist, delicate and deliberate, as though he's memorizing the feel of me. Calloused hands slip up my arms, spinning me around to face him. I can't see his face, but I know exactly what I would be looking at.

"Paedyn . . ." The water seems to still for his soft voice.

"No," I say sternly. "Don't do that. Don't go saying my name because you think it might be the last time you ever will."

He has the nerve to chuckle. "Your name seems like a good word to die with on my lips."

"Kai—"

"I don't regret it." His words are a rush, a confession he's clung to. "I don't regret you, or what was between us. And I don't regret kissing you on that roof. But I know I'll regret what I have to do to you for the rest of my life."

Water licks at my collarbones as I blink at his words. The words of a man staring death in the face, determined to have the final say. "Do you regret it?" he asks, voice urgent. His hands roam up my neck to feel my face, fingers trembling over my cheekbones.

"I . . ." My hands find his arms, cupping his wrists. "I regret not doing it right. And I regret not being what I'm supposed to be."

He strokes a thumb across my wet cheek. "I'm sorry you have to be anything at all."

I know it's all talk of a dead man. All confessions of two people suddenly aware of their imminent doom. But I melt at his words, mourn what could have been. And now I'll drown in the regret that is him.

The tunnel is filling with water, forcing me to tip my chin up and stand on my toes. I feel hopeless in his arms, as though nothing mattered before I was wrapped in them. There is no past, no future.

Just him. Just us. Just this moment and what we decide to do with it.

Death emboldens. The end initiates.

His hands tug my face closer until I can feel his breath on my lips. Water drips from his hair to splatter onto my suddenly heated skin. His pulse pounds beneath my fingers wrapped around his wrists.

My heart aches. Aches to be reunited with the piece he's stolen from me.

My nose brushes his.

"Pretend," I whisper against his lips.

I am recklessness incarnate. Until the very end.

My mouth meets his.

He tastes like longing. Like regret and relief. Like nothing matters but this moment.

It's fervent, like a sinner's final prayer.

And maybe that is what this kiss is.

Repentance.

CHAPTER 26

Rai

She tastes like a piece of the heaven I won't be going to.

Kissing her is relief.

It's a delicate sort of demand.

She pulls away, panting words between each kiss. "I hate you."

"I know," I murmur into her mouth.

Her palms push at my chest, pulling her lips away from mine to whisper again, "I hate you."

I run my hand slowly up her side. "Prove it to me, Gray," I murmur against her ear. "Hate me enough to use me."

I hear her breath catch, feel her heart racing against my chest.

I look away, ready to pull back and—

A hand finds my face, turning it back toward her to press my lips against hers.

Her mouth is crushed against mine, and it's her I'll breathe in for the last time.

My hands are cupping her face, fingers twining in her wet hair.

I kiss her frantically, memorizing the feel of her lips against mine,

It feels like finality, this kiss. This moment.

I kiss her harder at the thought, willingly breathing her in until the very end.

Her arms slide from my wrists to wrap around my neck. She's clinging to me as though I'm an anchor she's willing to sink with. I'm drowning with her, in her.

It's only when the water reaches her lips that she pulls away. "Kai," she whispers, "I never learned how to swim."

"You're okay," I murmur, pushing tangled hair from her face. "I've got you."

I wrap my arms around her waist, holding her against me. It's only a matter of time now. The water is at my neck and rising rapidly. It's not long before I'm treading water, trying to keep the both of us afloat.

"Wrap your legs around me," I order softly, staying calm for her sake. I feel her nod before her legs are hugging my waist, freeing my hands to help keep our heads above the water.

My head is nearing the ceiling trapping us down here. I focus on the feel of her hands around my neck, of her fingers fidgeting with my hair. "Are you scared?" she whispers, her lips close to my ear.

"I'm brave enough to admit that I'm terrified," I say quietly. It's a struggle to hold the both of us, though I won't need to do it for much longer.

I only wish I could see her face, could count the freckles splattering her nose one last time. I wish I could drown in those ocean eyes before the water gets the chance.

"Do you . . . ," she starts. I feel her arms leave my neck. "Do you feel that?"

I try to keep my voice steady despite struggling to keep my head above the surface. "Feel what?"

"The air . . ." Her hands are running across the crumbling stone above us. "There is air coming from up here."

Her fingers sound frantic. I hear the sound of scraping nails and muttered curses before I'm blinking at a thin beam of light streaming through the ceiling. "Kai." She's breathless. "It's a grate. It's covered, but it's there."

She throws the chunk of stone she broke off into the water, half laughing as she begins tearing at the ceiling. I'm dodging pieces of falling stone as she rips the crumbling ceiling apart. It's a struggle to keep her afloat with her constantly moving in my arms, not to mention the fact that my head is brushing the ceiling. "Quickly, Pae," I grunt.

Her spine goes rigid in response to that nickname, but she's quickly distracted by the more pressing issue at hand. "I know, I know," she pants, pulling at the jagged stones. She's uncovered several inches of the hastily covered metal grate, allowing sunlight to stream through the slits.

I'm forced to tilt my head back to breathe. "Paedyn," I gasp.

"Just a little more," she says, frantic. Only inches separate us from the ceiling. Her head is tilted, her cheek likely pressed to the stone she's clawing at. The grate is mostly uncovered now, and she's pushing against it while I'm trying to hold her up.

I can't. I can't hold her any longer. I can't stay afloat. I can't *breathe*.

"Pae," I manage. "Take a breath—"

I gulp down air before the water swallows us.

Paedyn untangles herself from me, using both her hands to push against the grate. I wrap an arm around her waist to keep her from sinking and shove at the grate with every ounce of strength I have left.

The sunlight teases us, speckling the murky water. A reminder that the only thing separating us from air is this damn grate. I ram my shoulder against it, feeling it budge. Paedyn pushes, pounds against our final hope.

I'm running out of air, and I know she is too. Her movements grow more sluggish with each second.

I will not let her die like this. I cannot.

With one final ram of my shoulder, I feel the grate lift. I'm forced to let go of her, using both my hands to slide the grate to the side. It gives a couple of inches, allowing me to grab the lip and fully push it open.

Then I turn, finding Paedyn slowly sinking toward the bottom of the tunnel. Her eyes have drifted closed, her lips stained an eerie blue. I swim downward, grabbing her by the waist and pushing off the floor to shoot us toward the light.

Then I'm shoving her upward until her head peeks through the grate.

I vaguely hear her muffled gasp, her choking coughs. Through blurry vision, I watch her pull herself up and over the grate.

She made it. She's breathing. She's alive.

I don't know that I'll be able to say the same for me.

My eyelids are heavy, blinking shut without my permission. In fact, my entire body is heavy, weighing me down as I begin to sink.

So this is it.

This is how the mighty Enforcer meets his end.

It could be worse, I suppose.

I don't bother fighting the water anymore. I'm too tired. Too ready to rest.

She'll be free of me now. She's probably halfway to a shadow she can melt into. The idea almost makes me smile.

I sink into oblivion, the thought of her my final prayer.

CHAPTER 27
Paedyn

Water spews from my mouth.

I'm retching onto the crumbling alley street I've crawled onto. Panting, I roll onto my back, blinking into the dying sunlight.

I'm alive.

I'm alive.

I'm coughing and spitting and drenched in Plague knows what, but I'm alive.

I laugh up at the sky, my whole body shaking with the action.

I can practically hear Death cursing my name. My ears ring, and I'm trembling from head to toe. Just pulling myself out of the tunnel was—

My heart skips a beat, stuttering in my chest.

He saved me. He practically lifted me through that grate. He . . .

I kissed him. Again.

And now he's dying at the bottom of a sewer.

I scramble to the edge of the grate, frantically scanning the cloudy water. I can just make out the faint outline of his body as it sinks toward the floor of the tunnel.

My mind races, my heart following.

I could leave him. I could leave him and be done with this. Because no one but him could catch me, no one but him could find me again once I disappear.

This is my escape. This is my freedom.

This is wrong.

I pull at my hair, my frustration taking a physical form. If I save him, I may be damning myself. And yet, that is exactly what he did. Saving me has him sinking to his death.

I shake my head at my reflection in the murky water.

And then I dive into it.

It's anything but graceful. My face meets the surface right as I remember that I haven't swam a day in my life. Panic pulses through me, but I push it aside and force my legs to propel me forward. With flailing arms and feet, I manage to swim deeper.

I scan the water, finding him drifting a few feet from me. I kick hard, forcing myself forward as I reach for him. I wrap an arm around his chest, my lungs screaming at me for air. When my feet find the tunnel floor, I push off it with shaking legs.

We cut through the water, heading for the open grate above. I kick with every bit of fight I can find, keeping my eyes on the sky above. My hand reaches blindly for the lip of the grate, fumbling for something to hold on to. With lungs burning in silent protest, I'm tempted to drop the Enforcer and climb to freedom.

But my slippery fingers curl around the ledge before I heave us upward. My head breaks through the surface, and I don't waste a second before gulping down air. With one hand now clutching his arm, I use the other to pull myself onto the street. Then I lie on my stomach, hooking both arms under his shoulders, and pull him upward.

His head bobs above the surface, his eyes closed and hair tousled like running ink. I grunt with the effort of trying to lift his upper body onto the street. Only now can I see what it was he brought with him into the sewer. A chain jangles around his neck, practically choking him. I pull it off, not giving it another thought as I toss it aside to continue pulling him up, inch by inch.

I'm panting before half his body is even lying on the cobblestones, the other half still soaking in the sewer. It's a struggle to flip him onto his back, but I somehow manage to roll him over. His head lolls to the side, eyes closed against the setting sun. I wait for something to happen, anything at all.

But he's not breathing.

He's doing nothing but dying.

Is that not what I've wanted?

"No," I mutter. "No. I didn't dive back in there for you to die." I pat his face. I pat harder. Then I'm slapping him like I've always said I would. Nothing. "No. *No.*"

My hands find the center of his chest and begin pumping, begin trying to purge him of the water he's swallowed. "Come on, Azer," I whisper. My vision has gone blurry, but I don't bother to recognize the tears welling in my eyes. "Don't be dramatic," I order. "Open your damn eyes."

I'm pushing hard on his chest, pleading with him. How pathetic. I don't know why I care. This is exactly what I should want. To have tried my best and still be free of him. This is the ideal situation. I can walk away from this moment without guilt dragging me back to it for the rest of my life.

So why am I fighting back tears?

"Come on," I whisper, continuing my rhythmic pumping. "Come on, you stubborn bastard."

His eyelids flutter open.

I jump away from him, giving him room to turn and retch. A

tear rolls down my face as I laugh shakily, relief flooding every bit of my strained body. "I almost gave up on you."

He drags himself fully over the grate, breathing heavily at the sky. His head turns to the side, eyes studying me intensely. He coughs before choking out, "I'm shocked you even bothered to try."

I nod slowly, allowing what I've done to settle in. "It's a regret I'll have to live with."

We watch each other, his gray eyes unwavering. It feels different, this look. The look of two people who now share another secret. Nothing has changed between us, and yet, nothing will ever be the same again. The things Death made us say, the kiss we shared thinking it was our last, can never be undone.

I've already failed twice at resisting him, and I won't let it happen again.

Hopefully.

He is my enemy, my captor, my escort toward death. I will not let him also be my weakness. Not again.

"Thank you," he murmurs, voice gruff. "You never cease to surprise me."

"Apparently, neither do you," I say softly, fingers brushing my lips subconsciously. His smile is swift, distracting one moment, then gone the next.

I look away, feeling annoyingly bashful. Wet hair is plastered across my face, and I take my time wringing out the strands. I ignore the very tangible feel of his gaze on me and focus instead on calming my breathing, stilling my shaking body.

I hesitate before lying down beside him. "Thank you, too." My voice is quiet. I fold my hands over my stomach, feeling suddenly conscious of the fact that I could easily reach out and touch him. "You saved me first."

He gives me a weak laugh. "I'm shocked you even admitted that."

I roll my eyes at the pink clouds above us. Then I sigh, spinning the slippery ring on my thumb. "Lenny would be calling me a cockroach if he were here."

"A cockroach?" He turns his head to look at me. "I mean, I've been called far worse, but—"

"I'm sure you have," I cut in. "Specifically by me."

His laugh is tired. "That I have."

I'm quiet for a moment, content to feel him watch me as I stare at the sky above. "He says I somehow always manage to survive. Lenny, that is. Though I'm still deciding whether that's a gift or a curse."

"Hmm," he hums. "If I were a different man, a better man, I might tell you that surviving is always a gift. But"—he chuckles darkly—"you and I both know that I'm not. And that I know better than most that surviving is sometimes more painful than death."

I nod slowly. Of course he would understand. He always does. "I am glad I survived this time, though. That was not how I'd planned on dying."

There's a serious sort of humor coating his voice. "You've planned your death?"

"I've planned my *ideal* death." I shrug. "I was born to die. And when you spend your whole life running from the inevitable, you think a lot about the end. I guess you could say I have a preference."

He's silent for several heartbeats. "And what preference would that be?"

"What, taking notes for when the king orders you to kill me?" I laugh lightly as though the thought hasn't kept me up at night. But I rush on, not waiting for his response. "I want an end like those I loved most. Stabbed through the chest with a smile on my face."

"Paedyn . . . ," he starts softly.

"That's what I want," I say flatly. "I want to feel what they felt. I want to feel like I'm with them one last time while I'm still alive."

"That's . . . admirable, in its own, twisted way." He's quiet for a moment, contemplating something. "And I'm sorry I was the first to start that pattern."

I'm suddenly sitting up, turning away from him. I wish he hadn't said that, hadn't apologized for being the first to stab someone I loved. I wish he had known it was my father who was his first mission. I wish he had lied. It would make hating him so much easier.

"Do you have a preference in how you die?" I ask, avoiding his apology.

"I've never thought about it."

I snort. "Of course you haven't. Because people like you don't expect to die anytime soon."

"Maybe," he says softly. "Or maybe I'm just trying to ignore the fact that I'm not immortal."

"How very wise of you, Enforcer." I wring out my hair one last time as I scan the alleyway we've crawled into. It's shadowy now, helping to hide us in the dying light. We're tucked into the corner of a dead end, the sewer grate still open at our feet. But even with the streets being slowly abandoned for the evening, I still have no intention of sitting here in plain sight of anyone who happens by this alley.

"It's not safe here," I start. "Those guards will be looking for us."

"Are we going to talk about it?" he asks, suddenly seeming much closer to me. He's sitting up now, combing back damp hair with his fingers.

"I have no idea what you're referring to."

A cocky laugh. "Is that so? I could remind you, if you like?"

"It was a mistake," I huff, turning to look into his face that is far too close. "This one and the one before."

"The only mistake was not making it sooner."

"I . . . That's . . ." I'm stuttering. He smiles in that way that makes me want to slap him. Then he's inching closer, slowly stealing the small space that separates us.

"No"—his fingers trail up my neck to trace my jaw—"the mistake was tasting you now that you likely won't let me do it again."

I swallow. Shudder. Suck in a breath.

Plagues help me.

His face is close enough for me to make a bad decision with little effort. Rough fingers are tangled in my hair, brushing the sensitive skin on my neck. Water drips from the tips of his hair, clinging to thick lashes surrounding the eyes staring heatedly into mine.

"You're right," I say breathlessly. "I won't let you kiss me again."

Lie.

I'm leaning in with every word falling from the lips that desperately want to meet his again. The corner of his mouth lifts, drawing my attention. "Are you sure about that?" His breath is warm, filling me with heat. I nod absentmindedly, my thoughts on anything but keeping my word.

A calloused hand is cupping my face, rougher than the reverence in which he held me earlier. I melt into his touch, leaning closer as his eyes drift to my lips. It's intoxicating, watching him drink me in.

He inches closer, his hand roaming down my neck.

My breath catches as his lips brush mine and—

Something clamps around my ankle with a click.

I pull away, looking down to see the metal chain he brought out of the sewer with him. A single ankle cuff occupies each end of the three-foot chain. And he's just fastened one of them to me.

"What the hell—"

I haven't even finished spewing the rest of my profanity before he's clamping the other end of the chain to his own ankle. My eyes drift from his end to mine, blinking at the short length tethering us together.

When I find my voice, it's deceptively calm. "What did you do?"

"I just ensured that my mission makes it back to Ilya with me."

I blink at him; at the blank expression he's plastered onto his face. "You . . . you chained us together?!"

He shrugs. "It was the only way to ensure you'd stay with me."

"And you . . ." My mind reels as I drag my fingers through my hair. "You planned this before we even left the prison. That's why you took this chain from the wall." I shake my head, scoffing as I turn away from him. "You bastard."

I feel sick. I feel used. I feel at fault for this. Because I did this to myself. Not only did I save the Enforcer, but I also let myself *want* him. But it was nothing more than distraction to the prince. A means to an end. And I was stupid enough to think it could have meant anything more.

The pathetic are punished. And now I'm chained to my captor.

"Paedyn—"

"Don't," I cut in quietly. "Don't say my name."

Hurt flashes in his eyes; there one blink and gone the next. "It was the only way," he repeats quietly.

"Your mission needs a bath," I say flatly. "And a bed."

He stares at me, seeming to search for something in my eyes. "Okay."

I stand to my feet and walk on shaky legs until the chain grows taught. It tugs at my ankle, already tempting to tear skin. I strain to take another step, yanking at his leg.

I turn around, pulling on a mask of my own to smother my anger and hurt. "Try to keep up, Prince."

CHAPTER 28

Kai

"Are you planning to ever speak again?"

We've been walking awkwardly through the city's back streets for nearly an hour now, and she hasn't uttered a single word. The chain drags between us, skipping over cracked cobblestone as a constant reminder of what I've done.

I'm not proud of it. Not proud of what I did to get that shackle on her ankle. I can only imagine what she aches to scream at me, what thoughts are echoing in her skull. I know how she thinks, so I know that she assumes it was all a ploy. Every touch, every word, every kiss.

And I wish it was. I wish I didn't have feelings clouding my focus, my judgment. Wish I didn't need her like I need to complete this mission. It's exhausting, fighting every impulse telling me to explain why I did this. Why I have to do this.

My life is not my own. And, for that reason, she can never be mine.

As if it would matter. I've broken any and all trust that was built between us. And now I'm nothing more than what I had been before—her enemy.

She silently led me to where her pack was still hidden beneath the rubble of a crumbling building, and swiftly pulled a scarf from within it to wrap around her identifiable hair. I pulled a damp bandanna from my pocket to tie around the lower half of my face, reminding her that we're both in danger if one of us is recognized.

She didn't deign to respond to that veiled threat, and simply swung the pack onto her back and gestured for me to lead her toward a bath and bed. And that's exactly what I've been doing for the past hour.

Thankfully, most of what we were swimming with in the sewer was the freezing water used to flush the tunnel out, but we are in desperate need of a bath and fresh clothes. Both of which will prove difficult with this chain shackling us together. But first, we find somewhere with a tub.

"I can't imagine you lasting much longer without saying anything." I sigh. The chain drags between us, scraping the ground to fill the silence.

She doesn't bother looking at me. Her eyes are on the bare street before us, sparkling blue in the final rays of sunlight. I suppose I deserve her silence. Although, to her credit, I didn't think it would last this long.

I turn us down a busier street, feeling the shackle bite into my ankle with the tension. Merchants are packing up their carts for the night, unashamedly running over the toes of anyone in their way. I head for the main market, feeling the chain tighten as I pull Paedyn, forcing her to pick up the pace.

The chain.

I stop abruptly, feeling her palms meet my back before her nose can. Turning to face her, she seems to be looking anywhere but at me. By now I've lost my patience, as per usual. My hand finds her jaw, gently turning her face toward mine. She smothers me with a stare that I do my best to ignore. "You're going to need to steal a skirt."

Her brows rise, the first sign of emotion I've seen from her since we left the grate.

"Don't worry," I say dryly, "I'm not asking you to talk. Just steal a damn scrap of fabric at the very least."

"I'd like to see you try, actually." She tugs my hand away from her jaw, seemingly surprising by the sound of her voice.

I crack a smile. "She speaks."

Ignoring me, she throws her hands up in mock innocence. "I've put my thieving days behind me."

I shake my head before glancing over my shoulder at the dying street. "Yes, you're a saint. Now, unless you want to end up in a prison again, I suggest stealing something to cover up the chain that will draw plenty of attention to us."

"And whose fault is that?" she asks, crossing her arms.

"You are," I say, taking a breath before continuing, "an unbelievably difficult creature."

She laughs harshly. "Maybe you should have considered that before chaining yourself to me."

"Yes, what a complete oversight on my part." I step aside, giving her clear view of the street. "Now go show me what you can do."

"I already have, Prince," she huffs, pushing past me. "When I stole from you, remember?"

Oh, I remember.

I trail behind her, watching as she peeks her head around the corner of the alley. I move to step behind her before her hand finds my chest, pushing me back without bothering to glance at me. I'm not used to taking orders, let alone being shoved aside. But I roll my neck, swallow my pride, and take a step back to lean against the wall and watch her work.

Several carts rumble by the mouth of the alley we're standing in, but she stays still, not wanting what they're selling. After several minutes, I see her shoulders tense, her body lean forward in anticipation. And then I see why.

When the next cart passes by, she doesn't hesitate before stumbling into it. With flailing arms, she knocks a pile of colorful skirts onto the ground. If I had blinked, I would have missed the subtle kick as she tucks a skirt beneath the cart.

"I am so sorry, sir!" Her voice has jumped an octave, sounding innocent and ignorant. The merchant swears before looking up to identify the culprit. I fight the urge to break the man's jaw when his gaze softens with each second spent greedily running his eyes over her.

"My fault, miss," he says silkily, moving to brace a hand on her shoulder. "Are you all right? That was quite the tumble."

"Much better now, thank you." My eyes roll involuntarily. She bends to pick up the pile of skirts before placing them back onto his cart. "I'm just so embarrassed!"

"No need to be, my dear." His hand is back on her shoulder, and I'm considering breaking it. "Say, if yer not busy right now—"

"She's occupied, actually."

Dammit. I just couldn't keep my mouth shut, could I?

The merchant's eyes meet mine, as though noticing me for the first time. He doesn't bother responding, only offering a curt nod of understanding. With one last lingering look at Paedyn, he turns to continue pushing his cart down the street, oblivious to the skirt he's left behind.

Paedyn quickly snatches the cloth from the ground before the man has a chance to turn around and see it. Then she steps back into the alley, raising an eyebrow at me.

"What?" I grind out.

She snorts. "Possessive, are we?"

"I chained you to me. What do you think?"

She ducks her head, smothering a smile as she begins unfolding the skirt. Lucky for us, the styles in Dor consist of breathable cloth made to wrap around the body. The skirt is nothing more than a large sheet of fabric adorned with a tie, making it easy for Paedyn to fasten on over her thin pants.

"There," she mumbles. "I'd give you a spin, but I'm afraid the chain won't allow it."

I skim my eyes over her, taking in the hem of the skirt that pools around her feet to cover part of the chain. "Much better," I say, stepping around her to examine further. "That's a great color on you."

I can barely get the words out without laughing. The skirt is dyed an atrocious shade of yellow, clashing with her tattered green vest and tan skin.

"You're hilarious. Really." Her dull expression matches her voice. "I'm glad I can amuse you."

I run a hand down my face, attempting to wipe the stupid grin from it. Then I'm crouching in front of her, glancing up at her in question. "May I?"

Funnily enough, those are the exact words I uttered before ripping the skirt of the dress she wore to the interviews. Though, I'm not planning to repeat history at the moment.

I push the skirt aside to pick up her boot. I hear the beginnings of a protest before I start wrapping the excess chain around her ankle. She quiets, watching as the length of links shrink between us until only a foot remains.

I stand, dropping the flowy skirt to let it drape over the rest of the chain still separating us. "There," I sigh. "It's hardly noticeable. But you're going to have to walk very close to me. Maybe put your arm in mine, convince everyone we're a couple." Her brows fly up her forehead. "Think you can handle that?"

"Do I have a choice?" she huffs.

"Good point." I nod. "All right, let's go."

She lurches forward when I take a shallow step. "Easy, Azer," she hisses close to my ear. The arm she folds around mine grows tighter in silent warning. "I'm wearing a hideous skirt *and* an ankle chain. Don't push it."

I pat her arm with my other hand, taking slow steps onto the street. "I wouldn't dream of it, Gray."

Saying her last name only reminds me that she doesn't want me to say her first. It hurt, losing that privilege. Losing the right to something as intimate as her name rolling off my tongue. But I will respect her wish, keeping her name trapped in the confines of my mind.

After several stumbling steps, we find a familiar rhythm, our feet falling in time together. Merchants hurry past, paying us no mind as they rush home for the night. It's not long before the street is eerily empty, and Paedyn is untucking her arm from mine.

The sun has slipped behind crumbling buildings, sinking down the horizon to sleep for the night. We walk silently through the shadows, following the street until a run-down inn towers over us.

I place a light hand on her lower back, guiding her toward the building. "Welcome to your bed and bath."

CHAPTER 29

Kai

"Dor's finest, I'm sure."

She sounds serious, as though this *is* the best Dor has to offer. And I don't disagree.

I lead Paedyn around the edge of the building to the line of windows accompanying the rooms inside. After already being captured once, I've determined that our safest option is to sneak into a room rather than show our faces to the innkeeper.

I test each of the windows, searching for one that may be unlocked. When one lifts easily, I peek my head in to find luggage scattering the floor. "Occupied," I whisper to Paedyn, who's standing on her toes in an attempt to see inside. We continue to the back of the building, pulling at latches until another slides open. I thank the Plague under my breath before turning to a wide-eyed Paedyn.

"Empty." She flashes a smile that's gone too quickly. I drop to a knee before her, reaching for her foot to unravel the excess chain from around her ankle. When I look up, it's into widening blue eyes. "I'm not proposing, don't worry," I murmur. "Step on my leg; I'll give you a boost."

"Right," she mutters, looking away quickly. "Is the chain long enough?"

"Probably not." I shrug slightly. "I'll figure it out."

She nods before placing a dirty boot on my thigh. Gripping the window ledge, she begins pulling herself up with shaky arms. I place a hand under her thigh while the other pushes at her lower back. "Watch it, Azer," I hear her whisper harshly from above me.

I smile. "Gentleman, remember? I'm simply helping you break into this inn."

"How very noble." She manages to drag herself over the sill and into the room beyond. The chain pulls taut before I have a chance to catch my breath. My leg is yanked upward, forcing me to jump and ungracefully grab the ledge. It's a struggle to pull myself into the room with the chain tangled and taut between us, but I manage to make it inside fairly unscathed.

I've toppled onto the creaky floor, ankle throbbing. She peers down at me in the darkness, her expression smug. "Was that you 'figuring it out'? Because it looked like it hurt."

"Like hell." I sit up slowly, running a hand through my messy hair. "Thanks for your concern."

She smiles, stepping toward the bathroom until the chain is yanking my leg in her direction. "I was promised a bath." She frowns at where I still sit on the floor. "Must I drag your ass all the way to the tub?"

"By all means"—I flash her a smile—"go ahead and try."

She tosses her pack onto the floor, glaring at me as she unravels the wrap from around her face. Silver hair slips from the scarf, tumbling toward her waist. My eyes trail up the length of it before meeting her piercing gaze.

"I loathe you," she says simply.

I blink. "Thanks for the reminder."

"I just want to make that very clear in case something happened that made you think differently."

I duck my head to shake it at the floor. "Like you kissing me?"

"Just so we're clear"—she takes a step closer, pointing an accusing finger at me—"*you* kissed *me*." A pause. "The first time."

"And then you kissed me the second time," I say, standing to take a slow step toward her, clearing the space between us in a single stride. "And I think you loathe *yourself* for wanting to do it again."

She huffs dismissively, turning away from me. "And what makes you think I have any desire to do it again?"

I shrug. "You've already done it twice. So look at me and tell me you won't again." She opens her mouth to do just that, but I cut her off with a tug of the chain that has her tripping closer. "Without tapping your left foot."

Her mouth snaps shut. I smile at the rare sight of her flustered. "I'm not doing this with you," she huffs, turning toward the washroom. "I want my bath."

I'm still smiling as she leads me to the rotting door separating us from the tub inside. She spins, jabbing a finger into my chest. "You're staying out here." Then she's pushing open the door to peer around the corner. "The chain should reach if you sit outside the door."

"How fortunate." That earns me a swift backhand to the gut. She steps into the washroom, dragging the chain under the door.

"Sit," she orders, giving me a stern look before swinging the door partially shut. I obey, sitting in the warped doorframe with wood poking into my back.

I struggle to ignore the sound of damp clothes hitting the floor. So, being the gentleman that I am, I trace the grooves in the wood, attempting to occupy my thoughts with anything but her. I pause at the sound of her muttering. "Everything all right in there?"

"Other than the fact that I'm trying to bathe with a chain around my ankle?" She continues her mumbling, momentarily distracted. "I'm going to have to wash these pants with the rest of me, since they're not coming off anytime soon. I think I have an extra shirt in my pack. . . ."

The sound of sputtering water and creaking pipes drowns out her words. This must be the only inn in all of Dor with running water. Maybe this really is their finest.

I hear her splash into the tub, the action pulling my leg halfway into the washroom. Silence stretches between us, only interrupted by the occasional sound of sloshing water. I lean my head against the inside of the doorframe, listening to her. "I can hear your teeth chattering from here."

"Yeah, well, the water isn't exactly w-warm," she grinds out.

I don't contemplate my next words before asking them. "Why did you dive back into the sewer for me?"

I can't see her face, but it's not difficult to picture the look of surprise that is likely lighting it. "I . . . I couldn't let myself take another life." Her voice grows softer with each word. "I have enough blood on my hands."

"Your fingertips, maybe. But not your hands," I say evenly. "Three lives are hardly enough to stain your soul."

I would know.

"You found the soldier in the desert, then," she says slowly.

"I did. Though, I figured he deserved it."

Water sloshes from behind the door. "That's what I keep telling myself. But it doesn't seem fair for one to decide their life is worth more than another's." I hear her take a shaky breath. "And that is exactly what I did."

"I know the feeling," I murmur.

She's quiet for several, slow heartbeats. "I was on the roof, you know. Watched you find the Imperial I'd killed."

My breath catches.

Swallowing, I attempt to keep my voice steady. "Really? Then why am I still alive?"

"Because . . ." A breath. "Because you were going to bury him for me. Just like you had with Sadie in that first Trial. And seeing you kneel there, seeing you carry that man over your shoulder for me despite everything . . ." She trails off, clearing her throat. "I just couldn't bring myself to throw that knife."

I can't see her face, and a timid part of myself is thankful for it. "You could have been free of me twice now. You know that, don't you?"

Her voice is small. "I know."

"Do you regret it?"

My question silences her for several seconds before she whispers, "I'll regret it in the morning."

The sound of my words to her in the dungeon has a slight smile tugging at my lips. I shut my eyes, content to let silence stretch between us. It's not long before she's standing in the tub, leaving me to listen to the sound of water dripping from her body. "Would you grab the shirt from my pack and throw it in here?"

The idea of refusing is rather tempting, but I reach for her pack instead. I'd already emptied it of the numerous weapons she'd stashed in there, leaving it mostly unoccupied. I dig around until I find a thin, gray shirt wrapped tightly around a worn notebook.

Pulling both out, I untangle the swaddled journal before thumbing through the tattered pages. "What's this book in here?" I ask as I toss the shirt through the cracked door.

She's standing right outside the door now, her shadow painting the floor beside me. "It was my father's. Mostly filled with the work and theories of a Healer."

I can hear the hurt in her voice, however hard she tries to hide it. And I hate that I'm the cause of it. When I can't find my voice, she speaks instead. "Yeah, I saved it from the house you burnt to the ground."

She says it lightly, as though unaffected by the event. "About that," I start, running a hand through my hair.

"Don't say you're sorry. Please." When she speaks next, her voice is soft, delicate. "It's easier that way."

I nod, knowing she can't see it. Knowing exactly what she means. Knowing that apologizing for what I've done to her only makes me more human. Makes it harder for her to hate me.

The door creaks open as she steps through it. The loose shirt hangs off her shoulder, growing damp from the tangle of wet hair falling down her back. With a frayed towel in hand, she steps back into the bedroom to dry her sopping pants.

After thoroughly wringing out her clothing, she wraps herself in the towel and plops down in the doorframe. "Your turn."

CHAPTER 30
Paedyn

I'm braiding my hair when he walks out of the bathroom.

Walks out of the bathroom, shirtless.

A strand of hair slips from between my fingers. I scramble to my feet, looking anywhere but at the tanned chest and damp pants hanging low on his hips. Beads of water are dripping from his hair to roll down his shoulders, trailing toward the body beneath. Not that I noticed.

"Do you ever have a shirt on?" I say casually, eyes on the braid I'm fumbling with.

"I washed it, so it needs to dry." Gray eyes flick up to mine. "If I'm distracting you, by all means, let me know."

I scoff as though that isn't exactly what he's doing. As I head across the room, he's forced to follow until I plop down onto the thin mattress. He towers over me, illuminated only by the moonlight streaming through the window, aggressively tousling his wet hair with a towel.

"You're dripping water on my bed," I say, scooting farther across the mattress.

He looks up at me from under the towel. "I'm sorry, *your* bed?"

"Yes, *my* bed."

"No, I heard you," he says simply. "I'm just trying to understand why you're saying that."

"Because I'm not sleeping with you." He gives me a look, to which I quickly rephrase, "I'm not sleeping in this bed with you."

He's making no effort to hide how humorous he finds this. "And why is that? It's not as though we haven't shared a bed before."

"So you keep reminding me." I turn my attention back to the neglected braid. "Yes, *before*."

Before every bit of betrayal that was brought between us.

"Well, you don't have much of a choice." He nods to the chain hanging limply between us.

"You could hang your head off the other side of the bed," I say sweetly.

"Why don't you, seeing that you're the one who's so desperate to get away from me?" He takes a step closer to the bed, his knees brushing the quilt. "I have no problem sleeping beside you."

I shake my head in annoyance, shifting to the other side of the bed that is suddenly too narrow for my liking. The mattress sinks when he sits beside me. Ignoring him, I take my time untucking the thin quilt and slipping beneath it to burrow in the covers.

It's freezing, the frigid air tempting my teeth to chatter. I'm not sure when it suddenly got so cold, but the damp hair sticking to my neck certainly isn't helping. I pull the quilt over my chin before shoving my icy hands beneath each thigh.

"You're shaking the bed," he says quietly.

"And you're more than welcome to roll off if it's bothering you so much."

I can hear the smile in his voice. "You've been shivering since your bath."

"You say that as though you care for my well-being." The chain clanks loudly when I shift onto my side and peer into the darkness.

"No, but I care for my well-being. And I'd rather not be kept up all night by you shivering."

"Spoken like a true gentleman," I scoff.

We fall silent, nothing but the faint chattering of my teeth to fill the space. He stills beside me, so much so that I assume he's fallen asleep. That is, until the mattress sinks behind my back, and I practically roll into him.

"What the hell are you—"

His chest meets my back.

I try again. "What the hell—"

"Shh."

My mouth falls open. "I'm waiting for a better explanation than that."

"Easy, Gray." A hand brushes my hip, making me jump against him. "I can't sleep with you shaking the bed, and you can't sleep when you're freezing. This is best for the both of us."

"Is it really?" I start. "Because I—"

"Plagues," he chuckles against my ear. "Just pretend. Pretend not to hate each other in these moments, remember?" I open my mouth to object, but the arm he circles around my waist has me snapping it shut. "All this means is that we're useful to one another."

I stiffen slightly against him.

Useful to one another.

The sentence stings more than it should. I hate myself for hating how it sounds rolling off his tongue. Because *useful* is the extent of our relationship. The most we will ever mean to each other.

"Fine," I say, annoyed at the sound of my voice quivering. "Pretend."

With that, I allow myself to melt into his warmth when he pulls me closer.

I'm tangled in his arms and wrapped in the chain tethering us together.

I blink in the hazy sunlight streaming through the window, feeling the warmth of it coat my face. His arm is warm against my cheek, fingers peeking from beneath my unraveling hair. I can feel his deep breaths stirring my hair, warming my neck.

He's comfortable. He's content.

He's pretending.

The thought has me untangling myself from him, starting with the arm slung snuggly around my waist. Grabbing his wrist, I toss it behind me, not bothering to be gentle. Then I'm sitting up, pulling strands of my hair from his fingers.

He stirs before quickly sitting up on his elbows. The quilt slips down his bare chest as he watches me with sleepy eyes, tracking each hand as I gather my hair over a shoulder.

"You missed a piece."

I glance up at the sound of his gruff voice. "Good morning to you, too." I run a hand over my neck, finding the forgotten strand falling down my back. He watches me while I pretend not to feel his gaze traveling over my face.

"What now?" I ask distractedly. "Time to drag me back out to the desert?"

The thought of returning to Ilya bleeds into an equally bleak one, and my heart aches at the sudden reminder of my selfishness. I've been so caught up in the Enforcer who holds my fate in his hands that I have yet to spare a thought for my friends; the Mixes living in squalor.

I worry for Lenny, Leena, Finn, and every other soul who was kind enough to help me. Believe me.

Please be safe. Please.

If I knew who or what to pray to, I would have.

"Not quite." The bed shifts as he stands to his feet, forcing me up as well. He walks over to the washroom, stepping inside to grab his damp shirt from the tub. I'm not sure why I look away when he pulls it over his head, but the action feels far too intimate.

"We are going to cut through Dor," he says, stepping back into the washroom. "And then cross the Sanctuary of Souls."

I let out a humorless laugh. "The Sanctuary of Souls? The rocky terrain infested with bandits?" I scoff. "I think I'd prefer the Scorches."

His voice is slightly muffled by the cracked door. "Father sent me out there plenty of times. We'll be fine."

I swallow at the reminder of his torturous training. "Well, were you chained up last time you visited?"

He's silent for several seconds. "I was always . . . challenged when I was out there." More silence. "So, like I said, we'll be fine."

When he steps out of the washroom, he's carrying a bundle of clothing in his arms, intending to dump it on the floor for the innkeeper to find. A flash of familiar olive green catches my eye, and I snatch the vest from his grasp. "Not this," I snap. His brows lift at my tone—a silent question. "Adena made it for me," I say quietly, clearing my throat self-consciously. "I—I made a promise to her."

He nods slowly, seemingly hesitant. "The final Trial. I . . . I saw it happen. Saw you hold her." A muscle ticks in his cheek. "Heard you scream."

I look away, feeling the emotion begin to pool in my eyes. "She made me promise to wear it for her." I run a hand over the rough hem. "And I plan on doing just that."

Clearing my throat, I shrug the vest over my shoulders. I hate the way he's watching me, like he's ready to collect the pieces when I inevitably break. He sighs through his nose, opening his mouth to say . . .

A loud bang at the door cuts him off.

"Aye! Who's in there?"

The man pounds at the locked door, rattling the rusty hinges. Kai nods to the window, his eyes still fixed on the door. I step lightly toward our escape while wrapping the scarf around my head, shoving the silver strands of hair into it. When we reach the window, I'm slipping on my boots and quickly throwing a leg over the sill before the rest of my body follows. Kai is right behind me, jumping from the sill as I hear the door burst open.

"Oi! Get back here, you bastards!"

We scramble from the scene on sleepy limbs. I'm tripping, trying to wrap the skirt around me while Kai flings our dirty clothes behind us. A laugh climbs up my throat before spilling from my mouth. The prince glances over at me, and I catch his smile before he pulls the bandanna over his face. I hear him chuckle as we duck into an alley, dodging rolling carts and swearing merchants.

"Stop them!"

I whip my head around, spotting what can only be the innkeeper. His face is red and splotchy with rage as he charges after us, pointing a thick finger in our direction. "Stop those two!"

The sight of him only makes me laugh harder, while the sound of that only makes Kai's smile widen beneath the bandanna. I squint in the rays of the rising sun, narrowly avoiding those milling about the merchant street.

"This way," Kai calls over his shoulder, grabbing my hand to yank me down an alley. He snatches a large hat from a passing cart—a sloppy attempt at thievery. The merchant shouts after us as we cut through several more streets, the chain scraping the cobblestone beneath us while I attempt to smother my laughter. I can't help but find this all very amusing, and I'm slightly concerned as to why.

"We need to lose him," Kai murmurs after another shout echoes around the corner. I'm about to say something when he suddenly pulls me down another alleyway and pushes me against the crumbling wall.

"What are you—"

"Pretend, Gray," he breathes, trapping me against the wall with his body. Before I get the chance to question him, he's untied my skirt with one hand and thrown it to the ground. I blink at the crumpled fabric at our feet before his hand is guiding my face back to his.

I see the order in his eyes, the need for me to listen to him, just this once.

So, I don't push him away when his hand trails down my neck to lift the scarf from my head.

Because this is pretend. This is a plan.

He pulls the floppy hat onto my head, tucking my messy braid within it. Then he's leaning closer, pulling the bandanna from his face. His free hand is tight on my hip, pushing my back against the wall. I take a quick breath when his head ducks beneath my jaw.

The brush of his lips has me swallowing.

His mouth moves lightly, trailing kisses across my skin. My breath catches when a hand cups my face to bend it down toward him and away from the street. He moves slowly down my neck, his lips growing less hesitant as they follow the path of my jagged scar.

"Kai . . ." My voice sounds breathy, though that wasn't at all what I intended.

"Pretend," he breathes against my skin, making me shiver.

At the sound of approaching shouts and pounding footsteps, he pulls my head and the hat atop it down farther. His body is pressed against mine, face buried in my neck and hidden beneath the brim of this hideous hat I'm wearing.

The group of men now on the hunt for us pass by without a step in our direction. We are nothing but a lovesick couple, after all. Just two lovers looking to be left alone.

Lovers.

The thought of others perceiving us as such has me swallowing.

He's made it to the end of my scar, kissing the hollow of my collarbone. Any farther down and his lips would find another scar etched over my heart, branding me till death. The thought has me pushing him away from me and stepping from his hold.

He takes a step back, breathing heavily. Gray eyes crash into mine, swimming with an emotion I don't bother trying to decipher. After a long moment, he blinks, giving me a curt nod of approval. I feel my cheeks burning and pull the hat lower to shield myself from his piercing gaze.

He watches as I dust the skirt off before wrapping it around my waist, giving time for my face to cool. Then he clears his throat before looping the chain several times around my ankle, closing the gap between us.

"Ready?" he asks casually, as though I'd imagined the last five minutes.

Fine. If he thinks nothing of it, neither do I.

So I adjust my hat, nod curtly, and hook my arm through his.

CHAPTER 31

Kitt

The little box on my desk is buried beneath piles of stained parchment.

I hide it there whenever I get the urge to think too long on my decision. The decision that Calum assured me was the right one. Though, reminding me of my father's three *B*'s to becoming a great king did help convince me further.

My fingers drum against the wooden desk, the sound hollow and harsh.

There's a quick knock, knuckles on the door that echo my fingertips on the desk.

"Come in."

Hinges groan before a masked Imperial peeks his head into the room. "Your Majesty. Excuse my interruption, but you informed me to—"

"So no sight of him?"

I hear the Imperial swallow. "No, Your Majesty. None of his men, either."

"And her?"

"Nothing, Your Majesty."

He should be back by now. It's been over two weeks, and he should be back by now. He should have brought her to me. Or maybe he brought her somewhere else. Maybe he never intended to bring her back. Maybe he ran away with her. Maybe they are running away from me—together. Because he should be back by now. Because—

"My Enforcer should be back by now."

"Yes." The man nods fervently. "He should be, Your Majesty."

"Keep searching the edge of the city."

"Yes, Your Highness." He looks sidelong at the door, practically begging to be dismissed.

"Go."

With a curt nod, he ducks out the door before closing it softly behind him.

I run an ink-stained hand down my face.

He always completed his missions. Well, he always completed his missions for Father. But I'm not him, am I? He reminded me of that every day. And then he'd spend the rest of that day training my future Enforcer. The one who should be back by now. The one who is running away with her. Or from me. Or his life.

I tear at the parchment littering my desk, digging until my fingers find that small box I buried beneath.

I look at it like I do every day.

The kingdom thinks I've gone mad.

I think I've gone somewhere. A darker place, maybe.

I hear servants whispering as they step past my door, watch Imperials eye me when I happen to walk the halls.

They think I'm mad with grief over a man who felt little more than disappointment and obligation for me.

How absurd.

How absurd to grieve a man who loved power more than his sons. How absurd to grieve a man who offered me no praise. How absurd to grieve a man who could never be pleased.

How unfair to grieve such a man.

So, I won't any longer. I'm done with it. Truly.

I miss who I was before finding him with a dagger buried in his neck. I miss the brother I was to Kai and Jax, miss sweaty days in the training ring. I miss running away from balls to drink until sunrise. I miss running from responsibility in general.

Kai and I were good. Especially so after Ava. We became impossibly closer with every night he spent fighting tears in my bedroom. I remember stealing alcohol from the cellar for the first time after it all, remember spitting out the first sip.

How odd that some of the fondest memories now were anything but in the moment.

Though I doubt I'll grow fond of the life I'm now living anytime soon. I may not even live long enough to look back and miss the days I hated.

My fingers brush the top of the box, feeling the significance of it with each swipe. I don't want to hate every day. Maybe I won't have to hate every day. Maybe this is for the best. . . .

I roll my shoulders, the ones now carrying the crushing weight of this kingdom.

And then I manage to find a relatively clean sheet of parchment.

This letter is for him.

For the man I'm sick of mourning.

This letter is addressed to the grief he's left me to grapple with.

The grief he doesn't deserve to make me feel.

The next letter is to her.

They usually are.

She makes for quite the muse.

Or maybe she's just easy to think about, easy to translate into words.

I pour my thoughts onto the page.

She should be back by now.

Another smudge of ink.

She should be back by now.

The paper tears beneath my pressing hand.

She should be back by now.

I add the parchment to the pile.

CHAPTER 32

Kai

"Slice."

My brow furrows, waiting for her to continue.

"Please," she manages from between bared teeth. I reward her politeness with a smile and a piece of apple lifted to her lips. Her teeth snatch it from my palm, narrowly biting me in the process. Which she's tried. Several times.

She glares at me from where she sits atop the roof. Early morning light dapples her face and the strands of silver hair peeking out from beneath her scarf. "Is this really necessary?"

She's talking about the rope I've bound her wrists with, of course. "Oh, you know exactly why it's necessary."

After a long day of walking to the quieter outskirts of the city, we managed to climb onto the roof of a run-down building where she had the nerve to pull a knife on me in my sleep. I woke up to the sound of her picking at the lock around her ankle before she held the blade to my throat. I'm slightly concerned that she managed to get ahold of a weapon without my knowledge. But the tiring scuffle ended with both hands bound behind her back with a strip of old tarp I'd found. Only then was I able to get some rest.

"Am I not supposed to try to escape my captor?" she asks, exasperated. "I'm not exactly the type to go quietly."

"Obviously not," I sigh, offering her another slice of apple. She takes it begrudgingly, hating that I'm feeding her.

"How long is this going to last?" She wiggles her fingers at me from behind her back.

"Until the urge to kill me dies down."

She huffs out a laugh. "So it seems I'll forever be tied up."

"What a shame that would be," I say distractedly, using the knife she found to cut slivers of apple for myself.

I catch the quick roll of her eyes. "Slice."

This is becoming rather unenjoyable for the both of us. I cut another piece for her before reaching over to lift it to her lips. "We're about halfway through Dor. If we make good time today, and don't run into any trouble, we might make—"

"Slice."

I shut my eyes, breathing deeply for a moment before I feed her another piece. "As I was saying," I breathe, sounding calmer than I feel, "we might make it to the Sanctuary of Souls in a couple of days."

"Perfect." Her smile is deceptively sweet. "One landmark closer to my death."

I look away to the street below us, not wanting to think about the possible truth in her words. I hate that I don't know what Kitt plans for her. Or worse, what he plans for me to do to her.

"Well, it's best not to keep the king waiting, hmm?" She struggles to her feet, looking down at me as she adds, "Especially since we're taking the long way back to Ilya. We wouldn't want him to think something happened to you."

Her tone is mocking, attempting to mask what she's truly feeling. I know better than most what that is like. So I say nothing as I stand to my feet, studying her face and the emotions she refuses to let me see. But it's the hand she waves at me from around her back that steals my attention.

"I need my arms to climb down."

I smile slightly. "I could just catch you at the bottom."

"This chain would pull me off the roof before you even got there."

"Fine," I say simply. "Then you'll beat me to the bottom."

A sound of annoyance climbs from her throat. I laugh lightly before closing the distance between us, watching her eyes flick between mine. She stills when I reach behind her back, brushing her sides before I grab her bound hands.

It's only when she opens her mouth to tell me off that I cut the tarp with my knife, holding her gaze all the while. Her hands break free with a snap, the sound stretching a soft smile across her lips. "So you don't want me to fall to my death?"

She's close, smelling faintly of the inn's cheap soap. I shrug. "Not if you're going to pull me down with you."

"Well, that's the only way I'd allow myself to die."

I'm smiling before I even get the chance to stop myself. Then I'm reaching up to tuck loose silver strands of hair into her scarf, my fingers brushing her temples. The feel of her skin has my mind wandering back to the alley where my mouth was on her neck, feeling her pulse race beneath my lips.

It's troubling, how tempting she is.

She tasted like a privilege, felt like a dream.

It was an effort of sheer will to step away, to pry myself from her.

But it was all pretend, after all. At least, that is what I keep telling myself.

I run a hand through my hair before pulling the bandanna over my nose. "Ready?" I ask, walking us over to the edge of the roof.

"It wouldn't matter if I wasn't," she says cheerily.

I shake my head and swing over the side of the building, gripping the tall lip of the roof while my legs dangle beneath me. Paedyn does the same, straining as she begins to carefully climb down. We struggle down the wall of the building, using every crack in the stone as a place to fit our fingers and feet.

The chain clanks between us when we finally leap to the ground. My hand stings, and I look down to find a thin line of blood blooming across my palm, courtesy of a jagged stone. Ignoring it, I watch her wrap most of the chain around her ankle before she straightens. Then she's hesitantly threading her arm through mine as we set off through the backstreets of Dor.

The edge of the city is eerily empty, housing only the homeless and crippled. To live this far from the main market streets is not a choice—it's a punishment. Outcasts are pushed to the outskirts, leaving them to fend for food or make the trek to the market alleys.

But it's safer to travel along the border where there are less people to recognize us, especially with the news of our escape from prison likely spreading. We make good time, only needing to dodge a few persistent peddlers as the day wears on.

It's only when we pass the fourth flyer of her face that she tears it from the shop's wall. "What?" she bites out, catching the glance I throw at her. "I'm sick of staring at myself."

She's about to crumple the poster when I snatch it from her. "Let me see this." I easily avoid the swipe of her hand, lifting the parchment above my head.

"You are insufferable," she huffs, finally giving up. "What could you possibly want with that?"

"Comparing it to the original," I say simply, holding the picture beside her face. She almost allows herself to laugh at that. My eyes flick between her and the poster, scanning each feature. I hand it back to her in a matter of seconds. "Not enough freckles."

"Not enough . . ." Her head whips in my direction, confusion crinkling her brow. "What do you mean, not enough freckles?"

"I mean," I say without looking at her, "they didn't draw enough freckles."

She huffs. "Yes, I heard that, but—"

A burly man steps out from an alley, blocking our path. Paedyn's arm tightens slightly around mine as his eyes skim over us, stopping at the sight of a chain clamped at my ankle. I take a step, urging Paedyn to move around him when his face suddenly splits into a smile.

"Damn," he bellows, "you've really got yourself a ball and chain, eh?"

For once, I'm relieved by such a comment. Let him think what he wants, so long as he doesn't know who we are. With that in mind, I play along. "Yes, and she's clearly quite the handful."

I'm going to pay for this later. I can feel it in the way she's squeezing my arm.

I rest my hand on Paedyn's back, guiding her forward as the man laughs. "You certainly put her on a leash!"

Her entire body tenses, ready to rip the man apart. I slide my hand around her waist, trapping her against me so she doesn't do anything rash. "Well, I can't have her running away from me, now, can I?"

His laughter fades behind us as we hurry past him and down the alley. I expect the elbow she throws into my ribs before the blow lands. "That," she says softly, "is the least you deserve."

"What exactly did you want me to do?" I murmur. "Tell him why you're chained to me?"

She doesn't bother answering as we step in time down the street. We walk in silence for several minutes, keeping our heads down and our pace even. It's only when a group of men step out in front of us that we falter.

There's four of them, all large and lumbering. A man steps forward with a jeering smile, the one we escaped from just minutes ago. "You know," he says, shaking a finger at us, "I thought you looked familiar, girl." He pulls a crumpled piece of parchment from his pocket, holding it up for us to see Paedyn's face staring back. "So this is the infamous Silver Savior, eh?"

I brace a hand on Paedyn's back when he takes a slow step toward us. "And that must make you the Enforcer sent to fetch her for your little king. We heard about your escape from Rafael. But he captured the both of yous easy enough." His smile only grows. "We'll get a lot for these two, boys. The Elite freak can't take down all of us. In fact, I don't think the Enforcer is half as powerful as we thought."

I glance to the right, eying the empty alley there. "I'd hate to say it, but . . ."

"I know," she murmurs back before lurching into a run.

We skid into the alley, tripping over the chain as Paedyn struggles to unravel it from her ankle. Shouts echo behind us, closely followed by the sound of thundering footsteps. I grab her hand as we zigzag through the uneven streets, focusing on keeping our feet beneath us.

"We won't lose them like this," she pants, pulling me in a new direction.

"I know," I say, swiping at the sweat stinging my eyes. The next right we make has us heading for one of our pursuers, forcing us to skid to a stop and turn around. "Any brilliant ideas?" I ask breathlessly.

"I was just about to ask you the same thing." She barely manages to avoid an old man who hobbled into our path. We turn another corner, this street more crowded than the rest. Without a word, she's tugging me toward a dimly lit building and throwing open the door.

We all but stumble inside, going from blinking in the blinding sun to being shrouded in shadows. I scan the room, taking in the velvet chairs and gaming tables. The space is smoky, helping to conceal the faces of the men drinking and gambling. Women prowl around the room in flimsy clothing, searching for an empty lap to sit on.

"You just pulled us into a gentleman's club," I murmur beside her.

"Of course you would know what this was," she whispers harshly. "What now?"

"Now," I say, letting my hand graze her lower back, "we blend in."

I pull the floppy hat from the pack slung over her shoulder and quickly rip the scarf from her head. Then I tug the hat low over her face, tucking the remnants of her messy braid into it. "Play along, all right?" I murmur, wrapping an arm around her waist. "Take off your vest. It's recognizable."

She obeys for once, folding the fabric into her pack to leave her with only a thin shirt hanging off a tan shoulder. Then I'm pulling her toward an empty chair seated at one of the many gaming tables. A few men encircle the game, peeking around the women on their laps to sort the cards in their hands, smoke puffing from the cigars hanging at their lips.

I sink slowly into the velvet chair before pulling Paedyn onto my lap. She sits straight and stiff until my hands find her hips to ease her back against my chest. "Loosen up, darling," I whisper against her ear. "Look like we belong here."

She nods slightly, the brim of her hat nearly hitting me in the face. I feel her melt against me, convincingly more comfortable with where she's perched atop my thigh. Keeping one hand slung loosely across her hips, I use the other to signal the table to deal me in. After throwing the few shillings I have onto the felt, a man throws me several cards.

She turns so her cheek is against mine and slowly wraps a lazy arm around my neck. It's just an excuse to whisper without looking suspicious, but I struggle to slow my racing heart, nonetheless. "What are you doing, Azer?" she murmurs, her lips brushing my cheek.

I swallow at the feel of it. "You pay to play," I breathe. "And not playing will only draw more attention to us."

She exhales against my skin in a way that has me clearing my throat. "Remind me to steal your money back at the end of this." With that, she's turning toward the table to watch the men lay their cards.

It would be a lie to say that I'm unfamiliar with a gentleman's club, though the one in Ilya feels much cleaner than this. But I know how these games are played and, much more importantly, how to win them.

"I doubt you'll need to do that, darling." I lay a card onto the worn table. "I don't plan on losing."

The men around the table take their turns, frequently swapping out the women decorating their laps. I feel Paedyn tense each time a girl is exchanged, hating how the men discard one just to run their hands over another.

It's not long before a woman slinks over to wrap her arm around my shoulders. Her voice is high and breathy as she offers to take Paedyn's place. But when I open my mouth to decline, it's not my voice I hear.

"This lap is taken," Paedyn says coolly, pulling herself closer with the arm still draped across my neck. With a huff, the woman nods and turns away to find another body to warm.

A sly smile spreads slowly across my face. I lean forward to look at her, but she's stubbornly ignoring me to instead focus on the game unfolding before us. Wanting to catch her eye, I drop my cards onto the table to drag her chin toward me.

"Jealousy looks good on you, Gray," I murmur, my fingers still cupping her chin.

Her eyes flick between mine, full of a familiar fire. "I'm not jealous."

My gaze lingers on her lips before traveling down the length of her. "Then you just look good."

She scoffs, turning her face from my hold. "Why don't you focus on not losing, hmm?"

I open my mouth to argue that it's her fault I'm distracted in the first place when the door suddenly bursts open, flooding the room with harsh light.

Two familiar men step inside, looming in the doorway and looking for us.

CHAPTER 33
Paedyn

"You brought your own, eh?"

I tear my eyes from the two men crowding the doorway to blink at the one beside us. The woman on his lap wears a feathered hat that sits precariously atop her head, likely knocked around by the handsy man she's perched on.

His comment has my cheeks heating. I despise this place. And I despise having to act like nothing more than a pretty toy.

Kai's hand tightens on my hip.

Don't be rash. We are being watched.

That is what I hear in his hold, in the way he pulls me back possessively on his lap. His silent order has me relaxing against his chest while peeking under the brim of my own absurd hat at the two men now perusing the room. They look innocent enough, as though deciding what table they wish to gamble at. But their eyes are searching, studying each person in their path.

"She's my good luck charm," Kai says simply, earning a few chuckles from the table. He's wrapped his arm fully around my waist,

leaning in to rest his chin on my bare shoulder. With his bandanna pulled from his face in the dim light, the stubble across his jaw tickles my skin, making me shiver.

"What do you think, darling?" he asks against my ear, holding the cards in front of me. He says this loud enough for the table to hear, as though this is a regular routine for the two of us.

"Hmm." I lean my head against his, feeling his breath on my cheek. Then I'm reaching up to tap a card. "This one."

"That's my girl," he murmurs, placing the card onto the table.

The game continues, though I'm paying no attention, with the way his fingers are splayed across my stomach. I glance up at the men looking for us, finding them slowly making their way to our table. I know Kai notices too when he ducks his face close to mine to hide subtly beneath my hat.

I can't help but stiffen with every step our pursuers take. I'm ready to hop from Kai's lap and run if it comes to that. My fingers fidget with the skirt currently draped over the chain at my ankle, bunching the fabric in my sweaty palms.

A firm hand runs down the length of my side, earning my undivided attention. "Relax, Gray," he breathes against my ear. His palm travels down my hip to the leg below, gripping me beneath the knee to pull me impossibly closer. "Pretend, remember?" His voice is a caress, mimicking the hand now running over my thigh.

Right. Pretend.

That is all anything is between us. Every touch, every look, every genuine moment.

Pretend.

I shift, turning sideways to fling my legs over his lap.

Pretend.

My hand finds the back of his neck, fingers combing through his hair.

Pretend.

Nothing means anything with him. And that's what I keep telling myself.

His focus is fixed on me and far from the game at hand. "Am I distracting you?" I ask sweetly.

"When are you not?"

"Hmm. Your heart is pounding, Prince," I whisper against his ear at the feel of it thundering beneath his chest.

"It's a close game," he murmurs. "And I'm not accustomed to losing."

I scoff softly. "No, you're used to that pretty face and title of yours getting you everything you want."

He pulls back enough to look me in the eyes, allowing me to glimpse the emotion peeking through the cracks in his mask. His gray gaze travels over my face, taking in every disheveled inch of me. "Not everything."

I blink. He stares at me until a man signals him to take his turn. It's only when I look to see the card he's played that I glimpse the two men walking toward our table. Kai's chin finds my shoulder again to conceal his face beneath the hat's brim. His hand brushes up and down my hip, helping to keep me relaxed against his chest.

Pretend.

That's what I do when the men stop to stand beside the table. I play with Kai's hair, wrapping my arms around his neck.

Pretend.

My free hand is running fingers over his unshaven jaw before finding their way down his neck.

Pretend.

I'm pretending to ignore the fact that the men are now looking right at me, watching the show I'm performing for them. I can feel their eyes trailing over us and the faces that are partially hidden. When I'm certain I should be jumping to my feet and running, they grow tired of us and turn to watch another table.

I exhale, tipping my forehead against Kai's cheek. "They're gone."

A muscle feathers in his jaw. "Good work, Gray."

I sit up slightly at his tone, at the reminder that this was all strictly to blend in. "Have you almost lost yet?" I say stiffly.

He's distracted. "Your faith in me is inspiring."

"Can you hurry this up?" I say quietly.

He places a card onto the table. "What, you have somewhere better to be?"

"Yes," I say dryly. "Not on your lap."

He ducks his head, chuckling against my neck. "Is that so?" I shiver when his hand slowly encircles my waist again, calloused fingers brushing the bare skin where my shirt is riding up.

I nod slowly. "I'm bored."

His lips graze my jaw. "No, you're not."

I fight the urge to turn and face him fully. "And what makes you think I'm not?"

"Call it a hunch," he murmurs against my ear before laying a card that has the men around the table groaning. The game ends with angry mutters and the pile of glinting shillings being pushed in our direction.

Kai quickly tosses the coins into my pack with an insufferable look of satisfaction. "Looks like you won't be needing to rob anyone today, darling."

"Too bad," I mutter. "I was so looking forward to it."

With a chuckle, Kai all but lifts me off his lap and onto my feet. He stands close behind, placing a firm hand on the small of my back. We make our way to the door at a casual pace, as though we aren't worth an outrageous amount more than what we just earned.

I throw one last glance over my shoulder to the men in search of us, finding them talking to a table on the other side of the room. And then I'm stepping through the door to blink in the blinding sunlight. We turn cautiously around the corner, scanning each street before we stride down it.

It takes nearly an hour of walking before we feel safe enough to slow our pace and lower our guard, but we keep our heads down when we pass the occasional straggler so far from the heart of the city. My feet drag with exhaustion, my eyelids threatening to flutter closed. Kai notices this, of course, and has taken to yanking on the chain when my steps grow sluggish.

"You did a good job back there," Kai says quietly, breaking our long stretch of silence.

I hum dismissively. "It's not very hard to sit on a lap."

"Oh, sitting is easy," he argues. "It's the looking pretty part that can be difficult. Well," he adds sincerely, "not in my experience. But I'm sure others may struggle with that."

I laugh despite myself. "You think so highly of yourself."

"Someone has to." His following accusation has my head whipping toward him. "Since you're still denying that you think I'm pretty."

"Well, I don't think you're pretty."

"You know, I almost believe you." He throws me a bemused look. "You are rather convincing. Especially so during your performance on my lap."

I turn my face away before he can catch the blush blooming across my cheeks. "Well, I've had plenty of practice *pretending.* I've been doing it my whole life."

At the mention of the sham that is my life, my Psychic ability, I'm only reminded of the many people who were dragged into it.

The ones who were unassuming accomplices, collateral damage in my performance. Soft green eyes and an easy grin flash in my mind. The new king was the latest victim of my charade, my betrayal.

I shrug the pack from my shoulders to pull out a half-eaten loaf I'd snatched from a merchant's cart—just like I have all our food. "Do you think he's worried about you?" I ask between bites of bread. When Kai raises his brows in question, I add, "Kitt?"

I swallow. That's the first time I've referred to the king by his name and not his new title. It feels foreign in my mouth, as though it belongs to the memory of someone I used to know. And in a way, it does.

"If he is worried," Kai sighs, "it's because I'm with you."

I snort. "What, he thinks I'm out to murder all the royals?"

He looks at me fully then, eyes roaming over my face. "He has no idea what you're out to do."

"I'm not out to do anything," I say defensively. "All I want is a unified Ilya. And I certainly had no intention of killing the king that day. He came at me, remember? As if he'd been waiting for the moment." I look away, shaking my head.

"You still killed the king. You're a criminal—"

My bitter laugh cuts him off. "And what does that make you? A saint?"

He stops abruptly, practically yanking me into him with the chain. "I've never claimed to be anything but a monster." His hands are gripping my shoulders despite his voice being deceptively soft. "But I also had no *intention* of killing your father that day. In fact, I had no intention of turning into the shell of a man I am today. But I did. And I pay for it every day."

I blink at him, at our abrupt shift in conversation. "What do you mean, you had no intention of killing my father?"

"I had no intention of even becoming a murderer that day." He pauses, letting go of my shoulders as though just realizing he was shaking them. "I didn't know what my first mission would consist of. And I wasn't going to go through with it once I found out." He runs a hand through his messy hair. "He was sleeping, and I wasn't going to do it. I was going to slip out of the door and deal with the consequences. But then he woke up. He looked me right in the eyes, and that's when I was suddenly driving the sword through his chest." A shake of his head. "He hadn't even reached for a weapon. Hadn't moved at all. And yet, I ran him through anyway. In my panicked state, I did exactly what the king hoped I would." He's silent for a long moment, swallowing his pride before adding, "I stumbled from the room and threw up before I even made it back to my horse. I didn't want to do it, Gray. I *wasn't* going to do it."

I take a step back, blinking back tears as I look anywhere but at him. "Not what you wanted to hear, was it?" he says roughly. "Makes it harder for you to hate me."

I turn away slowly, resuming my slow steps down the street.

"Harder, maybe," I say softly. "But not impossible."

CHAPTER 34
Kai

The edge of the city is eerily deserted.

With each step closer to the Sanctuary of Souls, the less people linger. It's to be expected, considering the bandits that haunt this corner of the city. We pass the occasional skittish stranger, hurrying to find their way back onto a crowded street.

I glance sidelong at Paedyn. She's been spinning that ring on her thumb for the past several hours while managing to look anywhere but my direction. I hate when it's like this. When we don't speak. When she acts like my prisoner.

"Your braid is falling out."

It's not, actually. But I'm pathetic and couldn't think of a better way to break the silence. Talking about her hair is better than not talking at all. She grips the brim of the hat, looking around to find any wandering eyes. When she deems the coast clear, the hat slips from her head to let the braid tumble down her back.

"Hold this," she orders, shoving the hat into my hands.

"There's those lovely manners," I murmur, watching as she struggles with the knotted tie at the end of her braid. It's unbearable to watch, really. "Just let me do it."

"Absolutely not." She laughs. "The last time you braided my hair, it was a mess, remember?"

"I was out of practice."

Emotion flits across her face. "Well, I'm sure you've brushed up on your skills since then."

I'm only confused for a moment before realization rams into me.

She thinks I've been with other women.

The thought almost makes me laugh, and yet, I play along.

"Does that bother you, Gray?"

She ducks into a dim side street, pulling me with her. "Are you going to fix this, or should I?"

She's still attempting to unravel the braid when I lean against the wall. "That wasn't an answer."

"What do you want me to say?" she huffs, whipping the braid behind her. "That you braiding another woman's hair bothers me? That's pathetic, and I won't say it."

I sigh, stepping behind her to gather what is left of the braid into my hands. "Well, I haven't." I manage to untangle the strap and run my fingers through her hair.

"Haven't what?" she asks stiffly.

"Haven't braided any woman's hair but yours," I say softly. "Well, yours and Ava's."

I feel her spine straighten against my fingers. "Ava?" She laughs humorlessly. "Let me guess, one of your many lovers? Perhaps one you actually liked?"

I'm silent for a long moment, swallowing back the emotion climbing up my throat. "Yes, I liked her. Loved her, even."

"Great to hear."

"She was . . ." I blow out a breath. "She was life itself. Every bit of good I lacked."

She glances over her shoulder, but I push her face back toward the wall. "Why are you telling me all this? To make me jealous?"

I smile. "There is no reason to be jealous—"

She cuts through my words. "Really? Because it sounds like—"

"Of my sister," I finish, talking over her.

I think I hear her jaw snap shut.

"I . . . ," she stutters, searching for words. "I didn't . . ."

"Didn't know I had a sister?" I say simply. "Of course you didn't. You and the rest of the kingdom weren't supposed to know."

Her hair slips from my hands as she turns to face me. "What do you mean?"

My fingers catch her chin, turning her gently back toward the alley wall so I can gather her hair between my fingers once again. "She was born eleven years ago—her birthday was nearly three weeks ago. For her health, my mother wasn't supposed to have any more children. But Ava was unexpected. Unplanned." I take a quiet breath. "The birth was . . . difficult. We almost lost the queen because of it. I remember sitting by the side of her bed, holding my mother's hand while the Healers did the best they could."

The braid is halfway down her back now, her hair slick in my hands. "Ava wasn't supposed to survive the birth, but she was a miracle despite all the odds."

"What . . . ," Paedyn starts hesitantly, "what happened?"

"She was sick. The Healers said she didn't have long to live. And because of that, Father ordered her to be kept a secret from the kingdom. He didn't want news of a frail queen and her sick child to spread. Apparently, ill royals are an embarrassment. A sign of a weak king and kingdom." I roll my shoulders, feeling the tension and anger building there. "So Ava was hidden, was a secret kept by the entire staff. Still is."

"And now?" Paedyn asks softly.

"She was four when the sickness took her away from me." I swallow. "I learned how to braid because of her. She was weak, and doing her own hair was something she struggled with. So I learned to do it for her. I used any excuse to spend time together. I'd endure every bit of training the king put me through because I knew she was waiting for me on the other side of it." I tie off Paedyn's braid with shaky fingers. "She had this beautiful thick, black hair. Big, gray eyes like my mother. Everyone joked that she was the prettier version of me. And when I looked at her, I saw the best parts of myself."

"Kai . . . ," Paedyn starts. "I didn't know."

"She wasn't supposed to ever step foot outside the castle that caged her in," I continue.

"Wasn't supposed to?" she asks quietly. "That sounds like she did."

A soft smile lifts my lips at the memory. "Oh, she did. I made sure of it. When it was clear that the sickness would take her at any moment, I snuck her out into the gardens one night. She splashed me with the freezing fountain water, picked as many flowers as she could." I pause. "And she laughed. Plagues, despite it all, she always laughed. Her very essence was contagious."

Silence stretches between us as Paedyn slowly turns to face me. "You never talk about her."

I look away, shrugging as if the sadness of it all isn't swallowing me whole. "It hurts too much. Kitt never brings her up either. He knows not to. But everyone loved her. Everyone knows not to talk too much about her when I'm around." I run a hand through my hair. "Even in death, she still feels like a secret. And I want to talk about her—I do. It's selfish, really. But every time I look at myself, I see a mangled version of her."

"I'm so sorry," Paedyn whispers, her fingers hesitantly brushing across the top of my hand. "I had no idea."

"Most people never will," I say bitterly. "Even after she died, the king—Ava's *father*—refused to tell the kingdom about her. She's buried beneath that willow in the gardens. The one you found me under that night during the Trials." I watch the realization widen her eyes. "I visit her as often as I can."

"That's why you were there," she murmurs.

I shake my head at the uneven cobblestones beneath my feet. "I wanted to tell you. But I never thought I actually would."

Her palm finds my arm, gentle and unsure. "Thank you for telling me." She sounds shy. "And I'm so sorry about Ava."

I smile slightly, desperate to lighten the mood and think of anything but my dead sister. "So, I've never braided the hair of a lover. And I hardly think my four-year-old sister is anyone to be jealous of."

A quick smile lifts her lips in understanding. She is familiar with the sound of a subject change. "As if I would be jealous to begin with."

I sigh in relief at her willingness to play with me. "It's cute when you pretend you're not."

A quick roll of her eyes before she's running her fingers over the braid. "Not bad, Azer. I'm not fully convinced you haven't been practicing on someone."

"Just you, darling."

"Hmm," she hums, flipping her hair over a shoulder. "How sweet."

I glance up at the setting sun. "Let's get moving. We can make it a little farther before nightfall."

I pick up her giant hat from where I tossed it onto the ground. She huffs when I push it onto her head and over her eyes. After lifting the brim to glare at me, she tucks the tail of her braid in before we set off onto the deserted street.

"You're stepping on my hand."

Her boot is crushing the fingers I have wrapped around the ladder's rung. "Oh. Oops."

"Yeah, *oops*."

"I can't see a thing up here," she whispers down to me.

The barn we've snuck into is swallowed in shadow, and the loft above the stables even more so. We are nearly out of Dor now, and anyone willing to brave the Sanctuary of Souls stops here for a ride through it. Horses bray softly beneath us, settling into their stables for the night.

The shackle rubs against my raw ankle when she pulls herself up onto the loft. I feel my way up the ladder until I'm met with surprisingly sturdy planks of wood. I roll onto my back with a sigh, breathing in the smell of hay and the animals who eat it.

Her shoulder brushes mine as she lies down beside me. The feel of it has my mind racing with the memory of her on my lap. I push the thought aside, just like I've done several times now.

"You don't think anyone saw us sneak in here?" she whispers.

I shake my head, stabbing hay into my hair. "I don't think there is anyone even out here to see us."

She's silent for a long stretch. "I keep hoping he'll find me."

Straw continues its stabbing as I turn my head toward her. "Hoping who will find you?"

"Lenny," she whispers. "Or any of the few people who still care about me."

"I'm sure they've looked for you," I say, ignoring the growing guilt I refuse to feel.

"Have you killed Mixes? Or just Ordinaries so far?"

I stiffen slightly at the hurt in her voice. "I haven't found any *Mixes* in Ilya. Well, haven't realized what they were if I had. But now that I know what their limited power feels like, I don't doubt that I will."

"And then you'll kill them."

"I didn't say that."

"You didn't have to," she spits. "They are exactly what you and the rest of the kingdom are afraid of—your powers dwindling."

I blow out a breath. "They are the beginning of the end of Elites."

"And what is so wrong with that, if it means everyone gets to live?" she whispers, pleading for me to understand.

Silence surrounds us, interrupted only by the muffled stirring of horses. "Your mother was an Ordinary?" I finally ask.

"Yes," she says simply. "She died of illness when I was a baby."

"And your father a Healer?"

"You already know that."

"So," I say slowly, "how is it that you're an Ordinary?"

"What are you . . ." A pause. "What are you talking about?"

I shrug, rustling the hay beneath my shoulders. "Shouldn't you be a *Mix*, then? That is, so long as your mother was, well—"

"Think very carefully about your next words, Azer," she says, deceptively calm. "Because if you were about to suggest that my mother was unfaithful, I would think twice." Her voice is suddenly soft. "They loved each other."

"I think you overestimate love," I say simply.

"You can't overestimate something that is infinite."

Infinite. How equally intimidating and intriguing.

I can just make out her outline in the darkness. "You can't tell me that you've never wondered why you're Ordinary."

Her tone is dull. "I guess I've been too busy surviving to figure it out."

I quiet, contemplating her words. After several long minutes, I clear my throat. "We'll sleep for a few hours before we grab a horse and head for the Sanctuary."

"Can't wait," she mumbles groggily.

"You going to attempt to stab me in my sleep?" I pause. "Again?"

Her voice is muffled against the pack she's stuffed her face into. "Well, it didn't exactly work last night, did it?"

"Still breathing," I assure her. "But it was a valiant effort."

"Don't mock. I'll push you off this loft."

"Then you'll be falling with me."

She rolls over. "It'll be worth it."

CHAPTER 35
Paedyn

Hay is stabbing me in the head.

And so is the finger Kai jabs me with. "You sleep like the dead."

I roll over, grumbling into the pack I've been using as a pillow. "Just practicing for when I inevitably am."

He makes a sound that might just be a stifled laugh. "Up. Now."

"I'm tired."

"So am I," he sighs. "Specifically of you."

"You're the one who chained us together," I mumble. "So you're not allowed to complain about my company."

"Up, Gray."

"Make me, Azer."

Shit. That was a mistake.

He swings his legs over the ladder, managing to drag me over to him. Then he's climbing down, yanking my back across the straw and toward the edge. "All right," I gasp when my head is nearly hanging over the wooden loft. "You're insufferable."

He stops long enough to let me shove the hat over my hair and fumble to pull on my socks before the accompanying shoes. "So you've told me. Many times."

Dull sunlight squeezes through the slits of wood the barn wears. The day is young, still scaring the shadows away. My boots find the ground with a thud that lifts a cloud of dust. Horses peer around the corners of their stalls, perking curious ears at the strangers staring back at them.

"This way," Kai whispers, leading me to the back of the barn. He nods to the animals lining the walls. "These horses are conditioned for long journeys. And we have enough food and water in your pack for four days."

"Yes, thanks to me," I murmur.

"Yes," Kai nods. "Thanks to you and your thievery."

"I prefer the word *skills*, but—"

A horse brays to my left, making me jump. "Damn these beasts," I breathe, heart pounding.

Kai chuckles. "These *beasts* are the gentlest ones you'll find."

He unlatches a stall and quietly pushes it open. The horse inside is a deep brown, his coat dull with dust. Kai absentmindedly runs a hand down his snout before grabbing a saddle from where it's thrown atop the wall.

"Come introduce yourself," Kai says softly, nodding toward the horse he's now saddling.

"I'm fine, thanks."

The bastard yanks the chain, causing me to nearly stumble into the beast breathing down on me. "Asshole," I hiss at him, straightening to find myself staring up at the horse.

"Oh, come on, Silver Savior," he mocks. "He won't bite . . . probably."

I roll my eyes at the prince before hesitantly raising a palm to the horse's snout. His nose is soft and warm as he gently nuzzles against my hand. I muster a small smile, swallowing my fear for such a formidable creature. Because something so strong is never truly tamed.

"Your bravery is inspiring," Kai says dully. "Now open the door so I can walk him out before the stable hands get here."

Annoyingly enough, I obey and step aside as he leads the horse out into the center aisle. Hooves clop against the packed dirt as we head for the barn door and final stretch of the city beyond. We are nearly outside when a shadow slips into the barn before the figure follows.

The man stumbles to a stop, taking in the horse and the two strangers stealing it.

"What the hell?" he stutters, eyes skimming over us.

Kai's gaze never strays from the giant man. "Get on the horse, Gray."

"But the chain—"

"Then put your foot in the stirrup and hang on."

I don't even have the chance to argue before the man is stepping toward us, gripping something that glints in his hand. Kai pushes me behind him before ducking under a punch the man throws at his jaw.

The fight is a blur I can barely see from behind Kai's back. The man grunts when he takes a hit to the temple but manages to have the Enforcer doubling over after sinking a fist into his stomach.

"Yeah, take your time with that saddle!" Kai calls behind him, narrowly avoiding another hit.

His sarcasm shakes me out of my stupor to struggle with the stirrup. When I watch him fight, it's hard to look away. It's a practiced precision. An alluring sort of chaos.

The toe of my boot teases the stirrup as I attempt to balance on one foot. I hear the scuffle and scraping of boots before Kai's back is ramming into me, knocking the wind from my chest and the feet from beneath me. I hit the ground with a thud but force myself up before I've even choked down air for my burning lungs.

I look up to find the man clutching his bloody nose and stumbling back from a hit. Kai doesn't waste a moment before turning to wrap a hand around my thigh and shove my boot into the stirrup. Then his hand is on my back, pushing me upward as I begin swinging my other leg over the saddle.

When the chain tightens, Kai grips the saddle and hoists himself up to sit behind me, stretching the chain between us. I glance at the man beneath us, now stumbling forward to grab my leg. I kick violently, trying to free myself from the clammy hands clamped around my calf. When he doesn't budge, I bend to grip his hair before driving his broken nose into my kneecap.

He howls, blood streaming down his face as he staggers back. I'm suddenly thrown against Kai's chest when he digs his heels into the horse's sides, spurring it into a run. It's only when we've flown out the barn door and into the streets that Kai slows our pace. Barely.

I'm gripping the horn of the saddle, squeezing my eyes shut with every turn. Kai's hands are resting on my thighs, his chin hovering over my shoulder as he grips the reins. This far from the main market, there are few people brave enough to live so close to the Sanctuary. But those who do find themselves jumping out of our path to avoid being trampled.

The sound of pounding hooves on cobblestone echoes off the surrounding brick walls. A gust of wind catches the brim of my hat, tearing it from my head and into the street. Silver hair is falling down my back, exposed in the daylight for the first time.

"Duck, darling." Kai's hand finds the top of my head, pushing it down before we ride under a fallen beam wedged between two buildings.

"Don't call me that," I say, straightening as I run a hand over my frizzy hair.

"Don't call you what?"

"Darling. That's what."

I can feel his smile against my neck. "Why? Like it too much?"

"I think *you* like it too much," I challenge.

He huffs out a laugh that stirs my hair. Wind combs its cool fingers across my scalp, and I almost sigh at the feeling. The open air is freeing, tempting me to stretch out my arms and embrace it.

I watch what is left of the city pass by in a blur, barely glimpsing the occasional person pointing in our direction. But before long, the street stretching beneath us grows rockier as the Sanctuary of Souls looms closer.

I swallow. This is it. This is the beginning of the end I've prolonged for so many years.

There is no hope of rescue beyond Dor. The Sanctuary is my death sentence. It is all hope dashed and fate sealed. It is destined doom.

Road turns to rubble, buildings into boulders. Kai slows our pace when we enter the narrow passage that is the Sanctuary of Souls. I can just make out the outlines of each shallow grave and cracked tombstone that earned this place its name.

"You don't believe what they say about the souls, do you?" I ask quietly, eying the crumbling stones carved with faded names.

"I don't know if the dead haunt travelers," Kai sighs. "But I can't say I haven't seen some strange shit happen out here."

"Like what?"

"It's better if you don't know, Gray," he says smoothly. "I don't need you scared of the horse *and* our surroundings."

The laugh that bubbles from my throat surprises even me. "You're not funny," I barely manage beneath the palm I've clamped over my mouth.

"Really?" Kai bends over my shoulder to look at me, his voice comically confused. "Because it sounds like I am."

I turn away, hiding my face from him. "No. I won't give you the satisfaction of making me laugh."

"But then you'd be depriving me of the sound."

I fall silent, dropping the hand from my face. He shifts behind me, clears his throat, feels unsure, as though he's surprised by his own words.

This is the part where I should tease him, should tell him that flirting is futile.

But his tone is familiar, feeling like dancing in a dark room and thumb wars under willow trees. The way the words rolled off his tongue felt like a light flick to the tip of my nose, like calloused fingers braiding silver hair.

It felt like Kai.

Like the man behind the masks who looked at me like I was extraordinary.

I blink at the crumbling rocks crowding the path, willing my mind to wander toward anything but the words that have me wishing things were different. But I am Ordinary. I am the embodiment of the weakness he has been taught to hate.

Ordinary.

The word echoes in my skull, sounding different from every time prior.

I knew Mixes must exist, seeing that the Elites were so afraid of becoming them and weakening their powers. But I had never questioned why I wasn't one myself, why I am nothing but Ordinary.

I look down at the ring I'm fervently spinning on my finger. I feel foolish for not figuring this out sooner. But what I told the prince is the truth—a rare occurrence for me. I suppose I was too busy attempting to survive.

"We'll ride until nightfall and lie low until dawn." Kai's words cut through my thoughts. "Bandits claim the dark, and we'll be hidden best on the ground."

"Right," I say absentmindedly. A soft breeze ruffles the hair falling around my face, drawing my attention to the braid he wove and the mess of silver it's become.

I haven't stopped thinking about Ava. Can't stop thinking about how gently he spoke of her, as though remembering how fragile she was. I could hear the love coating each word and the hurt echoing after.

I think of the first Trial, of Jax dying in his arms. He almost lost another sibling that day. There are few people he cares about that he hasn't watched die—or betray him.

The sun beats down on us, and I'm beginning to wish my hideous hat hadn't blown away. I roll up the sleeves of my shirt, exposing sun-drenched shoulders to the sky. We've been riding for a long while now, silently scanning our surroundings and sorting out our thoughts. Looming stones surround us, casting the occasional shadow into our path while they burn in the midday sun.

"I bet you could cook an egg on one of these rocks," I say, my voice rough from lack of water and use.

When I don't hear some witty response, I shift slightly, feeling a weight on my pack. With a glance over my shoulder, I glimpse inky waves resting against my back. I swallow, suddenly feeling his deep breaths, his hair tickling my arm.

He's asleep.

The action is so unbelievably *human.*

His body is limp, at peace.

And completely vulnerable.

I doubt he's slept more than a handful of hours these past few days.

But here he is, breathing deeply with his hands resting on my thighs, his fingers a loose fist around the reins.

I blink down at the leather that could lead me anywhere, could steer even the strongest creature.

My heart pounds against my chest.

This is it. This is hope.

Taking a deep breath, I begin gently uncurling his fingers from the reins, stopping at even the slightest stir. When his left hand is free, he reaches for something, flexing his fingers instinctively. I swallow, placing my palm atop his own before threading my fingers through his.

I hold my breath until he stops stirring, seemingly content to be holding my hand instead of the reins.

I make quick work of his right hand, freeing the strap to gather it into my own. There's a fistful of leather now clenched in my hand, and I haven't the slightest idea what to do with it. I pull to the left, hoping to convince the horse to turn.

Nothing.

I take a breath. Then I pull harder.

The horse shifts to the left, now walking closer to the wall of rocks. I swallow my frustration and prepare myself to tug even harder.

Because if I can get this horse to head back toward Dor, I could—

"I wouldn't."

A hand wraps around my wrist, halting my attempt.

I huff, looking up to shake my head at the sky. "Damn you."

"Good try, Gray," he says, lifting his head close to mine. "But you wouldn't have made it far."

I shrug, attempting to act unbothered. "Who said I was trying to make it anywhere? What if I just wanted to hold the reins?"

"And my hand?" he asks. "Just wanted to hold that, too?"

I had forgotten my fingers were still laced with his and quickly untangle them. "I liked you much better when you were asleep," I say sweetly.

"Good to hear you liked me at all."

Crumbling bread sticks to the roof of my mouth.

I take another swig of the water we're supposed to be using sparingly, washing the dough down. The fire Kai built is dwindling, no more than dying flames in the growing darkness. He sits beside me, chain stretched between us, occasionally picking at his bread after tending to the horse. The poor creature must be exhausted after carrying us all day in the heat. We only stopped when the shadows crawled toward us, slipping over the stones to swallow us in darkness.

"You know, this was meant to be a final resting place for the royals," Kai was saying, nodding to the rocky ground around us. "Hence the name, Sanctuary of Souls. The first queen was actually buried in a crypt within one of the caves, but when the bandits began to claim this land, they abandoned the idea." He takes a breath, reminiscing on the history of Ilya. "So, Mareena—the first queen—is buried all alone in this place."

I hum distantly. "She doesn't seem to be alone." I gesture to the graves littering the ground several feet away. "Just not with her fellow *royals*." The word is coated with a bitterness I hadn't intended to voice.

"She's not with her *husband*," Kai corrects. "Her *family*."

"Right," I say quietly, as if that passes for an apology. "So, where is the rest of the Azer family buried?"

Kai picks at his bread. "There is a cemetery on the castle grounds. Every king, queen, and child is buried there. Except one."

Ava.

With a slow nod, I shift, crossing my legs on the bedroll. Kai catches my wince at the movement. "What's wrong?"

"Nothing," I say quickly.

"Try again."

I sigh. "I'm just sore, okay?" A laugh climbs up my throat. "Plagues, Kitt asked you to bring me back to Ilya, not take care of me."

His eyes narrow slightly. "He doesn't need to tell me to take care of you."

"So why do it?" I lean forward, looking for any sort of crack in the mask he's wearing. "Since when do you do anything the king hasn't ordered you to do?"

His voice is calm. "What I felt for you went against every order I've ever been given."

"Well then it's a good thing feelings aren't getting in the way anymore," I say quietly.

He dips his head, suddenly interested in the loaf of bread still in his hands. I clear my throat, looking up at the stars winking down at us. "Why did you . . ." I pause to consider why I want to know the answer before I even finish the question. "Why did you tell me about Ava? You said you never talk about her."

He runs a hand through his hair, sighing at the crackling fire. "I think that question deserves a dance."

I choke on my scoff. "I'm sorry?"

"You know how this works, Gray," he says simply, as though it's painfully obvious. "We dance—you get your answer."

"Please," I snort. "This has to be a joke."

His head tilts slightly to the side. "Is that a no?"

"Why," I say, exasperated, "would you want to dance with me?"

"You're asking more questions, and yet, we still aren't dancing."

I shake my head, smiling at the sky. "Fine." I stand to my feet, brushing the crumbs from my shirt. "But only because I want answers. Because this is ridiculous."

He smiles slightly before standing to extend a hand I hesitantly take. "Let's see what you remember."

"I remember how to stomp on your toes." I smile, draping my arm over his shoulder.

"I'm sure you do." His hand finds my waist, fitting there in a way that's far too familiar. "Why don't you show me that you remember how to stand close to your partner?"

I fight the urge to deflect and force myself to step into his warmth. The corner of his mouth lifts as he takes my free hand in his own, lacing our fingers together. His palm flattens on the small of my back, making me swallow.

"Very good, Gray," he murmurs. "Being close to me always was the most difficult part for you."

"That's typically how it is when someone is insufferable, yes."

"All right, smart-ass." He's looking down at me, smiling slightly. A long moment passes. "Are we going to dance, or would you rather continue staring at me?"

I look away, cheeks burning. "I was not staring at you."

"Fine. You were admiring me, then—"

"You haven't answered my questions," I cut in.

"And you haven't honored my terms." He nods down to my planted feet. "We still aren't dancing."

"So start leading, Azer."

His eyes flick between mine before a smile lifts his lips at my challenge. "Yes, darling."

He begins a simple step, forcing my feet to stumble in time with his. After several counts and far too much concentration, I finally relax into the movement, letting my feet find the familiar rhythm.

"So," I say slowly, "my question."

"Which one?"

"Ava." I pause. "Why did you tell me about her?"

He sighs against my hair. "Do you . . . do you remember the second ball, when I was—"

"When you were belligerently drunk?" I say, tilting my head to look up at him.

His smile seems sad. "Yes, when I was belligerently drunk. Which was your fault, by the way."

"My fault?" I scoff. "How was that my fault?"

"You were dancing with my brother; that's how." He spins me then, surprising me into tripping over my feet. "You were giving him that look like you do."

"What look?"

"I'm not quite sure," he says quietly. "You never gave it to me."

I look away, uncertain what to say. He clears his throat. "Anyway, one thing I remember very clearly from that night was when I dragged you onto the dance floor."

"Yes," I smile, happy to have changed the subject. "I remember that very clearly too."

"I kissed your hand before we danced. Do you remember?"

I nod slowly, recalling how his mouth brushed my knuckles for everyone to see.

"And then my lips found the pad of your thumb." His voice is a murmur, a memory made words. "I hadn't even realized I'd done it." He shakes his head. "And until that moment, I hadn't done it in years."

"I remember that too." I search his face in the shadows. "I wondered what it meant."

"Ava was a Crawler," he says quietly, still dancing slowly. My mind wanders to the many figures I've witnessed scaling the crumbling buildings on Loot Alley, their ability allowing them to climb effortlessly.

"She was only a Defensive Elite," he continues, cutting into my thoughts. "Some people say that your level of power is due to how strong you are physically and mentally. And Ava was born weak." He spins me again slowly. "As she got older, using her power was difficult. She would grow tired and fall from the walls. Then she would cry, saying that all she wanted was to be strong." He sighs through his nose, looking up at the stars. "So, I would kiss each of her fingers to 'give' some of my power to her. She loved it. Made it higher up the wall every day. But she especially loved when I kissed her thumbs, told me it gave her extra strength. So that's what I did. I kissed her thumbs every day until Kitt helped me bury her."

I haven't realized there are tears in my eyes until one threatens to fall. "You loved her very much," I whisper.

"I did. I *do*," he says simply. "And I've never kissed a thumb that wasn't hers."

"So," I breathe, "why mine?"

He finally meets my gaze, shaking his head slightly. "Your spirit is familiar. You remind me of what could have been. In another life, I think Ava would have grown up to be like you."

I struggle to laugh. "What, you wanted her to be a criminal?"

"No," he murmurs. "I wanted her to be formidable. Recklessly bold. Powerful despite ability."

I stare at him, taking in each word.

"I am none of those things," I whisper.

He drops my hand to brush gentle fingers beneath my chin, raising my face up toward his. "You are much more than those things."

"You overestimate me."

"No. I just *see* you."

Adena was the only person who had ever truly seen me and stayed despite it. But she is gone. And it's the prince meant to kill me who now says the words she used to reassure me with.

I swallow the sentences I don't know how to say. "I've never cared enough to kiss someone else's thumb," he continues softly. "But my lips found yours that day."

"And look at where that got you," I whisper, fighting my smile.

My gaze travels over his face, from the gray eyes that see me to the soft lips that have tasted me. I feel myself falling into something familiar, like a trap I'm willingly walking back into. His hand is firm on my back, burning like a brand and pulling me closer with each step of this back-and-forth dance between us. Once again, I find myself walking the sharp end of a blade, knowing it will inevitably cut me in the end.

And yet, my fingers find his hair. My body presses against his. My heart beats to be broken.

He smiles in that way that has me suddenly smiling back. Dirt crunches beneath my boots as we dance in the dark, the chain wrapping around my leg to continually trip me. I huff, irritated with the damn thing. Kai chuckles when I stumble into him for the dozenth time, to which I glance up with a glare.

"Don't hurt yourself, darling." Before I even have the chance to respond, he's wrapping his arm fully around my waist and lifting me onto his boots.

"What the hell . . . ?"

He grins, flashing both dimples at me. "Let me dance for the both of us."

I swallow my protests, looking down at my booted feet atop his. The arms he winds around my waist are strong, secure in the way they hold me against him. "Kai," I whisper. "We shouldn't . . ."

"Shh." His mouth is against my ear. "Pretend."

The word floods me with a false sense of relief, as though I'm suddenly allowed to want this. To pretend that this is okay. I twine my hands around his neck, struggling to smile with all the emotion crowding my face.

He stops abruptly, searching my eyes. "What's wrong?"

"Nothing." I smile sadly, fighting the tears that threaten to fall. "I just . . . I used to do this with my father. That's why I never learned to dance properly." My laugh sounds pained. "Because he always just did it for me."

He nods, tucking a strand of hair behind my ear. "I'm sorry I did this to you."

I sniffle quietly. "Did what?"

"This hurt," he murmurs.

We sway in silence for a long while before I finally allow my head to rest on his chest. He's a weakness. A comfort I shouldn't allow myself to seek out. But I let his feet guide mine, shutting my eyes against the flood of memories.

"He used to dance for me until I fell asleep," I whisper against his chest.

I feel him nod against my hair. "Then we'll dance until you're dreaming of him."

CHAPTER 36

Kai

Her head is crushing my arm.

And I fear I'd never move again if it meant she stayed beside me.

The thought is startling, creeping up from the depths of a feeling I don't want to dive into at the moment. So, I smother it, content to silently stare up at the sky streaked with pink clouds. The bedroll does little to disguise the feeling of uneven dirt beneath my back, and yet she sleeps soundly beside me. It's impressive, really.

She danced atop my feet until her eyelids grew heavy, her head slumped against my chest. I lowered her onto my bedroll before she could drool on my only shirt. Now I'm staring at what remains of the braid I wove into her hair, running a finger over the silver strands.

She's so very deceiving. So Elite in likeness. It's startling, feeling no power from her.

A sound slips past her lips, soft and sleepy. I fight the urge to wrap my free arm around her, to brush my lips across her neck.

Despite everything, I struggle to not want her.

Something has shifted between us, and yet, nothing at all has changed. She's the same Paedyn I knew before finding out she was Ordinary. The same Paedyn I knew before she killed the king.

The same Paedyn I was falling for.

And it's terrifying. Terrifying to know every terrible thing she's done and still want all of her in spite of it.

I just don't know if she can say the same for me.

I killed her father, after all. She defended herself against a man I loathed while I murdered a man she loved. And now I've chained her to her doom. She is the mission I'm dreading.

She stirs, and I still. When she flips to face me, a blue eye peeks open, blinking in the morning light. "You didn't wake me," she grumbles, puzzled.

"I don't bother trying anymore."

She laughs sleepily. "I would have thought you'd thrown me over the horse by now."

I lift the hand she's not currently crushing and flick the tip of her nose. "Traveling is only fun when you're constantly trying to escape."

I drop my hand to see wide eyes blinking at me.

Shit.

Once again, I hadn't thought about what I was doing until the deed was done.

I haven't flicked her nose since that final Trial where everything went to hell. That final Trial I was racing to finish just so I could find her on the other end.

I haven't flicked her nose since I was foolish enough to have feelings for her. Yet here I am, following the same fate. Falling into the same patterns. The same Paedyn.

She clears her throat, suddenly looking very much awake. "Would you like me to keep trying to escape?"

"It is rather entertaining," I say casually, despite feeling anything but.

"Good to hear. Because I wasn't planning to stop."

In one swift movement, she's grabbed a jagged rock from beside the bedroll and buried it against my neck as she leans over me. "This could do enough damage for me to escape, don't you think?"

My smile shifts into a grimace when her other hand presses against my hip as she props herself up farther. "Only if you're able to go through with it," I manage, blowing out a breath.

Her brows knit together with something deceptively akin to concern. "What happened? What is that face for?"

"Maybe," I bite out, "it has something to do with the rock digging into my throat."

"Oh, please, I'm barely putting any pressure—"

She leans her weight against my hip again, and I wince just enough for her to catch the movement. Her eyes dart down my shirt before widening at what they see. "Why are you bleeding?" Her head whips back up toward mine. "And why didn't you tell me you were bleeding?"

"It's just a scratch, Gray—"

"A scratch?" she chokes, dropping the rock. "You're bleeding through your shirt. I'd hardly call that a scratch."

"Are you worried about me?" She looks away, rolling her eyes. "You seem worried."

"Yes," she says simply, meeting my smug stare. "I'm worried you'll become a deadweight. And seeing that we're chained together, I'd rather not have to drag your body back to Dor."

"How thoughtful."

Her eyes have already returned to my stained shirt. "I didn't stab you, so who the hell did?"

"Stable hand. He had a small blade between his knuckles. The wound wasn't deep, but it must have reopened last night."

She shakes her head at me, disappointment drowning her features. "What the hell is wrong with you? Seriously." She half laughs. "I'd love to know. This could have gotten infected. Why didn't you tell me?"

"Because I've survived far worse, Gray."

Her gaze softens. "That doesn't mean you keep suffering just because you know you can."

I study her face, the way she bites the inside of her cheek in concentration or blinks rapidly in frustration. When her fingers curl around the hem of my shirt, I feel my heart stutter in my chest. "I need this up," she says softly, pushing the fabric to expose my stomach.

I swallow. "Always trying to get me naked, aren't you, darling?"

"No, but I am always saving your ass, Prince." She squints at the wound, struggling to see past the blood. "Yeah, it doesn't look too deep."

"He just grazed me," I say casually. "I told you it was shallow."

She gives me a look. "That doesn't mean it won't get infected." She fumbles for her pack, feeling around inside until she pulls out the disgustingly yellow skirt. Using her teeth, she rips a strip of cloth from beneath the waistband and sparingly soaks it in water from one of our few canteens. "We don't have any ointment, or the right plants to make some, so cleaning it up will have to do."

I watch her closely as she wipes the wound clean of blood. Watch her breathing quicken and her hands tremble slightly. She looks away, growing paler by the second. Her fingers sit atop the fabric, shying away from the blood she's sopping up.

"Suddenly squeamish, Gray?" I ask quietly, studying her ashen face.

Her voice trembles slightly. "Something like that."

Something is very wrong. And I'm pretty sure she doesn't want to talk about it. So I slowly lift my hand, placing my palm atop her wrist. "Let me."

I see her swallow, see her contemplate arguing before she simply nods and drops the cloth. She scoots back on the bedroll, putting distance between me and my wound. I tear my eyes from her to pick up the fabric, grimacing as I prop myself up on an elbow and continue cleaning the gash.

I look up at her, wanting to take her mind off whatever it is that has her looking so panicked. "Why didn't you ever leave Ilya?" The question has been burning in my throat ever since I discovered what she was.

She glances up at me, her eyes darting down to the wound before quickly looking away. "I don't really have a good reason. I think I was just . . . stubborn."

I chuckle, shaking my head. "Shocking."

The glare she gives me doesn't match the growing smile on her face. "I was stubborn and told myself that Ilya was just as much my home as it was the Elites'. Not to mention that I was too young to survive a trip across the Shallows or Scorches—I barely survived this time around. And I think Father would have wanted me to stay in Ilya. I mean, he trained me into a Psychic for a reason. He started the Resistance for a reason." She ducks her head, smiling sadly. "It was also my little way of defying the king and everything he said about Ordinaries. I was living against all the odds, right under his nose." Her eyes meet mine. "And something about that kept me fighting."

I nod slowly, sitting up slightly when I finish cleaning the wound. "Staying in Ilya was something you could control. It was your decision, unlike everything else in your life."

"You are the last person I figured would understand that." She laughs softly.

I shrug a shoulder. "In case you've forgotten, I also didn't have a choice in the fate I got dealt. So, I found my own ways to feel in control."

"Like what?" she asks quietly.

"Like never again taking the life of a child. I'd banish the Ordinary children with their families and lie to my father." My lips twitch into a smile. "That was my little defiance to the king. Back in Dor, I even ran into a little girl I banished who made it across the Scorches with her family. Abigail's the one who led me to you."

"So I have *Abigail* to thank for your appearance at my ring?" She's fighting a smile, and it's an adorable attempt.

"Someone needed to humble you, *Shadow*."

"Oh, is that what you did?" Her smile is sunshine incarnate, warm and bright and blinding. "Because I remember kicking your ass. As per usual."

"That's cute, Gray. Keep telling yourself that."

She shakes her head at me. "Sit up."

"Polite." I smile in that way I know she hates. "As per usual."

The look she wears makes me chuckle as I slowly sit up with a grunt. She's tearing more fabric with her teeth now, freeing a long strip from the skirt. Then she's hesitantly sliding closer to wrap her arms behind me, her face close. Feeding the fabric around my back, she winds it across my stomach several times before tying it off.

"There," she says softly, scrutinizing her handiwork. "Now I shouldn't have to worry about you becoming a deadweight."

The horse nickers a few feet from us, managing to tear my eyes from her and remind me of where we are. "He's ready to get moving."

"That makes one of us," she mumbles before standing to her feet and untangling the chain from her legs.

I follow, rolling up the bedrolls and stuffing them into the pack. Fiddling with the reins I knotted around a tall stone, I offer the horse an apple that he happily chomps down on. "You ready?" I say over my shoulder to where Paedyn is slinging the pack onto her back.

"No. I have to pee," she says flatly. I sigh, hanging my head at what I know she's about to say. "You know the drill, Azer."

I lean my forehead against the horse. "I don't know why you insist—"

"Are your ears plugged?"

I blow out a breath before covering my ears. "Yes," I probably shout. "Even though I don't get why."

Her yell is muffled. "Keep talking!"

"You know," I say, raising my voice. "I pee too. I don't understand why I have to plug my ears and shout every time."

"Of course, you don't." She's suddenly behind me, and I uncover my ears before turning to face her. "You're a man."

I blink at her, debating whether I want to know exactly what that means. She steps slowly beside the horse, reaching out a hesitant hand to run down his mane. Determined blue eyes find mine over her shoulder. "Teach me how to ride this thing."

CHAPTER 37

Kitt

Light spills through the windows lining each ornate hallway.

I almost wince at the sheer brightness of it all, having been locked within my dungeon—otherwise known as the study. Emerald carpet softens my steps while each stationed Imperial struggles not to stare at the sight of me.

I slipped the box into my pocket, though I'm not entirely sure why. I've come to the conclusion that the constant feel of it helps convince me that I'm in control of the situation. That I'm making the right decision. But the box feels heavy against my leg, slowing each of my steps.

Following the wafting smell of dinner, I turn down another hall, earning shy smiles from passing servants. I self-consciously run a hand through my hair, hoping I didn't look like the mad king they all whisper about.

I ventured from my study in the hopes that they would gossip about something else for a change. Perhaps about how I've scrubbed the ink from my hands and exchanged my crumpled shirt for a crisp new one. Or how I ate my meal this morning instead of dumping it

from the window. If nothing else, the fact that I left the study at all will earn their attention.

Warm light leaks beneath the kitchen doors, pooling around my feet when I falter to a stop. The knots in my stomach seem to tighten at the sound of her booming voice, familiar and frightening all at once. I've been avoiding her, and I'm not quite ready to deal with the consequences of that decision.

I turn, retreating down the hallway like the coward I am. A servant passes by on her way to the kitchen, averting my gaze when I attempt to meet hers.

Great. Now I've been spotted tiptoeing around my own castle.

I'm really not helping my case.

I have all of eight seconds before the cook has caught me.

"Kitt?" She says this with the tone of a question but the volume of a shout.

I spin, spotting her head peeking from between the kitchen doors. With a forced smile, I make my way back over to the bustling kitchen.

"Hi, Gail," I say, sounding far too sheepish for a king. She swings open the door, allowing me full view of her floured face and food-splattered apron.

There is a split second where I'm convinced she hates me, convinced I'm nothing more than the rumors. Nothing more than the mad king she is now forced to serve.

But the second passes, and in the next, I'm being pulled into a crushing hug. "Oh, my sweet Kitt!" Flour-streaked arms encircle me, flooding every cold crack in my heart with warmth. When she finally pulls away, it's with a wide smile on her face. "Come in, come in! I have somethin' for you."

I'm dragged into the kitchen, feeling like the boy she raised. Dozens of eyes widen at the sight of me before quickly darting away.

Servants scurry out of the way as Gail guides me to the counter where Kai and I typically loiter.

"I've been makin' some every day, hoping you'd come and see me." She pushes a covered plate toward me, lifting the napkin atop it to reveal a glistening sticky bun.

The smile that forms on my lips feels foreign. "Thank you, Gail." I clear my throat. "I'm sorry I haven't visited sooner."

Her gaze softens. "Well, you're a busy man now."

"Unfortunately," I say, as lightly as I can muster.

She eyes me, seeing something on my face that warrants her yelling, "All of you, out! Five-minute break before we plate the food."

No one questions the order. In a matter of seconds, each servant has filed out the double doors and spilled into the hallway beyond. When it's quiet enough to hear me bite into the sticky bun, Gail pins her scrutiny back on me.

"Heard you've been dumpin' my meals out your window." She raises an eyebrow. "Not up to your standards anymore?"

"No," I say defensively. Then again because her eyebrow continues its climb up her forehead. "No, of course not. I just . . . don't have the appetite I used to."

"Hmm." She nods at the sticky bun, silently ordering me to take another bite. It's only when I have that she says, "Is that why one of my girls told me you were walkin' away from my kitchen? No appetite for dinner?"

I nod, knowing that it's safer to do so than admit I've been avoiding this interaction. She nods back, though I doubt she believes me. "How are you doing, Kitty?"

Her question halts the sticky bun on its way to my mouth. This is the exact reason why I didn't want to face her. Because she'll make me talk about it.

"I'm better."

I think. Maybe. I actually don't remember what better is supposed to feel like.

"I know how difficult this has been for you," she says softly—a rare occurrence for her. "Not only about your father, but also . . ."

She hesitates at even the insinuation of how much I cared for *her.* How much it hurt when she betrayed me like she did, killing my father and more than a piece of myself in the process.

"Yes," I manage, "it's been difficult. But I've had help." I think of Calum and his guidance, of Kai and his effort to salvage the relationship I may have ruined.

She nods, rubbing a napkin across my cheek as though I'm still the toddler she once scooped into her arms. But I don't fight it. It's comforting, being cared for. Nice to pretend that Gail is the mother I never got to meet.

"Kitty, because I love you," she begins evenly, "I have to ask." There is a long pause before she gains enough courage to let the words spill out. "What do you plan to do with her once Kai brings her back?"

I almost muster a laugh. "*If* he brings her back."

"Don't you say that," she scolds, ignoring the fact that it's the king now standing before her. "Of course he will bring her back to you. And not because it is his duty, but because he loves you."

"And what if he loves her more?"

The words tumble from my mouth, conjured from my deepest fears. I've barely allowed myself to think it, let alone speak of it. But what's worse is the way that Gail's face never changes. Her expression is blank, her back straight and eyes unblinking. As though this isn't her first time hearing the question. As though she's asked herself the same one.

I look away, desperate to focus on anything but the question hanging between us. My eyes land on a thin candle tucked into the corner of a counter. I nod toward it, desperate to change the subject. "Is it someone's birthday? There is a cake candle out."

"Oh," Gail says slowly, walking over to snatch up the candle. "I found one for Kai, but it was too late. I meant to put it away a long while ago."

"For Kai . . . ?" Realization cuts off my question. I run a hand down my face, shaking my head at the ground. "Ava."

I'd forgotten. I'd forgotten despite knowing exactly how important her birthday is to him. I've never missed a morning under the willow. Until now, that is.

I swallow, feeling emotion begin to sting my eyes. The urge to pour my thoughts onto a page is suddenly overwhelming. I blink at the kitchen, wishing I had never left the comfort of my study—my dungeon. As I back away from Gail, the doors swing open, spilling servants into the room. I don't hesitate before pushing my way through the chaos, watching bodies leap away from my frantic form.

Let them think I'm mad. Maybe I am. Maybe it's better that way.

I hear a shout that resembles my name.

I don't look back.

CHAPTER 38
Paedyn

"Look, there's another one. Wedged between those stones."

I point to our left, turning slightly in the saddle to see Kai's gaze following the length of my arm. He nods after finally catching sight of it. "So get us there, Gray."

I had a feeling he would say that after spending the entirety of the day teaching me how to steer this beast. The reins are slick in my palms, forcing me to tighten my grip as I pull the leather to the left. I smother my smug smile when the horse obeys. We walk over to the nestle of rocks where I pull on the reins, halting the clopping hooves.

"Good work." Kai pats my thigh firmly before jumping down from the saddle. "I'm a great teacher."

"Or," I say, softly stroking the horse's mane, "I'm just a fast learner."

"Yeah, a fast learner that steered us into at least a dozen boulders."

"Just get the damn arrow," I order before he has the chance to continue.

His shoulders strain as he struggles against the caught arrowhead. When he finally manages to free it, he straightens out the crooked tip before adding it to the others sticking out of the pack he now wears.

"That's five," I say, feeling the saddle shift when he steps into the stirrup. "At this rate, there has to be a discarded bow out here."

"I wouldn't be surprised," he says, placing his palms back onto their usual spot on my thighs. "With all the bandits passing through, there are likely weapons scattered all over this place."

I run my gaze over the wall of rocks on either side of us, creating an uneven tunnel. "And these bandits have yet to make an appearance."

"And let's pray they don't."

I stuff the reins in his hands, suddenly too curious to steer. "I didn't peg you as the type to pray, Prince."

I feel his shoulders shrug against my back. "I didn't used to believe in a God."

"And now?"

There is a long pause followed by a softening of his voice. "I found proof of a paradise."

I glance over my shoulder to find his eyes already on me. "And what was that?"

His gaze glides over my face and down the length of my braid. "You'll know when you see it."

Plagues. Pretty boy. Pretty words.

When his eyes trail back to mine, I turn away to look at anything other than him. His hands are resting on my thighs while his chest is brushing my back with each breath, and the feel of it is drowning out every rational thought.

I wish I could douse myself in cold water and shiver until I shake off this feeling. This feeling of falling for something I know I should be fighting.

I take a deep breath, forcing myself to focus on the wall of stones sliding past. We ride in silence—the type that's far louder than uttering a word. The day crawls by, dragging the sun across the sky until it starts to sink.

My eyes skim over the stones, studying the shapes to pass the time. I squint against the sun, catching something glinting from where it's wedged between two looming rocks. "Do you see that?" I ask, finally breaking the silence.

"See what?" he sighs against my hair.

"Whatever that is that's shining up there." When he doesn't respond, I reach behind to grab his jaw, stubble biting into my fingers as I turn his face in the right direction.

"Thanks for the help." I feel his mumble against my hand. "It's pretty high up. Which one of us is going to climb up there and—"

I'm already swinging my leg over the saddle. "Thanks to you, both of us have to go, *darling*." I draw out his favorite word, making him chuckle as I rattle the chain between us. "You and your fear of heights have to come along."

I hear the smile in his voice as he drops down beside me, swiftly tying the horse to a jutting branch. "Yes, I can imagine that you and your fear of horses are terribly sad to be getting a break from the *beast*."

"If only I could get a break from you," I say sweetly over my shoulder. The towering rocks loom overhead, swallowing us in shadow. There are more trees scattered around in this cluster of stones than I've seen since setting off into the Sanctuary.

"This way," I say, staring up at the shining something. The trunk of a massive tree weaves up from between the stones, creating a sturdy foothold. My fingers curl around the rough bark of a branch beside my head, and with sore muscles straining, I slowly start the climb upward. Kai trails close behind, following the path of foot- and handholds I found.

I'm nearly level with the top of the stone beside me, stretching to see over it.

The tip of a bow juts between the rocks, its bronze cap blinding in the sun.

My face splits into a grin.

"Can you reach it yet?" Kai calls from beneath me.

"Yeah," I breathe. "I got it." As I lean against the rock, my fingers brush the length of the bow before I'm straining to free it. When the weapon leaps from the rock, I nearly fall from the tree I'm clinging to. "Found our bow," I pant.

"Too bad you won't be allowed to use it."

I sling the bow across my back. "Why? Your ego can't handle that I'm a better shot?"

"It's not my ego I'm worried about you wounding," he says smoothly. "It's the rest of me."

"Deadweight, remember?"

I'm about to start climbing down the stone when my gaze snags on what glints behind it.

I still, sweaty hands slipping and heart racing.

I don't hesitate before stretching a foot onto the stone and slowly convincing the rest of my limbs to follow. Kai sighs, not budging below me. "Care to explain why you're climbing over the rock if you already got the bow?"

"Because," I pant, "you'll never believe what is hiding back here." I'm on top of the boulder now and making my way down the back side. The chain tightens between us, stalling my progress. "Come on, Azer. At least try to keep up with me."

"It's not as though I have a choice, Gray."

The chain loosens as he begins to climb, allowing me to ungracefully slide down the short back of the stone and onto the plush grass below.

I blink at the beauty I'm beholding.

It's like a hidden world; a piece of perfection.

A grove of drooping trees sprouts from a bed of soft grass, their branches tangling together as though they've been holding hands for decades. Large roots break through the earth to weave between the vibrant foliage encircling the most beautiful thing of all.

A sparkling pool shimmers in the center of the scene, rippling each time a soft breeze blows through. Plants crowd the water to soak their leaves and bathe in the sinking sun.

This place is peace itself.

Kai is suddenly beside me, marveling at the masterpiece before us. "It's no wonder the bandits claimed this place."

"It's breathtaking." I sit beside the edge of the pool, dipping a finger into the cool water. "And so . . . out of place."

He joins me, examining the plants at our feet. "I'm sure this was here long before the Sanctuary of Souls became the burial road it is today."

I look over at him before my eyes trail back to the beauty beyond. "It seems the 'Sanctuary of Souls' had a very different meaning back then. Back when the first queen was buried here. It wasn't menacing—it was sacred. A place where the souls celebrated."

I can feel his eyes on me. "And what is it that souls celebrate?"

I shrug a shoulder, still not meeting his searing stare. "That someone cared enough to bury them."

My words hang in the air between us. My mind wanders to the Whispers where Kai buried Sadie during the first Trial. Not because he wanted to, but because he knew that I did.

His hand brushes mine.

He's placed his palm on the grass beside mine. I feel his fingers inching closer before they graze the tips of mine.

I don't dare look in his direction. My gaze is fixed on the glittering water as I occupy myself by counting each ripple.

On ripple three, he slides his pinkie beneath mine.

By seven, most of our fingers are woven together, tangled in the lush grass.

It's silly, really.

No, actually, it's bullshit.

It's complete and utter bullshit that he's able to make me melt with nothing more than a mere touch.

His hand should not have so much control over me. Tracing fingers should not be tugging on my heartstrings. But gentleness will be my undoing. There is an intimacy in being reached for.

His thumb strokes mine.

The feeling is comfort incarnate, tangible tranquility.

And that's why I pull away before I can change my mind.

"I'm getting in," I say, standing abruptly while rambling thoroughly. "Which means you also have to get in. Because you've made sure I can't do anything without you. So, *we* are getting in."

I pull the bow from my shoulders and toss it onto the ground. He's staring up at me, still not bothering to stand to his feet. "Is this all a plot to try to drown me?"

I look down with a smile, my vest already off one shoulder. "Now there's an idea."

He chuckles, head shaking as he slowly stands to his feet. When the pack is off his shoulders, he stares at me expectantly. "What?" I ask, unsure why I sound so defensive.

He gives me a lazy shrug. "I'm just waiting for you to tell me to turn around."

I blink at him. Then at the hem of my shirt still clutched in my hands.

I straighten slightly, staring him down. I'm not sure why I say it. Why I feel the need to prove something to him. But when I open my mouth, the words fall out. "What makes you think I was going to have you turn around?"

He crosses his arms over his chest. "Probably every moment we've spent together prior to this one."

Lifting my giant shirt up, I keep my eyes on his. "I'm full of surprises, Prince."

I pull the loose fabric over my head, leaving me standing there in a plunging, cut tank that cinches just below my breasts. It's the type of breathable bra I would wear while training, and the easiest to find and steal on Loot. I glance down quickly, making sure my brand isn't visible. It's bad enough that the scar trailing down my neck is always available for wandering eyes.

Pants hang low on my hips, exposing every inch of abdomen to him. When his eyes skim over me, I shiver despite the setting sun streaming through the trees. There's something about the way he's looking at me that makes it difficult to not want him to. His gaze is reverent, slow like an earnest prayer.

I swallow when his eyes find mine again. Take a breath when he swiftly pulls his shirt over his head. The cloth I wrapped around his stomach is splotched with blood, and he doesn't bother looking down as he begins unraveling it.

"Good to wash it out," I breathe, because I can't think of a single thing to say.

He nods, tossing the fabric to the ground. I hope he didn't hear me swallow at the sight of his body. I've seen him countless times without a shirt, and yet, I'm still struggling not to stare. His skin is tanned, every muscle defined. My eyes trace the crest of Ilya tattooed on his chest, the dark lines tangling atop his skin.

Plagues, I need to cool off.

My face burns, so I turn it in the direction of the pool. "You first."

He takes a step closer to me and not the water. "No, you go ahead, darling. You're looking a little flushed."

"You know," I say, "drowning you sounds more tempting by the minute."

His chuckle follows me to the edge of the pool where I pull off my boots and socks before dangling my feet above the crisp water. I suck in a breath when my toes touch the surface. The water is frigidly refreshing, and I quickly dunk the rest of my feet in.

The outer ring of the pool is shallow, the water blue and inviting. But the center grows darker and deeper, and I don't plan on exploring how much so. I hold my breath as I slowly sink into the pool, biting my tongue when the water laps around my hips.

I give myself several seconds to adjust to the temperature before tugging at the chain with my foot. "Come on. It's warm like your fancy palace bath water."

"Yeah?" His laugh is scoffing. "Is that why your lips are turning blue?"

My fingers fly to my mouth and the chattering teeth trapped inside. "They are not." I drop my hand to splash water at him. "Now, get in here so I can drown you already."

"How inviting," he mocks, stepping into the pool. "Shit." He hisses between clenched teeth when the cold water reaches his thighs.

"What's wrong, Azer?" I ask innocently. "You look a little cold."

"Oh, and you aren't?"

I circle a finger across the top of the water, creating ringlets. "Not a bit."

"Hmm." The look in his eyes has me worried. "Well, that just won't do."

And then he's wading toward the center of the pool.

It's not long before the chain tightens between us, and I'm being tugged behind him. I swallow my gasp when water splashes around my waist, inching higher with each drag of my feet. A laugh slips between my chattering teeth at the sight of goose bumps climbing up his muscled back.

I dig my heels into the slippery floor when water meets my collarbones. "Kai." Water laps around my shoulders. "Fine, Kai, I'm cold. We can stop now—"

My chin dips into the water and panic pulses through me. I'm splashing my arms, kicking the feet that barely touch the bottom now. Through blurry vision, I see Kai turn and rush toward me, splashing water with each step.

Strong arms circle my waist, lifting my head high above the water. "You're okay. I've got you." Concern crinkles his eyes as he looks me over. "I forgot how much shorter you are. Didn't realize the water had gotten so deep."

I cough, blinking water out of my eyes. "Still can't swim yet, asshole."

He shakes his head at me, breathing heavy. Water is rolling down his face, dripping from his eyelashes. He lifts a hand from my back to tuck a soggy strand of hair behind my ear. "Hell, with all that talk of drowning me, I figured you'd be a little more confident in the water."

I smile weakly. "I'm confident enough to hold your head under."

He chuckles, flashing a dimple at me. His fingers play with the end of my braid before tugging at it. "So, I've taught you to dance and ride now. Should I add swimming to that list?"

"Not if you're going to gloat about it," I mumble.

"I'm not gloating. Yet." He traces a finger down my wet braid. "Simply stating that I'm not sure what you would do without me."

"I would be free without you." I smile sadly. "I would be doing whatever the hell I want."

"Like fighting in cage matches and living in a crumbling building?"

"Beats rotting in a cell," I shoot back, my eyes on his.

His fingers find my chin, wiping away the water dripping from my lips. "I won't let that happen."

"Yeah," I laugh humorlessly. "Make sure to kill me quickly, please. I'd rather just get it over with."

He shakes his head, eyes on my scar. I flinch when his fingers brush the jagged line and turn away to hide it from him. "Gray . . ."

"Azer," I cut in firmly. "Don't pretend to forget who we are to each other. What we are to Ilya." I jab a finger into his bare chest. "Elite. Ordinary. Enforcer. Criminal." I shake my head, staring blankly at the branches swaying around us. "We are enemies with history. Enemies who hate each other."

I don't bother to look at him, but I know he's shaking his head. "You don't hate me."

"Oh, I have every reason to."

"But that doesn't mean you do."

I huff and push my palms against his chest. "Put me down."

He holds me tighter. "You know what I think?"

"No, actually, I don't give a damn what you—"

"I think you hate that you can't hate me."

My face is inches from his. "Oh, I can hate you just fine."

"Then hate that you feel something for me." His hand skims my thigh while the other presses me firmly against him. "Hate me for making you want this."

A raindrop pelts my cheek. I swallow, searching for words before settling on a shake of my head. I push weakly against his chest, blinking at the beads of water trailing down tan skin.

"Just pretend," he murmurs. "We deserve to pretend."

There's that word again—the one that justifies the feelings I'm fighting.

He's lifting my leg, guiding it until it's wrapped around his hip. Another raindrop finds my nose when my gaze lifts to meet his, our faces close. My heart pounds in my chest, raging a war with my screaming mind.

I shouldn't do this. He is a slippery slope that I am on the verge of tumbling down, a temptation I know better than to taste. Again.

But this is pretend.

This is a secret for the souls.

And that's what I tell myself as I wrap my other leg around his hip, his hands tightening across my back. Holding me against him, he takes a few slow steps back until the water laps around our collarbones. And I let him. Because I trust him more than I care to admit.

Rain begins sprinkling from the sky, creating a pattern of ripples around us.

"This is just pretend?" I whisper, melting into his hold.

"This is just us." A hand slides up my back and over my hair. "No titles. No obligations. No history."

I nod slowly as I place my hands on either side of his neck. Rain splatters onto our faces, falling harder with each second spent staring at each other.

"You going to kiss me, Gray, or just continue admiring what you see?" he murmurs, now running a thumb over my bottom lip.

"Still contemplating drowning you, actually." My voice is breathy, my own fingers wandering over the curve of his jaw.

"Oh, darling, I already am." His lips inch closer to mine, teasing me. "And I'm begging you to let me breathe you in."

I smile slyly. "I thought you never begged?"

"I'm getting used to it when it comes to you."

And then his hand slips behind my neck to pull my lips toward his.

His mouth is on mine, distracting from every echo of warning bouncing around my skull. He tastes like a mistake, and yet, I memorize the feel of his lips against mine. Some part of me knows I shouldn't be doing this, but I can't seem to remember a single reason why.

This kiss feels different.

This kiss feels like making up for lost time. Like every moment our bodies pressed together while our lips kept their distance. Every moment tension twined around us, yet we broke away.

Kissing him on the rooftop was intended to hurt him, to show him the extent of my loathing. Hatred coated the lips that met his, and anger enticed me to do it.

Our kiss in the sewer was initiated by impending death, spurred by panic. It was rushed and impulsive—everything that this moment is not.

This tastes like longing. It is passion parting my lips, desire deepening the kiss.

He takes his time doing exactly what he begged to do—breathe me in. A hand runs down my neck while the other explores the curve of my bare waist. He slows the kiss when my fingers curl into his hair before running over the length of his shoulders, feeling scars flecking his skin.

There is a certain reverence in his kiss, a gentleness in the way he holds my face. I've never felt such delicate passion.

Rain is pelting us now, soaking my hair and dripping from my nose. He kisses me harder despite it all, as though remembering how he hadn't the first time we were caught in the rain, outside the palace. I wrap my legs tighter around him, pulling him close enough to feel his heart hammering against his chest.

I sigh against his mouth when his tongue meets mine. That has him greedily tugging me hard against him with a calloused hand. The kiss grows impatient and demanding and desperate in the way that desire typically is.

His teeth pull at my bottom lip. Not with anger or loathing like I had atop that roof, but with wanting. The action sets my body ablaze, spreading fire through every vein. My mouth moves in time with his, matching every swipe of his tongue, every move of his lips.

His fingers are in my sopping hair, running down my neck—

Thunder claps above us.

Perhaps it intended to cheer us on, but instead, it tears us apart.

I'm breathing heavy, blinking in the streaming rain at him doing the same.

I squint up at the sky crowded with ominous clouds, occasionally broken by a strike of lightning. Loosening my legs from his hips, I clear my throat and force myself to find his eyes. He studies me for a long moment, lifting a hand to wipe a droplet of water from the tip of my nose. "You're shaking," he says, barely loud enough for me to hear over the storm.

I swallow. "I'm cold." His lips twitch at that. My fingers trace the swirling Ilya symbol tattooed on his chest. "Your heart is pounding."

"That tends to happen when you touch me, yes."

My eyes flick up to find a dimple peeking out at me. The twitch of his lips tempts me to press my own against them, but I manage to restrain as reality sets in.

Pretend. Distraction. Weakness.

All words to describe what shouldn't have just happened.

He gently grabs my wrist to guide it behind his neck, doing the same with the other. "What are you doing?" I ask hesitantly.

He steps deeper into the water, turning us in a slow circle. "You tell me, Little Psychic." I roll my eyes at him while he flashes a smile.

His next words mirror the ones whispered after placing me atop his feet to dance beside the firelight. "Let me swim for the both of us."

CHAPTER 39
Paedyn

I'm soaked to the bone by the time Kai lifts me onto the edge of the pool.

The rain is falling harder now, stinging my eyes and slapping my skin. Kai pulls himself onto the grass beside me, his hair a damp mess over his forehead. He sprawls out on his back, shutting his eyes against the persistent rain.

When I move to stand, he wraps an arm around my waist to pull me down beside him. I gasp before laughing as I roll my head toward him in the wet grass. Peace pulls at his features, softens his lips into a slight smile.

He looks like relief.

I doubt he's ever felt so free. There isn't a soul besides mine and those surrounding us who knows where he is. And there is a certain comfort in being willingly lost, hidden from life itself.

We lie there for a long while, basking in nature's shower. At some point, his hand finds mine. He loosely interlocks our fingers, an action that is somehow more intimate than our time spent in the

pool, as though he's content to silently exist beside me.

A bright crack of lightning has me sitting up, eyes flying open. I look behind us to the soaking pack sitting in the damp grass and quickly stand to my feet.

Kai attempts to reach for me again, but I jump away with a laugh. "Come on, that's enough laying around." I scoop my pack off the ground, watching it drip like the rest of me. "We need to dry off, and so does everything else."

He sits up, blinking in the rain. "Yeah, you're shaking the chain with each shiver."

At the mention of it, I shiver again. I turn, picking up the bow before backing into the strong body suddenly standing behind me. "I'll take that," he says against my ear. "My life has been threatened enough for today."

I begrudgingly let him pull the weapon from my hands as I pour the water out of my boots, just to slip them back onto wet feet. Throwing my soaked shirt over my shoulder, I walk toward the wall of stone and trees separating us from the road beyond.

Climbing the slippery slope is a humbling endeavor. It takes several tries to pull myself over the top of the stone before I can attempt to reach the tree beside it. Kai follows behind as I slowly make my way to the ground, sighing in relief when my feet sink into the damp dirt.

I squint through the steady stream of rain. "Where's the horse?"

Kai steps beside me, bow slung across his back. "The thunder must have spooked him. He's probably long gone by now."

I sigh. "I was just getting the hang of riding."

"Oh, is that what you call it?" Kai asks, lips pulled into a smirk.

I put a hand to his cheek, pushing it as I walk by. The action feels comfortable in a way I wish it wouldn't. So I keep my hands to myself as we walk down the flooded road, searching for shelter to wait out the storm.

We don't make it far before a cluster of rocks catch my eye. A large, flat stone stretches across the ones beneath it, creating a makeshift canopy high enough for us to sit comfortably under. "This way!" I shout over the storm, turning us toward shelter.

When we duck under the rock, I sling the pack from my shoulders, breathing heavy. I'm about to plop down on the patch of dry ground when Kai says, "I need to go get firewood."

Both our heads drop to the chain tethering us together. "All right." He sighs, "We need to go get firewood."

Forcing myself back into the rain is an effort of will. I drag my feet while Kai collects wood for our fire, breaking branches from trees and piling them into my arms.

My teeth are chattering by the time we make it back to our camp. "This wood won't be easy to light," Kai murmurs, arranging the wet branches for the fire we are about to attempt.

"We have two matches left," I say, digging around in my soaked pack. My fingers find the metal box and pull it out, relieved to find the matches still dry.

"This wood won't light on its own," Kai says, looking up at me. "We need something to help start it. Do we have any paper?"

I'm about to shake my head when my eyes snag on the journal tucked between damp bedrolls. I swallow, slowly reaching a hand toward it. I can feel Kai's eyes on me as I pull the leather book out and flip through the pages, finding them surprisingly dry.

"Here's some paper," I say quietly.

"No." Kai's voice is firm. "No, we aren't using that."

"It's fine." I nod, trying to convince myself. "I'm sure most of this is just research and notes. And I'd rather not freeze tonight so . . . it's fine." His eyes narrow, expression skeptical. "I'm fine."

That seems to persuade him enough to nod slightly. I turn back to the book in hand, taking a breath before skimming the first few pages. His familiar handwriting makes me smile, makes me struggle to swallow. I squint in the dim light, urging my eyes to adjust to the growing darkness.

The first page tears easily. It talked of recipes for various remedies Elites can use when they are unable to get to a Healer. The second page was more of the same, consisting of measurements and herbs for common illnesses. The third page was filled with ink, swirling with scribbled notes describing a difficult patient.

Every piece of parchment burns easier than it tears. I hand each shred of my father to him, watching his life's work go up in flames. It takes several pages to light the wood, and nothing but a weak flame to show for it. Kai tends to the fire, forcing it to grow despite the difficulty.

I wring out our shirts, laying them near the fire beside every other damp belonging. Then I lean against the stone to read over the remaining pages crinkled between the journal's leather covers. I thumb through it, stopping to read entries about the many people he helped heal in the slums.

My fingers fumble on a thick piece of parchment near the back and my curiosity has me flipping to what lies behind it. A journal entry stares back at me, slanted letters staining the page. But this one is different from the rest. This one is personal and dated, deep thoughts spilled onto parchment.

I sit up slightly, my spine stiffening in shock.

The action doesn't go unnoticed. "What?" Kai asks, fire forgotten.

"My father . . ." I shake my head at the page. "He kept a journal."

Silence. "Yes, I gathered that."

"No, I mean, he *kept* a journal." I look up, eyes wide. "His own thoughts and feelings. A log of his life."

"A diary," Kai says quietly.

I nod, looking down at the book in my lap. "The first entry is dated more than ten years before my birth," I say. The words are smudged and rushed, as though he thought it was wasted time to write of his own life. I look up to find Kai's gaze pinned on me. His nod of encouragement has me clearing my throat and reading the scribbled script.

"I suppose I'll just write about this, since it's treason to speak it to anyone else. The king offered me a job again. Well, more like threatened me with it. I was summoned to the palace to help his Healers during fever season, but I know his true intentions. He wants me out of the slums and into the upper city with the rest of the Healers. He doesn't want anyone tending to the poor or less powerful, for that matter. I wouldn't be surprised if he began another Purging, this time for the Mundanes. He thinks them to be weak like the Ordinaries, treating the slums like the scum beneath the shiny shoe that is his Elite kingdom.

"There is a reason no other Healer can be found anywhere near the slums. Greed is a plague that Ilya has yet to eradicate. But when the king offers each Healer more money than they could ever spend in their lifetime, they happily agree to whatever strings are attached. The conditions are simple enough—only care for the upper class and promote the idea that Ordinaries are weakening our powers through prolonged proximity due to the undetectable disease they carry.

"He is paying them off. What an expensive lie. Because no one will question what the Healers say they detect. For decades,

the king has been buying the support of the only people who know this disease to be a lie. And it has worked beautifully. It's not as though Healers care for Ordinaries. They may know that the 'undetectable disease' is a farce, but they also know that Ordinaries and Elites reproducing will dwindle our power and eventually cause our kind to go extinct. That alone is enough for their greed to promote the king's lie and ensure that Elites never allow Ordinaries back in Ilya.

"It's bullshit, but brilliant.

"And I'm the problem. The exception with a target on my back. The king is persuasive—I'll give him that. His bribes are very tempting to a resident of the slums, but I can't abandon the lower class, not when no one else will help with the sickness that spreads through the streets like wildfire.

"So the slums are where I will stay. The king will not buy my support."

I blink at the familiar writing, hearing his voice with each word I read. My eyes skim over the page again. And again. And—

"Did you hear that?" I blurt, looking up at Kai.

He's crouching in front of the fire, hands draped over his knees. He stares blankly at the flickering flame, nodding slightly. "I heard it."

"Do you know what this means?" A crazed smile tugs at my lips. "This is proof, Kai. This is proof that there is no disease detected by the Healers. And the king—"

"The king has been bribing them to lie about it," he finishes quietly. His gaze hasn't strayed from the dim fire. "That is, if any of this is even true."

"My father was no liar," I snap, harsher than intended. I blow out a breath before calmly continuing. "Don't you see? It all adds up.

Your father had all the Healers under his control, somewhere he could watch them closely. And he wanted the slums to suffer because even some Elites are too weak for his liking."

I hear him take a shaky breath. "No. No, that can't be right." He drags his fingers through damp hair. "I can't let that be right because I've justified everything. Everything I've done as the Enforcer. It was all to protect the Elites and Ilya from this *disease*, but if Ordinaries aren't weakening our powers . . ."

He trails off, running a hand over his face. I reach a hesitant hand toward him, unsure what to say. "Kai . . ."

"That would mean that he's been killing Ordinaries to prevent them from reproducing with Elites. He's been killing healthy, innocent people." He finally looks over at me, gray eyes icy. "*I've* been killing healthy, innocent people."

"You didn't know," I murmur. "How could you have? The king had every Healer spewing his lie."

I turn away, shocked at the sincerity seeping into my words. I never thought I would sympathize with the crimes he's committed against Ordinaries like me, but his head is in his hands, his hurt hidden behind the crumbling mask he wears.

Remorse is written all over his face. Anger is sketched into the stiffening of his shoulders, the storm raging in his eyes.

He's spent his whole life living a lie that helped him live with himself.

He shakes his head, his shadow doing the same on the wall behind him. "It can't be true." He won't look at me. "Are there any more entries? Anything else about this?"

I flip the page, finding more words sprawled there. "This one's dated a few weeks later. Here, look at this." I scoot closer to the fire, flooding the page with light and making it easier for us to read.

I had an idea while I was working in the palace today. A terrible, treasonous idea that shouldn't be written down. But I know there are Ordinaries hiding in Ilya who need help surviving. Probably Fatals too. And maybe it's naive to hope that there are Elites out there who believe killing Ordinaries to be wrong.

I want to find those few. I want to build a community, something the king can't ignore. I want to fight with the Ordinaries—for the Ordinaries and those alike.

I don't know how yet, but I'm going to try.

I stare at the smudged page. "He's talking about the Resistance." I smile slightly. "No wonder he hid this journal beneath a floorboard. It's incriminating."

Kai nods as I flip the page so we can read the entry that follows.

I've been searching the abandoned buildings in the slums and have found a couple of Ordinaries willing to trust me. I invited them into my home and told them of my plans to fight for their right to live in Ilya.

There are more of us now—at least a dozen. Our little Resistance is growing. I've started training Ordinaries to "adopt" an ability, help them join society instead of hiding in abandoned buildings. Most take on the Hyper ability since it's the easiest lie.

I'm still being summoned to the castle for fever season. The king's bribes are tempting, but I play my part as a Healer and return to the slums.

Every time.

I eagerly flip the page, finding a different topic scribbled there.

I met an Ordinary girl. Well, a woman. She caught the fever while living in the slums, which usually means death. But I happened to find her in time. She's beautiful—a complete distraction as I worked. Something about her soul seemed to call to mine. I'm determined to marry her.

I finally did it. I married her.

I'm going to be a father. Alice has been throwing up all morning with a smile on her face. She's convinced it's a girl.

Tears threaten to fall as I read of the mother I never met. Through blurry vision, a date catches my eye, forcing my frantic fingers to a stop. "This one's from three weeks before I was born," I say quietly, looking up to find Kai staring intently.

She lost too much blood. I couldn't stop it. I'm a damn Healer and I couldn't even save her. I buried her in the backyard with our baby. She was right. It was a girl.

My heart stops. Time slows.

"I buried her in the backyard with our baby."

I shake my head, ignoring the hand Kai places on my knee. "I . . . I don't understand. Father said she died of illness when I was a baby but . . ."

I trail off, tearing through the pages until I find the next entry.

I wasn't planning on writing in here after Alice. I wasn't even planning on having an "after Alice," but I woke to a bang on my door last night. Yet when I opened the door, no one was there. That is, until I looked down.

And there she was. A baby girl.

Someone left her on my doorstep. She can't be more than a few weeks old with a head full of silver hair and deep blue eyes. She's beautiful. Alice would tear up at the sight of her.

I'm going to be a father. This is what Alice would have wanted. She already had a name picked out anyway.

A tear splatters onto the parchment, drowning the ink.

I think Kai might be saying something, but I can hear nothing past the ringing in my ears. My head is spinning, heart pounding, breath catching in my throat because I can't seem to swallow it. I can't breathe. I can't—

"Hey." Kai's rough hands on my face rip me from my thoughts. "Hey, look at me. You're all right."

I reach around his arms to viciously wipe at the tears leaking from my eyes. "No, I'm not all right!" I finally suck in a breath, blinking back the flood of emotion behind my eyes. "This can't be right. I won't believe it," I sputter, repeating Kai's own words. "This means . . . I was an orphan before I even lost my father." A hysterical sob slips past my lips. "And that would make my whole life a lie."

Kai shakes his head, expression stern. "No. Your life isn't a lie, you hear me?" He lifts my face up, forcing me to look at him. "Just because you don't share the same blood, it doesn't mean he wasn't your father. He raised you as his own. He chose to love you."

Everything he's saying makes sense—and I hate it.

I want to rage, want to scream, want to sit here and feel sorry for myself. Because a part of me feels betrayed, feels deceived by the man I called Father.

I silently flip to the next entry as Kai's hands slowly slip from my face. I can feel his eyes on me, waiting for me to break.

But I'm tired of breaking. Tired of having to lug around pieces of myself that I'm too tired to fit back together.

I sniffle, returning my eyes to the page and continue reading numbly.

Without Alice, my only purpose now is the Resistance. It's all that keeps me going. That, and Paedyn.

Tears splatter onto the page once more at the sight of my name. The pad of Kai's thumb swipes across my cheek, stealing the tear from my skin. "Talk to me," he murmurs, leaning close enough that I can't ignore him.

I shake my head, struggling to swallow the emotion clogged in my throat. "The truth, then?"

He nods. "The truth, always."

I take a shaky breath, fighting tears between each one that follows. "I've spent my whole life accepting the fact that I would never truly be able to live it. I'm an Ordinary, and that's fine—I'm living with it. I've come to terms with what I am not, and I'll deal with it until the day I die. But—"

He takes my shaking hand into his own, urging me on with a single steady look. "But I've paid my dues, haven't I?" The words are a gasp, as though they were ripped from my throat. "Have I not suffered enough? I am already nothing, but now I belong to no one. The one thing in my life that was right and real and mine alone has been ripped away from me." I take a shuddering breath, blinking blankly into the fire. "Just like everything else."

He's shaking his head at me, reaching up a hand to push stray hair out of my face. "You cannot be nothing when you are everything to someone else." My eyes climb up to his, finding them avoiding mine. It takes several heartbeats for him to open his mouth, spilling words that sound unsure. "And that is what you were to your father. Whether or not he was your flesh and blood. He loved you more than most."

His words hit me hard—a reminder of how anything is better than what he endured by a man who truly was his father. I quiet, attempting to calm my breathing. Then I'm flipping the page, ignoring the unshed tears welling in my eyes. I force my eyes to focus, to continue reading. His words are my distraction, his handwriting a comfort.

I met a Fatal today in the streets. He pulled me into an alley and whispered that he wanted to help with my idea—which he only knew about because he happened to be a Mind Reader.

We talked for hours about the struggles he's endured and how he wants to see Ordinaries and Fatals free once again. But we first need to find those who are hiding in plain sight.

"Calum," I whisper, knowing exactly who this Mind Reader is. The next page is a hurried collection of several days.

Calum has found us three more Ordinaries already. He scours the streets, reading thoughts until he finds a mind that screams their secret. His method is much quicker than mine. We all met tonight to discuss our plans.

Several of our Ordinaries haven't been to a meeting in weeks. I'm beginning to worry that something has happened. Likely an Imperial's doing.

We've cleared out the cellar beneath the house to use for meetings. There are too many of us now to go unnoticed. I fashioned a bookshelf over the cellar door, concealing the entrance in case we get unexpected visitors.

I thumb through the pages, skimming over years of growing the Resistance.

I've appointed leaders to different sectors of the slums. We can no longer all meet at my house. Now, just us leaders hold meetings to discuss how the Resistance is doing. We have plans to confront the king and his lies, but we are much too weak to attempt that now. Maybe in the next few years.

"Gray."

He says my name softly, attempting to wake me from my stupor. Ignoring the concern crinkling his brow, I furiously flip through the remaining pages. Blank parchment stares back at me until my fingers still on a longer log.

I forgot about this journal. Apparently, it's been six years since I last wrote in here. There's not much to say other than how big Paedyn is getting.

It's clear now why she was left on my doorstep. She's Ordinary. Her parents didn't want to deal with hiding a child. And, damn, are they missing out on her.

She's got this fire about her. This quickness. I've been training her differently, more extremely. I never want her to feel anything but strong. And when I noticed how observant she was as a young child, I figured it was best to stick to her strengths. So I'm sharpening that little mind of hers into a weapon to protect herself with. As a "Psychic," she can do more than pass as an Elite, more than survive. She can live.

I told her about Alice. Except the truth of how she died. Pae thinks it's illness that took her away from us shortly after she was born. I've lost sleep trying to decide if I should ever tell Paedyn the truth. But I am the only father she's had, and even in death, Alice is her mother.

Ink smudges down the page, smearing as though he shut the book in a hurry. I ignore the look of growing concern painting Kai's face as we continue to read the next page dated several years later.

I haven't told her about the Resistance. I will. Eventually. It has gotten more difficult to hide it from her as she's gotten older. I don't know why I haven't told her. Maybe I don't want to get her involved. Maybe she's still just my little girl despite how strong she's become. Even though she doesn't need it, I want to protect her for as long as I can. And being a part of the Resistance is dangerous. The king knows of us now, his Imperials ordered to be on the lookout.

Maybe it's best she doesn't know until the Resistance is ready to make a move. Maybe it's best she stays my little girl for as long as possible.

I flip the page, my vision blurry.

Nothing.

My fingers fumble with the corners, tearing through each piece of parchment only to find them empty.

When my thumb meets the back cover, I stare at the leather binding representing the end of his life. The closing of a chapter. "That's it," I whisper. "That's the last entry he wrote."

I'm tired. Too damn tired to find the energy to feel anything more. So I slump against the stone, shoving the journal back into my pack.

Kai watches, running his eyes over me. He looks hesitant to interrupt my lack of thoughts. "Are you okay?"

I rub my hands over my eyes, feeling tears tickle my fingers. Then I settle my blank stare on him. "I always find a way to be."

CHAPTER 40

Rai

It's unnatural for her to be so quiet.

She hasn't spoken since she shoved the journal into her pack and curled up against a stone for the night. I doubt either of us got much sleep after tossing and turning on damp bedrolls until dawn dappled the ground, sneaking beneath our stone fort to wake us.

I look over at her, hair slipping from its braid to fall around a tired face. Her eyes are shut against the light pouring over her, hands curled beneath her cheek.

"I know you're awake."

I whisper the words, aware that she's paying close enough attention to me to hear them. And still, she doesn't stir. I sigh, shifting closer to her until we are sharing the same air. "Don't be stubborn, Gray. I know you're listening." I lift a hand to tuck a silver strand behind her ear before running my fingers down the length of her neck. "I've gotten rather good at reading your body language."

That has her eyes flying open to grace me with a glare

"Then you should know that I was ignoring you," she mumbles against her hands.

"As you normally do."

I watch her struggle to fight a smile, and the sight of it has me doing the same. "I just . . ." She runs a hand over her face, suddenly serious. "I just have a lot on my mind. Barely slept."

I nod, understanding how she's feeling. We both discovered things last night that have our minds reeling, lives unraveling. Everything I've been taught to believe, everything Father told me to be true, is suddenly crumbling beneath the weight of scribbled words. All that I've done, all that I've justified . . .

Now I am nothing more than a monster without a cause.

"I know," I say quietly. "I was awake beside you." I feel her eyes on me as I take my time gathering our damp shirts.

"You had just as much to think about, I'm sure." She tilts her head, watching me closely. "I've always believed I wasn't diseased; I just had no way to prove it. But you . . . This is all very new to you."

"I blindly trusted the Healers," I murmur. "Trusted men who have known me since I was a child. But it seems the real problem was still trusting my father after everything." I almost laugh. "Then again, the journal could be wrong." She opens her mouth to argue, but I continue quietly. "Which is why I intend to find out what the real truth is. Interrogate every Healer if I have to." She's quiet for a long time, allowing me to sit with my thoughts. "And I'm going to tell Kitt."

The words slip past my lips before I can swallow them. She sits up slowly, watching me closely. "You're going to show him the journal?"

I nod. "He should know."

"Do you think it will make a difference?"

"I don't know anymore," I say softly, shaking my head at the ground. “I feel like I don’t know *him* anymore. He lived to please our father, and now that the king is gone before he feels he did . . .”

“He’s spiraling.”

“No, he’s fine,” I cut in sharply. “He’s going to be fine. He just needs to adjust, that’s all.” I look away, nodding to convince myself. “Kitt will come back to me.”

“Right,” she says quietly. I know she’s only agreeing to spare me from spiraling as well. Because the thought of Kitt as a crazed king keeps me up at night, keeps me hoping for my brother to return.

“We should get going.” I open her damp shirt and push it over her head.

She sputters, batting my hands away. “Thanks,” she mumbles, glaring as the shirt hangs limply around her neck.

“If you’d rather continue wearing that”—I nod to the skimpy tank cut low enough to be a distraction—“then, please, by all means.” I smile at the flush painting her cheeks.

“Don’t do that,” she huffs, pushing her arms through the sleeves and tugging the shirt down.

“Do what, darling?”

“That. The flirting.” Her eyes sweep over me accusingly. “The dimples.”

I laugh before I’m able to stop myself. “You know, I can’t really help that.”

“Help what?” She crosses her arms. “The flirting or the dimples?”

“Yes,” I say simply.

She shakes her head, hiding a smile while stuffing the bedrolls into her pack. “Well, no more. Of any of it.”

“Why?” I place a hand on the pack she’s fighting to throw over her shoulder. “Worried you’ve stopped hating me?”

“I could ask you the same thing.” She leans in, face close. “I’m no longer diseased. Ordinaries were *never* diseased, actually. So, you have no excuse to hate what I am anymore."

I blink at her. "I never said I hated what you are."

"Fine. Hated what I wasn't."

I open my mouth, her name ready to fall from the tip of my tongue. But I stop myself, honoring her wish to not use it again. "Gray. When I look at you, I see a strength that no Elite possesses—and it called to me long before I ever discovered what you were or were not."

Her eyes flick between mine, full of an emotion I can't decipher. "And yet, you're still dragging me back to Ilya."

"Duty," I murmur. "Not choice."

"Right." Her voice is stiff. She slings the pack over her shoulder and ducks out of the shelter. "So don't make this harder than it has to be."

I follow behind, pulling my shirt on before adding the bow across my chest. Puddles litter the damp ground, the morning sun reflecting off what the storm left behind. "I'm not the only one making this difficult."

Her scoff echoes off the stones. "We wouldn't even be in this position if you'd have let me disappear and start a new life."

"Duty, remember?"

She stomps in front of me, rattling the chain between us. "Doesn't mean you're not ruining my life, remember?"

"You did that yourself the moment you plunged a sword through the king's chest, remember?"

"He came at me, *remember*?" She spins to face me. "And this kingdom is far better off without him. Maybe you'll start believing that after all you've learned."

My palms are suddenly planted on either side of her face as I shake my head. "You are a pain in the ass, you know that?"

"Why, because I'm right?" she breathes.

"Because you're dangerous."

Her eyes never stray from mine. "I would have thought you'd gathered that the first time I kicked your ass."

"Oh, I did." My thumb brushes her cheek. "But it was when you kissed me that I truly feared what you'd done to me."

She shuts her eyes. "I told you to stop that."

"This is honesty, not flirting."

"Well, your right dimple is still showing, so—"

"Is that why your eyes are closed?" I laugh, ducking my face so it's level with hers.

"We should keep walking," she blurts, turning away from me. "You're on a tight schedule and my feet are already hurting—"

"Don't deflect, Gray," I call behind her.

"Do you think it will rain today? I'd rather not be drenched again. I'm still drying off from yesterday."

"We kissed." I see her back stiffen beneath the damp shirt sticking to her skin. "Three times now."

She turns, looking tired. "Why are you telling me this as if I'm not constantly avoiding thinking about it?"

"Because this is already more difficult than it should be," I say, taking a step toward her. "You're not just a mission to me. You're not just another enemy for me to find. You're something even more terrifying."

Her voice is little more than a whisper. "And what is that?"

"A need."

We stare at each other, both surprised by the words that pushed their way past my lips. Sunlight is streaming through her hair, making her glow like something far too heavenly for me.

"I thought you had found your courage," she says softly.

I smile slightly. "Maybe I'm fine with being a fool. So long as it's for you."

She shakes her head, backing away from me. Her mouth opens to argue, and—

A twig snaps faintly to my right.

Instinct has me angling toward her, shielding her body as I clamp a hand over her mouth.

I whip my head toward the sound, searching for any sign of who I fear may have found us.

It's only when piercing pain erupts in my shoulder that I know I was right.

Bandits.

CHAPTER 41

Paedyn

Kai grunts against my ear, pain ripping the sound from his throat. His hand slips from my mouth, unmuffling the sound of my scream.

"Kai!"

He slowly sinks to his knees, displaying the deep gash stretching across the length of his shoulder. I saw the flash of an arrow before it tore through his skin, splitting flesh in an instant. I drop down beside him, hands on his face and heart in my throat. "Are you okay?"

"Bandits," he strains, ignoring my question. "I won't be much help." Another arrow wizzes past my head.

"I can see that," I say, carefully pulling the bow from his back. He hisses through clamped teeth when I bump his wound. "We need to get out of the road. Now." I nod to a cluster of stones no more than a few yards away. "Can you make it there?"

"It's my arm, darling, not my leg," he grits out.

"Perfect." I stand to a crouch, pulling him up with me. "Then you should have no problem keeping up."

We run toward the rocks, hearing arrows whistle past us. Kai pushes himself between me and the persistent arrows, blocking my body with his own. That's why I gasp in surprise when the tip of an arrow manages to graze my calf.

It stings, sending searing pain shooting down my leg. I can feel the blood tickling my skin as we duck behind the rocks, stealing refuge from their size.

Ignoring my own wound, I turn to his far more worrying one. Blood stains his skin, engulfing the shoulder underneath. The sight has me suddenly swallowing my rage, seeing a shade of red that has nothing to do with the blood running down his skin.

He's hurt. And I hate it.

That realization might just anger me more.

Because it is then that I understand just how terribly I will hurt anyone who dares hurt him.

My eyes trail back up to his, my stomach churning at the sight of so much blood—the blood that someone so carelessly spilled. The thought has me slipping on a mask of my own, smothering everything but the icy anger cooling my features.

I ignore the feel of his eyes, focusing only on the task at hand. I arrange the arrows so their feathered shafts can be easily grabbed from the pack before I sling it onto my shoulders.

The bow is hot in my clenched fist. My eyes drift back to his, finding something akin to awe on his face. My voice is even, my face cold. "I'll be sure to make them pay."

I watch him take a heavy breath. "Can't stand to see me wounded?"

I take a step back, my eyes on his. "Only when it's my doing."

The last thing I hear as I step from behind the rocks is a fervent "Be careful. For me."

And then I'm pulling an arrow from my pack, settling it onto the bow, blowing out a breath, and firing at the first figure I see.

The man crumples when my arrow sinks into his chest. I quickly crouch back down, ignoring the fact that I'm aiming to kill. But I only have four more arrows, and I can't afford to waste a single one.

A cool sort of calm settles over me as I step out into the road. My movements are practiced, my mind still. It all happens so fast that I hardly register nocking another arrow.

I duck behind a set of boulders, feeling an arrow skim past my head. Knowing which direction the arrow came from, I stand and fire at the shoulder sticking out from behind a stone. The arrow hits close enough to the heart that he collapses quickly.

I stride back out into the road, hearing nothing but the gravel grinding beneath my boots. Instinct has me turning to fire at a shadow, finding a man with a bow trained on me. It crumples to the ground with the rest of him when my arrow meets his heart.

It's quiet. Too quiet.

I find cover behind another group of stones, scanning the surroundings until an arrow comes flying toward me. I duck before it can sink between my eyes. "Found you," I whisper, nocking my arrow.

When I stand, he fires another, narrowly missing my shoulder. I don't hesitate before letting an arrow fly toward the head that appears over the rocks. I watch the point tear through his neck, severing tendons and spraying blood.

I hear the thud of his body hitting the dirt.

It's that sound that wakes me from my stupor.

I shiver despite the icy anger melting away. The road I now stand in seems to spin beneath my feet. Ears ringing and heart racing, I squeeze my eyes shut, as if that could hide me from what I've done.

The bow grows slick in my sweaty palm. I drop it numbly to stare at my hands. I can almost feel the blood coating them. The blood of those I *killed.* When Father taught me to fight, I know this is not what he had in mind.

No, not my father. Not truly.

Even still, I'm a failure. More than a disappointment to him. I'm a disgrace. A mockery of everything he taught me to be.

I've taken lives. Multiple lives. Seven, to be exact. And I can hardly breathe under the weight of guilt crushing me.

"Hey."

I spin at the voice, raising my loaded bow into the face of another man.

Kai.

It's Kai. I'm okay. I don't have to hurt him.

His fingers are warm beneath my chin as he guides my face to his. I blink slowly, taking in his crinkled brow and icy eyes. "You're done, okay? You did it." He tucks a strand of hair behind my ear, more gently than I deserve. "I wish I could have done it for you. My soul is already stained enough for the both of us."

His voice sounds far away, separated by a flood of thoughts. I shake my head, swallowing hard. "I think you underestimate how much I've stained my soul as of late."

I could drown in the bodies now beginning to pile at my feet. I never wanted to be this. I am nothing, and yet, I've taken everything from others. Maybe this is how I've managed to evade Death for so long—by satisfying him with souls that aren't mine.

Kai's smile is soft, forcing my focus back to him. "The fact that you even care about your soul means you're still far better than most."

I stare at him for a long moment, letting his words sink in. Letting myself pretend that I believe them. It's only when he moves to lean against a stone that I remember he's wounded. The arrow gash is deep and long, dripping blood down his back.

"Shit, Kai, why are you talking about my soul when you're bleeding all over the place?" I shake my head, moving to crouch behind him.

"I like talking about your soul," he grits out as I gingerly touch the skin around the gash.

"And why is that?" I say distractedly.

"Maybe," he breathes, "I'm envious of it."

I swallow. "There is nothing about me to be envious of."

"Then you don't know yourself well enough."

"What," I huff, "and you do?"

He's suddenly struggling to his feet with a grunt. "You can deny it all you want, but we both know I do."

"And where do you think you're going?" I ask beneath him. "Well, where are *we* going?"

"I want to be at least slightly comfortable while I bleed out." He extends a hand to me that I don't bother taking before standing to my feet. "I'm hoping for a cave."

"You're not going to bleed out. . . ." I pause, skeptical. "We are nearing the caves?"

He nods. "We're almost at the edge of the Sanctuary now. The stretch of caves is right before the field separating us from Ilya."

"Perfect," I say dryly. "Almost home."

We step out from behind the stones and back onto the path. Walking in silence, I glimpse the first body slumped over a cluster of rocks and quickly look away. My stomach twists at the reminder of what I've done, at every body I now have to face. The weapon I killed with is back in my hand, sweaty and seemingly harmless as it dangles toward the dirt.

Though, in a way, it is. A weapon is only deadly if it's used. And a bow only kills if I fire the arrow for it.

Even with my eyes on the ground, I know each time I pass a body. I feel the weight of what I've done with each step. Kai stays quiet beside me, knowing exactly what this must feel like. What it is to kill and live with each ghost.

I hear dirt crunching beneath a boot behind us.

I spin at the sound, lifting an empty bow.

He's scrawny, much smaller than his fellow bandits—it's no wonder I missed him among the rocks. He holds a bow in shaky hands, straining to keep it trained on Kai.

And before I can blink, he fires.

I don't think before stepping in front of the prince I'm supposed to hate. Time seems to slow as the arrow flies toward me. Reflexes take control of my body, forcing me to raise my empty weapon.

I swipe the bow through the air, hearing wood connect with the arrow's shaft before I've even registered what's happened. The arrow falls to the ground in a blur, its tip buried in the dirt.

I look up to find the man's expression mirroring my own. Utter shock is etched across his face at what I've managed to do. I take advantage of his hesitation and reach behind me to slide an arrow from where it sticks out of my pack.

It's laid across my bow a heartbeat later.

My fingers curl around the string—lungs constricting, breath catching in my throat.

I loosen my grip on the bowstring, ready to let the arrow fly—

A blur cuts through the air, flipping until it sinks into the man's chest.

I blink, looking down at the arrow still notched on my bow.

When my eyes trail back up to the man, he's clutching his chest where the hilt of a knife now protrudes.

I turn, finding Kai standing beside me, clutching his wounded shoulder. "There," he says, sounding pained. "That's all taken care of."

I glance back at the man falling face-first into the dirt. "How did you . . . ?"

"Left arm," he says casually. "Still hurt like hell though."

"I had that handled." I look away, avoiding his gaze. "I was . . . I was going to do it."

He steps between me and the man, blocking my view of Death coming to claim him. "I know. I know you had it handled. You made that very obvious when you batted an arrow out of the air." He shakes his head at me, a smile drawing out his dimple. "But, like I said, my soul is stained enough for the both of us. And you've killed enough for me already."

I look away, unsure what to say. Unsure how to tell him exactly how much that meant to me. So, I settle on a soft "Thank you."

"That sounded painful," he says, smirking like the asshole he is.

"Well, thanking you isn't exactly something I'm used to doing."

"I think it's just manners in general that you aren't used to," he says, starting down the path again.

He pulls me along while I shake my head at his back, aware that this is all just a distraction from the death happening behind us. "Oh, and you are so well-mannered?"

"Considering that I've had numerous tutors and years of education, yes, I would say so." His voice is strained with pain. "I've been taught how to hold myself in court and amongst nobles. How to speak to women and—"

I snort. "You mean flirt?"

"No, that's always come naturally, darling."

I've finally caught up to walk beside him. "Does being an ass come naturally too, or is that something they taught you in the palace?"

His lips twitch as he considers my question. "Naturally. But I can't take all the credit." He looks me over. "You bring it out of me."

I look away, scanning the stones as an excuse to look anywhere but at him. The terrain has grown rougher, impossibly rockier. The walls on either side of us are high and dotted with scattered hollows. Most are too small to call a cave, but my eyes snag on the mouth of one that looks promising. I vaguely wonder which one of these is home to the first queen herself.

"How's that one?" I point.

Sweat beads on his brow; pain pulls at his mouth. When he simply nods, not offering any sort of sly comment, I know he's in a great deal of discomfort.

The sun beats down on us as we slowly make our way to the cave. Blisters scream at me with each step as skin rubs against boot. I bite my tongue, knowing that what the Enforcer feels beside me is much worse.

Shadows drape over us when we finally step into the cave. Light seems to be swallowed up in here, making the cavern feel as though we've stepped into the evening.

"Sit," I order sternly.

He keeps his eyes on mine as he obeys, lowering himself to the ground. "What are you doing, Gray?"

I crouch behind him, carefully lifting his bloody shirt to examine the wound. "What does it look like I'm doing, Azer?"

"It looks like you're caring about me," he says with a smirk seeping into his voice. "And it feels like you're undressing me."

I huff. "Don't be too flattered. I can't have you becoming a deadweight, now can I?"

He grunts in pain when my fingertips brush the tender skin around the wound. The smell of blood stings my nose, forcing me to take a deep breath before saying, "I don't have anything to stitch this up with. All I can do is wash it out and wrap it."

"Great," he grits out. "Let's get it over with, yes?"

"But it needs to be stitched," I say sternly. "It could get infected."

"We'll be back in Ilya by tomorrow," he says calmly. "The bandage will stop the bleeding long enough. I'll heal myself when we get there."

"Right." I nod, swallowing at the sight of blood. I grip the hem of his shirt to carefully pull it over his head. He hisses when it tugs at his wound. With a gentle hand on his back, I urge him to lie on his stomach.

Back bare and stretched out before me, thick blood pools on his skin. I can barely see the slice beneath it, and the metallic scent stings my nose. "Tell me something," I manage weakly.

"Tell you something?" His laugh is pained. "Is this really the best time for—"

"Yes," I cut in. "It can be anything, just . . . just talk to me."

I squeeze my eyes shut, needing a distraction from the feel of his blood on my fingertips and the sight of it spilling over his skin. Something in the way he stills tells me he's starting to understand.

"All right." His voice is strained. "The truth, then?"

"The truth, always," I murmur.

A long pause. "Sometimes I'm envious that you were the one to kill my father."

My eyes fly open to blink bewilderedly at the back of his head. "W-what?"

He manages a sigh. "I've spent my whole life fantasizing of doing what you did. I'm not proud of it. But every time he would cut me, scream at me, or force me to face a fear over and over again, I fought the urge to hurt him back. And Plague knows I could have." He quiets, voice strained. "It consumed my every thought. Because before I hated him for everything he did to me, I hated him because he hated Ava. He never admitted it, of course, but I knew. I knew he hated that she was weak, knew that he thought she was a disgrace to the family name."

I reach slowly for one of the canteens we refilled with rainwater, distracted by the secrets spilling from his lips. "But I couldn't ever bring myself close to doing it." He sighs. "No matter how hard he trained me or hated the people I loved, he was still my father. Blood and duty run deeper than hatred."

I'm quiet for a long moment, eyes fixed on the dimly lit wall of stone before us. "And I did what you secretly wish you could have done yourself."

"And the worst part," he murmurs, "is that I'm supposed to hate you for it. But you are much harder to hate than he was."

We have little water left to spare, and horrifyingly, I don't hesitate before pouring most of it over his wound. Because, despite it all, I've come to realize that there is little I wouldn't sacrifice for him.

I don't allow myself to dwell on that sudden discovery.

"Shit," he hisses, feeling the water sting as it seeps into his gash. "I take it back. Maybe you aren't so hard to hate," he grits out.

Blood is dripping down his back, staining his skin red in the dim light. My hands are covered in it, every finger sticky and smelling of the death I'm all too familiar with.

I don't play with him. I don't tease or take his mind off the pain. Instead, I look away as I wash out the wound, unable to stare at the stream of red. I rip fabric from what's left of my skirt with shaky hands. I use bloody fingers to tuck the makeshift bandage beneath his chest.

Breathing heavy, I lean over his back to pull the fabric around the wound.

My braid slips from behind my shoulder, swinging until . . .

It drags across the pool of blood beginning to well again atop his wound.

I suck in a breath before clamping a hand around the middle of my braid, ready to toss it back over my shoulder.

My hand sticks to the hair inside my palm.

I look down slowly, my whole body shaking.

Blood is streaked through my hair, dripping from the ends and smeared from my hand. I swallow the growing lump in my throat as I tug my hand away to stare down at the blood coating it.

I smell nothing but death, hear nothing but the ringing in my ears.

I think Kai is saying something, but I ignore him as I fumble with the fabric, bloodying it as I rush to cover the wound.

I tie it off with a muffled gasp, reaching for the canteen. I manage to drain the last few drops of water into my palm before violently scrubbing my hands together. Blood swirls over my skin, running down my wrists and—

"Gray."

His voice is stern enough to snap me out of my frenzy. I'm not sure when he sat up, but he's facing me now, resting a gentle hand on my leg. "What's going on?"

I shake my head, fighting the tears that threaten to fall. "It's nothing. . . . It's . . ." My gaze falls to my hands and the blood coating them. The same hands that held the dying bodies of those I loved most. The same hands that are forever covered in their blood.

"It's the blood," he says softly. "You never used to be squeamish until . . ."

My heart thuds against my chest, making me feel faint.

All I smell is blood. All I feel is guilt.

"I . . . I can't anymore," I pant. "I can't feel like this anymore. It's all too much."

I look down at silver hair stained red. The sight of my braid has me stilling, has me hating how much power blood now holds over me. It's an effort to slow my breathing, to steady the beat of my heart.

A numb sort of anger suddenly smothers the panic coursing through me. I take a deep breath, lifting my gaze to his.

"Cut it off."

His brows crinkle at my words, "What?"

"I want you to cut it off," I say quietly. My face is blank despite the tears still clouding my vision. I run bloody hands over the length of my braid, staining it with each swipe.

Kai's eyes follow my fingers, widening slightly in understanding. "Gray, maybe you should—"

"I want you to cut it off," I whisper. "Please."

"Hey, look at me," he says softly, his hand straying to my face. "I will wash your hair, okay? The blood won't be there forever—"

"Yes, it will," I cut in loudly, my voice shaky. I blink back tears, forcing myself to hold his gaze as I do. "Yes, it will," I repeat, whispering this time. "The blood will always be there. The blood of my father. The blood of my best friend. The blood of every person I have *killed*. It's always there." My voice cracks. "And I'm drowning in it."

He shakes his head, running a thumb over my cheek. "Adena's and your father's deaths were not your doing."

"Just because it wasn't my doing doesn't mean it wasn't my fault," I whisper.

"No, that's not—"

"Please. I know you keep my dagger in your boot."

He stills at my soft words. "I don't want you to regret this."

I shake my head at my bloody hands. "You don't get it. This hair holds memories. And it's *heavy*." I turn slowly until my back is facing him, the loose braid hanging down the length of my spine. "Please, Kai."

Silence.

Until there isn't. Until I feel him reach for his boot. Until my braid is held gently in one hand while the other holds my father's blade against it.

I feel his breath on my neck, hesitant and unsure.

A tear rolls down my cheek when I nod.

Lifting the braid from my neck, he begins dragging the blade through it.

Every bit of composure I had left crumbles at the sound of my hair being sliced off.

Tears tumble down my cheeks. I cry for my past, for the little girl who held her father's hand until it grew cold. For the little girl who struggled to survive in a kingdom that hated her.

I cry for Adena—my sun in the darkness I was drifting toward. I can still feel her bloody body in my arms, see her broken fingers bound behind her back. I cry because death is undeserving of her. But she deserves my mourning, my every tear held back.

I cry for every time I felt as though I shouldn't. For every time I felt as though it made me weak.

I feel the whisper of loose hair falling down my back, weight lifting off my shoulders.

When he pulls away, I hear the dagger clatter against the cave floor. I move my head, feeling light without the heavy curtain of hair cascading down my back. The freshly cut ends barely brush my shoulders, tickling my skin.

His hand is on my arm now, gently turning me around to face him. I put up a pathetic fight, not wanting him to see me like this. Eventually, he pulls my hands into his, grabbing our last full canteen from the pack. I watch as he uses his teeth to tear more fabric from the skirt before pouring a precious amount of water onto my stained hands.

He sits in silence, washing the blood from my hands. His touch is soft, as though I'm delicate, not fragile. As though he's treating me with care because I deserve it, not because I need it.

He swipes the fabric across my palms, between my fingers, spending extra time around my fingernails. It's only when my hands are spotless that he puts the fabric down and looks up at me.

Everything he does is intentional, a type of intimacy I've never felt before. Simply being so cared for has another tear rolling down my cheek before I can stop it. That's all it takes for the flood of emotions to crash into me again.

I'm practically choking on my tears, breathing uneven. "Shh," he murmurs. "You're all right."

He reaches a hand to my face, intending to wipe away the tears there. I shake my head, pulling away. "No, I don't want you to see me like this. I don't want you to wipe my tears away."

He nods slowly, taking in my words. "Okay. Then I won't."

His hand slowly finds mine from where it sits in my lap. I watch in confusion as he picks it up and lifts it toward his mouth.

Another tear escapes my eye when his lips brush against the pad of my thumb.

The action is so small, yet so significant. Now that I know the meaning behind it, I swallow at his willingness to share something so special with me.

But then he takes that thumb and guides it toward my cheek to wipe away a tear there. Then he pulls it back to his lips, kissing it again before using it to wipe away another one of my tears. "You're strong enough to wipe away your own tears, but too stubborn to let someone care for you," he murmurs.

He continues to kiss my thumb, helping me wipe away every tear decorating my face. My eyes are puffy, face splotchy, but he looks at me with a reverence reserved for religion.

When he's kissed my thumb for the last time, I'm being pulled into his arms. My back is pressed against his bare chest, and he holds me tight despite his wound. A hand is running over my short hair, fingers brushing my neck.

"Thank you," I whisper, placing my hand on the arm wrapped around my waist.

He leans his head against mine. "Are you feeling better?"

I'm quiet, considering his question. "For the first time in a while, I feel like that's a possibility."

CHAPTER 42

I haven't been to the west tower since visiting the little girl who once occupied it.

In her place now lies a woman. A queen. A mother—perhaps partially even to me.

I set a quick pace across the plush carpet, content to avoid the many curious looks that follow. Servants smile politely; Imperials stare shiftily. Glancing at one of the many windows lining the hall, I attempt to catch a glimpse of my reflection.

Instead, my feet falter. My throat dries. My vision blurs.

I have yet to visit his grave. Yet to force myself to stare at the patch of dirt he's buried beneath.

The small cemetery stretches beyond the window, tucked against an intimate corner of the castle. Decades of kings, queens, and their lineage have been laid to rest beneath the soft grass. Carved stones sit atop each grave, marking what decaying body lies beneath.

The breath I take is shallow, rattling in my chest.

Several pairs of watchful eyes prickle my skin, and I straighten at the feel. Because I am their king. I am not mad. And I will not cause a scene.

Tearing my eyes from the fresh, upturned dirt that now swallows my father, I quicken my pace down the hall.

Head high. Back straight. Eyes clear.

In the days since my eye-opening conversation with Gail, I've visited the willow tree and apologized to Ava for missing her birthday. Hell, I apologized for more than just that. I likely looked every bit the mad king as I mumbled to the roots twining beneath my feet.

That's when Calum found me, reminded me of those three *B*'s. At the thought, I bury a hand into my pocket, finding the cool box beneath my fingers. I run the pad of my thumb over the velvet absent-mindedly, recalling the much-needed coaching Calum has offered.

"Look the part of the king, even if you don't quite feel it yet. For the sake of your plan, your people."

I round the corner, finding an equally packed hall filled with prying eyes. My hand tightens atop the box, finding courage in the three *B*'s it represents. Blowing out a breath, I stride evenly through the throng of servants and Imperials.

Head high. Back straight. Eyes clear.

I don't have the chance to wonder whether I look kingly enough before I'm standing beneath the looming stairwell that climbs up to the west tower. This wing of the castle is reserved for the infirmary—otherwise known as isolation.

Steps creak beneath my feet, groaning against my weight. Trekking up the multiple winding stories has me quickly winded.

Damn, am I really this out of shape?

I suppose my lack of endurance shouldn't be shocking after being holed up in my study for so long. But I'm panting by the time I reach the worn door at the top of the stairs.

My fist lifts, readying to rap my knuckles against the wood.

I hesitate.

There is a reason I have yet to visit the queen. She is my mother in name alone, and I suppose part of me always despised her for not being the woman who died giving birth to me. For not being the woman I so desperately wish I could have met.

But Father loved her greatly, and she him. It is the reason she is so ill in the first place—grief. At least we have those two things in common.

Until I find the courage to face father's grave, I will sit beside his wife's deathbed.

I knock. The door swings open.

I'm met with shocked looks from several physicians. They don't bother asking why I'm here. Only one patient occupies this tower.

Within a matter of seconds, I'm being ushered across the room, passing crisp beds blanketed with dust.

No one has been up here in years.

Even when Kai and I tore each other up in the sparring ring, the injuries were hastily fixed by Eli in our bedrooms. Because this wing of the castle is reserved for the wounds that run far deeper than a Healer can reach.

My eyes trace a particular cot tucked into the corner; its linens folded neatly. I distantly wonder whether Kai has seen that bed without Ava's body to occupy it.

"Kitt!"

Tearing my eyes from the cot, I find brown ones warm at the sight of me. "Jax," I say, forcing a smile. "I didn't know you were up here."

The grin he returns is far brighter than my own, contrasting against his dark skin. "I didn't think I would see you here. Or, uh, anywhere."

I watch the sadness settle onto his features and am desperate to eradicate it. "Sorry about that, J. I've been a lot busier than usual."

He nods, shifting on his gangly limbs. "Yeah, I bet." Then he throws a glance at the occupied bed behind him. "She's been asking about you."

I clear my throat. "Do you come up here often?"

He nods, looking sheepish. "Almost every day. I . . . I owe it to her. She's the one who took me in after my parents . . ."

I nod when he trails off, not needing him to remind me of his parents' shipwreck on the Shallows. I'm suddenly clearing my throat again, feeling slightly awkward. Something has shifted between us, and it's left me oddly off-balance.

I suppose that would be my fault. I'm the only one of us who's changed. The only one who is now king.

"Well," Jax says slowly, "I guess I'll leave you to it."

My hand finds his shoulder when he begins to step away. "Plagues, have you grown an inch every day since I last saw you?"

The joking tone of my voice, the glimpse of the prince he grew up with, has a smile splitting across his face. "Pretty soon I'll be looking down on you, Kitty."

"Oh, I hope not," I say pointedly. "Because then I wouldn't be able to do this." I reach forward, hooking an arm around his neck before ruffling his short hair with my free hand.

He laughs in that boyish way I've missed. Carefree and wholesome. After finally untangling himself from my arms, he stands before me, beaming. The sight has my chest constricting at the reminder of what things used to be like.

But maybe there is still hope of happiness in the future.

After managing to scruff up my hair, Jax takes several long strides and slips out of the room with a laugh. Shaking my head and smoothing the blond strands atop it, I turn my focus toward the woman already watching me.

Her once sleek, black hair looks dull sprawled atop the white pillow. When I make my way to the edge of her bed, she attempts a weak smile. "Hello, Kitt."

The voice that escapes her cracked lips is little more than a rasp. Gray eyes roam over me, looking so much like Kai's. She clears her throat, sounding stronger as she says, "I've heard that you haven't been doing too well recently."

My smile is sad. "I could say the same about you."

When I take a seat in the rigid chair beside her, she reaches for my hand, grasping it far tighter than I figured she was able. "Just silly rumors, then, hmm?"

She smiles, and I smile back. "Yes, just rumors."

Growing suddenly serious, she says softly, "I didn't think you would come to see me."

I press my lips together, nodding slightly. "If I'm being honest, I didn't think I would either."

"I can't blame you." Her smile is sad. "I never made much of an effort to have a relationship with you." Tears well in her gray eyes. "And for that . . . I am sorry."

I swallow, unsure what to say. Thankfully, she's speaking again before I'm forced to come up with anything. "Plagues, you look so much like him."

My eyes crash into hers. Reaching up a shaky hand, she brushes a strand of hair from my forehead. "You are exactly what he looked like when I fell in love with him."

"Really?" I breathe, desperate to learn more of the man I idolized.

"Really." She laughs, though it sounds pained. "You know, we didn't like each other very much at the beginning. My father was a trusted adviser to the king, and when your mother passed giving birth to you, I was the easiest option for him. He wasn't obligated to spend months courting me." She nods, remembering it all with a slight smile. "I didn't want to marry him. Truly. It was clear that all he wanted from me was another heir. But something began to blossom between us as time went on. Love. He was different with me. Kind and caring." Her eyes slowly meet mine. "And now, here I am. Dying because I no longer know how to breathe without him."

"I know the feeling."

The words are out of my mouth before I can swallow them. "I know you do," she whispers. "You loved him very much."

My voice cracks. "I just want to make him proud."

She squeezes my hand. "And you will, Kitt. You will rule this kingdom for him. He believed in you, and so do I."

"Did he?" I whisper pathetically.

She stares at me for a long moment. "He left you letters." My breath catches, and I hold it as she continues. "Just in case something . . . happened to him. They are meant to guide you, tell you exactly what he would have wanted for the kingdom. I haven't read them, obviously, but you should. I believe they are in his bottom desk drawer. Well, *your* bottom desk drawer."

I had yet to open any of those compartments for the sake of my sanity. Because it hurt too much seeing a quill he held or a note he scribbled. But now . . .

"I'll find them," I breathe. "Thank you."

She smiles. "Of course."

I stand to leave. She coughs. I wince.

"Kitt?"

I turn back toward her frail form. "Yes?"

"Visit me again?" She swallows. "You look so much like him."

My throat burns.

I nod.

CHAPTER 43

Her legs are tangled in mine, her head pressed against my beating heart.

I've lost track of the time, content to hold her until my entire body goes numb. We've fallen into a silence that sounds like contentment, peace of mind.

I don't dare move, too afraid to ruin the moment when she's likely frightened of having it. It's clear that she doesn't know what to do with me. Doesn't know what to do with me because of what I'm doing to her.

We are a day away from Ilya now. A day away from handing her over to Kitt—the king—to do with her what he will. And I don't exactly know what Kitt is capable of anymore. I don't even know how he will react when I show him the journal, the documentation from a Healer the king couldn't buy.

He likely won't believe it. Hell, I'm not quite sure what to believe either.

I've lived my entire life believing that the Ordinaries are diseased and dooming us all. But this lie falls in line with father's character, with his hunger for power and control. Not to mention how many Ordinaries were living among us for decades with no noticeable effects on our abilities.

It seems like such an obvious lie when you haven't been living it your entire life.

She shifts against me, pulling her legs to her chest. A flash of red catches my eye, and I reach out to grab her leg. She's about to protest when I lift her calf toward me to see torn pants and the arrow slice beneath.

"Why didn't you tell me about this?" I say calmly.

Her voice is as stiff as her body has become. "Because it's just a scratch."

"It's bleeding."

"No." She sighs. "It bled. And I was doing a fine job at ignoring it until you brought it up."

She shifts so I can see her face grow paler in the dim light as she stares at the dried blood. I grab the mutilated skirt and tear another strip of fabric from it. Then I carefully lift her leg over mine before rolling up what fabric remains of her pants.

I feel her eyes roaming my face as I wrap the strip of skirt around the wound, winding it tight before tying it off. "There," I say simply. "Now you don't have to look at it."

She manages a small smile. "Thank you."

My lips twitch. "That's the fifth time you've thanked me now. Seems to be getting less painful to say."

"What," she scoffs, "you're keeping track now?"

"I wouldn't if it wasn't such a rarity."

She shakes her head, hiding a smile as she looks up at me. Short hair suits her. Though I'm quite sure there is little that doesn't. But I like her like this—hair messy and lips quick to smile at me.

Her leg is still draped across mine, forcing her to sit sideways. I study her for a long moment before saying, "It was Adena, wasn't it?"

Everything about her seems to shrink at the mention of her friend. "What about Adena?"

"The blood," I say softly. "You never had a problem with it before . . ."

"Before she died," she says bluntly. "Something about being covered in the blood of those you love—more than once—makes you unable to bear the sight, the feel, the smell of it. I guess . . . I guess Adena's blood was my last straw."

I nod, understanding in my own twisted way. My eyes travel over her, taking in the strength she fails to see. Her own piercing gaze is sweeping across my face, though I doubt she sees strength. Perhaps sin. Allegiance at best.

"We should get going, yes?" Her voice is deceptively cheery. "We mustn't keep the king waiting longer than need be."

I know that tone. She uses it every time there is talk of taking her back to Ilya.

Which is my duty. Taking her back to Ilya is my duty.

She untangles herself from my lap to stuff everything into her pack. The chain clanks when she stands to her feet, the sound a constant reminder of what it is I'm doing with her.

I follow, carefully pulling the bow across my uninjured shoulder. Glancing over, I find her gaze fixed on the ground, eyes wide with emotion. I follow her line of sight to see the dagger lying beside what was her long silver braid.

It feels as though she left a version of herself on the floor of this cave, another ghost to roam the Sanctuary of Souls. I bend to pick up her dagger, feeling the silver swirls press against my palm. How odd it is to hold a weapon with so much history in my hand.

"I won't ever get it back, will I?" she asks dully.

I begin heading for the yawning mouth of the cave. "One day," I promise.

"Bury it with me, will you?"

Her words make me stiffen, and it takes every ounce of strength to ignore them. When we step outside, it's into late-afternoon sun. The road is rocky enough to jostle my shoulder and stretch the already throbbing wound there, making me dread each step. We walk in comfortable silence for a long while before she breaks with a casual, "You're hurting."

"Oh, am I, Little Psychic?"

She looks unamused until she says, "Let's just say I've gotten rather good at reading your body language."

I chuckle at my own words spit back at me. "That is how you did your little Psychic trick, isn't it? You read people."

She nods. "That's the gist. It sounds a lot easier than it is, if I'm being honest. It takes years to hardwire your brain to string details together in a matter of seconds."

"I believe it," I sigh. "You were—still are, I suppose—very convincing."

I feel her gaze on my face. "So, you never . . . questioned my ability?"

I laugh lightly. "Of course, I did. That's kind of my job." Shaking my head, I glance up at the blue sky above. "But you were *distracting*. It's as though the moment I considered your ability, you'd do something to turn my thoughts in the other direction. And I am still discovering new powers, especially when it comes to the Mundanes. So, a Psychic didn't seem too far-fetched."

Her smile is smug. "I am very good at what I do."

"Don't go getting cocky, darling."

She turns to look fully at me, her expression blank. "You have a blister on the inside of your left foot." Her eyes fall to the growing scruff on my jaw. "You don't keep a beard because you hate the way it feels. And . . . you wore a ring back at the castle, but you took it off before you came to find me."

I shake my head at the ground, trying my best to hide my astonishment. "You got me, Gray. That all sounds about right." I flex my hand like I have been ever since leaving the castle. "It was the Enforcer's ring I was wearing. Big, gaudy thing I'm not used to. The feel of it between my fingers bothered me. So I figured a mission was a good excuse to take it off."

I glance over to find her staring at the ring she spins on her thumb. She scoffs at the sight of it. "My whole life I thought this ring represented the marriage of my *parents*, not strangers."

"They were your parents," I say sternly. "Blood doesn't equal love. Jax is just as much my brother as Kitt is, despite us not sharing the same parents."

She nods, understanding but not fully believing. "It makes sense. All of it." She manages a weak laugh. "I'm the daughter of some Ordinaries who didn't want to deal with me. That's why I'm not a Mix. I guess . . . I guess I just never thought about it until now."

"Why would you?" I say simply. "When a father loves you, you don't feel the need to go looking for another one."

She nods, falling silent. The sun hangs above us, hot against the back of my neck. I say nothing about my aching shoulder or the burning blister she's already aware of that rubs against my boot.

We walk in an easy silence for a long stretch of the remaining road. The last of our stale bread is quickly devoured and washed down with warm water.

That's when the ground begins to even out, tufts of grass appearing all around us. Shielding my eyes, I squint against the falling sun, spotting the flood of green we are heading for.

"We're almost to the field," I say, shattering the silence. I can already see the castle's towers looming over the horizon.

"Great. Last stop before Ilya."

There's that tone again.

I clear my throat. "Have you ever been to the field?"

"Considering that it's near the castle—and I hadn't been anywhere close to there until the Trials—no, I've never seen the field."

"Good." I throw her a smile. "I'll be the first to see your reaction."

Her mouth is hanging open, just as I suspected.

"What . . . what is that?" she gawks, feet falling faster against the dirt.

"That would be the field."

A hand smacks me in the stomach. "I know that, smart-ass." She smiles sweetly as though she hadn't just knocked the air from my lungs. "I'm talking about the flowers."

I straighten, hand pressed against my stomach as I stare at the sea of bright red. Every petal bleeds into the other, creating a blanket of color to warm the grass beneath.

"Poppies," I say, smiling when I see the look on her face.

"I've never seen such a bright flower," she blinks. "They're orange and red and *everywhere*."

I can't seem to tear my eyes from her. "So? What do you think?"

She glances back at me, her smile worrisome. "I think you're slowing me down."

With the words barely out of her mouth, she turns and bounds toward the field. I manage to start running before the chain has the chance to try to yank me off my feet. I watch her spread out her arms to embrace the wind as her boots find the edge of the field.

I haven't seen her this carefree since the day I followed her out into the rain, plucking a forget-me-not to tuck behind her ear. Seeing her enjoy life makes surviving mine suddenly worth it.

"At least try to keep up!" she calls, poppies crowding her legs with each step. "I think you're out of shape, Azer!"

"Is that so?" I laugh, gaining on her.

She realizes too late what is happening.

A squeal slips from her lips when I cut in front of her, bending to catch her legs and throw the rest of her body over my uninjured shoulder. I bite my tongue at the sting that still shoots down my body, but the sound of her laugh is healing, capable of making a man forget his own name, let alone his pain.

"What are you doing?" she laughs against my back, arms flailing.

I spin us around. "Showing you just how out of shape I am."

She giggles like a girl who hasn't had to grieve her father and best friend. Like a girl who hasn't struggled to survive, stolen when she was starving. Like a girl who isn't chained to a man she's meant to hate.

There is such beauty in resilience, in the ability to laugh despite it all.

"All right," she pants, "you made your point. You can put me down now."

"But I'm giving you the best view of the flowers," I say with a smile she can't see.

Her voice is slightly muffled. "No, you're dragging my head *through* the flowers."

I laugh, crouching as I wrap an arm around her back and flip her over my shoulder. Lowering her slowly to the ground, I lay her down so flowers circle her as she smiles up at me.

The setting sun drips golden rays across her face, blue eyes burning bright against the vibrant red of each poppy. It's hard to believe that something so beautiful would willingly stare at the likes of me.

I feel undeserving of her gaze, of the way her eyes roam over my face. I shake my head, still staring down at her. "Don't look at me like that."

"Like what?" she asks softly.

"Like I'm worthy of being seen."

Her lashes flutter at my words. She swallows, lifting a hand to cup my face. My eyes drift closed at the feel of her palm against my skin, the privilege to be touched by her.

"Dance with me?" she whispers.

My heart skips a beat at the timid question.

I open my eyes to find hers fixed on my face, giving me that look I don't deserve. "For however long you want, darling."

I help her to her feet before guiding her arms around my neck. My hands find her hips, holding tight as I lift her feet atop mine. She gasps in surprise before a smile splits her face, fingers curling in my hair.

I sway with her body pressed against mine. My hands roam up her back, unused to the feel of it without her heavy curtain of hair. I tilt my head toward hers, taking in the mess of silver falling to her shoulders.

I tuck a wavy piece behind her ear, running my fingers down the short length of it. "You don't regret it?"

She shakes her head, her smile sad. "No."

"Good," I murmur. "Because I've always had a thing for short hair."

"Oh, really?" She laughs as I sway us in a circle.

"It's true. Among other things, of course." I shrug a shoulder. "Short hair. Ocean-blue eyes. Twenty-eight freckles. And"—I pause, examining her with a tilt of my head—"how tall are you?"

She blinks in confusion. "Umm, about five and a half feet?"

"Five and a half feet," I continue evenly. "The terrifying ability to kick a man's ass. Stunning smile. Ridiculously stubborn. Hair like molten silver. Quick to threaten me with a dagger." I smile down at her. "Should I go on?"

"What's next? A ballad in my name?" Her voice holds a challenge, but her face wears a smile.

I pull her closer, my hand fitted into the curve of her waist. "Are poets not just fools with fancy words?" I duck my face until our foreheads meet. "I think I qualify, darling."

She laughs softly, looking down at the flowers crowding around our legs. We're swaying in the sunset, her boots atop mine with a field of flowers to witness.

I watch her gaze climb up and across the sea of petals reaching toward the sky. I don't need to turn my head to know what she's looking at. "Last night," she says quietly.

"Last night," I echo.

She nods, winding her arms tighter around my neck. "Then we might as well enjoy this while it lasts."

We sway in silence until she whispers, "Pretend, right?"

I swallow, hating the sound of the lie that slides off my tongue. "Pretend."

CHAPTER 44
Paedyn

We sit in a bed of red, the type that's sweet and soft, not sickening and sticky like I'm so used to.

I stretch out my sore legs in front of me, feeling petals tickling my skin. We walked much farther across the field after finishing our dance, Kai's toes likely numb in his boots. I keep my back to the castle that is now very near, choosing to ignore the inevitable.

"How the hell did you do that?"

Kai's frustration seeps into his voice, something I'm sure he's unaccustomed to allowing. He's lying sideways, propped on an elbow as he wrestles with poppy stems. I snort at the sight of what is supposed to be a flower crown, watching it crumple in his hands.

He nods to the nearly completed crown in my lap. "How is yours not falling apart?"

"Maybe," I say slowly, "because I'm doing it right."

The dull look he gives me has a laugh bubbling from my throat. Petals slip between his fingers as he fumbles to wrap the stems together. His words are a mumble under his breath. "I can wield a sword in

both hands, but I can't get these damn flowers to stay together."

"To be fair," I say, twisting the final flower into place, "I've had a lot of practice. Adena and I used to make these all the time out of dandelions."

The thought brings a sad smile to my face as I admire my handiwork. I plop the crown on his head, adjusting it atop his black waves. "There. Back to being a prince."

He smiles, distracting me with his dimples. I lie on my side, mirroring him as I prop myself on an elbow and stare up at the crown. The bright flowers contrast with every one of his features, soft and dainty where the rest of him is anything but.

"Here." He pulls a half-crushed flower from his hand. Fingers brush my hair as he tucks the stem behind my ear. "Pretend it's a forget-me-not."

That night of the last ball flashes in my mind, along with the memory of a kiss we almost shared. And to think we've shared more now, when we truly are meant to be enemies. "We are quite good at pretending," I murmur, watching his face.

He opens his mouth, as if to free words he's been trapping inside.

But his eyes drift down the length of my neck, following the curve of my exposed shoulder. The oversized shirt and tank strap now hang loosely down my arm from lying ungracefully on my side.

His eyes narrow, looking like chips of ice as a storm begins to brew within them.

The heart beating beneath his gaze stutters at the realization of what he sees. I sit up swiftly, yanking the shirt back over my shoulder. I press a hand to the fabric, ensuring that it's covering the mutilated mess beneath.

"Gray." His voice is cold. "What the *hell* was that?"

I shake my head at him, hating the way I'm shrinking away. "It's nothing."

"Then let me see," he says, deceptively calm.

He reaches a hand toward me, and I don't think before blocking it with my forearm.

His eyes fly up to mine. A heartbeat passes. "What was that?"

"That," I say coolly, "was a block. Would you like me to demonstrate a punch?"

He chuckles humorlessly. "You can't be serious."

"Try me."

He shakes his head, bewilderment painting his features. When he reaches again for the sleeve of my shirt, I push his hand down before sending my free fist flying toward his stomach.

He blocks it easily, slowly letting his eyes climb up to mine. "Are you really trying to fight me right now?"

"Depends on whether or not you're going to keep your hands to yourself," I say, hiking my sleeve up farther.

His eyes flick between mine, his words a whisper. "What did he do to you?"

That question has every bit of pent-up rage rushing to the surface in the form of a swift punch to his jaw. I barely manage to nick the side of his face with my knuckle before he dodges.

We are both on our knees now, breathing hard.

"Hey," he pants. "I just want to know what happened—"

Another punch to his stomach, followed by one to his jaw that I manage to land. When I pull back for another, he grabs my wrist before I can do any more damage.

"I'm not going to fight you," he says sternly. "I won't."

Frustration tears from my throat, sounding like a growl. I push his chest with my free hand, hard enough to have him tilting back on his knees. Slamming my body against his, I send us toppling over poppies and onto the ground.

I'm straddling him, panting down at the worry he's wearing. "Why won't you fight me?" My voice cracks, tears suddenly crowding my vision.

"Because the next time I lay a hand on you, I only ever want it to be in a caress," he says softly.

I duck my head, squeezing my eyes shut against the flood of emotion there. I feel a calloused hand on my cheek and shake my head at the comfort I don't deserve. "Please," he whispers. "Show me."

I let out a shaky breath, opening my eyes to the gray ones already looking at me. Then I slowly climb off him as he sits up, swallowing my pride to gently pull the layers of clothing from my shoulder.

A cool breeze kisses my collarbone, as if to offer its sympathy. I haven't felt the sticky air on my skin since the king sliced me open outside the Bowl.

Kai's expression doesn't waver, as though he slipped on a blank mask. There's a crack, though. There always is. I catch the muscle that twitches in his cheek, the flex of his hands. "How did he do it?"

I attempt to swallow the lump in my throat. "A sword."

He sighs through his nose.

"After he dragged the blade down my neck," I continue, lifting my chin so he can see the familiar scar in the pale light, "he told me he'd leave his mark on my heart, so I never forget who it was that broke it."

He inches closer, eyes trained on the mangled skin beginning to scar. His voice is icy, sending a shiver down my spine. "It's an *O*."

I nod. "For—"

"Ordinary," he finishes, disgusted. "He tortured you, and you didn't think to tell me?"

"Would it have made a difference?" I say, throwing my hands in the air. "That doesn't make me any less of a criminal."

"It would have made you less of a murderer," he says harshly. "Why did you hide this from me?"

"Because . . . ," I stammer. "Because I can barely stand to look at myself! Don't you understand?" Tears sting my eyes, but I push on. "He *ruined* me. Marred me. For the rest of my life, I will look at this scar and think of the man I hated most. The man who had my father killed. The man who mercilessly killed Ordinaries like me. The man who tried to murder me himself." I shake my head, looking anywhere but at him. "I couldn't let anyone else see how he branded me. See the damage he did. I . . . I just couldn't."

The hurt held in his gaze is almost too much to bear. "Gray . . ."

"Say my name," I whisper. "Please."

I know he hasn't said it since we escaped the prison. Since I told him he lost the privilege of calling me it. And he's respected my rule ever since.

But I crave the sound of my name on his tongue. I want him to shout it from a rooftop, whisper it in my ear, trace it on my skin. I want my name to form a familiar shape in his mouth, tasting of my lips.

I want him to own my name and still beg when he says it.

Or maybe I just want him.

Surprise seeps through his crumbling mask before relief washes it all away. A hesitant smile lifts his lips, as though I've just uttered the most beautiful words he's ever heard.

He says my name like it's been on the tip of his tongue, whispered into every breath he's taken. "Paedyn."

Then he opens his arms.

A quiet sob slips past my lips as I crawl into his lap.

Strong arms fold around me before I bury my face in his bare chest. He runs a hand down my short hair, holding my neck as I shake against him. "He didn't ruin you, Pae," he murmurs against my ear.

The nickname sends a tear rolling down my cheek to splatter his chest. "But you thinking so means that even in death, he wins. That scar is a testament of your strength. A testament of *who* you are, not what."

I nod, curling closer against him. Flowers swallow us as we sit there in silence, creating a pretty wall of petals. His body is warm, his arms a heavy comfort around me.

We sit until darkness settles over us, his palm stroking my hair all the while. When the moon hangs low over us, and my eyelids grow heavy, he gently slides me from his lap to lay out a bedroll.

He all but lifts me onto it before lying down beside me, his shoulder brushing mine. I roll onto my side to face him despite the darkness. "Thank you."

He turns his head with what I'm sure is a smirk on his lips. "That's six times now."

"And likely the last," I say with a smile.

He looks back up at the stars winking down at us. "Scars."

I blink. "What?"

"Scars," he repeats. "Something else I've always had a thing for."

Laughter seems to stutter in my throat, as if unsure whether it should come out of my mouth. He reaches over and gently flicks the tip of my nose, making me giggle in a way I didn't know I could.

"Plagues, I love that sound," he murmurs, making me fall silent. "I would tattoo it into my skin if it meant you'd laugh at me for doing it."

"And I would," I say quietly.

He chuckles before his lips press against my forehead, the kiss soft and sweet. Then he pulls me closer as I turn my back to him, allowing an arm to hook around my waist.

"Try not to dream of me, Pae," he whispers against my ear.

"You first, Prince."

CHAPTER 45
Kai

Today is the day.

The panicked thought pulls me from my sleep.

I open my eyes only to squeeze them shut against the blinding sunlight.

I run a hand through my messy hair, roll my sore neck from a night of sleeping atop thick flower stems. Blinking up at the clear sky, the sun tells me we've slept plenty long enough.

My eyes wander to the shadow spilling from its castle sitting far too close. The end of this mission is so near, and yet, I'm not sure if I have the strength to finish it. But I'm chained to duty, created to command. I was made for the king, not for her. I could never be worthy of her.

My gaze sweeps back down to the crushed flowers.

As to be expected, Paedyn is still fast asleep against my chest, hands tucked beneath her face and hair strewn impressively in every direction.

Paedyn.

I earned her name back. It's a relief to let it roll off my tongue after days of it trying to escape my lips.

She's nothing but a tangle of limbs beside me. I hesitate to wake her, if only so I can stare at her longer. But I'd rather her company than anything else.

I shake her shoulder.

Nothing. Not surprising.

I try again. This time, it earns me a grumble against her hand.

The next attempt to wake her is met with a middle finger raised over her back. I chuckle, continuing to shake her. "It's both impressive and alarming how you always manage to sleep so deeply."

"If you can sleep in the slums," she mumbles, "you can sleep anywhere."

She rolls over to face me, blinking groggily. I can't help but smile at the sight of her, so obliviously stunning. After several large yawns, she props herself on an arm to pick the flowers that droop over us.

Looking down at me, she begins threading the flowers into my hair. A smile parts her lips, the type that is concerningly contagious. "Making me pretty, Pae?"

She rolls her eyes. "As if you need help with that."

As soon as the words leave her mouth, she's pressing her lips together, regret coating her face. I smile at her in the way I know she likes, making her huff in annoyance. "I always knew you thought I was pretty."

"Plagues," she mutters.

"Tell me," I say smoothly, running a lazy hand up and down her side, "how is it that you've been able to resist me for this long?"

Her laugh alone could cure the most corrupted parts of me, and that is exactly what it's done since the day I met her. "Well, it hasn't been very difficult, Prince."

"I find that hard to believe."

There's that laugh again. "Maybe cocky bastards just aren't my type."

"Then tell me who you want me to be for you."

Her hand stills in my hair, petals falling from her fingers. I watch her gaze soften with each silent second that passes. "I don't want you to be anything that you're not."

"But what I am is not good enough for you," I murmur, looking up at the clouds shifting above us.

"And what about what I am not?"

Her question has my eyes flicking back to her face. "What are you talking about?"

She slides her hand from where it was tangled in my hair. "Have you forgotten what I am? What you are meant to do with me?"

I sit up, forcing her to do the same. "And what is it you think I'm meant to do with you?"

"Hate me!" she shouts harshly, seeming to surprise herself with the outburst.

"Is that what you want?" I ask, my voice low. "You want me to hate you?"

She swallows her answer, saying nothing.

"Look me in the eyes and tell me to hate you, Paedyn."

Silence.

I stand to my feet, laughing bitterly. "Because I will. I will hate you if it means you spend the rest of your life thanking me for it."

She stands slowly, avoiding both my gaze and the question she won't answer.

I take a step toward her. "Five words. That is all I'm asking for. Five words for you to tell me how you feel."

I watch her eyes trail their way to mine. Then I listen to the five words that fall from her lips. "Please just hate me." A pause. "Asshole."

Under different circumstances, I would have laughed. But instead, I breathe, "Why?"

She shuts her eyes. "Because it is easier that way. Easier to stay enemies than become anything more."

I take a deep breath. "It's a little late for that, don't you think?"

When she says nothing, I grab the bedroll and stuff it into her pack. A numb sort of mask slips over my features, keeping my face blank and voice even. "Fine. We should be on our way, then."

She shakes her head, having found her voice. "Don't do that to me. Don't go hiding under one of your masks so you can pretend not to see this."

I run my hands through disheveled hair, shaking my head. "You want me without a mask?"

Her voice is strained. "That is the *only* way I want you, Kai Azer."

I take a step toward her, feeling stripped bare under the weight of her stare. It feels unnatural to let emotions paint my face, frustration crowd my features. But I let the mask shatter for her, leaving only the monster beneath it. "Fine. Here is me without a mask, Paedyn," I say, breathing heavily. "I don't know what you want me to do. I don't have a choice—"

"You always have a choice," she says harshly.

"Not in the life I was born into. The missions I'm sent on." I'm practically panting as the words tumble from my mouth. "You."

She hesitates. "Me?"

"Yes, you. Something else I've always had a thing for." I let out a bitter laugh. "I had no choice in the matter. Do you think I could have stopped it if I tried?"

She shakes her head at me. "Stop what?"

CHAPTER 46
Paedyn

"Stop myself from falling in love with you!"

I choke on my next breath, air clogging in my throat.

His chest is rising and falling in time with my own. My heart sputters back to life, beating hard against my rib cage. I shake my head at him, taking a step back. "No. No, don't say that. I asked you not to make this harder than it has to be."

"And I told you that it already is," he says, voice harsh. "Dammit, the minute you threw a dagger at my head, I knew I was done for. There was no longer a before you, only what I wanted *with* you."

"And what could that possibly be?" I laugh bitterly. "I'm an Ordinary. You're Elite—"

"Not out here I'm not."

I stare at him, startled by words I never thought I'd hear fall from his lips.

"Out here I am Kai and nothing more." His throat bobs. "Out here I am powerless. A monster without an ability to hide behind. An Enforcer free from his masks. A man shouting his love for a woman."

"Kai . . ."

"Pae."

My name from his lips is a weakness I shouldn't let him hold over me.

"I think I would fall on my sword if it meant you mourned me," he breathes. "And it's terrifying to think you hold that much power over me."

He closes the distance between us, tilting my chin up so I meet his gaze. "You asked me what my favorite color was once. I'd never even pondered the answer to that question before you. And yet, I realized in that moment that it was blue." He bends to brush a kiss to my temple, a murmur against my skin. "It is your eyes."

I take a shaky breath, feeling his on my face.

"Tell me you hate me, and I'll still count every heartbeat, every freckle, every shiver of your body, if only you say it with a smile." He backs away, freeing my face from his hands. "I may be a monster, but if you cut me, I'll bleed. And if you break my heart, Pae, you'll break me. So, if even a sliver of your soul longs for mine, I'll spend the rest of my life trying to deserve it."

My eyes are glassy, rimmed with tears I'm too stubborn to let fall. The plea in his gaze is poetic. He flexes his hands at his side, as though it's an effort to keep them off me. I take in his hair of petals and eyes of ice that only seem to melt when they fall on me.

"Maybe you really are a poet," I whisper.

He smiles softly. "Or just a fool for you."

"Pretend?"

My voice is small, soft like the breeze blowing through my short hair.

"Never."

"None of it?" I ask quietly.

“Darling”—he smiles—“I have never had to pretend to want you.”

His words have my heart stuttering before realization hits me. “What about our fathers?” I blurt. “What we did to one another?”

“I won’t spend the rest of my life hating you for saving yourself.” He sighs deeply. “I know why you did what you did. And I hope you understand why I did the same.”

“I . . .” Words I thought I would never say are suddenly caught in my throat. “I forgive you, Kai. I think I might have a while ago. Because I can forgive you for what you didn’t even know you were doing.”

His eyes flutter closed in relief.

“I wanted to kill you,” I whisper, forcing his eyes open. “I wanted to be your undoing. But even then, I knew I wouldn’t be able to live with myself if I had.”

He inches toward me, head shaking and eyes roaming as though overwhelmed by what he is seeing. “Oh, but you are my undoing. My deliverance. My downfall disguised as a deity.” Another slow step. “You are my ruin.”

I’m dazed, unable to do anything but let a smile tug at my lips.

“Call us even. Call me crazy. I don’t care. Just . . .” His eyes are pleading, brimming with emotion. “Just call me yours.”

We stare at each other for several thundering heartbeats.

“Flicking my nose,” I breathe.

His brows crinkle. “What?”

“Flicking my nose,” I repeat simply. “Something I’ve always had a thing for. Among others, of course.”

Understanding lights his eyes as a slow smile spreads across his lips, accompanied by dimples on either side. “Go on, darling.”

“That reminds me.” I nod. “Calling me ‘darling.’ Cocky bastards. Long, dark eyelashes . . .”

I could melt from the heat in his gaze.

"Knowing what I need exactly when I need it. Ripping my dresses. Dimples that make me—"

In a single step, he's closed the distance between us and pulled my mouth to his.

He kisses me deeply, breathing me in. I melt against him, memorizing the feel of his hands running over my body. I press a hand to his cheek while one of his finds my hair, threading it between his fingers.

I pull away just far enough to pant, "Have you really counted my freckles?"

"All twenty-eight of them," he breathes before kissing me hard. "Though, you might have more now from the sun." Another quick kiss. "I'll have to do a recount."

My laugh has him pulling me closer, nipping at the tip of my nose with his teeth.

I wrap my arms around his neck. He is my anchor, and I am willing to sink, so long as it is with him.

With each kiss, he captures the three words I'm too scared to say. I hope he can taste them on the tip of my tongue, read them on the curve of my lips. Because uttering the words feels like a death sentence. Every person I've ever loved has left me.

I'm cursed to lose in love. But that is what I feel for him, what I've felt even when I hated him. Because hating him was easier than hating myself for wanting him.

So I bite my tongue. I fight the urge to shout those three seemingly harmless words at him. Because wherever I love, people die. And I'd rather love him silently than mourn him loudly.

He pulls away, breathing heavy. "You need to get out of here."

Slipping my dagger from his boot, he crouches before the chain tethering us together. "What about you?" I stammer. "What about your mission. And Kitt—"

"Don't worry about me." He wedges the blade between the seam of the cuff around my ankle, trying to pry it apart. "I can handle Kitt. He already thought I wouldn't be able to bring you back anyway."

"He did?"

He huffs humorlessly. "Yeah. He figured I would do exactly what it is I'm doing now—letting you go." He strains against the handle of my dagger. "It seems he was right to doubt me."

I drop down beside him, crushing poppies beneath me. "What does this mean?"

He doesn't answer, eyes trained on the stubborn chain.

"Kai. What does this mean?"

He stops long enough to look up at me. "It means you are going to get as far away from here as possible. I'll stall the search for you as long as I can, but you need to find a way to get to Izram by then."

I shake my head. "No."

"Yes, Pae."

"No." My voice is stern. "No, I'm sick of running. And I won't spend the rest of my life doing it unless it's you I'm running back to."

"Then I'll spend the rest of my life tracking you down," he says quietly. "Glimpsing you in the shadows. Fighting you in the streets. Dancing with you in my dreams. Because living without you is only bearable when I know you are out there still living too."

"Please," I whisper.

"Kitt won't let me stop hunting you." He puts a hand to my cheek. "You have to—"

He stops abruptly, his head tilting slightly to the side.

"What?" I ask hesitantly. "What is it?"

He says nothing, a muscle ticking in his cheek the only movement.

"Kai?"

His eyes meet mine suddenly. "They're coming."

"Who is?"

"Kitt must have my men searching the edge of the city for me," he mutters under his breath. "They spotted us. Two Flashes, coming fast."

My throat goes dry.

Kai slings the pack over his shoulders before pulling the bow across his chest. He reaches up to touch my face but thinks better of it when he glances over his shoulder.

I see them now, two blurry figures speeding toward us. It feels odd to see abilities at work after spending so many days without them. So many glorious days where everyone was equally as Ordinary as I was.

"Hey, look at me," he murmurs. I turn to meet his hard gaze. "I need you to play along. Can you do that?"

"Playing a part is something I'm rather familiar with," I say evenly.

He nods. "Be smart. I'm going to fix all of this. I promise."

Now it's my turn to nod. His eyes flick between mine, and it's a struggle to not throw myself into his arms. "You are my proof of a paradise," he murmurs with a quick flick of my nose.

Then he turns toward the figures closing in on us, mouthing a single word I barely catch.

Pretend.

CHAPTER 47

Paedyn

"It's about time you spotted us out here."

Kai's voice is cold, callous in a way I forgot it could be. He walks ahead to meet the men, dragging me carelessly behind him.

"Y-Your Highness," one of them stutters, bowing quickly while the other follows. "We were expecting you days ago. Thought something might have happened . . ."

Kai stares the man down for an uncomfortable moment, crossing his arms over his chest. "You're new."

The Imperial shifts on his feet. "Uh, yes, sir."

Kai—the *Enforcer*—nods. "So, you haven't yet learned that questioning my abilities is a sure way to lose your tongue." The man grows paler with each word. "So let this be a lesson. A warning."

I've seen him treat his Imperials like this before, seen how obvious his disdain for them is. But I hadn't realized how much of it is a facade, a show of power and control. The line between respect and fear is a fine one, and after this disaster of a mission, he's reminding everyone exactly who he is.

"Now get this chain off me," he says simply.

The men stumble forward, sliding swords from the sheaths at their sides. I lift my chin as they look me over, the disgust on their faces mirroring my own. The especially ugly Imperial spits at my feet, and I don't hesitate to do the same—only, at his face.

Blood sprays from my lip when his palm meets my cheek. My head whips to the side where I spit blood to match the poppies surrounding us.

When I turn my head back toward the man, I find him face-to-face with his Enforcer. Kai's eyes are like chips of ice, so cold they burn. "Touch her again," he snarls, voice low, "and I'll slit your throat. She's *mine*."

A shiver crawls down my spine at his cold words. He said something similar to his men back in the Scorches, but this time it sounds different. It sounds like unspoken words and secret longing. Like he was speaking to me in a language they would never understand.

The Imperial nods repeatedly until Kai steps away. I gasp when pain sears across my ankle and look down to find the other Imperial wedging the blade of his sword into the cuff.

He carelessly cuts my skin, trying to pry the cuff apart. I bite my tongue to keep from crying out, to keep from giving him the satisfaction of knowing he's hurting me.

I can feel hot blood spilling from the cut to pool in my boot. The feel of it has my heart pounding, has my eyes searching for Kai's. He glances up at me, remorse flickering in his gaze. His look alone begs for my forgiveness, pleads with me to hear his unspoken word.

Pretend.

I look away, blinking down at my boot. The pain only ends when the cuff breaks open with a satisfying click. I blow out a breath as the Imperial lifts his sword from my torn skin. His face is close to mine, white mask obscuring most of it, with the exception of the smirk he flashes at me.

Ignoring him, I attempt to roll my stiff and sticky ankle. My foot feels foreign without its restricting jewelry weighing it down. The urge to run is overwhelming, an instinct that consumes every rational thought.

"Don't even think about it, girl."

The Imperial must have read the thoughts right off my face. He leers at me, daring my feet to take a single step. "You can't outrun me, Ordinary."

I startle at his words. Not because I'm shocked he knows what I am, but because I've spent my entire life dreading the sound of those words from an Imperial's lips.

I straighten, refusing to cower. "I've been outrunning you my whole life."

His hand twitches, fighting the urge to smack me across the face for the second time. He thinks better of it when the Enforcer steps close beside him. "Cuff her."

Both Imperials nod before the quieter one begins clamping iron around my wrists. My gaze lifts to Kai's, his mask cold and unfeeling. I think of every moment I told myself I hated him, every moment I was determined to do to him what he did to my father. And then I wear it all on my face.

Pretend.

"There is a horse waiting for you when we get back into the city, Your Highness."

Kai turns to the Imperial. "Good. Let's get moving."

The other Imperial shoves me forward, nearly sending me face-first into the poppies beneath us. I roll my eyes at no one in particular. "Use your words, boys. Us Ordinaries don't speak another language, and I'm also quite capable of walking without being pushed."

"And why would we waste our breath on you, traitor?" the ugly one says, snickering beside his friend.

"If you don't know any big ones, that's okay," I say sweetly. "I find that most Imperials don't."

I ignore the hatred burning in their gazes and instead focus on the flowers beneath me. The cuffs clank on my wrists, weighing down my arms and chafing against my skin.

We walk in silence, the castle looming closer, until the Imperial to my left feels the need to open his mouth again. "I'm looking forward to the king ridding us of you."

I keep my expression blank. "Yes, I'm sure his highness is most excited about my homecoming."

He smirks. "All of Ilya is looking forward to it."

I swallow, eyes flashing to Kai's bare back ahead of me. He doesn't dare turn, his shoulders tensing with each step.

It hits me then. The reality of my imminent death.

I don't know how I'll cheat him this time. There is nowhere for me to run. Death can only be fooled so many times before craving revenge.

Our pace is steady, and I pass the time by watching the flowers slowly begin to wilt beneath our feet. The poppies dwindle with each step, seeming to shrink toward the earth and hide from the city beyond.

It's not long before what's left of the field turns to gravel, which then turns to familiar, uneven cobblestone. Several Imperials linger at the edge of the city, all bowing at the sight of their prince and Enforcer. He nods dismissively to the group of men before climbing atop the horse waiting impatiently for him.

A rough hand on my shoulder tears my gaze from Kai and pins it on the Imperial dragging me behind the horse. He holds a long rope in his other fist, the end of it tethered to the saddle Kai sits on.

I'm not sure why tears prick my eyes as the Imperial ties the rope around my cuffs. Or why I nearly let them fall when the horse begins moving, dragging me behind it.

Maybe it's the humiliation of it all. Of being escorted to the king like an animal as I stumble behind one. Or perhaps it's the Elites that file from their fancy homes to jeer at the traitor. The murderer. The Ordinary.

I've never seen this side of the city. The side where the Offensive populate—the only ones worthy enough to live so close to the castle. I gawk at their homes as I pass. These Elites live in excess while those with less power live in squalor beneath them.

I wouldn't be surprised if Mundanes are declared the new Ordinary, just as Father suspected.

People point, praising their prince in the same breath they use to curse my name. I shut my eyes against the hatred they wear, tripping over stones as we parade through the streets.

"Traitor!"

". . . part of that Resistance cult!"

"King killer!"

"Who will save you now, *Silver Savior*?"

I keep my face blank, willing it not to crumble with each insult spit at me. The cuffs rub my wrists raw while the sun beats down on my damning hair.

I keep my eyes on the castle, on the doom I'm slowly approaching. The chants follow us, quieting with each step toward the awaiting king. Perhaps they, too, fear what it is I've turned him into. What sort of king did I leave them with?

When we step into the shadow of the palace, I know it won't be long before I find out for myself. The horse's hooves clop against the cobblestone covering the courtyard. My eyes snag on a cluster of forget-me-nots crowding the stairway into the castle.

Memories of a soaking dress, rain dripping from his lips onto mine, forget-me-nots tangled into my hair, come flooding back. I look up to where Kai sits, finding him staring at the same patch of courtyard where our lips brushed for the first time.

And now I doubt they will ever brush again.

We slow to a stop beside the stairs I hoped to never have to climb again. All is quiet as Kai swings from his saddle, nodding at an Imperial. The man fumbles with the knotted rope, fingers slipping against the tie.

Kai steps beside him, sliding the Imperial's sword from the sheath at his side to cut the rope with a single swipe. I hear the man swallow, and I almost smile despite my circumstance. Kai then pushes the hilt of the sword into the man's palm without a single word before wrapping a familiar, calloused hand around my arm.

He leads me over to the staircase, quickly swiping his thumb across my skin.

Pretend.

Words burn in my throat; words I wish I could say to him before it's too late. I glance over, trying my best to memorize the planes of his face, not knowing if this will be the last time I see it.

Or maybe he will be the last thing I see.

The one to drive a sword through my heart.

CHAPTER 48
Kai

What am I walking her into?

Heavy doors swing open at the top of the stairs. Imperials greet me with a bow.

Duty. That is what I'm walking her into.

Because this is no choice of mine.

I could have ripped out that Imperial's throat for laying a hand on her, so what is it I'll do if Kitt orders me to do something much worse?

I can hardly stand the way she looks at me, hatred burning in that gaze I love. But this is pretend—the only time I've ever pretended *with* her.

Every touch, every dance, every kiss disguised as distraction was anything but. Because before I loved her, I longed for her. She was a want I wasn't worthy of. And I'm afraid I'll never get the chance to deserve her.

Because now that I have her, I'm giving her away.

We step through the towering doors and into the ornate hallway beyond. She looks around, taking it all in as if doubting there will be another chance to. I hate it, hate that she's already accepted a fate of her deciding.

The emerald carpet beneath our dirty boots looks out of place, as does my lack of shirt and Pae's filthy one. My first mission as the Enforcer certainly hasn't failed to make me look bad. But I hold my head high, feeling the familiar burn of eyes searching for imperfections. I roll my shoulders, straighten my spine, slip an unbothered mask over my features.

Because power is portrayal. And respect is demanded.

We continue down the hall, a fleet of Imperials following behind. The gilded doors grow closer, beckoning us to discover what waits on the other side. *Who* waits on the other side.

I don't know what version of him awaits us beyond these doors. Perhaps the brother I know, or the king I now serve. He's unpredictable, unprepared to rule so young. Or rather, unprepared to lose a father.

And Kitt without his compassion is a man I don't recognize.

I glance over at Paedyn's blank expression. But it's her fidgeting fingers that give her anxiety away, relentlessly spinning that ring on her thumb.

For her sake, I pray to whatever will bother listening.

I pray for my piece of paradise.

Her eyes are pinned on me, wide and full of worry.

I don't dare change my blank expression, not with so many Imperials standing several feet behind her.

But I dare to lift my hand. Dare to raise it up to her nose, her body blocking the movement. Dare to flick the tip of it one last time, hoping she hears my words hidden within the action.

I love you.

And then I push open the heavy doors.

The throne room is packed with familiar faces. Every person of importance seems to occupy the large room, some stepping from behind marble pillars to stare at us dirtying the shiny floor with each step.

Noble men and women, advisers of all ages, startle at the sight of us. Not because they didn't know we were coming, but because we likely look as though we journeyed through hell to get here.

I'm aware of the many makeshift bandages wrapped around my body, each of them stained with blood. I remember promising Father I wouldn't walk into his throne room again without a shirt, and yet, here I am, half-naked before the entire court.

Though Paedyn doesn't look much better. Blood drips down her leg from the deliberately careless Imperial I plan to make pay later. Her shirt hangs from her shoulder, though she's ensured her tank strap covers the scar my father gifted her. The mere thought of it makes my blood boil—not that anyone would know, with the blank mask fastened over my features.

Dozens of eyes flick over my figure before slowly finding hers. Disgust burns in each gaze that crawls over her, taking in the scar down her neck, the split lip above, and the short hair that undeniably belongs to the once Silver Savior.

I yank her forward by the arm.

Pretend.

I am cold and callous and could not care less about the prisoner staggering behind me.

Pretend.

The chains binding her wrists clank with each uneven step she takes toward the throne. People part to make way, and I meet every gaze that strays to mine. This crowd is too proud and proper to shout their loathing like those we passed in the streets, but the various looks on their faces speak volumes.

Despite holding her head high, Paedyn's feet begin to drag with each step closer to his throne. The throne our new king now occupies.

She's scared.

The thought sends anger shooting through me, though it doesn't reach my face. Try as she might to deny it, I know this version of Kitt scares her. This version that she likely blames herself for.

I force her to her knees when we reach the bottom of the dais.

Pretend.

Shackles smack the marble floor; a sound associated with a traitor. She lifts her head slowly, daring to meet his gaze.

But his eyes are pinned on me, swiftly skimming over my body. I do the same, taking in the crown atop his head and throne beneath the ass I used to whoop in the training yard. I'm not sure I'll ever get used to the sight of him sitting in father's shadow.

"Welcome back, Enforcer."

His smile is small, and I'm not sure whether the formalities are due to the court being present, or if this is to be the extent of our relationship for the rest of this shared life.

"I was beginning to worry," he says softly. "You were expected back several days ago."

It doesn't sound like a slight, but it stings, nonetheless. At least I always knew when father was undermining my abilities. "As you can see by the looks of us"—I gesture to my body and Paedyn's below—"we ran into some unforeseen circumstances."

Kitt nods. "I see. You made it home, regardless."

"Of course I did." The words fall harsher than they should have. "Your Majesty," I add quickly.

"And your men?" he asks with a tilt of his head.

I fold my hands behind my bare back. "Unforeseen circumstances."

"Ah." Kitt drums his fingers on the large arm of the throne, looking uncomfortable in the seat. "And her?" he asks suddenly, nodding toward a kneeling Paedyn. Leaning forward, he glides his gaze over my face. "Any other unforeseen circumstances I should know of?"

CHAPTER 49
Paedyn

He hasn't looked at me.

I've been kneeling on the floor before him, and he doesn't even have the decency to look at me.

His hair is disheveled, dull against the golden crown atop his head. It looks uncomfortably heavy, consisting of what must be a dozen gold strands all twisting between one another. I recognize the familiar tangled pattern to represent Ilya's crest and the use of all powers working together.

I fight the urge to roll my eyes at the utter bullshit of it all.

"And her?" he suddenly asks. "Any other unforeseen circumstances I should know of?"

The silence filling the throne room is suffocating.

His words ring in my ears, hang in the air between us.

But it's the unspoken question that has my eyes widening.

He's asking if something happened between the two of us.

I fight the urge to look over at Kai and instead keep my eyes pinned on the king who can't be bothered to look my way. The court surrounding us doesn't seem fazed by the question they only know the half of.

I can't imagine we look as though something happened between the two of us. In fact, I would argue that we've never looked more like enemies than in this moment with my bloody, kneeling body at his feet.

"I brought her back, did I not?" Kai says evenly.

"That's not what I asked, Brother."

I still at the title, feeling the significance of it.

That one acknowledgment of what they still are to each other is enough to have Kai's voice softening. "No. No other unforeseen circumstances."

The lie slides off his tongue, sounding of sincerity. They stare at each other for a long moment, allowing me time to study this king I'm kneeling before.

Dark circles smudge beneath his eyes, aging him with nothing more than lack of sleep. His hair is ruffled, sticking up between the strands of his crown as though he's been running his hands through it. Wrinkled clothes lie below an unshaven jaw while slightly mismatched socks tell me that servants haven't been tending to their king. The faint outline of a box draws my attention to his right pocket, though I can't make out what it is that lies inside.

Ink subtly stains his hands, as though he's scrubbed them vigorously, leaving his knuckles cracked and dry. Fingers drum against his chair, his only sign of fidgeting, though his knee occasionally bounces. And his eyes . . .

His eyes are suddenly pinned on me.

Green and crisp like fresh dew on a blade of grass.

Green and swimming with emotions.

Green like those of the king before him. The king who carved his mark above my heart. It seems to sting at the reminder of those familiar eyes full of hatred.

But this green gaze I hold is considering, scrutinizing in a way that seems too harsh for the Kitt I once knew. But this is not that boy. This is what is left of him.

"Good," he says to Kai, though his eyes stay fixed on me. "Because I have special plans for her."

Everybody in the room seems to lean closer in anticipation. This is what they have all been waiting for—my punishment.

I swallow, forcing myself to hold his gaze as he stands to his feet. "Ladies and gentlemen of the court, let me reintroduce you to who it is that kneels before you." His voice is soft in the way that powerful people can afford to be, forcing everyone to listen closely. "This is Paedyn Gray. Once a contestant in the Purging Trials where she ranked quite highly for a Mundane. And to think a *Psychic* became such a threat to Offensive Elites."

I catch the shaking of heads in my periphery, but keep my eyes fixed on Kitt as he continues. "But she isn't exactly what she seems." Grunts of agreement echo throughout the room. "Not only was your Silver Savior an Ordinary in disguise, but she was a traitor under our noses. Paedyn." His eyes flick back to me. "Do you confess to not only being a Resistance member, but to conspiring with them as well?"

I blink, still shocked at him addressing me by name. My throat has gone dry, voice raspy as I manage, "Yes."

The crowd gasps dramatically, as if they hadn't already known all this. I'm tempted to tell the king to spare us the theatrics and sentence me to death already.

"Not only that," he continues quietly, "but do you admit to . . . killing the former king of Ilya?"

My eyes never stray from his. "I do."

That has the people murmuring around me, cursing my name between breaths. Kitt nods, looking down at the marble floor reflecting my dirty face. The stretch of silence that follows is deafening, and I bite my tongue to keep from filling it.

When the king looks up, I see Kitt shining through his expression. The sudden shift has me blinking in surprise, blinking at the familiarity of that face. And when I see Kai straighten slightly beside me, I know he sees it too.

"This woman—Paedyn Gray—has committed atrocious crimes," Kitt says, looking around the room. "She killed my father, your king, plunging his own sword through his chest before her dagger through his throat. She conspired with the Resistance, a radical group of Ordinaries, helping them find a passage into the Bowl Arena." His eyes find their way back to mine, memories clouding that green gaze. "She lied. She killed. She betrayed."

The sting in his voice has me dropping my gaze to the feet that slowly carry him down the steps of the dais. "And I have grieved. I have stepped suddenly into the role of your king while still mourning the former. And, yes, my reputation as a crazed king has reached my ears." My eyes lift to his while the throne room grows thick with tension. Uneasy glances flick between the Elites, breaths held as they wait for their king to continue.

"But I assure you," he finally continues, allowing everyone to breathe again, "that my future decisions are anything but crazed. And I will explain them all to you in due time."

When his eyes land back on me, I know my time has come.

"Paedyn Gray . . ."

I duck my head, not wanting to see the words form on his lips.

So this is how it ends.

Not by the Trials. Not by the Scorches or bandits or sewer

attempting to drown me, but by the mere word of a king.

A king that I created.

I wonder if he will make Kai do it. Maybe re-create the death of his father. That only seems fitting.

"Stand."

I almost don't hear him over my deafeningly dreadful thoughts.

It takes several stuttering heartbeats to finally scramble to my feet, wincing at the pain shooting up my sliced ankle.

The king's eyes travel up the length of me before landing on my gaze.

He pulls that box from his pocket, small and velvet between his fingers.

The lid lifts, snapping open to reveal . . .

Nothing could have prepared me for the words that fall from his lips.

Not even a real damn Psychic.

The ring sparkles against the black velvet it sits within.

"You are to be my bride."

EPILOGUE

I think I'm drowning.

But not into her blue eyes like I happily would.

No, I'm sinking into the floor, letting it swallow me whole.

I can hardly breathe under the crushing weight of Kitt's words.

My ears ring. My heart pounds.

The command echoes in my skull, though I have no idea why he would want this. Why he would want her. Not now. Not after everything.

And yet, I still want her after everything.

I'm surrounded by the entire court and the only thing I can focus on is not falling to my knees beside her.

Marriage.

Marriage to someone who isn't me. Marriage to someone I will spend the rest of my life serving.

I'll lose her forever while being forced to watch.

I can't even look at her.

I'm a coward, morphing back into the monster I was when she found me.

My vision is blurry, eyes fixed on the dais above.

This is how I lose her.

Not by death but by something just as binding.

The command rings in my head.

And to think I wasted so much time trying to hate her.

To think I won't have enough time to love her.

My heart aches because every beat belongs to her.

And I may never get to tell her that.

Is this how she will remember me? Escorting her to this fate? Bound by duty alone?

I could laugh. I could cry. I could burn this palace to the ground like I did her house, just for a chance to confess my love before the flames consumed me.

Because I am bound to her very being. Hers until the day she realizes I don't deserve to be.

The king's eyes are on me while mine are somewhere far away. Somewhere with her. A place where I am nothing and no one and happy being powerless, so long as she is beside me.

My gaze falls from the fantasy, finding its way to her.

This is not how I will remember us. Not as enemies or traitors or monsters, but as two people dancing in the dark, swaying beneath the stars. Her feet atop mine, her head on the heart that beats only for her. Just Pae and Kai.

I step away from her kneeling form, masking every emotion with a blank stare. I'm leaving her to face him. Her future husband.

I melt into the crowd, standing at a safe enough distance to prevent myself from stealing her away.

This will be the rest of my life. Forced to love her from a distance. Mourn the loss of her each day.

But I will.

I will smother every emotion but the one that belongs to her. I will love her until I am incapable of the feeling.

She is the torture I may not survive.

Eagerly, she is my undoing.

Her gaze lifts, meeting eyes that are not my own.

Eyes of the man who gets to have her—if she allows it.

She was supposed to be my forever.

Now I'll watch her become someone else's.

Because the beast doesn't get the beauty.

Acknowledgments

It would be a lie to say I haven't skimmed through several of my favorite authors' acknowledgments, trying to study up on the best way to go about this. Because I'm convinced there is a secret formula to follow, one that keeps you—the lovely reader—engaged while I—the rambling author—attempt to express my admiration to the people who made this book possible. And maybe by the end of this, you can let me know if I figured it out or not.

After the sudden success of *Powerless* (which I will forever thank you for), writing book two suddenly became a daunting task. Within a matter of months, this series I had begun out of passion alone, abruptly shifted into something far larger than I could have ever imagined. And for that reason, *Reckless* terrified me. The pressure of making it perfect weighed heavy on my shoulders. But when my fingers met the keyboard and words began spilling onto the page, it felt as though I were back in my childhood bedroom, writing *Powerless* to fulfill the big dreams I had as a little girl.

It was a privilege to return to this world with so many people eager to dive back in with me. I have loved growing with this series and the characters that are so dear to my heart. As equally fun and heart-wrenching as *Reckless* was to write, it was typing the final word that was my favorite part. Because I proved something to myself that night (at approximately four a.m.):

My story—my dream—did not end when I finished *Powerless* at the age of eighteen. And I have now gained the courage to keep dreaming. Keep writing. Keep doing what I love.

All right, enough about me. I can confidently say that I wouldn't even get the chance to practice my acknowledgment-writing skills if it weren't for a handful of incredible people. For starters, I have the great privilege of working hand in hand with not one, but two incredible Simon & Schuster teams. Even with my scarily overactive imagination, I never could have dreamed of having a group of people in both the United States and the United Kingdom that care so deeply for me and my stories. I wish to give each of you a kiss on the cheek but seeing that several thousand miles separate most of us, I will have to settle for typing your name with the utmost admiration.

Starting with the lovely UK team, it seems only right to begin my gushing with Yasmin Morrissey. As one of my brave editors, you have endured countless voice memos, emails, and Zoom calls about all things *Reckless*. You have been there through every stage of this book, and I cannot thank you enough for your constant support. Even my impostor syndrome and self-criticism are no match for you! I genuinely fear what would become of me without your diligence, and I look forward to many more lengthy voice memos in the future!

But there are several other members of the UK team I have the honor to thank, starting with Rachel Denwood and Ali Dougal—my managing and publishing directors. Laura Hough and Danielle Wilson have championed my work with UK retailers while Loren

Catan, my in-house designer, came up with the gorgeous cover design for *Powerful.* Miya Elkerton and Olivia Horrox in marketing along with Jess Dean and Ellen Abernethy in publicity. The fantastic rights team, led by Maud Sepult and Emma Martinez, who have found incredible international homes for *Powerless.* Last (but certainly not least), Nicholas Hayne and everyone else. Thank you.

As for my equally lovely US team, I must first shower Nicole Ellul with immense admiration. Being my other fearless editor is no simple task. You have helped guide me so graciously through each publication process, and your faith in my work is appreciated more than you know. Thank you for every idea and ounce of input that has made this series what it now is. Your enthusiasm alone is an inspiration to me.

Continuing on to the rest of the marvelous US crew, I have Jenica Nasworthy to thank for keeping everything organized as my managing editor. But there are several others who deserve a huge general thank-you, at the very least. Chava Wolin, Lucy Cummins, Hilary Zarycky, Alyza Liu, Justin Chanda, Kendra Levin, Nicole Russo, Emily Ritter, and Brendon MacDonald—you all are incredible at what you do. Thank you.

At this time, feel free to take a break from my ramblings to drool over the gorgeous artwork and map in the front of this book. And, yes, the rumors are true. It is all hand drawn by the insanely talented Jordan Elliot. I cannot think of a better person to bring my world to life, and I am incredibly honored to continue working together. Here's to more jaw-dropping art!

To my unflinching attorney-agent, Lloyd Jassin, I must give my obvious gratitude. Thank you for helping me navigate through this world of publishing—I cannot imagine tackling any of this without you. You are a pleasure to work with, and I hope to continue doing so for many years to come.

Besides the incredible S&S teams who helped assemble *Reckless*, there are several others at work behind the scenes. And I happen to be related to those individuals. Firstly, I can humbly admit that none of these dreams would have come true if it weren't for my parents. Mom and Dad, you have supported me every step of the way and believed in me when I found it hard to believe in myself. Thank you for trusting your little girl enough to let her pursue this passion. I am so blessed to have you both, but especially a mother who happily juggles being my confidant, assistant, and bookkeeper.

Being the runt of the family, I suppose there are a few older siblings to acknowledge. Jessie, Nikki, Josh—you have all supported me in your own ways. I deeply appreciate every encouraging text and proverbial pat on the back. Thank you, Foos.

Aside from my family, there are several friends who ensured I stayed sane during this writing process. I would like to give a general thank-you to every person who had to put up with me rambling about this book. Each of you have helped and encouraged me in your own way, and I am eternally grateful for your unending support.

Now onto the daunting task of attempting to express my admiration for a certain boy. Zac, I cannot thank you enough for your encouragement and willingness to help. Whether it's cooking me a meal or offering a shoulder to cry on, I can always rely on your comfort. You are truly my fictional boy incarnate, and I hope to write our story one day.

As stated in the back of *Powerless*, I'd like to thank the One who gifted me my love of words and the desire to write. I truly would not be where I am today without my Lord and Savior, and I thank God for the opportunity He has given me.

Now it is your turn, dear reader. Did I hold your attention up until this point? Were you waiting for me to finally acknowledge you?

Because it is all thanks to you that I made it to this very page. I am honored to be on this journey together, and even more so that you took the time to read my story. You are my inspiration, my reason for every word. And I hope to hold your attention for many years to come.

Here's to more dreams, and the stories they create.

XO, Lauren

About the Author

When Lauren Roberts isn't writing about fantasy worlds and bantering love interests, she can likely be found burrowed in bed reading about them. Lauren has lived in Michigan her whole life, making her very familiar with potholes, snow, and various lake activities. She has the hobbies of both a grandmother and a child, i.e., knitting, laser tag, hammocking, word searches, and coloring. *Powerless* was her debut novel, and she hopes to have the privilege of writing pretty words for the rest of her life. If you enjoy ranting, reading, and writing, Lauren can be found on both TikTok and Instagram @laurenrobertslibrary or her website laurenrobertslibrary.com for your entertainment.

THE NEW YORK TIMES BESTSELLER
Hunted. Hunter.
Destined for each other.
POWERLESS
LAUREN ROBERTS

A POWERLESS Story
POWERFUL
New York Times Bestselling Author of Powerless
LAUREN ROBERTS